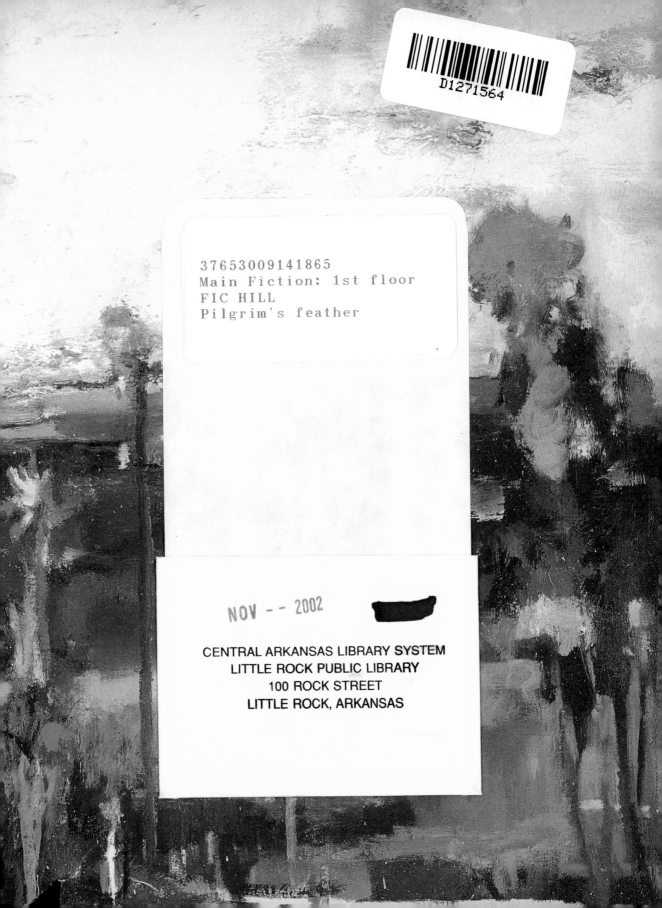

PILGRIM'S FEATHER

PILGRIM'S FEATHER

by R. Nemo Hill

ILLUSTRATIONS BY

Jeanne Hedstrom

The Quantuck Lane Press

Printed in Hong Kong by South China Printing

The text of this book is set in Poliphilus with display type in Blado.
Both are derived from Monotype typefaces.

Design by Antonina Krass

Composition by Gina Webster

ISBN 0-9714548-0-9

First Edition

The Quantuck Lane Press
Box 317
Quogue, NY 11959

In memory
of
Julius Eastman

I had heard that there was a bird called Phoenix, the only one of its kind in the whole world, whose feathers and flesh constitute the great and glorious medicine for all passion, pain, and sorrow...

This bird I could not hope to obtain entire, but I was seized with an irresistible longing to become possessed of at least one of its smallest feathers; and for this unspeakable privilege I was prepared to spend all my substance, to travel far and wide, and to endure every hardship.

Michael Maier

Contents

Part One THE RIDDLE

1 The Boy in the Nest   3
2 The Forest of Riddles 29

Part Two THE ELEMENTS

3 Hoop of Fire, Heart's Desire 47
4 City of Pirates 83
5 A Certain Distance 137
6 The Fall 167

Part Three THE GARDEN OF JEWELS

7 Through the Torn Curtain of Howling 221
8 In the Raven's Head 241

Part Four THE RETURN

9 The Great Goldman and His Flying City of the Sun 297
10 Requiem 333

ILLUSTRATIONS

Frontispiece	p. ii
The Boy in the Nest	p. 5
Nicolas Departing	p. 27
The Ram and the Reflection	p. 37
The Queen of the Shepherds	p. 49
The Volcano	p. 63
Nicolas Gathering Ashes	p. 69
The Sleeping Queen and the Salamander	p. 77
The Tattoo Artist	p. 93
The Seaport	p. 105
Nicolas Adrift	p. 121
Underwater	p. 133
Stargazing	p. 146
The Albatross	p. 156
An Uncomfortable Position	p. 169
Overlooking the Garden	p. 179
The Stairway	p. 212
Now You May Enter	p. 220
The Queen and the 21 Cats	p. 223
Guarding the Temple	p. 225
One Step at a Time	p. 227
The Fishmarket	p. 229
Everyone Must Pay to Cross the River	p. 231
Gillam's Ghost	p. 233

The 4 Serpent Kings   p. 235
Morning Glories and Hummingbirds   p. 237
Nature Morte   p. 239
Outside the Cave   p. 245
Inside the Cave   p. 252
Landscape with Bridge   p. 305
The Flying Citizens of the Sun   p. 315
Jungle of Parrots   p. 327
The Phoenix   p. 330
Nicolas Returning   p. 334
Caught Beneath the Wing of Sleep   p. 347

PILGRIM'S FEATHER

Part One

THE RIDDLE

The Boy in the Nest

He grew up among birds. The intricate chains of birdsong bound him to his cradle, the quiver and coo of pigeons roosting was his original lullaby. All his earliest memories were winged. Perhaps that's true of everyone.

The aviary where he found himself lay far from any human habitation. Deep in an unnamed forest, beyond the end of any trail marked on any map, isolated even from the temper of the seasons with their violent changes of weather, it seemed an island in time as well as space, and there was no one, no one at all, who could explain exactly how it was that the boy, Nicolas, had appeared there one quiet and otherwise uneventful day.

The hundreds of species of birds that found refuge there, the jays and loons and gnatcatchers, larks and owls and swallows, thrushes and warblers and wrens and tomtits, the bare-throated bellbird, the boat-billed heron, the red-winged blackbird, the sulfur-crested cockatoo, and the short-tailed babbler, all of them might come and go at will, appear and disappear, without occasioning the slightest mystery. They could fly, after all, and the power of wings needs no explanation. But a young boy, an infant, curled up naked upon the bare ground without so much as a basket or blanket for shelter, so far away from any known place that no number of miles could possibly measure the distance: how was the arrival of so helpless a creature to be explained?

It did not concern Nicolas. Sometimes in the night, tired of sleeping, he would stretch his memory, not because he needed to know, but only because the memory is a muscle like any other and thus delights in exercise. Lying perfectly still in the darkness, he would attempt to steer his thoughts, turning them back, back. . . . Mother? The bright red wing of a flustered cardinal would sweep across his mind's eye. Father? The splash of a kingfisher's sudden dive would startle and distract him. Home? With just a trace of light on the horizon, birdsong would shatter the night of memory into the million shiny pieces of a relentless present. Nicolas would be on his feet immediately, every dawn's orphan, scattering seed corn among the roots of trees and the webbed feet of ducks and geese.

He'd never given any thought at all as to how exactly he'd managed to survive the dangers of those years of lonely infancy. Defenseless against predators, unable to feed or clothe or shelter himself, he'd nevertheless managed not only to endure but to thrive. Old enough to crawl, then to stumble about on his pale little bowed legs, he'd grown accustomed to discovering the little gifts of food and piles of primitive garments, bowls of peeled fruit and boiled grains, vests and sandals woven of bark and grass and turkey feathers. Nature simply seemed to provide for him as effortlessly as it did for the birds and other creatures with which he was surrounded. There was no reason to question the fact. It was only when he'd begun to imitate and thus to educate himself that his hidden benefactor decided it was time for them to meet, in person.

It was the morning that Nicolas put the finishing touches on his very first nest, almost five years after his appearance in the sprawling forest aviary. For several months he'd been watching, studying, comparing. It was the hermit thrush that he eventually designated as his teacher, chiefly because of the pleasant odor of the spruce and cedar trees beneath which she habitually chose to build and rest. Nicolas had already grown fond of sleeping there—but whereas before he'd

simply collapsed on the ground, at the very most heaping up the fallen leaves and branches to serve as a fragrant pillow, there came a morning when he finally surrendered to the guidance of the nervous little nut-brown thrushes he'd been observing for so long. Rushing back and forth and back and forth with them for days on end, he collected bits and pieces of the same dried leaf and twig and petal, only larger, and cemented them together with the same muds and sticky clays, molding them into a sort of cup or cradle.

Nicolas heard a sound that morning as he stood surveying his finished product, his nest. He heard a sound over his shoulder that he did not recognize. It was a laugh. A single, low, good-natured laugh. And it was not until he'd actually climbed into his nest, to test it, and settled down comfortably, his head resting on its rim, that he saw, looming over him, for the first time, the singular bird whose call was that singular laugh: an old man, that old man who had, in fact, as the boy subsequently learned, nurtured him, anonymously, from the very first moment he'd come to the aviary.

"Well. It's a fine nest," said the old man, his hands in his pockets, his lower lip thrust forward in a feeble attempt to conceal his smile of amusement.

Of course the boy could not possibly understand him. He had, as yet, no command of this peculiar new language the old man spoke, although he'd already learned to recognize that laughing bird call he heard now for the second time in one morning. Unable to restrain himself any longer, the old man had set his smile free, and it was this broad grin more than anything else that seemed to put the boy in the nest at ease. There was something in the old man's manner, strange and unfamiliar as it was, that inspired not fear but trust.

Moments later, still smiling, the old man withdrew.

From then on, Old Gillam made no further efforts to conceal himself from the boy. He went about his business, with nothing any longer to hide. If Nicolas happened to be wandering or foraging in that portion of the forest where he was working, so be it. If he were to witness, through the branches of the cedar beneath which he slept, the salting and boiling of the grain or the removal of the empty bowl, that was fine. And if, rounding the blind corner of one of the huge whitewashed swan coops or swallow barns, they were suddenly to find themselves face to face in the bright sunlight, there could be no harm in it.

Nicolas, however, quickly outgrew such chance encounters. Though Old Gillam had not yet spoken again, his casual manner and easy smile emboldened the boy, excited his curiosity, and within a short time Nicolas took to deliberately following the old man for days at a time. Gillam moved at a much slower pace than that of the frantic little hermit thrushes. He walked like Nicolas himself, and as time went by he even waited. And so student followed teacher, surreptitiously at first, then quite openly.

In no time at all, they became inseparable.

All of this was long ago, of course, long before the story begins in earnest, long before the boy became the Pilgrim. But unlike his life before he'd come to the aviary, this was a recoverable past, and even long after Old Gillam was gone, Nicolas could relive those days of study and companionship as if they'd never been so grievously interrupted.

"Put a wing on anything, anything," said Old Gillam, "two wings, and see what happens."

The old man stood in one of the aviary's more remote meadows, a meadow dotted with clumps of white hibiscus, budding but not yet in bloom. Over one arm hung a bucket of cool water sweetened with honey. While his other arm was poised in midair, the red rubber bulb of a tiny glass eyedropper pinched between his fingers. It would still be a few days before the white trumpets of an army of hibiscus blossoms erupted en masse. In the meantime, he was feeding the hummingbirds.

"Anything, anything at all," said Old Gillam, gesturing with his eyedropper for emphasis, frightening the bird that hovered near its tip. Its ruby throat flashed in the sunlight as it darted away and then swiftly back, undeterred.

Though he appeared to be preoccupied, Nicolas was listening attentively. He was running here and there through the meadow grass, raising enormous clouds of dragonflies wherever he passed, their dry wings clicking in the still air of the warm afternoon. Less experienced and more impatient than his tutor, he would dart forward, and, thrusting his whole hand in and then out of the bucket of sweet water, he'd scatter droplets in every direction, attempting to feed the dragonflies before the click and rustle of their wings subsided and they settled down once again, motionless, onto the swaying tips of stalks and grasses.

"Even that log over there," the old man went on, pointing with his dropper, bewildering another hummingbird or two, "even this bucket, or that stone. Or your shoes."

Nicolas stopped running and looked down at his old shoes.

"Yes, yes, my boy, your shoes," teased the old man. "Imagine if they were winged, where would you be then, eh?"

Nicholas wasn't quite sure he understood.

Without any warning Gillam let go of his bucket and his dropper, swooped down upon the boy and, lifting him beneath the armpits, swung him up over his head and through the air in great graceful arcs. More than a few hummingbirds darted in for a quick taste of the sweet water still dripping from the laughing boy's wet fingertips as his teacher ran with him across the meadow.

He loved it when the old man made him fly. It became one of their favorite games, even though sometimes it was a long walk back to retrieve the fallen bucket, even though sometimes they searched for hours to find the eyedropper lost in the tall meadow grass.

Of course, not all of their lessons were so boisterous or gymnastic in nature, just as not all of the birds whose habits and legends formed the basis of the old man's prodigious body of knowledge were as perpetually excited as the hummingbirds and their kin. Sometimes days or even weeks would pass in more solemn study, or search. For instance, the pale blue shells of discarded robins' eggs that Old Gillam ground to a fine powder and kept in an enormous glass urn housed in one dark corner of the swan coop: these were exceedingly difficult to find. Nicolas had trained his eyes to pick out the bold red breast high overhead in the foliage and then to drop his gaze directly down. But his treasure map as often as not proved useless, his scavenging beneath the nesting robins netting not a single blue fragment of a shell. On more than one occasion, it was only when returning empty-handed that he stumbled quite accidentally upon what he'd been looking for all along. Marveling at the handfuls of shells that the old man had managed to collect in the same amount of time, some of them virtually whole but for a single bit pecked out one side, the boy, ashamed, would keep his paltry offering to himself, in his pocket. Gillam would already be hard at work inside the coop, grinding away with his mortar and pestle, and he'd console the boy with only a single pat on the top of the head and return to work.

"What do you need them for, anyway?" Nicolas had eventually grown bold enough to ask.

"Fetch me the funnel," was Gillam's only reply.

The boy held the funnel in place over the narrow neck of the glass urn as the old man poured the blue powder in and stoppered the jar without saying another word.

It was on afternoons such as these that Nicolas, despite his attachment to the old man, longed to be on his own, alone, and free to do as he pleased. Gillam was not at all insensitive to such a boyish urge to wander unsupervised. Yet though periodically left to his own devices, the old man's stories exerted such a pervasive influence on the boy that even his own innocent games seemed as if directed by his absent teacher. And so he'd spend entire days alone, searching, from sunup to sundown, for the fabled eaglet ejected by its parent from its nest.

"There are only two creatures in all the world who can look directly into the sun without averting their gaze," the old man had taught him, "the eagle and the falcon."

He pointed directly overhead.

It was almost noon.

"Go on, my little eaglet," he said, "try it."

Nicolas bent his head back and stared up into the glaring disc of the sun, then quickly turned his face away, squinting in pain. He heard the old man speaking, but he could no longer see him—his eyes were too full of burning sparks and black explosions.

"When she is in the nest with her young, the eagle forces each of them to stare straight into the shining sun. She tests their legitimacy. The child that turns away, or blinks, or is blinded, she tosses from the nest, presumably to its death."

It was a foolish quest, he knew.

He knew that eagles nest on high, on mountain cliffs or crests or the lonely tops of the tallest trees. He knew that there were no mountains to speak of within the boundaries of the aviary. The countryside was, for the most part, flat or barely rolling, ambling forest and meadow and marsh.

He knew this.

But it was not the part of himself that *knew* things which strode, on those solitary afternoons, directly into the sun, toward the myth of mountains, now and then deliberately burning his eyes with the light in the sky in an effort to strengthen his solidarity with the orphaned eaglet he never managed to find, dead or alive.

Exhausted by such games, dejected after all his fruitless efforts, he might, in the evening, remove from his pocket the various fragments of blue eggshell he'd failed to surrender over the years. They'd gradually increased in number, and he might amuse himself trying to piece them together, like a puzzle, as if, were he to find the proper arrangement, he might manage to construct one whole pale blue egg. Then again, too tired to play the shell game any longer, he might just lie under the open sky, and see, briefly, in the path of a shooting star, the fall of an eaglet, and renew his vow, even as he fell himself, into sleep, to set out tomorrow to retrieve it.

Old Gillam knew the boy's moods well. He could read them just as easily as he could read the migrations of birds, the movements of the stars, the wind in the leaves of the birch or the oak; just as easily as he could hear the secret blue eggshells crackling in the boy's back pocket whenever he walked or sat down next to him. He was well aware that Nicolas had been searching for the rejected eaglet all day and dreaming of it all night. Standing over him, watching him sleep, tracing the furrows in his child's brow by starlight, Gillam decided, then and there, to show the boy, the very next morning, the stone he referred to as his white crystal.

Actually, the stone was pale gold in color, the white of its name appearing only in the brilliant lines that traversed its surface. It was beautiful, undoubtedly. But what made it truly remarkable was that it had come, the old man swore, straight from the beak of a heron.

Nicolas rubbed the sleep from his eyes, trying to focus for a moment on the curious stone in the old man's hand.

"Come, come now, hurry up, we must get started."

It was scarcely light, the birds had barely begun their song.

"No, no, no, don't bother with that this morning."

The boy was reaching, out of habit, for the burlap feedsack.

"But the geese, the ducks, they—"

"Never mind them."

"But who'll feed them, who will—"

"Don't worry about them, they'll be fine," the old man assured him. "They only pretend to need us so that we don't feel too useless. Now come, come, follow me."

Nicolas trundled after him into the blue-gray light of dawn.

"Where are we going?" he asked after a while, but, receiving no reply, he merely trailed along a short distance behind, stopping to grab a handful of ripe berries from an overhanging branch, then catching up again. Two hours later, on the edge of the great marsh, they halted.

Old Gillam sat down on the spongy ground, on a patch of thick green moss, and produced his white crystal once again.

Nicolas gazed at the stone, expressionless.

"Hold it," said Gillam.

The boy reached out his hand, stained red from his breakfast of berries.

"It's said that one who carries such a stone acquires wisdom," quoted the old man.

Somewhere behind them the jarring call of a bittern echoed across the marsh and then ceased abruptly. After a few minutes of rest, they continued on, Old Gillam in the lead, Nicolas following with the milk-and-honey-colored stone clutched tightly in his hand.

They penetrated the marsh slowly. The ground was soft and uncertain and sucked at their ankles. It became clear to Nicolas that the old man was headed for the sandier expanse on the north side of the great marsh where the network of streams that fed its stagnant waters still flowed more swiftly before getting choked and bogged down in its low-lying pools. It was a lonely and desolate area, inaccessible, quiet, its series of elongated sandbars and sand islands frequented by slow and stately groups of herons, gray and great blue.

11

A solitary wedge of great blues passed overhead, their broad, slate-colored wings undulating, wave upon wave, the dark branches of their legs trailing reluctantly behind as if still earthbound. Almost out of sight, blocked by a stand of tall cypress interrupting the horizon, they wheeled back around gracefully, their formation trembling yet keeping shape, reapproaching as they gradually sank down and vanished beyond a bend in one of the larger streams just ahead.

Old Gillam beckoned.

Rounding the bend, they saw that the herons had landed. Ten or fifteen of them were scattered across the shallow streambed, their legs sprouting up from the clear water that mirrored their slate-blue plumage, their paler necks curved round or tucked in or extended, each a different silent letter of a silent alphabet, poised, watchful, over the surface of the stream. It was so still that Nicolas could hear, when he held his breath, the rippling of the water as it eddied around their dark slender reeds of legs.

It was here, in this inlet, that Old Gillam claimed to have found, or been given, his *leucochryse*, or white crystal. And it was here that he returned, formerly alone, hereafter with his young companion, to watch and to wait in seclusion for a second encounter with the stone and with the heron who held it in the tip of its long sharp yellow beak.

Nicolas was already aware of the rarity with which the heron uttered its harsh, croaking call. It seemed only natural, given the unpleasantness of the sound, that the heron should be reluctant to speak—but the old man had another, more novel, explanation for the bird's characteristic reticence.

"My stone," said Gillam, beckoning.

Nicolas handed his treasure back to the old man, who rolled it round and round in his palm.

"It confers wisdom," he said, "just as surely as silence does."

He paused, passing the stone from one hand to the other.

"And the heron, in its preference for the silent and solitary places of this earth, is a better teacher than I in this regard. Fortunate indeed are those students before which it stands with the stone gripped in its beak so as not to be able to utter a sound."

Once more the old man paused.

"Such a stone," he said, "is found nowhere else."

The herons went on feeding, staring into the current, stabbing from time to time at the water, breaking its surface with a sharp splash. To Nicolas it seemed more and more as if it were not just food for which they hunted with such strangely patient precision but something else, something small and simple, bright white and golden, which he and the old man passed silently back and forth, from hand to hand, between one another, all day long.

"Nicolas!"

The boy jerked upright, uprooting one of the dandelions whose greens he'd been harvesting, inadvertently pulling it right out of the ground.

"Nicolas!"

He swiveled, once, twice, trying to determine from which direction the shout had come. The old man rarely raised his voice—and yet now for the third time the boy's name came booming out across the low ridge and down the wooded hillside.

"Nicolaaas!"

He dropped his bundle of wilting greens and ran, nearly tripping in the tangle of low scrub, up the slope and then along the crest of the ridge. Almost immediately he spied the vultures, circling ominously in the air, and instinctively he veered off in their direction, down the other side of the hill, where the beech and elm grew thicker, where the shade was darker and cooler.

Emerging from the wood, he paused to catch his breath, leaning against the trunk of an enormous chestnut tree. From there he caught sight of Old Gillam, not that far off, standing by the shore of one of the lakes the wild swans favored for nesting. He was gesturing to the boy, but his eyes were glued to the ground at his feet, while all around him the vultures, their bald red leathery heads clearly visible now, were spiraling, and settling, apparently undisturbed by the old man's presence.

Nicolas approached as quickly as caution would allow. He did not want to interfere with or startle the birds. He'd seen vultures feeding before, their sharp, dripping beaks, their cold eyes. He'd no wish to get between them and their carrion.

"It's Argent, the old trumpeter," Gillam called out to him as soon as he was close enough to hear, and the boy's pace quickened as he hurried to the old man's side.

The enormous trumpeter swan lay dead at the water's edge, glowing in the center of an infernal ring of vultures like a pale fire in the darkest of hearths. Its eyes had already been pecked out, their clotted sockets swarming with insects, and the lake, where it lapped against its breast feathers, was veined with the pale pink of blood dissolving and disappearing into deeper waters.

Nicolas looked up questioningly into the old man's calm eyes, then back down at the violated swan. The hungriest of the vultures had already entered the chest cavity through a tear in the neck, submerging its entire head. Right before the boy's eyes the head reappeared, glistening with blood, a long tough string of gut stretched taut in its beak until it snapped with such force that the whole carcass of the swan recoiled, shifting under the impact, sending some of the younger, more timid birds scuttling a safer distance away.

Gillam knelt down, brushing the eager birds away with a wave of his hand. They seemed strangely obedient to the old man's terse commands.

"Dear old Argent," he mumbled, lifting the swan's long, limp neck with his fingers, gently turning its head to one side, then the other.

As a rule, the birds of the aviary did not receive names. The swans, however, were an exception. They were Gillam's personal favorites, and there wasn't a single swan in his care that had not been christened by the old man. Nicolas found it next to impossible to keep their identities distinct. But there was no mistaking Argent, by far the oldest and noblest of the wild trumpeter swans. Whether their relationship went back centuries, as the old man claimed, or only decades—in either case their intimacy had never ceased to astound young Nicolas.

"I heard him singing from the other shore," said Gillam, letting Argent's head fall back softly into the mud.

Nicolas knew the legend of the swan's song by heart: capable of piercing the veil between this world and the next by virtue of its prophetic gifts, its vision of heaven so entrances it that the swan bursts forth into a song of expectant rapture as its death draws near.

So went the official explanation. But down through the ages, pieced together from the scattered accounts of those few lucky souls who'd witnessed the swan's song firsthand, there gradually emerged another story, one that did not so much contradict the official report as embellish it. It was common knowledge, by now, that the swan's head, as it sang, was turned in equal measure both ahead and behind, hymning both the beauty of the world to come *and* the beauty of the world from which it was passing. It was this doubling of direction, this marriage in music, this harmony, that lent to the swan song its rapturous tone.

"All nostalgia is heaven bent," was how Old Gillam put it, whispering, and rising, as if in benediction.

The vultures, wasting no time, renewed their poking and tearing.

"We'll have to row him back across."

Nicolas looked around for the little skiff in which the old man had crossed the lake. It was moored to a willow just a few yards down the shore.

Neither of them moved.

"But how did he know?"

"Know?"

"When to sing, I mean," said the boy.

"It's no mystery, really," the old man assured him, "merely a feather, one of those tiny white feathers on the head. You see, it grows inward when death approaches, this feather, and it actually penetrates the swan's brain. It was that lightness of flight inside his head that warned him."

The old man slid his hand over his own scalp, letting it rest for a moment at the base of his skull.

"It's the lightness of flight inside the head that's the only warning," he repeated softly, "and there's nothing but song after that."

Moments later, Nicolas watched the vultures, in response to a single flick of the wrist, lift, circle, and then, as if dismissed, soar off, one after the other. The boy stood dumbfounded. He was glad to see them go, he detested the birds, they frightened him; but there was something sinister as well about this natural talent that the old man seemed to have for manipulating them.

"I'll need your help."

Gillam was on his knees again, attempting to raise the swan.

Nicolas knelt as well, facing Gillam across the bird's body, both of them placing their hands carefully beneath the muddied feathers and lifting. Together they managed to transport the corpse along the shore and lay it in the bottom of the waiting skiff.

The old man shoved off with one oar, and Nicolas had to wade into the water up to his knees in order to clamber aboard, tossing the bowline in ahead of him.

From out of nowhere, their royal escort appeared.

"King," said Old Gillam, "and Queen," greeting the two mute swans formally, by their given names.

Other than that, not a word was spoken until they'd completed their brief passage, moored the boat alongside the coops, unloaded the swan, and carried it inside. Nicolas looked back once, over his shoulder—the two silent swans had turned back immediately, they were already far away, King and Queen, two shining marks on the distant water.

Gillam let the door of the swan coop swing shut behind him.

"Did you know that they mate, not with each other, but with the wind?"

"Who?"

"The vultures," said Gillam. "You don't like them very much, do you?"

The coop was dark, the narrow vents high on its stone walls covered almost completely with scraps of thick patched sackcloth. Nicolas could barely see the old man. He listened to him rummaging around through the heaps of paraphernalia with which the room was stuffed full. It was only on rare occasions that Nicolas was thus invited to keep company with Gillam while he worked indoors. This was clearly the old man's private domain. And to be honest, the boy had always preferred their lessons outdoors in the bright sunlight of the open field and forest. The door had only been closed for a few moments, yet the temperature was rising already, it was stifling, and the boy was soaked in sweat.

"For five days the vulture must sit exposing herself to the north wind, who covers her."

For the first time in his life, young Nicolas felt skeptical of the old man's words. This unexpected colloquy with vultures had sown a seed of fear, even mistrust, in their relationship.

"But that's just a tale, just a legend."

He could scarcely believe he'd said such a thing to his teacher.

"It's a legend," the old man agreed. His face was hidden in shadow.

"But is it true?" the boy persisted, in spite of himself.

Apparently it was a lesson he needed spelled out for him, once and for all.

"All legends are true," pronounced the old man, "even those that contradict one another."

"Are *yes* and *no* the same then?" the boy demanded to know.

In the obliterating darkness of the swan coop, their conversation stumbled, headlong, lacking those concrete illustrations of nature normally at their disposal.

"Yes and no? The same? Of course not! How could they be?" answered Gillam. "But neither is what is true to be confused with the one or the other, the *yes* or the *no*, the *truth* being a third thing entirely, quite distinct from either."

Gillam held a match to an old stub of candle he'd removed from a ledge above the door, and the fantastically detailed landscape of the coop interior lurched into view to rescue them from such abstractions. His vision adjusting to the flickering yellow light, Nicolas gazed around the room, eyes ranging freely over the walls of warped shelving and the countertops stacked with bottles and boxes, baskets and jars, of every conceivable size and shape and design. The huge glass urn of powdered robins' eggs was there as well, glowing dully in the corner alongside rows of even larger jars Nicolas had never noticed before, each full of indistinguishable pellets and powders.

Old Gillam caught and followed the path of the youngster's wide eyes. "Quail feathers," he said, pointing, "elks' teeth, goose down, elderberries, owl droppings, pemmican, rainwater, dew, the wings of termites. . . ." He chanted on, as the boy's gaze strummed the rows of shelves as if they were the strings of a musical instrument, " . . . comfrey, bloodwort, arnica, crows' quills, nutmeg, fox fur, the thorns of the yellow rose, peppermint, lambswool, paraffin, fish scales, honey, quicklime, hazelnuts, corn, wheat, tadpoles, a spider's web, sage." Such a straightforward inventory was hardly in keeping with the air of reserve customarily maintained by the old man here behind the swan coop's closed door, and Nicolas was caught off guard by his candor.

On a table across the room, next to the inert swan they'd deposited there with its wings outstretched, the boy saw a series of skeletal shapes, hollow frames of some sort, no two alike, woven from sturdy straw or river reeds or the youngest branches of a tree, green and still flexible. Nearby lay the soles of at least a dozen pairs of shoes, silhouettes clipped out from the pale bark of the silver birch. And here and there were piles of what looked like bones, tiny slender bones, stacked up neatly against one another to form little teepees or pyramids.

"Ribs," said Old Gillam, "the ribs of the meadowlark."

His eyes growing more and more comfortable with candlelight, the improbable collection of artifacts that spilled from every available surface and shadow surrendered themselves more and more readily. And even those more prosaic objects, a ball of string, for instance, or a silver spoon, acquired a quality wholly alien when discovered in proximity to an abandoned beehive or a saucer full of mercury or a mallard's wing torn in two.

Then there were the nests.

Nicolas had never thought it possible for a bird as fiercely territorial as the swan to nest in a colony such as this one. On more than one occasion, chancing upon one of their enormous thronelike nests while rambling around the lakes, he'd been forced to flee the aggressive display of the furiously protective parents. "It's said that with its powerful wings a swan can break a grown man's arm," Gillam had warned him. Yet here, within the close quarters of the coop, these antisocial birds had built dozens and dozens of nests. The floor beneath the counters and tabletops was lined with them, some no more than a few feet apart.

"Argent himself was born right here." Old Gillam pointed to a huge nest directly below the table on which the dead swan now lay. "And King and Queen," he said, "over there." He cleared his throat. "That was a long time ago, of course."

Indeed, the mounds of nests seemed ancient to the boy, rising up from the shadows like the rubble of a ruined city.

Nicolas heard a fresh flutter of wings and felt a fanful of air brush, ghostlike, by his face. He spotted the pale white dove easily in the gloom, quivering, cupped tenderly in Old Gillam's agile hands.

"Hold her for me."

He passed the bird gently, and the boy held it, its wings pinned, its heartbeat vibrating against his palms, as Gillam dragged the heavy old stump of an oak across the floor, mounted it, and then reached up to free one of the narrow vents from its ragged curtain. A ray of light fell through the room, down the opposite wall, and out across the countertop that supported the dead swan, slicing it in two with a brilliant white line.

Nicolas handed the dove up to his teacher.

"A long time ago," said Gillam, stroking the bird between its tensed wings, "a dove just like this one was released out into a world even more barren than our city of abandoned nests in here."

He raised the dove up over his head, maneuvering it toward the open window.

"And she returned from the wasteland with an olive branch clenched in her beak, you remember?"

Nicolas nodded. He remembered.

There was a flash as well as a flutter of wings now, the dove's white feathers soaking up the sudden sunlight as it flew straight out the window from the old man's opened hands.

"Let's see what she brings us back this time."

The sackcloth fell back into place and the ray of light vanished. Old Gillam climbed down from his makeshift stool, crossed the coop, hesitated as if looking for something, then retraced his steps, and reached out for a small amber glass jar nearly hidden behind an open box filled with copper coins and cherrystones and fishhooks. Opening the rusty lid with some difficulty, he shook a portion of the contents out into his palm, then vigorously rubbed his hands together and sniffed them.

"Ahhhhhh," he sighed, "smell that."

Nicolas inhaled.

It was as if the ray of light had entered the room all over again, more slowly this time, with the speed of syrup, and the color as well.

"Cinnamon?"

"N-n-not quite."

The boy stole one more sniff before the old man withdrew his hands.

"Cassia," said Gillam, "from the nest of the Phoenix."

The old man was used to the hothouse atmosphere inside the closed swan coop, but the drop of water hanging from the tip of the boy's nose reminded him that he was streaming with perspiration.

"Well, I think that's enough of a sweat for one afternoon," he said, tossing the boy a rag with which to mop his brow and the back of his neck. "Why don't you open the door a bit—"

Nicolas did not have to be asked twice.

"Or better yet, why not just wait for me outside while I gather up a few things in here, and—"

The boy had already been swallowed up in the gust of sweet fresh air that rushed in through the open doorway.

Gillam laughed out loud.

"We'll see what he brings back to me when the time comes, we'll see," he muttered, "we'll see, we'll see," as he flitted around the coop, gathering up a jar here, a dented tin or a lidless carton there, stuffing them all haphazardly into one sack, then heading toward the door after the boy. Remembering the candle, he turned back, hesitating before the outstretched body of Old Argent. Reaching out slowly, thoughtfully, he lifted the swan's head, as before, examining it, turning it this way and that. Shaking his own head then, he let the swan's fall back to the table with a soft plop, quickly blew out the candle, shouldered his sack, and scampered out the door.

"This way!" he called to Nicolas.

They headed toward the open meadow.

Old Gillam talked as they walked, producing another mysterious perfume from his tattered sack, warming it in his hands, softening it, then passing it to the boy.

"Frankincense."

"It's sticky," said Nicolas, smelled it, and smiled.

"Another favorite of the nesting Phoenix."

The boy pretty much knew when to ask questions and when to remain silent.

"What does it look like?" he asked.

"Hmmm?"

"The Phoenix. What does it look like?"

"Let's stop here," said Gillam.

They sat down on the grassy bank of a small creek edged with fern and laurel and a tide of wild strawberries that crept around roots and rocks, avoiding the moisture and the shade, flowing from one patch of bright sunlight to the other. The old man emptied his sack immediately, talking quietly all the while, letting the sound of his voice merge with the babble and gurgle of the water flowing alongside them.

"I've never seen the Phoenix," he admitted.

"Never?"

Nicolas assumed that his teacher had seen everything, once, at least.

"Well," he explained, as if to excuse himself, "there is only one, you know, only one in the whole wide world."

"Only one?"

"That's right."

Gillam had spread out his collection of rusty, cracked containers in a sloppy ring around them. And now he proceeded, methodically, to open each in turn, offering them one by one, after the briefest preparation, to the boy, who sampled them.

"They say that its neck is golden," he said as he worked. "They say that its feathers are a deep purple, and that its head is crowned with an exquisite crest."

Nicolas leaned in to smell the resin beneath the old man's thumbnail.

"Myrrh," said Gillam.

The boy exhaled.

"But, if there's only one, then, then how . . . ?"

"Musk," said the old man, working quickly.

The boy's eyes were watering, and he almost sneezed.

". . . then what happens then, when, then when it dies?"

"Well," said Old Gillam, "that doesn't happen very often."

The boy lowered his brow almost to his chin and just stared, perplexed, drunk and dizzy with perfumes.

21

Old Gillam took a deep breath.

"You see, the Phoenix lives for a very, very long time, and when it is about to die—"

He held out his hand once again.

"Mmmmm, cedar!"

Nicolas recognized that one.

"—when it is about to die," the old man continued, "it builds itself a nest of cassia and frankincense and fills it with every sort of fragrant herb and spice. All of these," he said, with the sweeping gesture of a merchant in a roadside bazaar, "all of these, and more."

Nicolas was a quick learner, and by now he'd begun sampling the wares on his own, without assistance. He especially enjoyed scratching the surface of the little block of sandalwood to release its fragrance, and crushing the essence from the pale jasmine petals. It was a gorgeous afternoon, the bright blue of the sky crossed by a few thick white lazy clouds and crisscrossed more quickly by garlands of songbirds, finches and bobolinks and waxbills, racing from tree to tree. On the far side of the creek several deer had come to graze and drink, and Nicolas could see a cowbird or two, and some sparrows, hopping excitedly about on their backs, pecking at fleas or bits of thistle, then fluttering up and resettling near the tail or on the head.

The old man's voice melted in and out of the creek's continual comment.

"And when the nest is completed, the Phoenix places itself in the center and begins to flap its wings at the sun, generating more and more heat."

From far away the fanatical hammering of a woodpecker started, stopped, and started again.

"Finally the nest bursts into flame, blazing up, consuming itself. And the bird is burnt to ash along with it."

"Honeysuckle!" shouted the boy, recognizing yet another perfume.

The deer loped off across the meadow, frightened by his outburst, their attendant cowbirds hovering above them, fluttering, unable to land.

"Yes, honeysuckle," said the old man, smiling, sniffing at the dried flowers himself.

He leaned forward, placing his hands on the boy's shoulders.

"The bird is burnt to ash," he repeated, "and from this ash is born a worm."

"A worm?"

Nicolas wrinkled up his nose, recoiling.

The old man's hands fell from his shoulders.

"Yes, a worm, a very special worm."

"A *worm*?"

"And from this very special worm grows a young bird that takes up all that remains of the nest and its parent, and flies away with it to a sacred city of the sun."

Nicolas was wide-eyed, but the sudden arrival of the dove prevented him from questioning the old man any further.

"Well, what have we here?" laughed Gillam. "Back from the wasteland already?"

The dove had perched right on his shoulder.

"Look!" cried Nicolas in alarm.

A bright red drop had fallen from the dove's beak, staining the old man's shoulder.

"What has it brought?"

It was a feather, a tiny, wet, red feather, soaked in blood.

The bird lingered only a moment before rising again into the air, realighting on a narrow peninsula of rock jutting out into the creek. As they watched, Gillam from where he sat, Nicolas from where he'd run to for a closer look, the dove gently dipped its head into the stream, then lifted it back out again, its dark round eyes blinking as the cold water beaded up and rolled from its feathers. Again and again it dipped, and blinked, the dark eyes ever unfathomable, betraying no emotion, not even patience. Each time, the feather in its beak grew paler in color, until finally, its baptism completed, it shone brilliant white, whiter even than the dove's own plumage.

The bird rose into the air, landing once again on the old man's boney shoulder. Grazing his ear with her beak, she released the soaked white feather, leaving it plastered to his skin. Gillam reached up and with his fingertips peeled the wet feather from behind his ear and held it up to his eyes.

"I might have looked for days around the lake and never found it myself," he marveled.

The dove was grooming herself, cooing quietly. She shook the remaining water from her feathers, flapping her wings and sprinkling the side of Old Gillam's head. It seemed to Nicolas that the old man rose to his feet as quickly, and at precisely the same instant, as the dove rose into the air—although the coincidence ended right there, for they both headed immediately in opposite directions. The old man mumbled something over his shoulder, something about work to do, slippers to finish, barley to roast, cherries to stem and pit, music to transcribe. Nicolas wasn't really listening. He knew by his tone of voice that Gillam was talking only to himself. He was quite content to be left on his own for a while, right where he was, reclining on the grassy bank in his ring of fragrances. It had been a full day, exhausting, really, and it felt so wonderful to stretch out in the sunlight, with nothing to do and nothing in particular to think about, that he dozed right off, jasmine in one hand, sandalwood in the other, and slept for the rest of the afternoon.

The boy sat hunched over with his head in his hands on the old, crumbling stone stoop out behind the swan coop. He'd stopped crying, finally. With one foot he was tracing some sort of pattern in the bran and the millet that had spilled out onto the ground. The feedsack had split at the seams right where he'd dropped it. He was telling himself over and over that he couldn't possibly cry anymore than he already had, while his bare foot moved mechanically to and fro in front of him like a pendulum.

And then he started to cry once more, and the tears seeped through his clenched fingers, and they darkened the spilled bran, and moistened the loose soil, and muddied his absently moving foot.

Near the horizon, the very last heron was setting out from its nest, the morning mist that still clung to the earth falling back from its ascending form like a loose sleeve from the pale arm of a woman reaching out for something too far away to touch. Only last night, the boy and the old man had sat together on this same stoop and watched the herons, returning, dipping into rather than rising out of the mist, as they flew home to roost for the night. Any bird's flight, any bird's call, could elicit from Old Gillam yet another facet of his infinite knowledge of bird lore and legend. The previous evening had been no different from any other, except that it was the last of such evenings he and the boy were ever to spend together.

"The herons," he'd said, pointing with his chin, "returning."

He traced a circle in the dust at his feet.

Nicolas sat quietly, attentively, waiting for the inevitable anecdote or fable to follow. But Old Gillam remained obstinately silent, watching the birds sweep back to their nests from all quarters of the sky like iron filings converging on a single hidden magnet. An hour later, alone now, Nicolas was surprised to find himself returning to his own nest beneath the cedar tree. Though, for sentimental reasons, he'd never allowed it to fall into disrepair, he had long since outgrown the habit of sleeping there. But that night, moved by the old man's mysteriously mute circle in the dust, he'd been drawn back to the nervous sleep of his original teachers, the hermit thrushes, and though he was by now too large to fit in the nest, he curled up on the ground beside it and drifted off, his breath keeping time, all night, with the slow beat of great blue broad wings.

It seemed an eternity ago, that peaceful night's sleep. It seemed as if a wall stood between last night and this morning. Through his tears, Nicolas looked down at that patch of ground where the old man's circle had been sketched, and he saw instead his own muddy foot and the straight line it had traced, over and over again, as it marked a different sort of time, one without curve or comfort.

Nicolas flung himself to his feet, kicking at the ground in a rage, obliterating the line he'd cut into the earth. And yet no wall came tumbling down. No circle reappeared, curling round to meet itself. Something was broken, blocked. And beneath a sky tilting irrevocably toward the blind blue of noon, a sky from which both mist and heron had at last evaporated, the boy stood trembling with grief.

He remembered the old man's words.

"Never forget, my boy, that even a single feather of the fabled Phoenix is said to be the remedy for all the anger and grief the heart and mind of man is heir to."

Nicolas had, dutifully, never forgotten.

But he had never really understood, either, for understanding is not a matter of duty, but of something else.

Like any child, Nicolas had had his share of disappointments and frustrations. But this misery that had opened now like a wound in the depths of his soul was wholly new. It burned his heart with anger and paralyzed him with despair. It could not be endured, and yet it went on and on, through one spasm of tears and one tantrum of anger to the next, unrelieved, unrelenting.

"Never forget, my boy, this great remedy. I will tell you a secret."

Nicolas sat perfectly still.

"We two-legged creatures, birds and men, we share a common religion."

For a long time Nicolas stood staring at Old Gillam lying flat on his back, dead, inside the swan coop. I'm nothing without him, he wept aloud, nothing at all. I have no arms, no legs, no voice, no eyes or ears. I'm nothing, nothing but tears. An hour later, still crying, he fled the coop, and stood staring out across the lake, crippled, not just by his own sorrow, but by all sorrow—that shared sorrow from which nothing and no one could escape as it passed from stars to stones to birds to men, to fathers to sons, and back again. And it was then, and only then, that the fabulous Phoenix truly arose for the boy for the first time in all its painful splendor. *For the eagerly coveted medicine remains lifeless until animated by that anguish for which it is the only sure cure.*

The boy turned his heavy head and wiped the tears from his red and swollen eyes.

Where before there had been only the whitewashed walls of the coops and barns and incubators, chalked and limed with their encrustations of bird droppings, where before there had been only dwellings, there now appeared this strange thing called a path, which led out into the world beyond the boundaries of the familiar forest, a world about which Nicolas, despite all his studies with the old man, knew next to nothing. That very morning, that very moment, Nicolas vowed to find the Phoenix, and to return, triumphant, with that great and glorious medicine for all passion, pain, and sorrow. Even the smallest, the most insignificant of its feathers would suffice. And for this unspeakable privilege, he told himself, he was prepared to spend all his substance, to travel far and wide, and to endure any hardship.

It was as if the wise old man had already known of the Pilgrim's path. Next

to his lifeless body on the coop floor he'd left gifts for the sad young man. The black blindfold. The bright yellow slippers lined with birch and stitched with dried berries. And the two bags, fully packed, resembling wineskins, but in fact made by a mysterious process from the carcasses of dead swans.

Old Gillam had often alluded to the swan bags, making veiled promises to the boy to teach him, always at some later, undisclosed date, the secret of their manufacture—and now here they were, two of them, lying on either side of the old man who'd taken their recipe with him to the silence of the grave. Nicolas knelt on the threshold of the swan coop and reached out to touch one of the bags, stroking its feathers as if it were still a living creature.

The boy wasted no more time in mourning.

He was possessed by his vision of the Phoenix.

Donning the yellow slippers, the blindfold poised in his trembling hand, he took one long last look around—and no matter in which direction he let his eyes roam, always, radiating out from where he stood, like spokes from the center of a wheel, was the path, the same path, proceeding.

Everything seemed to stand still in anticipation of his first step. The wind withdrew, birds swallowed their songs, the foliage of the trees in the distance seemed to hang like ascending smoke arrested in midair. Even the fox that normally worried the coops, day and night, stood motionless, exposed in broad daylight, not so much looking as listening for that first footfall.

The aviary vanished as he slipped the blindfold down over his brow, the power of his eyes gradually draining into his other senses, filling them with sight. Through the soles of his slippers he could feel the stones in the path beneath his feet. He heard the fox trying not to breathe and smelled the fresh droppings of the geese. His own sighs were deafening, booming in his ears like water in a cave.

The soft down of the swan bags tickled his wrists and his palms as he hoisted them up from the ground. They were heavy, and where his fingers curled around them, pressing up against their throats, he even fancied he could detect the last remnant of a pulse or the last lingering note of a song, not quite stilled.

His cheeks were wet.

His blindfold was soaked in tears.

CHAPTER TWO

The Forest of Riddles

Day and night went on alternating, no doubt about it, but to the blind-folded boy their stark contrasts were reduced to little more than a change in temperature. Certain sounds and sensations were added or subtracted—the hooting of an owl withdrawn to make way for an oriole's whistle, the wrinkles in cricket song smoothed and polished to the hard sheen of locusts whining, sun and moon trading sweat for dew, and the wind changing its direction, or its odor, from north or south to east or west, from mold or peat to mint or briar rose.

Under the circumstances, sleep was not to be thought of, nor was food. Such kindly old habits, which might have marked the hours in some recognizable order, were out of the question. And as for counting them, the hours, the days—that would have made him feel too much like a prisoner, which, after all, he was not. He was a pilgrim. And so he counted nothing, measured noth-ing—except that distance, hopefully decreasing a step at a time, which lay between himself and the Phoenix, between his aching heart and its promised balm.

More than once he stumbled, dropping to one knee or to all fours, one time even sprawling out with his chin in the stones. But he always raised himself up again and continued on.

It was impossible to say exactly when he became conscious of the sound. It had been there all along, perhaps, and thus experienced along with all the other sightless sense impressions. Yet for some reason it had suddenly raised itself up out of that dark sea and broken the surface, like a bubble from the depths, or one's own voice in a crowd. ˙

Except after stumbling, or falling, Nicolas had never stopped walking in however many dark days and nights he'd been traveling so far. But stop he did now, abruptly, standing motionless as if rooted to the spot. Tired, half starved, crazed with grief, his feet numb, his wrists and shoulders stiff with pain—he just stood there, waiting blindly, listening.

Until he heard it again.

Far in the distance.

Immediately he began to charge back and forth through the darkness inside his head, attempting to dress the sound in whatever came to mind. Was it a bronze gong or a hound's howl, a roar or sigh or moan, the ring of an anvil, part of a loon's laugh, or just the wind trumpeting through a dead tree trunk's hollow? It had, as yet, no form, nothing with which to support the weight of even the simplest, lightest garment. It merely crumpled up into itself at the touch of each potential image, and vanished into the very air that every sound is made of. It was only natural for the boy from the nest to rely, when all else failed, on the hollow skeleton of a bird. It was within such a delicate cage that he trapped the sound at last, clothing it with every form of feather imaginable—arriving, at last, at the most obvious of conclusions, one that made his heart leap and set his feet in motion once again.

It was the call of the Phoenix.

Of course!

Never mind if it sounded like no other birdcall he'd ever heard before. That was to be expected. "There is only one," the old man had told him, "only one in the whole wide world."

It seemed to Nicolas that all more familiar sounds faded away then, as he strode blindly through the forest, listening for that one sound like no other. And he wasn't disappointed, for the strange call rang out with increasing frequency, reorienting the boy each time, changing the direction in which he was headed, luring him on irresistibly.

It was a single low dark note, but bright around the edges, like an object eclipsing the sun, all shadowy in its center, all fiery around the rim. It played tricks upon the boy, rising and falling in volume, approaching, then suddenly receding, coming first from one direction and then from its opposite, sometimes, through the mischief of its echo, coming from two different directions at once. Nicolas never hesitated, nor did his path falter. They were one, he and his path, like the spider and the sticky thread it spins from its own self. Perhaps he was walking in circles, doubling back, retracing his steps. Perhaps he was only walking a web. Perhaps he would even end up right back where he came from, in the aviary, this queer ringing in his ears his sole trophy. That was of no importance to him now. He would follow this call wherever it led.

There came a moment, ultimately, when the sound erupted with such force, and from so many directions at once, that Nicolas felt as if he'd somehow entered right into it, and it into him. It was everywhere, vibrating in each and every particle of the air, and he breathed it in, in great startled gulps, until he was filled with it, until he could hold his breath no longer, and the sound came rushing back out of his gaping mouth. As he cried out under its spell, anyone might have sworn that the strange sound issued from the boy himself, that it was his own voice—that it was not the call *of*, but rather the call *to*, the fabulous Phoenix.

For one gasping instant there was no air at all, and no sound. Such strange music had apparently shattered and stolen its own instrument. Another music, another call, arose in its place.

> *The blindest season's tricks*
> *But lend circumference to the ring.*
> *Seek now that deeper point*
> *From which the horn's wide music springs.*

Nicolas froze.

He felt as if he'd been struck physically, boxed in the ears, or slapped right across the face. Accustomed as he was by now to his blindness, he nevertheless found his head spinning like a top, searching without sight, trying to fix the voice, trying to anchor it at a safe distance from his panic.

"Wh-who is it?" he asked feebly.

There was no reply.

And so he tried again, "Who's there?"

Once more the voice split the stillness.

> *It is not ordinary water*
> *But a pool of dew*
> *That shall afford the one who seeks himself*
> *The clearer view.*

"But I do not seek myself," blurted out the blindfolded boy, "I seek the fabulous Phoenix who is burnt to ash and from a worm reborn . . . " Nicolas had a strange sensation, as if the voice knew in advance what it was that he wanted to say, as if it had finished his sentence for him, " . . . and a single one of whose feathers will be strong enough to lift this heavy stone from your heart."

Had he spoken aloud?

He could not tell.

All he knew for sure was that his feet were wet, that he suddenly found himself standing in water up to his ankles.

"Not ordinary water, but dew," he corrected himself, but once again it was as if his voice were not quite his own, as if there were another voice that spoke through him, or in him, of things about which he could have no knowledge.

Nicolas backed up carefully until he was standing once more on dry land.

"Perhaps," he reasoned with himself, lifting his feet up one at a time and letting the dew drain from his waterlogged slippers, "perhaps there is no other voice at all, perhaps it is *all* only *inside* my head."

He did not recognize the laughter that took hold of him then, and shook him ever so gently.

32

"That's not me laughing," he insisted.

"Then who is it?" he wanted to know.

"It's you," he said.

"And who am I?" he asked.

The boy's face reddened, as the question, apparently someone else's, nevertheless fell from his own lips. *Hoo-mm-aiii, hoo-mm-aiii, hoo-mm-aiii,* it echoed in the distance, a phrase of birdsong repeated over and over again, haunting him from within even as it taunted him from outside.

"Just what is it you wish to know?" he asked himself.

"I want to know who is talking."

"When?"

"Now."

"When you are talking?"

"No, not when I am talking but when you are talking."

"You want to know who is talking now?"

Nicolas stamped his foot. In his exasperation, he'd forgotten which of the two voices was most his own.

"Ohhh, if only I could see," he sighed.

It was the first time his eyes had complained since he'd blindfolded himself and set out what seemed like so long ago.

"See what?"

"What is outside," he said. "Then I would know."

"Know what?"

"What is inside, or which is inside, or—"

Once more someone else's laugh rose up in his throat and tickled the roof of his mouth.

"Absurd! Look out and see in, no doubt look in to see out, why not just look at, you've never thought of that?"

How he yearned to be free of all this vertiginous chatter, how he yearned to hear once more that mysterious call, that long, lone note whose trail he'd followed so earnestly, and then lost, all at once.

"How can it be that I have gone so far astray?" he asked himself.

"You're tired."

Nicolas felt as if the bags he carried doubled in weight with each passing moment, and though he could not tell, in his habit of darkness, whether his eyes were open or closed, their lids lay heavy as sand or stone.

"Yes," he admitted, unable to resist his hidden conversational partner any longer, "I'm tired."

"And you're hungry."

"I am, I'm so hungry."

He sighed, dropping his shoulders, hanging his head.

"Who are you?" he whispered, softly.

In darkness, like a ripened pearl,
I am the hunter's eye.
I'm the question whispered in the ear of grain.
Who am I?

There was no mistaking *this* voice for his own. It seemed to come from infinitely far away, and though it whispered, almost tenderly, it thundered as well, frightening a flock of dark, swallowlike birds, flushing them up from the treetops in one startled mass that swept back and forth across the sky like an enormous scythe composed of thousands of smaller blades. He couldn't see them, but he could hear them, each rhythmic stroke of their sharp curved wings harvesting another shrill cry of *hoo-mm-aiii, hoo-mm-aiii, hoo-mm-aiii.*

Nicolas winced, recognizing their song.

He expected them to calm, and gradually settle. He expected the voice to slip back into its claustrophobic disguise and resume its nagging burlesque inside his head. But the birds increased in number, swarming, their cry swelling to such a pitch that it seemed as if all four corners of the earth echoed in unison.

Nicolas covered his ears, but it was no use.

"*Hoo-mm-aiii, hoo-mm-aiii, hoo-mm-aiii, hoo-mm-aiii, hoo-mm-aiii, hoo-mm-aiii, hoo-mm-aiii, hoo-mm-aiii, hoo-mm-aiii, hoo-mm-aiii, hoo-mm-aiii, hoo-mm-aiii, hoo-mm-aiii, hoo-mm-aiii, hoo-mm-aiii, hoo-mm-aiii, hoo-mm-aiii, hoo-mm-aiii, hoo-mm-aiii. . . .*"

He'd never realized just how insanely repetitive the song of a two-legged creature could be.

He didn't remember untying the blindfold.

It was as if it had dissolved, or grown transparent, all on its own. It was as if it had been forgotten, rather than removed.

Nor had he any idea how long he'd been standing there, paralyzed with fatigue, riddled with birdsong, his chin on his chest, his head far too heavy to lift.

The boy's vision returned so unexpectedly that at first he could scarcely see at all—all he saw was himself, his own reflection, but then that had been the riddle's rude secret all along. His own face just appeared before him, blossoming out of the darkened depths, and like anything that just *happens*, it trembled imperceptibly, as if painted upon some surface only momentarily stilled.

Nicolas stared into his own watery eyes.

He'd never seen himself so clearly before. There had been other reflections, tentative portraits in the lakes and ponds and overflowing buckets of the aviary. But they had been murkier mirrors, in them his face had had to contend with all sorts of foreign matter, bits of mud and algae, rotting leaves or branches half submerged, bubbles or ripples, or distorting waves.

The pool of dew in which the boy's face now appeared was free of all such obstruction and distraction. The dew was, by its very nature, devoid of every quality whatsoever. It was liquid in its infancy, passive, a perfect mirror, and in it Nicolas saw his head suspended, motionless, yet alive. It might have been the reflection of a ripe plum ready to drop with a splash from an overhanging branch.

Slowly he felt the heaviness in his head and his limbs drain away. He felt his muscles relaxing, one tensed fiber at a time. The ache in his neck, the ringing in his ears, the throbbing in his back and his thighs, all seemed to seep away. Even the pounding of his heart surrendered and was tamed.

When he finally raised his head from his reflection, and turned to look around, it was with a body grown so light he could scarcely feel it at all.

He had indeed traveled a long way. The forest in which he found himself was not the forest from which he had come. That forest had been open, this was closed. It was dark and damp and still, and it seemed to grow in two directions at once—up with the long slick trunks of slender trees, dark oily bamboo and warped palm, and then down again, its pale bloodless vines and creepers strangling the air and sucking at the gloom itself as if it were a stretch of soil or a patch of light on which to feed.

The rustling and the rattling in the thick blue-black shadows of the canopy overhead remained sourceless. Whatever it was that moved there refused to show itself. Except that with each disturbance, a few fat cold drops of water would be dislodged from some invisible leaf or frond high above, and they would fall slowly through the air, finally striking the wet earth, each with its own soft popping sound.

"Where am I?" the lost boy whispered to himself.

"You are in my pool, you are in my pool of dew."

He'd hardly expected a reply.

Wheeling around he found, to his astonishment, that he was not alone. Close behind him sat a great grain-colored ram, with white hooves and horns, and white ears, a white nose, and snow-white lips.

Caught between the Ram and the pool of dew, Nicolas backed up the few available steps until he felt the clear cold water behind him, lapping at his heels. The Ram did not move. With its pale legs tucked up comfortably beneath its body and its eyes shut tight, it appeared to be sleeping, and the boy hesitated before initiating conversation, unaccustomed to any sort of cooperation between sleep and speech.

"Excuse me," he said finally, and then again, a little louder, "Excuse me," hoping to wake the beast gently, respectfully, by degrees.

But the Ram did not respond.

The boy just stood there, not knowing quite what to do. A drop of water falling from the dark roof of the forest struck the Ram's broad back with a dull plop, then ran away in a little rivulet, darkening and matting the dirty golden hairs through which it negotiated its way. How long had the beast been sleeping there, Nicolas wondered, still as a mound of earth, never moving a muscle?

"Excuse me!" he repeated, even louder this time, for here at last was a creature he could question, a creature as strange as this strange new land into which he'd wandered. Surely the animal could guide or advise him. He must not let such an opportunity pass.

"Who are you?!"

Nicolas hadn't meant to shout, and he dodged his own echo as it came bouncing back at him.

"You are the boy, Nicolas," said the Ram, without opening its eyes, "come from the nest, come from the great sorrow in the aviary, come to seek the Phoenix, no matter what the cost."

The Ram remained perfectly still. Only its snowy lips had moved.

"I know who I am," the boy attempted to boast, mustering indignation at this invasion of privacy.

"Thanks to the dew," the Ram reminded him.

"The dew?"

"The pool of spring dew, the sacred oasis of which I am the guardian. . . ."

Nicolas turned to glance at the pool behind him.

". . . at your service," concluded the motionless Ram.

Something prevented the boy from speaking, something he'd seen out of the furthest corner of his eye. He turned back to the pool and then away again several times in quick succession. Each time it seemed to him as if his reflection were waiting there for him. Each time it seemed as if it remained behind when he'd again turned away. But if he were there, in the water, then who—?

"Do not be alarmed," said the Ram.

For the first time since the disappearance of his blindfold, Nicolas looked down at himself without the aid of the Ram's reflecting pool.

"Where am I?" he cried out, for his body was not there.

"In my pool," the Ram reminded the boy yet again, with the patient sigh of an ancient teacher of stubborn children.

Nicolas spun round, flailing his arms, kicking out his legs.

"Now do as I suggest," said the Ram, "and revel, without fear, in this temporary lightness of limb."

It was the oddest of sensations, but it was sensation nonetheless. He knew that he still took up space, he could feel it, but it was a different kind of space, it was a different kind of feeling, it was lighter, more buoyant. And it was clear, perfectly clear. Nicolas was sure of that because he examined every part of himself, from head to toe, one transparent inch after another. He was nowhere to be seen.

"My bags, my swan bags!" he suddenly cried aloud, terrified.

One look at his invisible hands revealed that their baggage had disappeared as well.

Swiftly he turned to face the oracular pool, his question unspoken on the invisible tip of his tongue. There was his reflection, just as he'd left it, staring back at him. Filled with dread, fearing the worst, he began to raise his arms, slowly, watching as they appeared gradually over the rim of the pool, first his shoulders, then his elbows and his wrists. He paused for a moment, closing his eyes before allowing the movement to complete itself, not opening them again until his arms, upstretched like the wings of a bird, could reach no further. There they were then, the two precious swan bags, floating in the blue dew, hanging like pale pendants from his tightly closed fists. The boy's arms grew tired, but he did not wish to lose sight of his precious cargo. He raised his feet, one at a time, marveling as his bright yellow slippers stepped out across the surface of the pool without the slightest splash or the smallest ripple.

"What is it that you carry with you, in the bodies of swans?"

Nicolas had nearly forgotten the Ram.

He lowered his arms at last, sufficiently reassured, and turned to face the beast who'd still neither stirred nor opened its eyes.

A growing suspicion took hold of him. Perhaps, he thought, the Ram was a reflection as well, and while it sat here, motionless, seemingly asleep, its body was in fact wandering through the forest, grazing contentedly, nibbling at the lichen-covered rocks, gnawing the sweet wet bark from the trunks of trees.

"Is an oracle all answers, then, and unable to question?" asked the Ram. "Why do you not reply?"

Nicolas could not reply. He'd no idea what the swan bags contained. It was not he who'd packed them but Old Gillam. He'd merely hoisted them up, and set out on his journey. And all these days and nights he'd traveled, carrying he knew not what, his arms and his shoulders aching, his muscles straining against this burden that his grief and his haste had kept hidden from him.

"How foolish I've been," he thought.

But the Ram banished the thought from his head.

"On the contrary," it said.

"But all this time, all this trouble," whined the boy.

"A wilderness," agreed the Ram, "incoherent and untidy."

"And all along maybe there's been, right here in my bags, something that might have helped me, something I might have—"

"Perhaps," snapped the Ram, its white lips curling back to reveal its whiter teeth, "but promise me something."

The boy waited, but the Ram had fallen silent.

"What?" he asked, "what must I promise?"

"You must promise first, then I will tell you."

"But—"

"That's the gamble of wisdom, my dear boy."

Nicolas melted. It was the old man's voice he'd heard, for it was Old Gillam whose *dear boy* he had always been and would always remain.

"I promise," he said.

"That you will never," the Ram swore for him, "under any circumstances, open the swan bags."

"But what if inside—"

"No matter what silly emergency seems to pressure you into what drastic action, you must never attempt to utilize their contents."

"But if—"

"Likewise, you must never part with them, but must keep them with you always."

Nicolas kept quiet for a moment, phrasing and rephrasing his objections over and over again in his head, searching for an expression for them that would not violate the solemnity of his oath.

"But if I heard it again, like before," he said at last, imploring, "the call of the Phoenix, then mightn't I search through the bags for some gift from Gillam that might help me to—"

"You heard no Phoenix calling, my boy, but only my horn."

Nicolas turned his back to the Ram, resisting his words.

"It was I who called to you, it was I who drew you in, into the dew."

And it was in the dew that the boy now saw himself struggling to hold back his tears of disappointment.

"Then I am no nearer my goal," he muttered under his breath, "and no further from grief than when I began."

"Come from the nest, come from the great sorrow in the aviary, come seeking the Phoenix," whispered the Ram, teasing, "no matter what the cost."

Nicolas whirled around.

"Tell me, then," he demanded, a warrior trying to wrest from the oracle of victory its crucial secret, "tell me of the sound it makes!" He dropped to his invisible knees. "How shall I recognize the call of the fabulous Phoenix?"

"I really don't know," said the Ram, "I've never heard it."

"Never?" croaked the boy.

"There is only one, you know," the Ram reminded him, and once more it was the old man's voice that echoed through the dark wet wood, "only one in the whole wide world."

Nicolas sighed, at his wit's end.

"There *is* one who might be able to help you."

The boy fixed his eyes upon the Ram's snowy lips, watching the unfamiliar word they held and then released, studying the shape of it as it fell out into the air.

"Neema."

"Neema?"

"Queen of All the Shepherds," said the sleeping beast, "perhaps she can show you the way."

"And where shall I find her?" cried the boy, leaping to his feet, light as air.

"Where the animals gather," replied the Ram.

"But where do the animals——?"

A sudden stab of pain cut Nicolas short, a sudden weight bruised the air in his lungs, stifling him. He couldn't even scream, as he swooned, crashing to earth, clutching one foot.

So preoccupied had he been with the Ram's words and the pictures in the dew that he'd paid no attention to the equally articulate movements in the shadows, to the snake that had been approaching stealthily for some time now, spiraling softly down to the ground from its hidden lair high overhead in the rustle and rattle of the wood's dark canopy. It struck swiftly, sinking its fangs into the boy's left foot—releasing its venom all at once, in a split second. As he plummeted to the ground, Nicolas caught only a glimpse of the serpent's tail as it sped away, slithering back into deep shadow, escaping.

It was as if all the heaviness of his body poured back into him at once. The wound's bright spark of pain burst into a thousand brilliant fragments that illuminated the inky darkness stealing over him, its fireworks congealing, as they cooled and fell, into the familiar patterns of his own returning flesh. Even with his failing eyesight, the boy could see that his body had resumed its accustomed color and character—it had reappeared. At the same time, before he blacked out completely, he saw the Ram's body shimmer as in a mirage, its liquid surface ruptured by that same bright meteoric pain that had so brutally plumbed his own depths.

The beast shattered, and evaporated.

And the boy was left stretched out in a dark, empty wood beside the blank surface of a small, still pool. He was blind again, and all alone.

Nicolas struggled to awake, as if from a dream, a nightmare, though it was not sleep, but something darker, that held him tight. The experience of blindness was familiar by now, and the sounds that penetrated his dark prison were embroidered more elaborately than ever before, even the simplest among them assuming fantastic shapes and associations.

The hardest of gems, a diamond, fell with a single clink onto a sheet of glass, which cracked with a long hiss that forked into several streams of steam at once, each one whistling off in a different direction and fading. The petal of a rose, heated in a furnace, yielded a thick squeaking syrup that deepened to a sob as it cooled and hardened. A hum of blue frost squeezed a steep sigh from a single white hair, which split in two with a loud, sharp snap. Ordinary windsongs or birdcalls, perhaps, warblers or gales or larks or breezes or sparrows—but not to Nicolas, who fought his way through their sonic jungle, holding fast to his hope of hearing the Phoenix call, drawn in by but rejecting each successive sound as unworthy of such a royal designation, then using those rejected sounds as the rungs of a ladder upon which he climbed back toward not only that light he'd lost but that light he'd not yet known as well, that mythical city of the sun toward which the newborn Phoenix must fly. It was as if there were only one sound, only one song, that was constantly transformed by his hallucinating ear into the next sound and the next and the next.

It was the barking of a dog with which the series at last ended, not because his imagination or the eloquence of the world of phenomena had exhausted itself, but because of a decreasing opacity in the air, a graying around the edges of his eyes, that caught his attention, and made him realize that somehow, sometime, during his struggle, his blindness had become mixed with, then replaced by, a simpler night, a night that was apparently drawing to its close now. Nicolas attempted to rise, balanced upon his Tower of Babel as if on stilts, wobbling, almost toppling, reaching desperately up and out of unconsciousness for this innocently barking dog. But, in the end, it was on his own two feet that he had to stand, and so he crashed back down, several times, gasping in pain.

By now the darkness had thinned to a deep granite haze or dark steel smoke through which the shapes if not the textures of things could be discerned with some effort. He began to remember to look as well as to listen. The forms of two crumpled swans on the ground on either side of him were the first things he recognized, reassuring him that his precious cargo was safe, that the oath he'd sworn remained unbroken.

Bending over, searching for the pain that had crippled him, he saw that his left slipper was soaked in blood and, removing it, discovered his entire foot to be raw and swollen, the flesh splitting open where the snake had struck.

The urgent barking of the dog made him look up. He could almost distinguish its shadow from the other shadows crowding together in the distance. At the same time, he realized it was not the sun rising over the horizon that was restoring his sight but rather the full moon, immense, lifting itself with a strange hesitant grace from out of its dark bed in the treetops.

"The treetops," exclaimed the boy to himself, "but how?"

He pictured to himself the dark closed canopy of the Forest of Riddles, then looked up, amazed, scanning this wide-open sky of a million stars.

"Then I have traveled already," he told himself, "and so I must be able to walk, I must go on."

Nicolas forced his wounded foot back into its bloodied slipper and stood, picking his swan bags up with him. He shifted his weight to his right foot, attempting a few painful steps. Had it not been for the barking of the dog, he might have collapsed again, discouraged. But there was something so passionate in the dog's appeal, the way it ran ahead and then returned, as if pointing out the way, waiting impatiently, then running on again, and stopping just before it was out of sight.

"Where the animals gather," Nicolas whispered to himself, remembering.

Looking straight ahead, he saw a thin black line, a black path stretching out across the moon-silvered field of vision. It was his blindfold. Though it had grown infinite in length, still he recognized its narrowness as that of his own brow—and it beckoned to its pilgrim, who set off after the dog, limping through the moonlight.

Part Two

THE ELEMENTS

CHAPTER THREE

Hoop of Fire, Heart's Desire

For a time, confused, mesmerized, all the boy could concentrate on was the woman's pale hand, patting and stroking the dog who lay perfectly still in her arms, as if turned to stone.

"Poor thing," she crooned, "he's exhausted, he's already fast asleep."

Nicolas blinked, hard, to see if the woman might vanish as suddenly as she had appeared.

"Fast asleep . . . " she went on whispering.

And though the bright green stone in the ring on her pale hand flashed, and even smiled, her features were impassive, her face averted. It lent to all her tendernesses a touch of infinite distance.

Freeing himself from her hand's hypnotic lullabye, Nicolas opened his eyes past the emerald ring, past the dog that had so suddenly leapt from the darkness of the road into the pale cradle of her arms. He saw that the woman herself stood alone in a strange silvery enclosure, a corral of some sort, woven from tree trunk

47

to tree trunk with thin strands of a mysterious substance, a drenched yarn or silken spittle, a moist thread the color and consistency of fog, or moonlight, or the powder rubbed from a moth's wing. It seemed but a single thread that returned continually to itself, and veered away again, doubling back and around, crossing and recrossing, weaving a map as light as air.

"You must eat and you must rest," said the woman calmly.

The boy recognized her at once as Queen of the Shepherds, and himself as one of her flock.

"You'll find the ground soft and quite comfortable," she assured him, turning her head for the first time, and smiling without moving her mouth. "It is a beautiful spring morning, there's a possibility of aqua and ripe melon in the sky, and a ghost of lavender in the melting mist, not to mention the greens that even in a single leaf cannot be counted. If only you would drop your burden and—"

"No!"

Nicolas hugged his swan bags to his chest, gripping them tighter than ever in his aching hands.

"Ahhhh, yes, you have already promised." She sighed, nodding her head. "I understand."

Nicolas believed that she did.

"I have seen a certain bird protect the egg in the nest beneath her through a storm that uprooted the very tree in whose branches she perched. Washed down a mountainside, swept across a river and out to sea, even set upon by wild creatures ten times her size, still she could not be budged."

She was staring directly into the boy's eyes.

"But you *must* sit, please, and you *must* eat something."

Nicolas did as he was told, dropping first to his knees, then shifting to a cross-legged position, finally finding it necessary to stretch out on one side so as to avoid irritating his wounded foot. He dared not remove his slipper, though it pinched horribly and burned, fearful lest he be unable to put it back on when the time came for him to be on his way.

"The milk of a goat, the seeds of a sunflower, and a tea brewed from the roots of sassafras and comfrey," said Neema, indicating three large wooden bowls on the ground beside him, "these will restore your strength."

Nicolas hesitated.

"Go on," she insisted, watching him lift the bowl of fresh warm milk to his lips, "and then you must rest, *you must sleep.*"

She watched him as he ate and drank, lowering her eyes occasionally to the swan bags lying safely on the grass beside him or to his bloodstained slipper.

Nicolas did not know exactly how or when it happened, but at one point, peering up at his shepherdess from over the rim of a bowl, he was surprised to see that the black dog was gone and that her arms, though still folded across her breast, were empty. Suddenly he was overwhelmed by a feeling of intense gratitude toward this beast that had rescued him from the dark depths of the forest and guided him to this warm, bright oasis of morning. And as always, when gratitude flooded his heart, the image of the old man swept over him as well. Some debts were incalculable.

"You must not worry," insisted the Queen of the Shepherds, "the dog is quite safe."

"And poor Old Gillam?" thought the boy to himself, trying with his mind's eye to brush away the dust and the swan's droppings with which, by now, his teacher's abandoned body must surely be littered. The last of the milk in the bowl trembled as he lowered it solemnly to the ground.

"You must sleep," Neema was whispering. But Nicolas was not listening to her. He was listening to other voices, distant voices.

"The flame's gone out," they sang, "it casts no light. . . ."

He turned his head, searching for the source of the sad song he heard echoing in the distance. "There," he said, pointing.

"Yes," said Neema, turning her head away.

Nicolas caught no more than a glimpse of them before they disappeared into the trees—two men in red leather vests and high black boots, heads bowed, shoulders hunched, struggling with the weight of a third man whom they carried, one gripping his ankles, the other his wrists.

The boy turned back to the woman and would have questioned her, had he not spied the tear rolling silently down her smooth white cheek. As he watched, she turned her back to him and, facing the horizon, raised her pale arms high into the air and waved once, as if signaling. Looking past her, Nicolas was astounded to see that the Queen's graceful semaphore had set the stationary hill-sides into motion. What the boy had assumed were the tall trunks of distant trees and the flowing colors of valleys of shadow began to detach themselves from the landscape and move off. With their tall, slender staffs and their long, flowing robes, great crowds of shepherds were dispersing to the four quarters of the earth from which they had been summoned.

"That song . . . " mumbled the boy.

But the music had already faded, swallowed up by birdsong, by *chirr-up* and *peeep* and *ta-weet.*

"Ah yes . . . the requiem . . . " said the Queen, turning back to her guest, the long lashes of her red-rimmed eyes shaking off their tears.

She hesitated.

"It is completed, for now."

Nicolas still gazed, intently, at the constantly shifting pattern of shepherds fanning out across the distant fields and slopes. But the warm milk and the strong hot tea were beginning to take effect, and his eyes were swimming, unable to focus, as when one wishes to return to an image once found and then lost among clouds.

"Not every pilgrim arrives on the morning of such a momentous night," said Neema. "But you must rest now. You must sleep."

For a moment Nicolas said nothing.

Neema leaned forward to see if perhaps his lids had closed already. But the flickering light of the departing shepherds was still reflected in the dark pupil of each barely opened eye.

"Why?" asked the boy at last. "Why is it so important that I must sleep?"

"Because everything has its other half," she began, "and because one must drink deeply of the river of forgetfulness before one can cross to the other side."

The boy went on watching the crumbling clouds and crowds of shepherds, and listening.

"Because there are two great kingdoms, and everything that lives, lives in both at the same time. Because each moment of surrender opens up, on that other side, like a Kingdom in a Grain of Sand whose palaces of fragrant smoke and whose whispering walled gardens are as vast and labyrinthian as the long winding paths and spiraling stairways of each moment of that other Towering Kingdom of Effort. Because it is soft, sleep, it is infinitely soft, like the silk of the cocoon that crowns the toil of the worm with colored wings only when all its striving has ceased. Because there is a land on the other shore in which beauty sleeps and, by sleeping, grows more and more inconceivably beautiful with each motionless moment passing. Perhaps you have heard the tale, the tale of how the whole kingdom sleeps with her . . . waiting . . . patiently . . . "

The lids of the boy's tired eyes rose and fell along with the colors gliding up and down the distant hillsides, the long, slow strokes of his lashes washing his weakening gaze in layer after layer of a gradually dissolving spectrum.

"How the king and the queen," she droned on, "still seated on their thrones in the great hall, fall asleep with their chins on their chests, the decree the king is about to sign yellowing with age in his hands, the ink evaporating. How outside in the stables both stallions and cart-horses cease their whinnying in their stalls, how the dogs lie down and sleep alongside the castle gates and in the shade of the castle's great stone arches, and how dawn after dawn passes and still not a sound emerges from the thousands of gilded birdcages that hang from every branch of every tree in the royal gardens . . . "

The auburn hills deepened to violet before the boy's closing eyes, their ascending slopes falling . . . falling . . .

"How nothing moves, nothing at all. Neither the long lace curtains that hang before the palace windows without a breath of wind to stir them, nor the leaves on the branches of the trees outside those windows. Even the flies on the ceiling sleep soundly, even the spiders in their empty webs and the rats in the cellar walls, even the steam rising from a hot cup of tea hangs paralyzed in the air, a puff of pearl smoke suspended in the silence . . . waiting . . . waiting . . . "

Nicolas was fast asleep by the time the last of the shepherds had departed and the hillsides had ceased moving.

"Welcome," whispered the Queen, and without moving from her silvery cage, she covered her eyes with one jeweled hand, and went to meet the boy where beauty was busy ripening.

The pomegranate with which they returned was far too heavy for either Pilgrim or Queen to carry alone. Though it was not large and would have fit in the palm of either's hand, the multitude of seeds it contained made its weight tremendous. In the morning, when Nicolas awoke, it lay in a fourth wooden bowl on the grass beside him.

"Open it," said Neema, lowering her hand from her eyes.

Without attempting to lift it, he tried for several minutes to enter, finally resorting to a heavy rock with which he split the fruit wide open.

"And eat," commanded the Queen.

Nicolas was staring at the rock he'd tossed aside, at the bloodlike stains the juice of the ruptured fruit had left on its jagged edge.

Neema waited.

The first seed spurted as he crushed it between his teeth, its tough, thin skin resisting like the hide on the underbelly of the sacrificial animal resists the knife, then gives way, in a flood of warmth. But in this case the deep red released was cool, almost cold. As the juice trickled over his chin, Nicolas stared down at the swarm of seeds that lay exposed in the shallow bowl like the hidden life of worm and larva and mole and mineral in the freshly turned earth of a plowed field.

"It's the only fruit already ripened at this distance from the harvest," said Neema. "Eat as much of it as you can, for you will need all your strength for the long climb ahead."

Dawn was breaking, and as the first rays of light crept toward them, the webbed walls of the woman's mysterious corral, which had grown virtually invisible in the darkness, came alive again. Now one strand, now another, absorbed the morning's soft light and reflected it back, until the whole network grew quietly luminous once more. Small groups of birds settled down on its glowing wires to sing, a handful of finches displaced by a family of quarrelsome grosbeaks, a pair of speckled turtledoves cooing contentedly, a solitary song thrush breathless with excitement. Like the skin of a bubble, Nicolas kept expecting the fine sun-spun threads to give way at any moment beneath the restless weight of the birds, but instead it was the birds who seemed to grow lighter, as if the weightlessness of those threads on which they were perched flowed right into them, or through them, emerging with their songs, which grew more and more effervescent with each dizzily ascending note. Nicolas had never in all his life heard such a morning of birds.

"Have I slept all day *and* all night?" he marveled, confused, for it was morning when he went to sleep—and morning, now, when he awoke.

"Perhaps," said Neema.

He crushed another of the pomegranate's many seeds between his teeth, swallowing the bittersweet juice.

"Or perhaps you slept for several days and several nights, perhaps you slept for years, or perhaps it is always morning here, just as it is always night in the depths of certain forests, and it is always noon, there, high atop the highest of all the mountains of fire."

She had not turned, nor had she pointed. Yet the Pilgrim knew on which side of morning to look for the mountains she had described. He rose to his feet, ignoring the stab of pain that pierced his wound, and turned to face the horizon, where, far beyond those low hills across which he'd witnessed the exodus of the mournful shepherds, there rose the harsher profiles of other, sharper peaks from whose depths a concealed flame belched forth enormous plumes and funnels of poisonous green smoke.

"Fire lives in those mountains," said Neema.

"Volcanoes . . ." whispered the boy, and as the word brushed across his lips they grew instantly dry and parched, his throat tightened, beads of sweat broke out on his brow, and a terrible thirst took hold of him.

"I have heard of a certain bird," said the Queen, her eyes lowered, "a singular bird, that nests fearlessly in the crater of the highest of the volcanoes, in its steep ring of fire—a bird whose tail, it is told, extends all the way from heaven to earth, a bird whose tail burns with a billion eyes, as if the very stars in the sky had outlasted the gloom of night and went on shining, tens of thousands of suns, brilliant even in the blinding blue of the brightest of days."

Nicolas reached for his swan bags automatically. Once more he knew where he was headed and was impatient to be on his way. Neema herself had at last raised her eyes to the horizon, but reluctantly, as if it pained her somehow. And even the half-eaten pomegranate in its bowl seemed, by now, to be staring off into the distance, the dark red of each of its many eyes kindled to the irresistible brightness of flame.

The boy's thirst grew with each passing moment.

"But to which of the volcanoes . . . ?"

"Your heart's desire will show you the way," said the Queen of All the Shepherds, sadly, "for it is a ring of fire . . . "

Her voice trailed off, and she turned away once more, her eyes fixed now upon the fruit burning in its bowl—for the remains of the pomegranate, its blood heated to the boiling point, had burst into flame. A single crimson petal of fire rose from the spilled seed, unwavering, as if it would burn, peacefully, forever.

"It is the ring of fire," Neema went on at last, her head bowed, "it is the ring of fire through which you shall, undoubtedly, pass."

And then she sighed, exhaling with such strength that the steady flame atop the fruit flickered, briefly.

"Go now," she said.

Swinging the full heavy swan bags over his shoulders, Nicolas set off toward the smoke on the horizon, certain that he would pass through the hoop of fire and find the Phoenix, even surprising it, if necessary, in its burning nest. "I cannot fail now," he told himself over and over as he strode forward, "I cannot, and I shall not fail."

He looked back only once.

The pomegranate still burned tirelessly in its bowl, the Queen of All the Shepherds still stood stoically in her web of cool light.

But a tranformation was in progress. The glow of the flaming fruit was contagious. Its heat and its light bled through the air. Its fire was reflected or absorbed by the filaments of the Queen's web, which rapidly increased in temperature, blushing scarlet, until the Queen seemed hemmed in by red hot wires, by the walls of a magical furnace in the center of which she stood, serenely impervious to fire.

As Nicolas watched from a short distance away, the birds that were perched there, strung along those suddenly glowing wires like colored beads, rose up into the air in alarm, unable to bear the heat. In one flock they took flight, a single swirling mass in which all species mingled together—singing madly— as they approached the burning fruit in its bowl and, hovering there, began to circle frantically in the air above it, spinning round and round the tip of its ascending tongue of flame like electrons whirling insanely about a glowing nucleus.

It was a long time before their shrill voices faded to silence behind him, as he trudged forward across the fields and slopes of the Queen's vast pasturelands.

Nicolas had never before seen a herd of skunks. He'd never thought such a thing possible. Yet there they were, twenty or thirty of them at least, scurrying through the underbrush right toward him, their black and white tails quivering ominously in the air as they approached. Not long afterwards, the skunks left safely behind by a swift detour, he chanced upon an even larger group, this time of porcupines. More courageous now, he chose not to alter his course but waded right through them, their sharp quills scraping against his ankles as they hurried on their way.

At nightfall Nicolas stopped to rest, to enter that kingdom of sleep whose affairs of state his shepherdess had admonished him not to neglect for more than a day at a time. Selecting a suitable spot, a patch of grass sheltered by an outcrop of rock and a few flowering shrubs, the boy lay down with his head propped up upon his soft swan bags. But he couldn't seem to doze off. His foot was throbbing, his mind racing ahead to tommorrow's urgent progress. And the unfamiliar noises all around him set his nerves on edge and kept his tired eyes wide open.

He decided to build a fire.

Gathering a bundle of branches and a handful of dry grass, he selected two sturdier sticks and sharpened the first as best he could against a rock, notching the second, then placing the one inside the other and twirling it between the palms of his hands with a swift and steady rhythm. It had been Old Gillam who'd taught him this trick of fire-making. In those days Nicolas had been younger, and not as strong, and so student and teacher had alternated, passing the stick back and forth to one another. "My turn!" the boy would cry out, despite the fact that his hands were already badly chafed, his wrists numb. Afterwards, in front of their campfire, they'd sit for hours before falling asleep, talking quietly, trying to distinguish between a shower of sparks and a cluster of fireflies, or just staring wordlessly into the depths of the blaze until, overcome by drowsiness, they drifted off to deeper and deeper sleep.

The boy worked alone now, vigorously twirling the stick, faster and faster and faster, till the dry splinters of wood began to smoke and the dried grass smoldered and then caught fire. An hour later he sat staring into the flames that leapt up, crackling, into the darkness. But he remained uneasy. He felt as if he were surrounded on all sides, stalked by all sorts of strange wild creatures that sniffed and scratched around his little protective ring of firelight.

"Try to sleep," he kept telling himself, growing more and more frustrated. "Try . . . to . . . sleep . . ."

The words were still on his lips when he awoke the next morning, the charred remains of his campfire smoking beside him.

"I've been dreaming," he mumbled aloud.

Suddenly he remembered the pale dog. Though he'd hardly noticed it at the time, it had been sitting there beside Neema, quietly, watching—just as it sat here beside *him* through the long hours of darkness, watching him as he dreamt, guarding him against the terrors of the strange new night.

Nicolas opened and closed his eyes several times, attempting to clear his head. He stretched and yawned.

And then he stood.

"Owww!"

The pain that tore through his foot took his breath away, but not his pilgrim's resolve.

Hearing the gurgle of a stream somewhere nearby, he hobbled about until he found it, then dropped down on its bank, and, removing his slipper, carefully, painfully, he thrust his wounded foot into the cool rushing water, not wanting to look at it for fear that even a single glimpse might discourage him and plunge him into despair now that his goal was so near. "I cannot fail now," he repeated to himself, "I shall not fail." And he turned away from his foot and fixed his attention on the slipper instead, soaking it too, holding it underwater and watching its color return as the dried blood with which it was encrusted dissolved and swirled away downstream.

The cold water numbed his foot to the point where he could at least stand on it, and he decided it would be unwise to attempt to put his slipper back on. Twisting and braiding a few reeds into a sturdy cord, he looped it around the wet yellow slipper and slung it over his shoulder along with the two swan bags, then clambered as best he could back up the way he'd come. As he passed by the little grotto where he'd slept and dreamt, he almost expected to find the faithful dog waiting for him there beside his path, and he hesitated before continuing on up the slope, limping but determined.

The dog was a gift from Neema, he realized as he climbed, a shared guardian, a gatekeeper. It was a satisfying thought, and he was smiling to himself as he rounded the top of the hill, and gasped, unprepared for the shock of what he saw.

Stretched out below him was a vast and utterly treeless plain, the entire surface of which was in motion. As far as the eye could see it was covered by huge herds of every imaginable creature, every inch of ground teeming with life, all of it flowing ceaselessly forward, toward him, in exactly the opposite direction, Nicolas realized, than the one in which he himself must travel. Even the sky, as he watched, began to fill with enormous flocks of birds that spread out across the heavens, fracturing the light of the sun with their silhouettes and shadows.

Suddenly Nicolas caught sight of a solitary eagle soaring overhead, slicing through the tightly knit flocks of birds that crowded the sky. Standing atop the hill, his wounded foot raised slightly, not quite touching the ground, his eyes stretched wide in disbelief, the boy felt faint. Far in the distance the dark humps of several volcanic peaks towered up into the sky, wreathed in tepid clouds of pink and green, in bluish mists of steaming rain and ashes. And it was there, as he watched, as his faintness turned to fever, that the regal bird disappeared at last, swallowed up in the mists enshrouding those steep dark slopes that, in his heart, the young Pilgrim knew he must climb.

"If only I could fly like . . . " but he did not allow himself to finish. It was an envious dream, a dream of ease and comfort, unworthy of a pilgrim. He looked down at his bare wounded foot still suspended in the air—and placing it firmly, defiantly, on the ground, resting his weight directly upon it, he hitched up his loose slipper and his two unopened swan bags and set off into the crowds of animals sweeping toward him as if to bar his path.

The massive herd of sheep into which he was immediately plunged eliminated all possibilities of navigating the terrain below his feet. He was pathless, the earth lost beneath him, lost beneath their miles of ragged itchy wool, their warm black runny noses, their thousands of mud-encrusted hooves. Submerged in a bleating sea, not much more than his head and shoulders visible above its surface, he floated with all the groundless determination of a cork on the rolling dirty white waves of their backs. It was only by looking up and keeping his eyes fixed on the volcanic peaks rising in the distance that he managed to steer at all. Had they been traveling in the opposite direction, he might have clung to the back of one or the other and merely allowed himself to be carried along with the current. As it was, he was forced to struggle on against their tide as best he could, until the last of them had passed, only to be replaced by thousands of camels following directly in their wake, beasts whose prodigious height, eclipsing the horizon and his volcanic compass, obliged him to bend his attention back to the ground, and once more seek his path below.

It wasn't long before he discovered that he could make far more headway if he actually dropped to his hands and knees and crawled on all fours beneath the camels, dragging his bags and his aching foot behind him. Emerging, over an hour later, somewhat bruised and battered from this vicious forest of enchanted camels' legs, he found himself belly to the ground and eye to eye with an ocean of wood rats and frantic field mice that extended for miles in every direction. Nicolas jumped to his feet, shuffling as best he could through the scurrying rodents, many of which attempted to travel right over him, crawling up the backs of his legs. He tried to ignore their tiny claws and feet as best he could, but occasionally, annoyed, he'd snatch a rat up by its long tail, and swinging it around, send it flying through the air.

The rats were followed by herds of zebra, their bold black and white stripes blurred to a single vibrating color as they sped past him. And the zebras in turn by an army of bronze-backed turtles, across whose hard shells Nicolas passed, hopping from one to the other. Then there were the cheetahs, which terrified him at first, with their sleek, harsh cries and glaring eyes. But they passed swiftly, so swiftly that in his amazement Nicolas hardly noticed the hosts of ladybugs that succeeded them, until, looking behind him, he saw his own red footprints—for each of his steps had demolished thousands of the bright tiny beetles, staining the ground with their crushed red wings. And then even before the carpet of ladybugs had thoroughly unraveled, a swarm of nervous white hares erupted, hopping in every direction at once, colliding with him over and over again no matter how hard he tried to stay out of their way.

The hares were followed by slow, heavy herds of musk oxen, and they by masked raccoons, and they in turn by nervous gerbils, their eyes stretched wide in perpetual surprise, by screeching hyenas whose tireless jaws stank of rotting meat, by clouds of dragonflies thousands of times larger that any he'd ever seen in the peaceful meadows of the aviary. And there were rolling fields of giant pandas and snarling streams of mongeese, swarms of croaking bush-frogs, a fierce battalion of miniscule red ants, and then one massive pride of lions, walking slowly, turning to sniff the air in amazement, so densely laden was it with the odor of every possible variety of game.

Nicolas could scarcely stand when night fell, could scarcely summon the energy to light the fire in whose safe haven of flickering light he knew he might sleep. Long before any spark or smoke arose, with the stick still twirling hypnotically in his hand, he fell sound asleep. When he awoke, the pale shepherd's dog sitting still as marble alongside the gateway of dream, he found himself lying in a field of snow.

Or at least it seemed like snow.

"But that's impossible," he said to himself, wiping the sweat from his brow. For the first time he realized just how hot it had become.

Reaching out with one sleepy hand to feel the cold powder melt against his skin, he pulled away in alarm, for this snow was soft and warm to the touch. A moment later the whole field began to stir as the thousands of pure white ermines that had settled down to sleep all around him rose up, refreshed now, and began to move off. Nicolas sat rubbing the dream from his eyes as the sheet of stainless white fur glided away. No sooner had the ermines departed than a troop of sulky-faced baboons took their place, grunting and spitting as they waddled by.

Day after day, he continued on, five days, ten, more, buffeted back and forth by hordes of creatures, large and small, wild and tame, stopping only to sleep. It had become easier and easier to navigate, for the steadily increasing heat, as well as the rising ground, told him clearly and simply that he was indeed traveling in the right direction. "Steer toward the fire in the air," he told himself, "and climb—and sooner or later you will reach your goal." So he trudged on, holding always to the ascending path, seeking always the higher and the hotter ground.

At last the herds began to thin and separate.

The air had grown unbearably hot, gritty and sour. It scorched his lungs and the inside of his throat, and he had to stop every hour or so to catch his burning breath and wipe his boiling brow. It occurred to him that all along the animals were perhaps fleeing this terrible heat, and that only those hardy enough to withstand such extremes of temperature had stayed behind on these increasingly charred slopes.

The skies emptied first.

A loud, raw splash of screaming bluejays that swooped down from on high and swept rudely past him—these were almost the last birds he laid eyes on. The animals below, those without wings, disappeared even more dramatically. In the course of a single hot afternoon, he witnessed their herds reduced solely to those species that nature had seen fit to crown with horns. Whether curled, crescent or spiral, straight as arrows, or branched and webbed, every beast that he encountered from then on held its crowned head high.

Antelope and swift springbucks, tufted dik-diks, sure-footed mountain goats and ibex, rock-dancing klipspringers, hartebeests and kudus and striped bongos, red and white-tailed deer with their shy spotted fawns, even the normally glacial caribou—all of them were gathered together now, no longer fleeing, but quietly grazing on the nearly barren slopes, nibbling at the tough rubbery moss or sharp thistle that spread like a pale green stain wherever it found sufficient shelter from the waves of heat that billowed down from the mountain's fiery crest.

Nicolas stood mesmerized by the volcano's black summit.

Further up its forbidding slopes raced a herd of some lean fleet-footed animal, gazelles perhaps, or impalas—they were too far away for the boy to be sure, obscured by the great dry clouds of dust that their sharp speeding hooves struck from the parched earth. Rising like smoke, hanging listless in the scorched air, the hot dust dissolved into pale patches of mist through which a single running pink stitch of bright flamingos threaded its illusory way. The birds seemed ghostlike somehow, unreal, the opposite of those achingly present bluejays whose painful cries had heralded the emptying of the skies. Appearing and disappearing, swallowed up and then resurfacing, the distant rose of their plumage was transformed, its color echoing passionately around the blackened base of the volcano's uppermost slopes, reflected in a steamy mirror of fog as in a burning lake of magenta fire.

Higher up, always higher, Nicolas observed what looked like a herd of cattle scattered across the blackened hillside. Beyond them, all detail was lost at last, the whole mountain towering up into one terrible cloud, the cloud itself bursting from time to time, releasing fitful showers of oily water that boiled and hissed and rearose as steam long before it ever reached the ground.

Dizzied, he lowered his eyes once more to the herd of cattle that appeared to be grazing on the dark, steep slope. Their calm seemed miraculous to the boy. He didn't see how it was possible for them to survive such barren heat.

"Of course!" he thought to himself, remembering in a flash one of Gillam's old stories.

He squinted, trying to see if it might be true, and the glint of what he assumed to be a golden horn convinced him that these were indeed the cattle of the sun itself, those same cattle who'd been stolen or disturbed by so many gods and heros in the course of mythic time.

"And it was only a boy, an infant, really, who was their most celebrated thief of all."

Young Nicolas looked doubtful.

"You don't believe me? Oh, but he was a clever boy, the cleverest."

Nicolas leaned in closer, ready for the tale to unfold.

"And do you know how he managed to fool the great and wealthy sun?" asked Old Gillam, smiling delightedly.

Nicolas shook his head.

"By walking backwards," said the old man.

He burst into a loud peal of laughter, while his student sat stoney-faced, thinking, figuring.

"They searched in the wrong direction, of course," he explained, "foolishly believing that a man moves only in that direction in which his toes are pointing."

Nicolas looked down at his own wriggling toes.

"And that's not all," Old Gillam went on, warming to his subject. "Do you know what this mischievous infant said when he was lifted from his cradle and interrogated by the king of the gods himself?"

The old man raised his arm up to his face and, placing his lips against the crook of his elbow, breathed out with such force that the resultant sound exploded like the blast of a broken trumpet.

The boy stared in disbelief.

"He farted, my boy!"

"No!"

"It's true!" the old man insisted through his laughter. "He was an infant, after all, with no control."

They laughed for a long time.

Of course, there had been other, more serious marauders, Gillam had gone on to explain—starving men who'd killed and eaten, strong men who'd dueled and dared—and they had fared far more tragically. And of course, in the end, the infant Hermes had relented and had returned the precious cattle to their rightful owner.

"But that is not the point of the story," the old man had avowed, "for no one *that* clever need concern himself with the mere *possession* of anything."

It was almost dark when Nicolas finally arrived at the edge of that coal-black pasture in which the notorious cattle lay so serenely. Enormous bulls they were, with large, graceful horns that glowed golden, shining as if refined in the furnace of their own lord and master, dazzling as the sun itself. Nicolas had always pictured them grazing contentedly in lush ambrosial fields of lily and asphodel, surrounded by the heavenly industry of bees and butterflies. But so hot was this field that it had been purged of all such delicacies, reduced to a harder and purer nectar, a blackened honey of ash upon which these bulls of the sun fed casually without arising from their positions of eternal repose.

Nicolas decided to camp there that night, and, careful not to disturb them, he lay down among the solemn, heavy beasts and closed his eyes. In the morning when he awoke, not a single one of them had moved.

Standing, brushing the black dust from his skin and from the pale feathers of his swan bags, he looked around him at the hundreds of pairs of bright horns and dark eyes, confident that he'd not harmed a single hair on a single sacred head, satisfied that he'd done nothing to incur the wrath of the heroes of heaven. The enormity of his task, however, the mere presumption that a young boy might find the fabulous Phoenix and pluck even a single of its smallest feathers from its body, filled him with anxiety—and the rumbling of the earth beneath his feet did little to allay his fears as he tiptoed across the field, wading through drifts of black ash that reached, at times, as far up as his knees.

Five days later, not a single living creature in sight, he reached the summit of the volcano, or at least as close as he was ever destined to get. He would have continued further, climbing and climbing, had the entire mountain not started to shake with such force that he was nearly thrown from his feet. Nicolas stood his ground, waiting for the tremor to pass—but instead it grew more and more violent, the entire landscape shuddering and heaving all around him. Still the boy remained stationary, resisting each new convulsion, and his eyes remained anchored to the peak that growled and smoked and spit and threatened above him. He was certain that the Phoenix would appear at any moment, swooping down in glory from its nest of flames, bearing the feather of salvation for which he'd fought so hard and won.

"I cannot fail now!" he shouted triumphantly up to the mountain's summit. "I cannot and I shall not fail!"

A sudden gleam overhead, as if the clouds had caught fire, convinced Nicolas that his pilgrimage was at an end. So hypnotized was he by this prospect of imminent victory that he stood transfixed, making no effort to protect himself from the river of burning lava that bubbled up from the crater of the volcano and swept speeding down its slopes straight toward him.

He felt the heat increasing, he saw the brilliant burning water gushing down the mountainside, he waited breathless for it to veer off and up into the air on broad powerful wings of roaring flame.

Before he knew it, it was there at his feet—but still swimming along the earth, still wingless.

The boy was blistered almost senseless with pain as he watched the molten river of lava gurgle and clot, collecting in boiling puddles and pools, flooding every available dip and crevice, then swirling angrily around his foot. A single moment of its fiery touch was sufficient to communicate all the raging heat of the entire volcano to the boy's frail body. Nicolas felt as if his hair had caught fire. He saw little bouquets of flame spurt from his skin, dancing like wild will-o'-the-wisps out across his bare arms.

Turning, in terror, he saw that where it touched him the river of fire had been transformed, its colors cooled from reds and yellows to greens and blues that flowed, thicker and slower, all the way down the mountainside, fanning out behind him like an enormous glittering tail.

"A peacock's tail!" he cried out in anguish, and knew too late that he'd been deceived.

A bird whose tail extends from heaven to earth, he remembered, a bird whose tail burns with a billion eyes. Of course! He should have recognized the peacock from its description! He should have known in advance that this was not the Phoenix he was so desperately seeking!

"How could I have been so blind?" he wailed.

But there was no time for regret, and his lament was as swiftly ignited and burned away to nothing as were his dreams of glory and his tears of disappointment and everything else within range of the volcano's burning breath. Nicolas felt the flames licking at his wrists, and, turning in alarm, he saw to his horror that his swan bags were ablaze, burning in his hands, their pure white feathers already blackening in this raging fire that consumed all that it touched.

Nicolas ran.

Down, down the steep slope he ran, as fast as his legs would carry him, and when they would carry him no faster, he tripped and tumbled, falling down, always down, descending in hours those slopes it had taken him weeks to climb.

It was hopeless.

Despite the fact that he rolled over and over with them in the dust of the earth, despite the fact that he flailed at them with his hands, trying to smother the flames or beat them into submission, still the swans went on burning.

Once or twice he thought he spied the wings of the eagle overhead, beating as hasty a retreat as his own, abandoning him no less certainly than if he had been tossed, unworthy, from its nest.

When he finally came to rest, sprawled out nearly senseless at the bottom of the slope, even before trying to catch his breath, his eyes were groping for his precious cargo—for the two swans, coal black now, that had emerged with him from the flames, and that stared back at him with their red roasted eyes.

"Perhaps," thought the boy, panting, "all is not lost."

He reached out as gently as possible.

"Perhaps . . ."

But the bodies of the two black swans crumbled at the slightest touch, dissolving along with their mysterious contents into piles of fine gray ash.

Nicolas collapsed in a heap beside them.

Several times the strong young green branches slipped from his hands as he attempted to bend them into shape. Several times, forced too far, they cracked or splintered or snapped back more defiantly, bruising his thumb or his forefinger. At each new mishap Nicolas would despair of the whole project and dash it furiously to the ground—only to pick up the pieces again as soon as his anger had cooled, as soon as the pain in his injured hand had subsided.

And then he'd resume his work.

He really didn't know what else to do.

For a long time he'd merely lain on the ground beside the piles of ash, sifting them through his fingers or drawing in them with the tip of a twig or the stem of a leaf, rearranging them into piles of varying sizes, patting and pushing, and staring as if at nothing.

Moments of resolve would sweep over him.

He would stand, and then he would sit down again.

Suddenly in a terrible hurry, he'd begin frantically stuffing the ash into his pockets. Then he'd stop, almost as if he'd forgotten what he was doing, and empty them again, slowly now, and carefully, so as not to lose a pinch of the precious powder.

He knew that he must go on.

He *would* go on.

But he didn't know why and he no longer knew where.

All he knew was that in order to go on he would need a vessel of some sort in which to carry his ashes, something to transport the remains of his swans, those swans he'd vowed never to part with.

Never.

And so, always looking over his shoulder to reassure himself of the where-abouts of his pitiful treasure, he'd managed to collect an armful of slender branches, still green and resilient, and he set about constructing two small cages in which to house the piles of ash. Holding the tops of seven or eight branches in his hand, he squeezed them together as he tried to tighten the cord he'd looped and knotted around them like a noose. At the last minute the cord tore, the taut branches sprang violently open, and, cursing, the boy once more threw the entire cage across the clearing in which he knelt, and threw himself face down on the ground, his chin smudged by the soot in which it rested. Five minutes later he was attempting to secure the cage's wooden bars once again, this time successfully.

They were fine pieces of workmanship when completed, the two domed bird-cages. But sitting back, surveying them, Nicolas could summon no pride in his work.

Several mountain bluebirds that had been flitting about all day, annoying him, began to dart around the bars of the cages, as if trying to enter in. He swatted at them, trying to scare them away, but they kept returning, poking their heads through the bars and fluttering their wings.

"Go away!" he snapped. But like himself, the bluebirds seemed to have no place else to go.

Nicolas looked down dejectedly at his feet. He shook his head and sighed. "I have lost my slippers," he said aloud, only then realizing, in horror, that he no longer had in his possession a single one of the gifts Old Gillam had bequeathed him for his journey: the swan bags, the slippers, the blindfold, all were lost. Even that path that had appeared, as if by magic, beneath his feet, had vanished—and with it, not only the way forward but the way back as well.

"The eggshells," he gasped, remembering, "the blue egg. . . ."

He began digging feverishly in his pocket, as if it were his entire past that was contained there, his trembling hand emerging with those few fragments of blue shell that had survived the ordeal by fire. They smelt faintly of smoke, and of the aviary.

This, then, was what remained of his wealth.

"No!" he cried, and boldly, bitterly, without thinking twice, threw the few blue scraps over his shoulder, into the air—turning back, like a miser, to those other, more mournful riches piled up on the ground before him. Scooping up one handful of what remained of his hopes, he pressed it to his breast, as if the beating of his heart might revive the burning desires that lay dormant now in the dark ash. Behind him, the falling shells fluttered briefly, like the wings of those persistent bluebirds, before settling, like blue seeds, to the ground.

He did not look to see what he had planted.

Nor did he know, unaccustomed as he was to the fertility of such sorrows as he now endured, just how quickly it would grow and bear fruit. Looking back on things later, Nicolas would, however, conclude that it was from that moment on that he felt as if someone were following and watching him.

But he did not turn around, not just yet.

He stared instead at his swollen foot, blackened with soot.

"I will need some sort of shoes if I am to go on," he told himself, passionlessly, as he scanned the clearing in which he sat, assessing the materials at hand. Not far away, he singled out a suitable tree, a birch whose bark would do quite nicely.

Nicolas pounded the strips of papery bark between two rocks until they were smooth. He lined the flattened sheets with fresh leaves and blades of grass, then wrapped both his feet tightly and tied them around with the same cord he'd used to secure the bars of his cages.

He stood up, taking a few tentative steps in this direction or that, testing the new slippers.

"They'll do," he said.

He now had vessels for his ash, new slippers for his feet, he was even standing, ready to set out, ready to continue on his way. But where? Which way should he go? He still hadn't a clue.

Bowed down for most of the day over one task or another, the boy raised his head now and looked about himself. Before he'd seen only the pliant reeds and saplings, the papery birch bark, those things he could use, the tools for whatever task was at hand. But now he saw the lovely and useless hills, gentle rolling hills that served no apparent purpose, pale as sand dunes in the foreground, soft green and then scarlet in the distance. They seemed to the sad young man only larger and brighter versions of his own small, somber piles of ash.

It was all ash, he assured himself, gripped by melancholy, it was an entire landscape of ash just waiting for the disaster of his first pathetic step to shock it past dust and crumble it to nothing at all.

"Ash," he insisted to himself, "all ash."

But if in truth it *was* a world of dusts, they were enchanted dusts, splendid dusts, magnificent and alluring dusts, dusts heaped up and hollowed out so exquisitely, sculpted so seductively, rising in drifts and mounds of such strikingly beautiful hues that they seemed to have been ground to powder from the petals of dried flowers or from the translucent depths of precious stones.

Nicolas tried to ignore the peacocks.

He dropped once more to his knees, he turned his head away, he busied himself once more with his piles of ash, smoothing and scraping and scooping.

"A dangerously beautiful bird," was how Gillam had once described the peacock.

There were several of them now, pacing idly through the dry weeds and grasses, foraging for crickets or beetles, occasionally cocking their heads, glancing absently in his direction.

"They've come to laugh at me," the boy convinced himself, refusing to look up, refusing to acknowledge their undeniably glorious plumage.

"The proudest of all the two-legged creatures," the old man had gone on, "of all but one, that is."

Nicolas was gritting his teeth. Head bowed, he was grinding the ash to an ever finer powder between his tensed fingertips, working so intently that he did not notice the two horses as they entered the clearing. They stood among the unavoidable peacocks, a white horse and a black horse, staring expectantly at the miserable boy and waiting. It was a long time before Nicolas raised his eyes and returned their gaze.

"A blindfolded horse," he marveled, rising to his feet in astonishment. For though he could see the wide eyes of the dark horse glistening even from a distance, he soon realized that the dark stripe across the face of the other horse was not, as it had seemed at first glance, a natural marking, but rather a strip of black cloth.

The boy approached cautiously, taking a few steps and then stopping. The white horse stamped its foot, gently, several times, and what looked like a puff of smoke rose from the dry ground whenever its hoof descended. Encouraged, Nicolas crept forward until he stood close enough to feel the horse's steamy breath condense on the skin of his outstretched hand. For several moments they just stared at one another. The horse was indeed masked, yet the boy did not doubt for a moment that the beast was looking directly at him.

It was the horse itself that closed the gap between them, taking those last few remaining steps, then swaying its head in a heavy downward arc and nuzzling the boy beneath his arm.

It was the sign that Nicolas had been waiting for.

Limping, almost tripping, he hurried back toward his little cemetery, the low, gray mounds of ash rising from the surrounding turf like the humped backs of a family of freshly filled graves. As the horse waited, patiently, the boy gathered up what remained of the sacred swan bags and transferred them, a handful at a time, to the cages he'd constructed. Satisfied, at last, that not a pinch of ash remained upon the ground, he hoisted up the cages, which weighed next to nothing, and limped back to the expectant horse.

By the time he reached the horse's side, the pain in his infected foot was crippling—just a few more steps and he might have fallen. So it was with great relief that he found himself comfortably astride the horse's broad white back, his birdcages full of ash strung across the powerful muscles of its long neck.

As the horse began to move beneath him, Nicolas glanced up at its partner. The dark horse did not return his gaze. It seemed, rather, to be looking over his shoulder. It seemed to be looking at something, or someone, behind him.

The white horse slipped into a steady, even gait, needing no command or instructions. Nicolas heard the second horse, after a moment's hesitation, fall into step behind them. He could not tell whether it was the white horse that pulled him or the black horse that pushed him along a route he would never, at this point, have known how to travel alone, on his own two feet.

Riding along, with little else to do but watch the slow passage of earth and sky, Nicolas had plenty of time to question himself as to what had happened.

Such a fall as he had suffered was difficult to measure in terms of distance. "I have gone up and I have gone down." This, naturally, was the diagram with which he started. But there was a problem. If indeed he had returned to the base of that very mountain he'd climbed so laboriously, why was it that he recognized nothing? And if he hadn't returned, exactly what sort of slope was it that did not end where it began?

Mile after mile, he strained his eyes, searching for some sign of those huge herds of animals and dense flocks of birds through which he'd ascended earlier. The cattle of the sun and the ghostly pink flamingos, the skunks and rats and rabbits and bluejays, all had vanished without a trace.

More importantly, where were those volcanos whose dark, smoking peaks had commanded the horizon for as many days and nights as he'd been traveling through these vast pasturelands?

The creatures had fled, it was possible. Unlikely, given their great numbers, but possible nonetheless. Yet was he then to suppose that the mountains of fire themselves had moved off, thundering into the distance like a tribe of enormous burnt black bison, rolling and rumbling over the earth? It was as if he had fallen not merely down the slope but off the map as well, that map whose mastery of the horizontal was unquestionable but whose ability to chart the heights and the depths was another matter entirely. Nicolas was so puzzled that he began to hope, despite all evidence to the contrary, that he *was* somehow retracing his steps—if only so that he might find the Queen of the Shepherds once again and question her.

And what about this infernal peacock's tail? The Pilgrim had to confess to himself that he bore a slight grudge in this regard, that he harbored a growing suspicion that all along Neema had been well aware of the painful and costly detour to which she had subjected this innocent member of her flock.

"I need to speak with the Queen," Nicolas leaned down and whispered into the ear of the blindfolded white horse. When the horse made no move to change course, he felt confident that he was indeed retracing his steps and would soon arrive back at the webbed walls of the Queen's mysterious palace.

After hours of uneventful travel, the horse stopped at the edge of a small, slow-moving river and was leaning down to drink.

At first the boy did not even notice her.

Deceived by distance, he'd seen in the curves of her reclining body no more than another low hill, this one speckled unevenly with weeds and splattered with bright wildflowers. He'd read, in the rhythmic rise and fall of her breasts and shoulders, no more than the life of wind, never suspecting the breath of royalty.

"All this fuss and bother about a big blue bird."

Startled by the voice, Nicolas turned sharply, grabbing a handful of the horse's long pale mane to balance himself.

That was when he saw her.

"Excuse me, your majesty?"

Though the voice he'd heard sounded too harsh, the boy assumed that it must be the Queen who had spoken.

"Your majesty! Well, now, isn't that rich!"

The horse raised its head, sniffing the air, then paced slowly over to where Neema lay, on her side, in a grove of beech trees on the river's sandy bank.

"Burning with curiosity now, aren't you?"

The Queen of All the Shepherds lay perfectly still, her head pillowed lifeless on her arms, and her eyes bandaged as tightly as the eyes of his horse with a strip of thick white cloth.

"But you are asleep!" exclaimed the boy.

"Asleep? Why, I'm as wide awake as you are!"

Resting on the sand, directly in front of the face of the sleeping Queen, sat a small, ugly creature, tough skinned and slimy, a lizard, who was indeed very much awake, despite the fact that the narrow slits of its eyes had to struggle constantly to remain open beneath the weight of their heavy swollen lids. It was this creature who was speaking in such a rude and unpleasant tone.

"Well, boys, what can I do for you?" snapped the salamander.

Nicolas heard a noise behind him, almost as if someone had jumped or fallen to the ground.

"Boys?" asked the boy, uneasily.

Something, he didn't know what, still prevented him from turning around.

"I almost didn't recognize you without your proud tail," sneered the salamander, and the thick lids of its eyes swelled shut once, then reopened.

Nicolas disliked this beast immediately.

"But of course that's all behind you now."

The lizard's low, mischievous chuckle was cut short by the boy's exclamation.

"My slipper!" he cried.

There, on the sand beside the salamander, lay one of his lost slippers. There was no mistaking it—a few of the berries with which it was stitched still clung by a thread or two to its curled toe, its sole was still stained by those last traces of blood that the stream's water had been unable to wash away.

"Excuse me, your majesty, but that is my slipper, the slipper I thought I had lost."

"She can't hear you, obviously."

"But . . ."

"She's asleep, you told me so yourself."

"But how did it get here?"

The salamander shrugged.

"One step at a time. I suppose."

Nicolas would have retrieved it at once, but his mistrust of the salamander made him unwilling to dismount from his horse. And so the slipper remained out of reach.

"Of course, there are many means of transportation and transformation, and one must, *alas*, resist the temptation to play critic. But I ask you, all this walking, walking, walking, this endless series of steps, always one at a time, one after the other, it really is too slow, too tiresome, such a travesty of progress. I really don't see how anyone could put up with the pace of it."

Nicolas wished there was some way to wake the Queen.

"Well, at least you've shed that weight of birds."

"What weight?"

"Those bags of yours, those, those birdbags."

Nicolas lifted their caged ashes from the horse's neck and held them close, to protect them from the withering arrogance of this meddlesome creature.

"Heavy as lead they were," said the salamander, shaking his pointy snout in disapproval.

"No one asked *you* to carry them," barked the boy, offended by such irreverence.

"No one ever *asked* me to carry anything," retorted the salamander, "and yet here I am carrying even this conversation."

"I don't see why you have to—"

"No one asked salt to bear all the flavor of the food either. And I don't remember hearing anyone asking permission of the soul before burdening it with all that body."

"But—"

"Not to mention that poor, poor path of yours, crushed by that same tired step over and over again. It's no wonder it's disappeared, sunk back down into the earth or wherever it sprang from."

Nicolas couldn't get a word in.

"If you ask me, you should be thankful that your burden has been lightened. There's a lesson in *that* loss." The salamander laughed, then sighed. "Just give it up, that's all I have to say."

"But I have sworn *not* to give it up!" Nicolas exploded.

"Calm down."

"But you don't understand!"

"Perhaps I don't," agreed the salamander, "perhaps I've given up even that along the way. But I can assure you—oh, never mind, what's the use."

The beast wagged its head from side to side.

"Pilgrims!" it snorted, exasperated.

Nicolas just stared at his caged ash.

"Look. Don't think of it as a loss, but as a leap."

Nicolas said nothing.

"Or think of it as a sort of fireproofing."

Still Nicolas said nothing.

"Am I talking to myself here?"

The salamander shifted its weight, smoothing the sand behind it with one quick sweep of its tail.

"You should have been there in the old days. Why, whole kingdoms, whole cities and nations and everyone and everything in them were put to the torch, nothing but smoking ashes as far as the eye could see. They're the crown of time, kid. Now move along."

Nicolas was tempted to leave, right then and there, and he might have, had the Queen not stirred slightly, her whole body heaving with one long, gentle sigh.

"Excuse me, your majesty, but if I might just talk with you for a minute—"

"I thought I told you she was asleep."

"But I have so much I want to ask her."

"Look, I'm answering the questions here. Now if there's something you want to know that isn't completely stupid and a waste of time. . . ."

Nicolas bit his lower lip, trying to control his temper.

He lowered his ashes, stringing them back across the horse's neck, and waited in vain for the Queen to stir once more.

"Where am I?" he demanded to know at last.

"Hey, that's *your* hoop of fire. I said I'd answer questions, not do tricks. You're on the far side of your most recently frustrated desire, just like the rest of us. And if you're smart you'll rub yourself with its ashes like your friend over there, and quit sulking, so that you'll never have to burn through this one again."

The salamander had gestured with its tail, pointing to a boy that had appeared by the river's edge when Nicolas wasn't looking.

"Who . . . "

Without approaching, he could see that the boy bore an uncanny resemblance to himself.

"He's been following you," said the salamander, as Nicolas stared, "like a shadow."

Indeed, the color of one boy's skin seemed the shadow of the other's pale complexion. It seemed as if he had, as the lizard suggested, anointed himself with that gray ash that accompanied them both. Yet this was not the only difference between them, and it was almost with envy that Nicolas eyed the two enormous wings that sprouted from his shadow's back, enormous pale wings that extended all the way to the ground, their downy tips dragging along the earth whenever he took a step.

"What is he doing?"

The gray boy hadn't turned around but stood absorbed at the river's edge, staring at its far bank or into its lazily flowing waters, a long, thin pole gripped in both his hands.

"Is he pointing at something?" Nicolas wanted to know.

The salamander laughed.

"Never forsake the obvious entirely, kid."

Nicolas studied his shadow.

"He's fishing," said the salamander at last.

"Fishing?"

79

"Fishing."

"For what?" asked the boy.

The salamander began to laugh once again.

Nicolas was more anxious than ever to wake the sleeping Queen and question her.

"Your majesty, if I could please just—"

Once more the boy's earnest plea proved ineffectual. And for the first time since he'd arrived he became aware of the subtle change that had come over the Queen.

It was her skin.

Milky before, with the faintest trace of peach, it had taken on a distinctly gray tint, as if she too had been rubbed with ash, but an ash finer and paler than his, a cooler lavender ash, lighter and more ancient than his own dark residue. Her motionlessness began to disturb the boy, haunting him like that terrible calm before a storm when the wind withdraws and the earth falls silent and the air itself begins to gather shadows from out of nowhere.

He looked back at the salamander, glaring directly into the slit of its eye.

"Did she know?"

"Hmmm?"

"Did she know?"

"Know what?"

"Did she know where she was sending me, that it was only a peacock and not—"

"All this fuss and bother about a big blue bird," said the salamander, "and what's *knowing* got to do with it, anyway?"

"But if she knew—"

"Have you ever really stopped to think about how all those many colors spring from the same simple white of a single egg?"

"But if she knew, why didn't—"

"*Only* what's hidden," continued the beast, "could bloom so magnificently."

"But if—"

"The question is really one of direction, I think—to conceal, to make manifest—when you come right down to it, each is really the bud and the bloom of the other."

"But—"

"Blossom and decay, blossom and decay," the salamander began chanting delightedly, thumping its tail in the sand, "it's the only true way to pass through the day."

Nicolas flew into a rage.

"I think you're a perfectly horrid creature," he spat.

"Well I'm not here to win a contest, kid, I'm only here to make a few suggestions."

"No thank-you," snarled the boy.

"Keep burning, keep walking, see if I care," the salamander snarled right back, "see if she cares."

Nicolas felt his horse growing restless beneath him.

"Go on," taunted the beast, "measure everything with your own tired foot."

"I will!" shouted the poor young Pilgrim.

And he kicked the horse's flank to make him go, kicked him with such force that the pain that shot through his wounded foot almost toppled him from the horse's back as it broke into a violent gallop.

He listened, hoping to hear the other horse, and presumably its winged gray rider, struggling to catch up. He heard nothing, turned around to look, and saw that they had not followed. Grazing contentedly in the shade, the black horse had not even looked up. The shadow of a boy stood immobile, still fishing peacefully, still staring out into the depths of the river.

Neema, of course, slumbered on.

So swiftly did the horse travel that before long she was reduced by distance to just another heap of ashes in whose center the salamander stood out, in silhouette, like the final ember of dark fire that rules a cold hearth.

"My slipper!" cried the boy suddenly, realizing too late that, possessed by his anger, he had left it behind.

There was no stopping the horse now. Faster and faster it charged on, through forest and field, crashing through the underbrush, splashing through shallow streams, its hooves pounding the earth, until sweat began to stream in torrents from its flushed flanks and from the furrows of the boy's brow. They were both drenched, horse and rider, as they sped on and on in a sort of senseless exultation, racing blindly, as the salamander might have put it, between blossom and decay.

"The question is really one of direction," the spirit's beast had remarked with the brutal vertical wisdom of the pyre.

But there was a pilgrim's parallel wisdom as well, a wisdom of patient circles that grouped all directions under a single heading. "On!" Nicolas might have shouted to his horse, had the horse not known already of the rider's choice to take always the longer and more humble path, the path of experience.

CHAPTER FOUR

City of Pirates

"Gold, my boy! Gold!" rasped the one-eyed man, grabbing Nicolas roughly by the collar. "Now there's yer treasure! Mark my words, boy, there's yer blasted rainbow's end!"

"Where are we going?" croaked the boy. The man was practically dragging him down a narrow alley that seemed even darker, if that were possible, than the one they'd just emerged from.

"Never you mind, it won't be there till we get there, you just be trustin' old Phineas, I ain't steered a boy wrong yet."

Nicolas tripped and stumbled in the dark.

"But I can't see anything," he protested.

"Navigatin' is me life, boy, now don't you be insultin' an old ship's eye like I. Why, I recollect one storm she come on so thick and black she lay cross sun and moon and stars for four, for forty days and nights. I steered 'er through that one aright and so won't be needin' no compass on these streets I know better than the lines mapped on me own hand. Say now—" he stopped suddenly, pressing his face up close to the boy's and narrowing his unpatched eye to one dark slit, "you be carryin' any money?"

"Money?"

Nicolas shrugged, confused, timidly lifting up his precious birdcages full of ash.

"Agghhh," sighed the old sailor, and spit into the darkness, "never you mind, my boy." He slapped Nicolas so hard on the back that he almost lost his footing. "Never you mind," crooned the old pirate, as he pulled from his pocket a filthy rag in which was wrapped a single battered coin that seemed to glint, even in the inky blackness, with a light all its own. "You be my guest tonight, now there's the fact of it."

"But where—?"

"And once we get to celebratin', then we'll see about this bird, then we'll hear all and no more 'bout this bleedin', burnin' bird o' yers."

But Nicolas could be dragged no further. Despite the hand at his collar, pulling him on, he sank to his knees, protesting, "I . . . I'm sorry sir, but I can't . . . I mean, I don't think I can go any farther."

"Can't go on? A strappin' young lad like you, now what can be the problem ailin' ya?"

"It's . . . it's my foot," groaned the boy.

"And what's the matter with yer foot, then?"

Phineas struck a match in the dark, and one quick glance at the boy's festering wound drew a whistle from between his clenched teeth.

"Well, then, he's a brave boy who's deservin' to be carried on me own back like a soldier, wound and all." Before Nicolas could object or resist, the sailor had hoisted him up like a knapsack and plunged forward into the darkness. The man's broad shoulder, upon which Nicolas could not help but rest his head, smelled of the sea, or of what the boy would soon learn was the sea, though as yet he'd neither idea nor experience of that vast pathless expanse from which such brutally mysterious perfumes arose.

Phineas had stumbled upon the marooned Pilgrim quite by accident. Always on the lookout for treasures, be they buried or otherwise, he'd spied a heap of something beneath the rotting planks of a little footbridge that connected two of the crooked shoreside streets of this ramshackle port he called home between voyages. He'd slid down the embankment through the mud to investigate, only to find his treasure was alive, and shivering, even in its sleep.

"Why, it's no bed fittin' fer a boy, this cold and stinkin' mud," he swore, quickly removing his overcoat and throwing it over the boy even before trying to wake him. "Aye, the mud's an inn aright, but an inn fer the age o' men, a grave's inn. Take it from one who knows 'is beds, lad. Take it straight from one who knows all 'bout the damned dreamin'."

"Whaa—"

"It's directions you be needin', then."

"Huhhm—"

Nicolas couldn't tell whether or not he was awake.

"And yer luck's upon you in me own person presently—Captain Phineas B. Bellweather, B as in barnacle, at your service, and aimin' first things always first to steal the shake and shiver outta yer young bones sure as I stand here up to me ears and years in mud!"

"But whaa—"

"And then we'll be hearin' yer tale o' woe sure enough, once we find the hard bench and the good solid table that'll hold our glasses fer a whole night's worth of ale an' tellin'."

Nicolas had been too tired, too lost and confused, to be frightened—even of the ragged black patch that completely covered the man's right eye, even of the thick, plum-colored scar that shot down the side of his face from cheek to chin. He'd let the old sailor drag him up the embankment, he'd followed him as best he could through the maze of crooked streets. What else was he to do? Where else was he to go?

It had already been quite dark when he'd arrived, a dark and moonless night. He'd been filled with foreboding, and hadn't wanted to enter this strange city on foot, but at the edge of town he'd been unable to coax the white horse any further—it had refused to budge. And so he'd been forced to dismount, and, carrying his cages of ash with him, he'd set off, almost reluctantly, to explore. Quickly losing his way in the dark labyrinth of streets, he soon found himself crippled by the pain in his foot. He scarcely remembered settling down to sleep at all, there beneath the bridge. He might even have fainted, he might have fallen—it all seemed like a dream.

"And what is it could be lurin' a lad like you to these parts of ours?" Captain Phineas B. as in barnacle Bellweather had hazarded to ask.

In his exhaustion, Nicolas could be nothing other than matter-of-fact.

"I am searching for the remedy for all pain and sorrow," he said, gripping his voice as tightly as possible, "and I shall find one feather, one feather of the fabulous Phoenix, and then I shall return to my home in the aviary, to my . . . "

Here his grip failed, his voice trembled, crumbling into a pained silence.

Phineas B. Bellweather had said nothing.

It was over an hour later, he was riding upon the captain's strong back, his arms locked around his neck to keep from sliding to the ground, his cages of ash lashed tightly to his belt. He'd stopped shivering, the pain in his foot had subsided—and he was busy peering into the darkness on either side of these winding alleys down which the old sailor blustered like a gust of north wind, unconscious of any obstacle whatsoever. Nicolas stared and stared, trying to ascertain just what sort of forest this was. He'd never been in a city or even a town before, he'd never seen so many walls, so many buildings in one place, and all huddled so closely together. Already it seemed as if there was scarcely room enough to pass between them, and yet with each fresh twist and turn of their path the alleys grew narrower, more crooked, less navigable. The old sailor never hesitated.

Every so often the gloom would relent, withdrawing momentarily from the dull glow of a window, a cracked and smudged old pane of musty yellow lamplight, a single honey-colored cell in the comb of an otherwise dark and hidden hive. He could sense the life within, he was convinced that there were more people here in this strange dark castle of tilted walls and crooked corners than in any other place he'd ever found himself in his life. But the lamplit windows passed by in an instant, swiftly left behind, before he could catch even a glimpse of what lay inside.

And then, unexpectedly, he heard the voices. He heard them singing, and felt as if he was back in the forest at the edge of the Queen's infernal pasturelands.

"The flame's gone out . . . "

It was the same song, there was no doubt about it. He recognized those words. But there was more this time, there were other words that drifted toward him through the darkness.

"Frail boat . . . I sink," sang the disembodied voices, "into the sea . . . "

With no warning, the old sailor crouched down and let the boy slide, less than gently, to the ground.

Just as it had before, the music seemed to end no sooner than it had begun. And just as before—when his burning question had been extinguished by the single tear he'd spied rolling down the cheek of the Queen of the Shepherds— so now was his flood of questions staunched by the solemnity of the gesture with which the old sailor removed his hat and held it in his clasped hands, his head bowed down to the ground.

"The Requiem?" whispered Nicolas.

Phineas nodded, "Aye, lad, 'tis that and more, much more."

He pointed over their heads to a warped and weathered plank of wood hanging from the eaves of the building in front of which the Pilgrim had been deposited, in a heap, on the cold ground. A crude hieroglyph, which looked to Nicolas like the handle of a pump, was painted on the lower half of the sign, and above it, in large letters, their dark blue paint peeling, he read aloud a single, almost illegible word: "STILLWATERS."

At the very mention of that name Phineas B. as in barnacle Bellweather clapped his threadbare black cap firmly back onto his head.

"You see, my boy, outside in the cold and the dark o' the mud o' the streets, 'tis a requiem aright, god be restin' them souls every which way wherever they be a fallin'."

He grabbed Nicolas by the sleeve and yanked him to his feet.

"But inside," he hissed, "inside, there 'tis the same song, aye, but a differin' tune—God wake 'em now, them very same blessed and blasted souls—inside, my boy, inside 'tis a drinkin' song, and that'll be where we be a goin' and swifter than a man can swallow *amen*!"

And then they dove, into Stillwaters.

"Frail boat, I sink into the sea!"

The refrain was no longer mournful but triumphant, and deafening. Though by the time the boy's eyes had accustomed themselves to the smokey yellow light that filled the room, the rousing chorus had already stuttered to a halt, as every face in the tavern turned toward this strange pair of newcomers, the captain and the boy. Within moments, not even the scrape of a boot could be heard, or the clink of a glass.

Having traveled so long in darkness, unable to see one another clearly, Captain Bellweather and the boy were unaware of just how outlandish they appeared. Each of them was covered, almost from head to toe, with a thick dried layer of mud. They stood in the open doorway of the tavern like two ghouls, the whites of their eyes shining from behind their shadowy masks.

It was a mate of the captain's who broke the silence at last, for upon recognizing the glint in the eye behind the mask, he cried out, "If they be needin' a bath, the filthy strangers, then let 'em be havin' a bath!" And he sloshed a full pitcher of ale, from halfway across the room, directly into his shipmate's face, dissolving his mask, revealing his identity to everyone at once.

The uproar was tremendous.

They all knew Cap'n Barnacle Bellweather, who spluttered and spat and cursed and laughed as he chased his mate all through the tavern, overturning tables and glasses as he went.

Left alone there in the doorway, gazing around the room, Nicolas could scarcely believe his eyes.

Men with pictures on their skin! Men with one eye and one arm, and with rings through their ears and their noses! Women with their torn skirts hitched up over their scarred thighs, and thick black cigars clenched between their stained teeth! And rats, of course, scurrying across the floor and along the rafters, and barking dogs, one with a thick collar set with shining stones, another limping over on three legs to lick his hand and sniff at his wound, its fourth leg, a wooden peg, strapped to its body with a rope looped around its bent back. There was a talking parrot whose iridescent feathers flashed out through the smoke as it shifted from one sailor's shoulder to another's, all the while shrieking above the din of the crowd, "Take a bath! Take a bath! Take a bath!" And strangest of all, in one of the far recesses of the tavern Nicolas spied what appeared to be a huge brown bear manacled with a thick iron chain to the leg of the table at which it sat, its snout buried in one of the hundreds of empty glass mugs that were scattered everywhere.

And the maps! Every available surface was littered with them, maps of every conceivable inch of the unknown, maps to treasure, the boy would subsequently learn—but even now they seemed to have yielded up their fruits of search quite literally, piled high as they were with all the illicit cargo that found its way into the tavern via the deep pockets and quick hands and tempers of the pirates who drank at its tables and often slept in its dark corners. Everywhere there were piles of spice and remnants of silk, heaps of ivory and ebony and mother of pearl, and mountains of exotic tropical fruits unheard of to anyone who hadn't spent a lifetime crisscrossing the open seas. Sweet hairy rambutans and lychees, pawpaws and pine nuts and mangosteens, figs and dates from the desert, kelps and hiziki from the sea, and from the mountains a sour apple with the dry scaley skin of a snake.

Despite his involvement in his own games, Phineas had not forgotten the boy.

"Ladies an' pirates," he announced, smashing a glass against a tabletop to get their attention, "might I be introducin' to you this unfortunate pilgrim of yer own youth truly, now come ta tell us of 'is woes o' searchin', come to add 'is own page to the book o' the quest."

"Take a bath!" shrieked the parrot.

The boy could not but acquiesce. Before he knew it he'd been stripped naked, lifted up and then set down again in a large octagonal copper basin, where he stood, nervously, awaiting his baptism.

"Come now, lad," whispered Phineas, "don't you be shamed or afearin'." Nicolas was surprised to see that the old sailor stood stripped as well, in a basin identical to his own. "Naked as the day we was born," the captain managed to mutter before the bucket of hot soapy water that was dumped over his head cut him short, the mud melting from his skin, swirling away and collecting in the basin below, "and there ain't no harm in it nor can there be," he spluttered to a conclusion.

Moments later a stream of water sloshed down over the boy, warming his very bones.

And anyone passing by that night, cold and lonely, on the street outside the tavern, would have been witness, had he peeked in the grimey window, to a scene of such innocent charm as to have warmed him for the rest of his journey no matter how long that may have been. While the boy's smooth, pale skin glowed more angelically than the hard scarred crust of the gristled old pirate, still the two shone in the center of the tavern with a purity so delicately human that nothing could corrupt it.

Fresh dry clothes were brought for the boy, and he watched as an impossibly old man carried off his muddied shirt and trousers and began to wash them in the rusty sink behind the bar.

"Who's he?" Nicolas whispered in his captain's ear.

"Ahhh, the stories that 'un might be a-tellin' ya," he sighed, "and most likely all of 'em lies, beautiful lies."

He turned to his colleagues.

"He wants to be knowin' who it is there that's runnin' the pirate's laundry."

Suddenly, as one, they all rose, and as one they lifted their glasses high into the air and toasted.

"To the Knight o' the Rueful Countenance!" they bellowed in perfect unison.

The ancient man turned slowly, majestically, the boy's dripping singlet still clutched in one arthritic hand, and he bowed with an elegant flourish, and turned back immediately to his washtub.

"But I'm almost forgettin' meself," barked Phineas, "and me friend, me young friend, for you shan't be standin' a minute longer on that bloaty foot o' yers, my boy, but sit now, sit, and let us take the closer look."

Everyone in the tavern agreed that it was indeed a wound of the first caliber, although there were many who bragged of far worse—especially after Phineas got down to the other business at hand, and, withdrawing his old dented coin from the dirty rag in his pocket, he slapped it down onto the table with a loud crack, declaring, "Tonight, in honor of me newest o' mates, we'll all be a drinkin', all and every last stinkin' one of us, we'll all be a drinkin' hearty on me and me best coin!"

"By the fallin' skies, he be spendin' it at long last!" cried a woman who was walking toward Nicolas, tearing the bundle of cloth she carried into long thin strips as she approached.

"Now mind yer tongue, wench," laughed Phineas, "and be showin' a little respect fer the sailor who's carried such a weight in 'is pocket all these many long years o' thirstin'."

And so the boy's wound, his *pilgrim's ache*, as Captain Bellweather referred to it, was treated from both ends at once—soothed by the long soft strips of cotton in which his foot was wrapped like a mummy, and then numbed by the stream of burning whiskey that was all but poured down his throat.

The fire of the whiskey was quickly followed by a mug of cool ale, which left a pale crescent of foam across the boy's upper lip and a look of bemused contentment in his eyes.

"Now you be stayin' off that foot fer some days, me lovely," said the woman when she had secured the bandage, and downed her own glass of ale.

"But I can't," Nicolas erupted, "for I must be on my way to find—"

"You be hearin' that now?" cried the captain. "You be hearin' the search in 'is voice, and rememberin' how far from yer very own birthin' day you rascals been travelin' through yer own long an' lean pilgrim's ache?"

"Won't never leave you, my boy," confided one of the pirates who sat alongside him.

"One of us, 'e is, I'll be swearin' to it, aye!" cried the captain.

And on the other side of him another drunken rogue assured the boy, "It's just yer own heart lettin' you know fer sure it's still a beatin'."

"One of us!" the toast rang out through the tavern.

Captain Bellweather's glass was still raised high in the air, when suddenly he hesitated. "Whoa, then," he shouted, "but what sort of a tattoo is it you be sportin'?"

"Tattoo?"

"Tattoo! Tattoo! Tattoo!" the parrot took up the refrain.

Nicolas downed another mug of ale, wiping his mouth with the back of his hand just as he'd seen the other pirates do.

"Let us be seein' it—fer no lapsed pilgrim's without 'is tattoo, no, my boy, no one sets searchin' to sea without 'is picture of 'is heart on 'is sleeve."

Men with pictures on their skin, thought the boy, gazing around the room and understanding at last. He was feeling dizzy even before the next shot of whiskey went down, and, fortified by its burning vertigo, he seconded the cry for the tattoo artist that echoed off the tavern's walls.

Nicolas was drunk.

There were so many voices, voices shouting from across the room, voices whispering, up close, right into his ear. He could scarcely distinguish one from the other. All he knew for sure was that they were *all* talking to him. He was undoubtedly the center of attention—and there wasn't an old drunken soul present who didn't have the best and the only idea as to exactly what was the perfect image with which to draw the man from out of the boy.

"An anchor!" called out one of the assembled drifters, rolling up his own torn sleeve and flexing the muscles of his arm, his hand balled into a fist that remained undaunted, after all these years, by the meager handful of saltwater that was the only treasure its tireless grip on the waves of the sea had ever netted it.

"The full glass!" someone else cried out.

"The full bottle!" cried another, and promptly slid from his chair to the floor, smiling like an idiot.

Nicolas laughed aloud with the others.

The tattooist emerged silently from the crowd of drunks. He sat opposite the boy, directly across a low wooden table that he cleared of its maps and glasses and fruit peels with one sweep of his brawny forearm. From his breast pocket the man removed a neat bundle of deep purple velvet, stained and threadbare round the edges, and, carefully untying the cord with which it was bound, he laid it down flat on the table, folding back the fabric on each of its four sides with four precise gestures, thus exposing his inks and his needles for all to see.

Someone passed him a cigarette, and as he lit it, and inhaled deeply, another man approached, as silent as he. Stopping alongside the table, he paused for only a moment before tearing open the buttons of his shirt to reveal the tattoo of a helmsman's wheel that covered his entire chest.

"The pilot's wheel," he swore, more insistent than the others.

Nicolas stared at the enormous wheel that seemed to ripple slightly, like a reflection on water, with each breath the man drew. Beneath the painted surface he could count the old sailor's sharp ribs.

"Who's he?" he whispered, bending close to his captain.

"The Roamin'," Phineas whispered back.

The tattoo artist was busy picking up his tools one by one from their packet and arranging them on the table.

"Go on," urged Phineas, nudging the boy's shoulder with his half-empty mug, "ask 'im to tell it, ask 'im . . . "

Nicolas cleared his throat.

"He won't be startin' until you ask 'im . . . "

Of course they'd all heard the tale a million times, but then a tale wasn't a tale till it be told again and again and again.

"Tell me," was all Nicolas managed to say, and not a few of those present muttered with approval at the terse wisdom of one no more than a boy.

"Midnight it was, aye, and all of us, every soul o' the crew, sleepin' sound as babes, trustin' in 'im like always—fer 'e was the best o' helmsmen ever sailed the seven seas, and the best o' friends ever there was as well."

Once more glasses were raised.

"The best o' helmsmen!"

"And the best o' friends!"

"Aye!"

"Aye, 'tis too true, but that there was a devil in the sleepin' that night, but that the jealous sea 'erself was a devil guised as sleep an' whisperin' in 'is ear—but for just that he'd a been here right now, drinkin' with 'is mates one an' all."

Nicolas leaned over and whispered, "Who—?"

Phineas held one finger up to his lips.

"Not that he'd be havin' any of 'er seducin', not our pilot, not Pal'nurus, whose eyes never closed but that once, and now'll never be closin' no more s'long as I got me hands to hold 'em open tight."

The man dropped his hands, palms up, exposed, and Nicolas saw the wide-open eye tattooed on each one, staring at him.

"The pilot's eyes," whispered Phineas in the boy's ear. "No tattoo is more painful."

"But—"

The storyteller went on.

"Trust in a calm sea, 'e says to 'imself, bah! Trust the peaceful face o' the waves, a long an' low swell, an unchangin' world moored by the movin' harbor o' sleep, bah! ... *Cease yer toilin', pilot, close yer eyes,* she whispers, *I'll man yer tiller for the while* ... Bah!—I heared 'im say it meself—don't ask me how, me being sound asleep in me captain's berth at the time, but still I heared 'im curse 'er devil's bill an' coo just as loud an' clear as you be hearin' me yarnin' this very minute."

No one doubted it for a moment, least of all Nicolas.

"Fer our sake it was 'e cursed 'er, fer the sake of 'is ship an' 'is mates! Is no peace to compare to, that peace 'e give us after the long hard day o' work tarrin' and bailin' and trimmin' the sail or plyin' the blasted oar like a sea slave in the galley, and we a sleepin' sound, knowin' the ship safe come hell come highwater, knowin' no harm could come to 'er or to us with Pal'nurus pilotin' our dreams ... "

For a moment, the room fell silent. The cigarette that had burned down all the way to his fingers fell from the tattooist's hand without his having moved a muscle.

"But she don't rest, the sleep o' the sea. She don't rest till she's ev'ry last one o' us poor souls breakin' down and sinkin' 'neath 'er waves. That midnight clear even the eyes of good Pal'nurus was swimmin' in 'er still mirror o' the starry sky, caught up in 'er double moon tide—and bent weary 'gainst the ship's rail, over the side she tossed 'im easy and never even waked 'im afore he drowned. And on we sailed, and would be sailin' still, a ghost ship 'neath the waves, but for the boomin' o' the surf on the reefs that waked me and dragged me up deck to the empty wheel, those reefs we never even nightmared near so long as my poor pilot held an' helmed our dream."

"My poor pilot!"

"Poor Palinurus!"

The toasts were renewed.

And tears were shed, not the least of which were the beads of sweat that Nicolas spied rolling down the palms of the storyteller's hands, moistening the pilot's eyes he carried there.

"Man overboard!" shouted Nicolas, raising his glass on high, too drunk to be frightened that he had overstepped the bounds of pirate's propriety, of which he'd no doubt there was such a thing.

"Man overboard!" echoed the parrot, and the sailors laughed, their common sorrow turned, in a moment, to delight—their moods no more changeable than those of that sea they both loved and hated.

The tattooist was staring straight at the boy, waiting, as, one by one, recovering from their shared loss, the pirates again began shouting out their suggestions. Hours passed, and still they went on crying out image after drunken image, and still the tattoo artist sat waiting patiently for Nicolas to make up his mind.

"The cutlass!" someone snarled.

"Or the cannon!"

"Nay, let it be the crossed swords!"

"And the both of 'em drippin' blood!"

"Now don't be loadin' down the lad with yer own bloody troubles right from the start, but leave off the fightin' fer once in yer lives."

"Take care, lad, else you lose yer dreamin' in the shoals of squabblin' all the world's aboundin' in."

"Aye!"

"Aye, 'tis well spoke!"

"And well spoke he as well who says let 'em make it the full cask itself that he be imagin' in skin's ink, the broke open cask o' gems and jewels."

"Gold, my boy!"

"The gold's the thing!"

Nicolas recognized the captain's voice.

"Make it the bright coin, brighter even than me own that yer drinkin' on right now!"

"Nay, a chain!"

"Make it a chain, then, a chain o' gold, aye! Make it a chain thicker than me own neck an' skull!"

"Tie it true 'round yer own arm lad, and in the goldest o' gold inks!"

"And with a lock an' key o' gold to hold its fever hard by!"

"Nay! Not a chain, boy, but a crown!"

"Aye!"

"Well, then, let it be a crown then!"

"A crown then!"

"A crown o' gold!"

"A crown o' gold!"

A deeper, harsher voice rang out suddenly through the crowd of unruly men. It was the voice of a woman.

"Leave off yer crownin', ya scurvy wretches!" she growled.

"Crown o' gold! Crown o' gold! Crown o' gold!" shrieked the parrot.

And a bottle flew across the room, shattering against the far wall and missing the bird by only an inch or two.

"There'll be no coronatin' in my place!"

"Aww, Hecabee, we's only sportin' an' don't be meanin' no bit o' harm."

This time the bottle flew so close to their hats and heads that every pirate in the place ducked.

"Ya don't know *what* ya mean, any o' ya, ya louts—and yer youngster all puffed up with ale and tale, 'e don't know neither how 'is luck is with 'im only till the searchin' be over an' done, how she'll vanish soon enough in the curse o' the findin' an' the havin' . . . "

The woman turned away in disgust.

"And the losin' . . . " she muttered under her breath.

"Who's she?" Nicolas asked in his captain's ear.

"Now you be steerin' clear of 'er, my boy, you be promisin' me that. Fer she's got more salt in 'er than the sea."

Nicolas gazed at the woman, whose back was still turned.

"They say she had it all once," Phineas continued in a hoarse whisper, "all there was to have and more, lad. They say she was like to a queen, with 'er own palace and armies and gold by the shipful."

"And now?" whispered the boy.

"Only this," shrugged Phineas.

"This?"

"Aye, it's 'er place here we do our drinkin' in, and no other."

"But why, if—?"

"They say she's salts the ale with 'er tears, lad, and fer a sailor 'tis no other flavor compares."

Nicolas was still staring at the woman's back.

"Hecabeeee," pleaded the boldest, or the thirstiest, of all the pirates, "let us be havin' another round then."

"And who'll be a payin' for it?" barked the woman.

But before they could answer, she was already busy at the keg, calling out over her shoulder, "Ah ya poor wretches now don't be diggin in yer empty pockets fer me coin just yet, fer the next is on me, yer credit's good at least here in me own place, that much at least ya poor wanderin' souls be deservin', fer ya can't get much closer to the bottom of it than at the bottom o' one o' me own dirty glasses."

Nicolas glanced around the room at the wealth of treasure heaped up on table-tops and in corners.

"How can they be so poor when there's so much—"

"The treasure ain't for the spendin', lad . . . "

Phineas caught the boy eyeing the empty rag his coin had been wrapped in.

" . . . 'cept under certain, well, special circumstances."

The Ram's solemn words echoed in the boy's head. "Never under any circumstances, no matter what silly emergency seems to pressure you into what drastic action."

"To the queen of sorrow," more than a few of the sailors were busy toasting behind the woman's back, quietly, so that she would not overhear.

But the parrot was both a quick and a slow learner.

"Queen of Sorrow! Queen of Sorrow!" it squawked.

And once more a bottle flew, though this time it passed so wide of its mark that the men were confident that the crisis of fallen royalty had passed, at least for the moment.

"But we be forgettin' our business to hand," said Phineas.

The tattoo artist still sat waiting patiently, his eyes fixed straight ahead on the drunken boy.

Another man spoke up now.

"A broken heart," was all he said, baring his arm.

And while a murmur of approval rippled round the room, Nicolas caught sight of something spilling from the cornucopia of fruit piled up on an adjacent table, something that startled him and forced the words from his lips even before he realized he was speaking.

"A pomegranate!" he cried.

The commotion in the room ceased.

"A burning pomegranate!"

The tattooist sitting across from him broke into a broad grin.

"Well, I'll be . . . " mumbled Phineas.

But the boy interrupted him, whispering in his ear more urgently than before, pointing to the man who'd spoken last and demanding to know, "Who is he?"

"Who?"

"That man, the man with the broken heart," replied the boy.

The captain hadn't time enough to answer. For Nicolas had chosen, and the tattoo artist had set to work immediately. Already the boy's sleeve had been torn off at the shoulder, his arm had been extended out flat on the table and swabbed with a tiny sponge soaked in whiskey. Motionless for so long, the tattooist moved now with a swiftness that astounded the boy almost as much as that first prick of the needle against his tender skin.

"The Sumerian," Phineas answered as soon as he could, hissing into the boy's ear, trying to distract him from the pain long enough for him to grow accustomed to it.

"Hhhuu—?"

"The man with the broken heart," insisted Phineas. "He's not from 'round these parts. They call 'im the Sumerian, they do."

"But we haven't heard your tale yet," said the Sumerian.

His voice and mannerisms betrayed the fact that he was, indeed, like Nicolas himself, from some distant land.

"A burnin' pomegranate," whistled one of the pirates, shaking his head in awe, "so what is it then *you* be searchin' fer, lad?"

"A b-bird," Nicolas managed to say, wincing with the pain of the busy needle. He and the man with the broken heart were staring deeply into one another's eyes.

"Is it a blackbird, then?"

"A raven?"

"Fer she's a dark fruit you be choosin' as mark."

The pirates slipped once more into their chaotic guessing games.

"Is it an albatross?"

"Or maybe a turnstone?"

"Or a skimmer?"

"A godwit!"

"A stilt!"

"A snipe?"

Nicolas did not respond.

"Is it the peacock?"

"No!" shouted the boy suddenly, vehemently, "that is, well, I've already found the peacock, or I—"

"Already found the peacock!"

The pirates were impressed.

For the first time, Nicolas noticed the bale of brilliant peacock feathers stacked up against the wall behind the bar. The notion of *treasure* was undergoing a constant modification in his mind.

The man with the broken heart spoke once more. "But what is it you carry with you? There?" he asked, pointing beneath the table. Parked securely between the boy's feet were his cages full of ash, never forgotten for a moment, despite his drunken state. "They're birdcages, aren't they?"

Nicolas nodded yes and then asked the man a question of his own.

"Who's heart is it that is broken?"

"My heart," answered the Sumerian, quickly.

Once more, it was his turn to question.

"And you will capture this bird you seek in those cages you carry? But they are already full."

It was the boy's friend, his captain, who came to the rescue, breaking into the conversation to give the truth its authentic ring of surprise.

"And ain't it full to burstin' aready, mate, this heart o' yers, broke open as it is, an' achin' to be filled? Ain't it so full o' the empty as to be overflowin'? And still you be ever searchin' to fill it up the more."

100

Everyone was delighted.

"Full o' the empty, we is, we is!" rang out the drunken pirate's chorus, as the ale poured down their throats. Indeed, the surprise of the truth, which was a treasure in its own right, made a playful mockery, like any treasure, of the very map that led to it—or else it was no treasure and no truth at all.

And yet, beneath all the frivolity, beneath the gleam of the gold, be it truth or treasure, there glimmered something else darker and deeper, something the two of them shared in silence. The faded heart broken open on the man's arm and the bright burning pomegranate taking shape on the boy's shoulder through the consummate artistry of the needle-bearer—this pair of images seemed enough to bind the two travelers together forever.

"I was born with the robe of power already draped around my shoulders," began the Sumerian, "a king, until the day my righteous brother challenged me, and revealed the garment for what it was, a rag that could not withstand the rushing wind of the love of one's adversary. But now that he is dead, how I long for it once again, that robe of power, how I search for that yard or two of gold and purple brocade in which I might wrap his cold corpse and warm it back to everlasting life at my side."

He shook his head sadly.

"For to rule without him," he concluded, "is nothing."

The pirates were whispering among themselves.

"What's that in 'is net?"

"What's 'e say?"

"Hang me with an eel if I be a knowin'."

"Not from 'round these parts, is 'e?"

Nicolas stared at the man.

"The Phoenix," he said aloud, but it was as if no one had heard.

"There now," said the tattooist.

"Look, my boy!" yelled Phineas.

"Aye!" cheered the pirates.

The boy looked down at his shoulder, where the flame of the burning pomegranate had just been completed, leaping up from the crimson fruit below it like all that which the embrace of the fruit could not contain, and yet longed to, eternally.

"It's a fine mark," they all assured him.

"A red gold!" they swore.

"And the gold's the thing," they still insisted.

"Aye, the gold!"

"The gold!"

"Aye!"

"No matter what it's bleedin' hue."

The night in the tavern had ended with a song—of that much he was certain. It was only the pounding of the alcohol in his head, drowning out his voice with its own, that stopped him from singing at last. Standing still then, or as still as possible given the drunken tilt and sway of the ground beneath his feet, he tried to remember exactly where he was and where he was going.

All he could remember was the clang of the great loud ship's bell that Hecabee had rung from behind the bar. "Tide's out," she'd howled, as she chased the bellowing pirates out the door of her tavern and into a fog that lay so heavy on the streets of the town that there was no telling what hour of the day or night it might be.

They'd been singing, yes, they'd been singing at the top of their lungs. Blinded by the fog, they'd stumbled, perhaps for hours, up and down one crooked street after another, clutching at their bottles of ale. Nicolas could see his own bottle clearly enough, gripped tightly in his hand. He could feel other bottles, empty or still unopened, wedged into his deep pockets. And he could feel, as well, the rasp and scratch of his throat, which was raw with song—that song which, now that he'd stopped singing it, even for this moment or two, he could no longer recall a single note or word of, no matter how hard he tried.

He looked around for the others, especially his captain. But there was no sign of them.

It was then that he remembered how the fog had seemed to separate them, how their voices had grown distant, one from the other, as they'd wandered up and down these blind drunken alleys trying to reach the shore, where the tide was set to carry their anxious boats out to sea.

"They've left me behind," Nicolas gasped all at once.

Staring into the fog, his heavy gaze throbbing, he felt the stale alcohol shifting from side to side in his head like a bit of filthy seawater trapped in the bottom of a rocking boat. Raising his bottle to his lips, he took a swig of the flat ale and swallowed defiantly.

"Perhaps it's not too late," he hoped aloud.

Checking to see that his cages of ash were still with him, which, of course, they were, lashed once more to his belt, he ran off in the direction in which the fog seemed thinnest.

The fog was indeed thinning, burnt first to a pale haze, then dispersed almost completely by the strengthening sun. It was almost midday. The night had slipped away completely, along with its luminaries, its stars and its pirates. Drawn by the sound of voices, a low hum of voices as opposed to last night's heroic clamor, Nicolas emerged at last from the thicket of streets into the harbor itself, where the more legitimate business of the sea was already in full swing.

Huddled together, in small groups of varying sizes, men and women were trading, wheeling and dealing in products and promises, weighing one against the other and hoping to come out ahead. The drunken boy stood unsteadily, watching these stable clumps of merchants that seemed to have sprouted up here and there like so many tiny flowering shrubs, anchored to this thin sandy soil at the edge of the earth.

He smelled the sea before he saw it, and thought of the captain's strange, warm shoulder. Then he felt it, the sea, over his own shoulder, behind him. He felt something too large, something that had been waiting for too long, and he turned and stared past the handful of low-lying islands scattered across that calm shallow inlet that led out to endless depths and distances.

Nicolas approached the water's edge reverently, wetting his toes first, then wading forward tenderly until he was standing up to his calves in the great sea. He was vaguely aware, as he took a swallow of ale, of a stinging in his foot as the salt water soaked through his bandage and into his wound. He was vaguely aware, as well, of a cautionary voice or two calling out behind him. But he ignored both warnings, draining his bottle to the dregs and flinging it into the air, watching it land with a loud splash a few yards in front of him. It began to tip almost immediately, and, weighed down with the water pouring in through its narrow neck, it soon sank beneath the waves, lost to sight.

Nicolas uncorked another bottle, took a swig, and went on staring out to sea. When at last he turned back to the profits and losses of the activities on shore, it was as if to a mere game in a gambling parlor in which both dealer and deck were the same infinite, and every profit and every loss merely a drop in its ocean of swallowed efforts.

Then he saw the horse, the white horse that had carried him here to the border and boundary of all solid things. It was standing quietly, still blindfolded, just where he'd abandoned it when he'd set out on foot the night before. He called out eagerly, waving his arms over his head, trying to attract the horse's attention—but to no avail.

"White horse! White horse!" Nicolas shouted as he ran toward the beast, for he knew of no other name to call it. So intoxicated was he that he was sure, could he only reach the horse's side, and mount him once more, that the beast would whisk him away and carry him across the waves of this or any other sea.

They would gallop madly right across the water!

But the boy tripped and fell flat on his face even before he'd traveled a fraction of the distance that lay between himself and his magical horse.

"Seems you're in an awful hurry there, son. Can I do something for you?"

One of the merchants had darted over and begun to interrogate him even before lifting him all the way up from the ground.

"That's my white horse!" cried Nicolas.

"Yes? Well . . . don't reckon he's worth much . . . "

Nicolas spluttered with indignation.

"Let's see . . . a blind horse, well, maybe a few chores or a little light plowing. Hmmmm . . . I'll tell you what. You being a fine young boy and all, I'll give you, I'll give you ten pieces for him."

The man had already removed a little leather satchel of coins from his vest pocket.

Nicolas just stared, incredulous.

"Alright, alright, fifteen, fifteen pieces . . . sixteen pieces, but that's my last offer."

It was the horse itself that interrupted, thwarting the deal. It tossed its head, snorting to get their attention, and as both of them watched, it suddenly wheeled around and bolted off into the trees without looking back.

"Stop!" cried the boy, and tripped and fell once again.

"Well, let's not be too hasty here," muttered the merchant under his breath, as he quickly and quietly repocketed his coins.

Nicolas sat right down on the ground where he was.

"You alright, son?" inquired the man. Surely he would be acting on behalf of all his colleagues and associates if he tried to determine just exactly what this boy's business was here. Anyone with eyes in his head could see that most likely he was up to no good, that he was dirty, and perhaps even drunk, and certainly he was a foreigner. They'd had their share of troubles, they had their investments to protect, and really one could never be too careful.

"When did the ships leave?" Nicolas demanded to know.

"Ships, which ships, ships leave here all the time, son, every hour there's—"

"The big ships!" shouted the boy. "The pirate ships!"

"Ahh," was all the man said, frowning.

For a moment neither spoke.

"When did they leave?" insisted the boy.

"What's that you're drinking there, son? I think maybe you've had a little bit too much. . . ."

He tried to lift the bottle from the boy's hand, but Nicolas twisted away, resisting with surprising strength, and he raised the ale to his lips now, swallowing once, twice, and then again, coughing as the liquor flooded his throat too quickly.

"Gold!" he howled, scrambling to his feet. "I must catch up with them, for they say that its neck is of gold and its head is crowned with an exquisite crest and I don't know where else to go."

"Catch up with who?"

"Captain Bellweather," exclaimed the boy, "and The Roamin' and the man with the broken heart and the three-legged dog and . . ."

"Hmmmm."

The clever merchant was thinking, or at least calculating. Perhaps, he congratulated himself, I shall be able to kill two birds with one stone here. No doubt it would be best to get rid of this dirty drunken boy, but then why should I not be entitled to make a little profit in the process, just a humble handful of something extra for my efforts. . . .

He spoke aloud now, to the boy, "So then, son, you'll be needing a boat, I reckon, a boat of some sort if—"

"Don't you see?" Nicolas explained, "I've searched everywhere, everywhere—I must set sail now, I must, for it can only be on the far side of the sea that I shall find them."

"So you'll be needing to buy a boat!" repeated the man.

For a moment Nicolas's face went blank.

"A boat," he whispered to himself, and repeated it aloud, shouting, "A boat! Yes! A boat! A boat!"

It had never occurred to him that he might actually possess a boat of his own.

"Then I can leave now, right now!" He was running back and forth in front of the merchant. "Where can I find this boat?"

"Well, it just so happens that I myself have a boat that I *might* sell, that is, if . . . "

"Where? Where?"

"Now hold on a second, son," said the man, "just what is it that you were intending to pay for this boat with?"

"Pay?"

"Pay, yes, I mean, pay. You do have money, don't you?"

Nicolas said nothing.

"Well?"

The boy shook his head.

The merchant shook his head as well.

"Where does one find this money?" Nicolas wanted to know.

"*Where* exactly is it that you come from?" was what the merchant wanted to know, his eyes widening in disbelief.

But Nicolas had already darted away from him.

"Hey!"

The boy walked quickly, rushing over to a small group of nearby traders. "Where do I find—?"

The merchant was right behind him. "Sshhh," he hushed the boy. For there was a delicate transaction in progress, the value of a skein of the finest cashmere being weighed against that of a musical instrument of some sort, a kind of gamelan with keys of ivory and an intricately carved frame of ebony and rosewood.

"From the royal court of the Sultan of the Greater Archipelago," swore the owner of the exotic musical instrument.

"But I need to find—"

"Sshhh." This time it was the traders themselves who hushed the boy. They were at a crucial impasse in their negotiations, and a strict silence was essential as each awaited the other's next offer.

Impatient, Nicolas hurried on, almost tripping over the horse before he actually saw it.

"The black horse!" he cried out, and immediately began to look around for its rider.

"Have you seen a boy with wings, a boy just like me, just like me, but with long pale wings?"

Nicolas spoke to two children, brother and sister, apparently, who just stood, arm in arm, and stared at him, uncomprehending, until their mother beckoned to them, insisting that they move away from this strange incoherent boy who was attracting more and more uneasy attention here in the marketplace.

"Now wait a moment, son, if you would just . . . " The merchant was still in hot pursuit. He'd sold nothing all morning.

Nicolas was crouched down examining the black horse. Not only was he blindfolded now, he saw, but his hind leg was bandaged. The animal barely moved and was obviously unable to rise to its feet.

"And this horse also is for sale?" panted the merchant, catching up at last.

But the boy was off and running once again, clattering across a low wooden bridge and stopping to ask a man approaching in the opposite direction, an old man with a crutch, if he'd seen a boy with wings, a boy fishing somewhere along the banks of this stream over which they were passing.

"The gout," was all the man said, indicating his lame foot.

And he shook his head with increasing vehemence as Nicolas rattled on and on, "Or a man with a wheel on his chest? Or the Knight of the Rueful Countenance? Or a talking parrot? A trained bear? Or my captain, or——?"

The old man limped past him without another word.

Desperate, Nicolas turned to a group of men and women at the foot of the bridge.

"What's in those barrels?" he demanded to know.

"Silver spoons," sang out a woman with her high black collar turned up against the cool wind that blew in from the sea. A man seated nearby, slapping the sides of his barrel, interrupted her. "Saaardines," he shouted, advertising his own wares, "fresh sardines from off the coast of the islands."

Nicolas was furiously disappointed.

"There's no money in those barrels?"

The entire group of people began to laugh, thinking the boy was joking. "Barrels of money!" they guffawed. But their faces soon dropped, their smiles stiffening in their confusion, as they realized, one by one, that the boy was not joking, but deadly earnest.

Once more he ran on.

Time was wasting. With every moment he was delayed, he could feel the pirate ships drawing further and further away from him. If he didn't find some money soon, he'd never be able to catch up with them.

"Wait, son, wait!" It was the tireless merchant.

"I'll swim if I have to!" bellowed the boy over his shoulder, and he tipped his bottle and swallowed deeply, hurrying on.

It was an enormously fat man sitting behind a large table in the field across the bridge that finally made it clear to Nicolas that money was not something one *found* but rather something one *made*.

"And it just so happens, lad, that I'm hiring this very morning."

The fat man pointed to a pale, high tower of a building that rose straight up into the air behind him.

"We're always needing strong young boys at the refinery."

"The refinery?"

So that is where money is made, thought the boy.

"Morning, Stade."

"Morning yet is it, Steele? Looks to be almost noon to me."

"Ahhh, and so it is, and so it is . . . "

The merchant had stopped beside the boy, ostensibly to pay his respects to his competitor.

"How's business?" asked Stade, the fat man.

"Fine, just fine," answered Steele, "and with you?"

"Can't complain," said Stade.

They were both eyeing the boy greedily.

"So you're looking to hire my young friend here?" said Steele.

"Looks possible," said Stade, "looks possible."

"But how long will it take," blurted out the boy, "how long will it take to manufacture enough money to buy—?"

The fat man's eyes widened in amazement.

"Where is it exactly you come from, son?"

"From the nest in the—"

"Uhhps," interrupted the merchant, pretending to bump the table by accident, tipping the bottle that Nicolas had set down there next to his cages of ash. The fat man leapt up from his chair as quickly as he could. The puddle of spilled ale threatened to drip over the edge of the table into his lap.

"Sorry about that, Stade," said Steele.

"Accidents happen, Steele," said Stade.

"It's alright," the boy assured them both, with dauntless innocence, "I've another," and he drew a fresh bottle from out of one of his many deep pockets.

Steele's eyes dropped suddenly to the ground.

"How long will it take?" the boy was insisting, as the fat man settled back into his chair.

The merchant crouched down and swiftly palmed an object that had fallen from the boy's pocket. "Tell him, Stade," he grinned, straightening up, "tell him how long it will take."

"Well," hedged the fat man, "you see . . . "

"Tell him."

"You see, we don't actually *make* the money *itself* in the refinery."

"But you said—"

"You see, we make other things."

"But it's money I want to make!" insisted the boy.

"And it's money you will make—"

"Tell him, Stade," said Steele.

"Afterwards," mumbled Stade, realizing that the match was all but lost.

"How long afterwards, Stade?" asked Steele.

"A week," muttered Stade, "or maybe, maybe . . . two . . . "

"But I haven't time!" shouted Nicolas.

He was already pulling away from the table in disappointment.

"Look here," growled the fat man, "everyone has got to wait for payday!"

"But I told you I haven't time!"

"Well, then, I guess that's that," snapped the merchant, and, grabbing the boy roughly by the arm, he swept him away before the fat man could object, hissing into his ear as he dragged him toward the shoreline, "I thought you told me you had no money?"

They stopped near the water's edge, where the merchant opened his hand and showed Nicolas what he held there.

"What do you call this?" he barked.

It was a tiny silver thimble.

The boy had no chance to answer.

"Silver! It's silver! And you told me you had no money."

"But I never saw it before in my life!"

"Then would you mind telling me how it fell out of your pocket?"

"*My* pocket?"

"Yes, *your* pocket, back there, the same pocket you pulled that bottle from."

"But—"

Nicolas cut himself short. Thrusting his hand into the pocket in question, he was surprised to find that it was far from empty even now. Fishing around in its depths, his hand surfaced with a collection of objects that nearly drove the merchant crazy with excitement.

There was a nutmeg or two, several chips of emerald, a scallop shell, a spool of blue silk thread, the shavings from the tip of a rhinoceros's horn, a few tarnished pieces of eight, some agates, a shark's tooth, and a rare black coral.

"Where did you get these?"

"But . . . but . . . these aren't even my pockets," Nicolas muttered, looking down and suddenly remembering, "these aren't even my clothes, I've only borrowed them."

Had the pirates known? Had Phineas and the others purposely loaded up his pockets with just that wealth they knew he'd need later on? Or was it only an accident? Or was it theft? The boy dug into another pocket, and, looking down to see what sort of treasure he'd unearthed this time, he was as surprised as the merchant was delighted by the small piece of delicately carved ivory. A tiny figure of a beautiful young man, naked but for a winged helmet atop his head, it lay all but buried, nestled in the handful of cardamom and coriander seeds cupped in his palm.

"Then I can have the boat?" he exclaimed, suddenly realizing the implications of his good fortune. The treasure itself had already been surrendered. It lay in the merchant's always opening and closing hand.

"Of course! Of course!" said Steele, as if he'd intended to let him have it all the time.

"Then where—?"

"Right over here," he purred, leading the way, "right here, son, I have just the boat for you."

Nicolas could not believe his eyes.

"This boat?" he marveled.

"This and no other," said Steele, "and a splendid boat it is, a bargain at twice the price, no doubt about it."

Which may or may not have been a lie but was of little importance to Nicolas one way or the other. True, its yellow was paler, and its berries had been replaced by fragments of seashell and chips of amber set into the wooden planks of its hull, but as he ran his trembling hands over the familiar birch bark with which it was lined, a sense of confidence settled over the boy such as he hadn't felt since he'd first stepped into those yellow slippers Old Gillam had bequeathed him so long ago, at the very outset of his pilgrimage.

112

"*Cygnus*," he read aloud.

After examining every other detail of the boat, he'd come at last to the word printed across its bow.

He turned to the merchant.

"*Cygnus*? What does it mean?"

"It's the boat's name," explained Steele, "every boat must have a name."

Nicolas nodded.

"And a fine name it is," sighed Steele, "a fine and a powerful name."

A mysterious change had come over the man. Something had come seeping into his words, moistening what had been until then the dry and practical voice of a salesman. The merchant was not a bad man, only hungry, and he waxed suddenly poetic now that he could afford to, now that his pockets were full of gem and spice.

"Cygnus was a king," began the merchant, "a king who was transformed into a swan."

"A swan!"

"You've heard the tale of Phaeton?"

"Son of the Sun!" cried Nicolas, raising his bottle and his voice as if to toast, as if he were once again back in the tavern with his drunken bards and heroes.

"And so beloved was he by his father," the merchant reminded him, "that the Sun could not deny the young boy's wish to drive his fiery chariot across the skies—even though he knew the outcome would most certainly mean disaster."

Old Gillam had told the boy this very story, warning him how the earth itself had been burnt almost entirely to ash as a result of this powerful relationship between father and son.

"Phaeton was killed," mumbled the boy, his bottle no longer raised on high but hanging now at his side, his lips scarcely moving as he spoke, "he was struck by a thunderbolt, and plunged into the waters of a river flowing far from his home."

"Yes," said the merchant, "there was no other way to quench that fire he'd unleashed."

"But who's Cygnus?" Nicolas still did not know.

"Cygnus loved Phaeton as much as the Sun did, though not as a father," said the merchant, "but as a brother. When he learned of the bright young boy's terrible death, he denied his kingdom, he denied all kingdoms, even that bright burning kingdom of the gods that had tempted the boy and then destroyed him."

The merchant was leaning against the boat as he spoke, one hand pressed up against the long curved neck of its bow.

"So Cygnus left the splendor of his home and palace and wandered all over the earth, grieving. And slowly, slowly, he was transformed. He grew paler and paler, you see, until finally the whitest of feathers began to sprout from his limbs, from his belly and breast, until they covered his entire body."

The merchant was stroking the neck of the little boat.

"And still he wandered, always avoiding, in fond remembrance of his fallen friend, the burning heights of heaven, seeking out instead the cooler depths, gliding silently out across the still and shaded waters of a home far away from home."

For a brief moment the merchant seemed too tired to finish.

"He had become a swan," he managed to sigh at last.

"I . . . I . . . must . . . be going . . . " whispered the boy, and his voice seemed to float forward as if from far away. Until with a jolt, the tale told, he returned to time and repeated himself, vowing more forcefully now, "I must be on my way!" Lifting himself up, ash and ale and all, he toppled headfirst into this ship that was somehow both swan and slipper as well as clever merchant's coin.

The merchant was already looking at his pocketwatch, and fretting, by the time Nicolas had uprighted himself. With his cages of ash and his bottles of ale stowed safely aboard, Nicolas sat inside the little boat, watching as the other marketeers began drifting down toward the shore, several of the stronger men eventually gathering behind the boat's curved prow and pushing, sliding the vessel backwards over the sand and out into the water.

Caught up by the current the moment it was afloat, the boat moved swiftly and smoothly, and the groups of silent and expressionless merchants planted on the shore began to diminish in size.

Several of the women were the first to turn away, for many were mothers who'd lost their own bold sons to the sea. Life near the shore was full of these agonizing and often final farewells, and there was nothing to be done about it, and nothing to be said.

No one waved goodbye.

The merchants returned to their tasks ashore. No one dared share his deep misgivings with his neighbor. Yet between this weight and that measure, between the counting of this coin and the next, each glanced surreptitiously over his or her shoulder for one last glimpse of the boy's boat, which grew smaller and smaller, until it was no more than a speck in the distance. And then it was gone. They told themselves they'd think no more of it, as they stacked and shined their silver spoons and shelled their scallops and dried and salted their strips of whiting and cod.

"How's business, Stade?" asked Steele as he passed by.

"Can't complain," lied Stade, scowling.

The merchant paused, shading his eyes and squinting, trying to catch a final glimpse of his old leaky boat.

"She's long gone by now, I reckon," said Stade.

"Mm–hmm," said Steele.

On either side of the boat, a series of smaller and smaller islands drifted by. Some were no more than piles of rock, slick and green with slippery seaweeds, others pale mounds of bleached coral and shell, or smooth dark bars of wet sand. Here and there, a tangled patch of tough sharp grass was dotted with a single yellow or vermilion wildflower flying like one last bright scrap of flag from the deck of a vessel lost at sea, a vessel whose crew members were all winged now—from the ungainly dark cormorants that perched with their wings outstretched and drying in the sun, to the black and white terns diving headfirst into the sea, to the gulls, herring and ring-billed and silver and black-backed and ivory, all of them darting back and forth, in perpetual agitation, feeding and fighting.

Back in the aviary, a lone gull or a migrating tern might appear in the sky over one of the larger ponds or lakes, but such a solitary call as it might make, mew or squeal or hollow lonely cry, was far different from this other raucous choir in the sky. Closing his eyes, it was easy for the boy to imagine himself surrounded once more by the strident bullying and brawling of buccaneers.

"Ahoy there!" he cried out, and in his drunken stupor he rose up as if to board one of these noisy floating islands. A stranger as yet to the roll and swell of the sea, he quickly lost his balance and toppled, falling flat on his back in the bottom of the boat. For a long time he just lay there, searching for the sails of his pirate ships in the dancing surf of gulls above him.

A swig of ale will stop this dizziness, he kept telling himself. Just one more swallow, he insisted, reasoning with the tyrannical logic of the intoxicated. Heaving himself up on to one elbow, then one knee, and crashing against the side of the little boat, almost capsizing it, he eventually managed to lift his bottle and swallow.

But the bottle was already empty.

Off the starboard bow, a flock of black skimmers raced toward him along the water, their bright orange bills opening wide, then snapping shut on their catch. Startled by a splash, he turned in time to see a lone brown pelican reemerging from the sea, its dark pouch distended, wriggling with dozens of small fish. Hampered by his shakey sea-legs and his unsteady stomach, his own techniques of the hunt were far less successful. Even a single bottle of ale seemed to elude him. One by one he lifted the empty bottles, overturning them, discarding them—finally discovering one that was at least half full, though whether with ale or only with stinking seawater he would never have been able to tell at this point, so mechanically did he swallow down the bitter liquid.

"To the gold!" he called out to the gulls whirling and gliding overhead. "To the gold!" he howled, raising his bottle into the air. He was certain that the birds had taken up his cry and were repeating it, over and over, as he slumped back down into the boat, bleary-eyed and nauseous.

"But what . . . what is all of this?" he muttered.

Collapsed in the hold, trying to make himself comfortable, the boat suddenly seemed far too crowded to the boy, and, pushing aside the piles of emptied bottles to make room, he soon realized that they were not his only cargo.

What were all these things? Buckets and ropes and rods, spools and reels, pad-dles, poles, and sharp iron hooks—all sorts of rusty tools he couldn't begin to guess the use of—as well as yard after yard of tough, tightly woven netting that kept getting tangled around his hands and feet as he crawled around the boat on all fours, investigating.

"I don't need *any* of this!" he shouted to himself, or to the gulls, as one after another he began to fling the objects foolishly into the sea. "I'm no fisherman," he was swearing, "I am a pirate and I'll—"

Suddenly he stopped.

At his feet lay an object more intriguing than any of the others.

"Something else that's fallen out of my pocket," Nicolas concluded, as he lift-ed the little roll of wet parchment from the puddle where it lay and ran his fin-gers over the strand of dried fish-gut with which it was fastened. Even before he'd snapped the tough string of gut between his teeth and unfurled the scrap of parchment, he knew that it was a map, a map to treasure!

Nicolas leaned in close, his nose pressed right up against the wrinkled surface of the paper, trying to focus. For a long time he found himself trapped and wan-dering in the intricate chain of flowers, beautiful blue morning glories, with which the entire document was hedged or bordered. He grew dizzy tracing the winding paths of their stems, his eyes colliding repeatedly with their countless bright blooms. In the end his eyes grew impatient and leapt, landing near the center of the map, in a strange seven-sided figure within which was printed the legend "The Garden of Jewels."

Nicolas looked up, opening and closing his tired eyes in an effort to stem the dull pain that was beginning to swell obstinately in his head.

"Garden of Jewels," he whispered to himself, "Garden of Jewels, Garden of Jewels," hoping to recognize or to coax some sense from the phrase, but it meant nothing to him as yet. Returning to his map, he scanned the page for some fur-ther clue.

At first he was confident that the short curved lines or crescents surrounding the mysterious Garden of Jewels on all sides were the waves of some sea, perhaps the very sea upon which he now traveled. But there was always the chance that those lines were not wavy at all, that they were in reality perfectly straight lines whose rigor was distorted, like all else, by the ale in which his eyes were by now virtually pickled. And then if he turned the entire map upside down, well, the sea of waves was transformed completely, the hollows became peaks, suggesting a range of mountains. It was a splash of red at the summit of the largest of the inverted waves that rekindled in the boy the memory of the volcano, *his* volcano. Such a discovery immediately bolstered his faith in this map that could predict the future and recall the past at the same time. He redoubled his concentration, following the bewildering array of arrows that crossed and looped the map in bursts of enthusiasm that paralleled his own and that seemed, likewise, to lead to a series of inexplicable anticlimaxes and deadends.

There were great walls, "Walls of Uruk," according to the smudged letters that wound along their perimeter, and there were several forests, and, most unlikely of all, a beehive, dripping golden honey. "Gold," whispered the boy to himself, and his eyes began to close, as he slipped slowly but surely into the depths of a small dense patch of black ink adjacent to the golden hive, a dark blotch beside which, in sinister and scarcely legible letters, was scrawled a single word: *cave*. It was only the cry of a gull, swooping down near the boat, that woke the boy at the last moment, just before he'd sunk completely into the darkness the map foretold.

He reached automatically for his bottle of ale, as if to pull himself up and out of the gloom with its aid, too drunk to suspect its complicity in this sleep that was closing over him no matter how hard he tried to resist it. But once more the bottle was empty, and he flung it overboard into the sea, turning back to the map.

This time it was one long jagged line that caught the boy's attention. "Lightning," he mumbled to himself, turning the map this way and that, experimenting, "or something cracked or split, or maybe steps, maybe a long flight of steps, a stairway . . ."

Soon after that everything went black again, or white—whichever end of the spectrum the dreams of a drunk will conjure in order to overwhelm the receding colors of a distant waking world. Crouched down in the boat, with his chin on his chest and his map spread out on his knees, Nicolas finally succumbed, and fell into a deep sleep.

Now and again, one torn corner of the little map that lay open on the sleeping Pilgrim's lap fluttered tentatively in a bit of breeze. But other than that, inside the little boat, silently adrift, nothing stirred, nothing at all. For hours and hours the only things that moved were the birds circling noisily overhead and the clouds that passed by and ushered in the faintly twinkling stars—and the sea, of course, which cannot be still, which rolls on endlessly, relentlessly, rocking.

Ship's Log - day two - have i made a mistake? - nothing but water too bitter to drink - if only it would rain - i am so thirsty - and still sick though my head aches less now - i must be lost - even the birds are turning back

Thus began the Ship's Log of the *Cygnus,* the events of its first miserable day at sea mercifully omitted from the record. Nicolas had awoken before sunrise. Lying, unable to move, in the bottom of the boat, he'd tried to separate the rolling of the waves outside from the rolling of the waves within, and, finding it impossible, he'd been forced to lift the entire ocean along with his head, which fell back several times, before he managed to hoist it, like a bag of wet sand, and prop it up on the rim of the boat. All of this he accomplished without even opening his eyes, for the weight of their pain would have been too much to bear and might have tipped the scale and pitched his entire head right overboard with no more than a single loud splash for an epitaph.

He dozed off again, for a few minutes, draped over the gunwale along with the reeking fishnets spread out beside him. When he opened his eyes, at last, it was upon a sea and sky that were virtually indistinguishable, one sour rose-colored infinite.

He gasped.

The sudden intake of sea air choked him, made him cough—a cough that was exactly the same color, the same bruised pink as the dawn.

One by one the various pains that plagued him surfaced, and then sank back down to make way for the next and the next in an endless relay—his aching head and his blistered eyes competing with the throb of his swollen foot and the twisting of the knot in his stomach. The itch and sting of the skin on his right arm proved more puzzling than painful, and, investigating, he was surprised by the bandage he found there, having forgotten entirely about his new tattoo until he lifted the frayed edges of the rag wrapped round it and caught a glimpse of the bright burning scab.

"I'm so thirsty," he said aloud, groaning—remembering far more clearly than he remembered anything else that there was not a drop of ale left to drink anywhere in the boat. Though he rose only to his knees then, rather than his feet, still he managed to trip and fall.

Convinced that his heavy, wet clothes were responsible for weighing him down, he began to tear at them awkwardly, stripping them away until he was almost naked, even removing the bandage from his foot, rinsing it as best he could in the sea and hanging it over the side of the boat to dry. Exhausted, he sank back down, leaning once more across the gunwale and falling asleep.

An hour later, he reawoke with a cramp in his neck and a film of bitter salt across his brow and his cracked lips.

Ship's Log - day three - how i wish i'd signaled the fishing boats when i saw them - now it is too late - now there is no sign of them - and no sign of phineas either

On that first awful morning there *had* been boats, three of them, not far off the starboard bow. They were heavily laden, lying low in the water, their slack white sails aglow as they caught the first few rays of sickly sunlight creeping across the bloodshot horizon. Nicolas had looked away, the bright white of their sails scalding his tired eyes.

Given the cloud of swooping and screeching gulls that hovered over them, he judged them to be fishing vessels. Yet he made no attempt to cry out or wave. They were not pirates, after all, but only fishermen, and it never occurred to him that these might be the last boats of any kind that he'd see for months on end. He did not as yet understand what it meant that he was drifting further and further out into the mighty solitude of the high seas.

Ship's Log - day five - clouds today - perhaps rain - i hope and hope - it must rain soon - i must have something to drink . . . another thing - the swan is still with me - is it a reflection as i thought? - then why does it remain even today when the sun is covered and casts no shadows?

Nicolas hadn't noticed the swan until the evening of his second day, although he suspected it had been with him all along. It was the reflection of his boat, of course, cast onto the water by the rays of the setting sun. With its long curved bow, *Cygnus* was itself a swan, after all. And though the postures of the two swans were quite different, the one outstretched with its wings spread flat as if floating dead on the waves, the other stiff and upright with its neck held high— still the limp head of the one and the proud prow of the other were both pointed in the same direction.

A reflection, then.

Preposterous.

Yet what other explanation could there be?

Ship's Log - day six - today a shearwater tilting low over the sea suddenly struck the surface of the swan with its sharp beak - it broke apart and re-formed - it sounds fantastic but the ripples through its body seemed a trembling from inside - as if the swan were shivering - gladly i'd forget all such mysteries if only i could have something to drink right now - am well prepared for rain - still waiting - why does it not come?

The boy had spent that entire day, the sixth, preparing for the water from heaven that would quench his terrible thirst. Working methodically, he'd rinsed each of his empty ale bottles in the sea and then dried them. By late in the afternoon he sat in the center of a boat filled with upright bottles, each one pointing, open and waiting, to the sky.

The bottles sang as the little boat rocked on the swell, clinking lightly against one another with each dip and roll and rise.

"I'll catch every drop," Nicolas assured the clouds that had been gathering patiently overhead for the past couple of days. Unable to move around the boat for fear of upsetting the bottles, he sat quietly for the rest of the day, gazing at the swan, or at nothing, until dusk, then dozing off fitfully until dawn.

Ship's Log - day seven - woke this morning to find two tiny black birds with white topped heads perched on the rail beside me - resting - does it mean land is near? - i don't know - still no rain

day eight - more birds today - a pair of petrels - they seem to actually walk on the water as their beaks fuss just below the surface and then they soar off out of sight - skinny legs dangling - like threads - thunder in the distance - one of the smaller white capped birds from yesterday is still with me - the other flew away some time in the night - i cannot stand this thirst much longer

day nine - rain at last! - it woke me this morning - a fine mist - but has been growing heavier all day - i am cold but my bottles are already half full

Nicolas endured the ensuing torrent stoically. He had no choice.

He and the small black noddy sheltered together under some old clothes and a small canvas tarp he'd found balled up in one corner of the *Cygnus*. For a day and a half they scarcely moved. Occasionally the boy would reach out for one of the water bottles and drink deeply, and once or twice he peeked over the side to check if the floating swan had survived the storm, but he could hardly see at all through the driving curtain of rain.

While the small plump bird blinked and shivered and slept alongside him, Nicolas crouched for hours on end listening to the strange siren song that the storm struck from the boat, for the pelting of rain and wind played the little ship full of bottles as if it were a floating xylophone. Listening to the strange high-pitched music, and to the deeper roaring of the wind which had the unobstructed expanse of an entire ocean across which to gather speed, the boy lost all sense of where he was.

Ship's Log - day twelve - "whitecap" still with me - too weak to fly - fed him a few bits of fish skin today - same as i ate myself - tommorow i will try my luck with the pole again now that the nets have brought me something to use as bait

Nicolas settled into a sort of routine once the storm had passed and his ample supply of drinking water was secured. He was a clever boy, both practical and imaginative, thanks to Old Gillam's vibrant lessons. He'd already engineered his Ship's Log from the tools at hand, scratching out his nautical diary on pieces of dried birch bark peeled from the inside of the boat, while a hook dipped in fish blood served as his pen. Scarcely a day passed when he did not record some observation, no matter how brief.

day fourteen - watched the swan for hours while fishing - rough seas made it seem almost as if it were about to fly - wings flecked with foam and bits of brown and green seaweed

It was his discovery of the golden cup lying in the bottom of the boat in a pile of coral and kelp and rotting sardines that convinced him there was more to this fishing than he'd at first realized.

"So maybe they *were* treasure seekers after all," he confided to the little noddy, remembering those boats he'd scoffed at that first morning, "maybe they *were* pirates." Nicolas often spoke thus to Whitecap. "It was my own fault, I should have signaled to them while I still had a chance . . . "

The boy noticed a few perfectly round white stones caught up in the tangles of one of the nets. He picked up one, and then another, running his fingers over their silky smooth surfaces.

"Pearls!" he exclaimed, staring off at the horizon as if searching for a sail. "Why, if only I'd—"

Whitecap made a single, barely audible sound, the first the boy had ever heard from him.

"But it's too late now," he sighed, shaking his head, gathering up the pearls and depositing them inside the gold cup for safekeeping. From that day forth, his technique with both net and pole improved markedly. Each day he carefully examined his catch to make certain that he'd not overlooked even the tiniest fragment of a treasure. Yet the golden cup full of pearls remained his only prize thus far.

day twenty - nothing really - always nothing - each day like the one before and the one after - each one the same - whitecap has proven as loyal to me as the swan - both are still with me

day twenty seven - whitecap can fly - today he lifted off into the wind and circled round the boat a few times before diving back in for a landing right on my shoulder - i can't imagine why he stays with me here - i would certainly fly off if i were able - perhaps then i might spot the ships bearing phineas and the others - but it's silly to pretend i might ever find them again now day forty - my shoulders are terribly sunburned - must remember to keep them covered - so hot in the daytime then often so cold at night - caught nothing today - whitecap and i both went hungry

day fifty eight - nothing - nothing - how big can this sea be? - why do i not meet up with anything but water? - nothing - nothing but this endless desert of water - i can't help wondering what lies beneath its surface

Seventy-five days at sea, tanned by the sun, toughened by the salt air, numbed by a monotony that seemed eternal, Nicolas sat staring at his little map, which was as torn, faded, and weathered as he. Surely some escape must be possible, surely marked here on the brine-stained parchment must be some channel or current that would lead him . . . where? It didn't matter where, not at this point. At this point anywhere would do—anywhere that was *somewhere*.

"You don't have to stay here with me," he assured Whitecap. "You know that, don't you?"

The little bird cocked its head in the direction of his despairing voice, as it hopped about among the tangled nets, picking at bits of dried kelp and fish scales.

"Are you a pilgrim, too, then?"

Nicolas had to admit to himself that it had been a very long time since he'd even thought of that word, much less spoken it aloud.

The little bird went on scavenging as he talked.

"Do you know about the fabulous Phoenix, Whitecap? Have *you* ever seen it?"

The swell of the sea was so strong this morning that sometimes when the boy looked up the bird was high over his head, and then at other times the boat tipped so low in the opposite direction that the bird sank far beneath him.

"Don't you sometimes feel so lost and so empty, and sad, so sad that you would fly to the ends of the earth if only you might find something, anything?"

The black noddy fluttered up momentarily into the air, then settled back down, clinging to the backbone of a fish bleached chalky white by long days of sun and salt and wind.

"Have you seen my tattoo?" asked Nicolas suddenly.

The scab had peeled off weeks ago, the bandage had been discarded, and the burning pomegranate shone forth now in all its melancholy glory.

"It's my heart!" crowed the boy, playing the pirate as best he could, "Aye! And it is on me sleeve forever!"

Phineas B as in barnacle Bellweather would have been proud of him. But what would Old Gillam have thought?

"A long time ago a dove was released out into a world even more barren than this one, and she returned from the wasteland, you remember?" Nicolas was not sure if he'd actually been speaking, to the little bird—or if he'd only been listening, listening to the old man's voice, which echoed tenderly across the waves of sadness in his head.

The noddy was busy with its fishbone.

"Why doesn't he fly away?" the boy was muttering to himself now, as he folded up the map with a sigh and tucked it into his waistband.

"Why? Why doesn't he fly?"

Ship's Log - day eighty eight - fell down today - i'd thought the wound on my foot much better - but i've been sitting for weeks - tried to stand and could not even support my own weight

day eighty nine - nothing to do but fish - and watch the swan alongside me - and talk to whitecap - why doesn't he fly?

day ninety - nothing nothing - not even fish - not even wind - nothing at all - always nothing

day ninety one - nothing

day ninety two - day ninety three - nothing - nothing

day ninety four - today i hooked something with my pole - very heavy - the pole bent so sharply i thought it might break - in the boat i realized it was only a rock - just a lump of coral - what a disappointment

Initially it was Whitecap whose interest was most captivated by the lump of black coral that the boy had fished from the sea. And had it not been for the fact that he'd nothing better to do than sit watching the bird pecking at his disappointing catch, Nicolas might never even have noticed the treasure it contained. It was just a momentary flash, the faintest of glimmers that caught his eye. But after two days of scraping and digging at this meteor from the sea, he'd managed to extract no fewer than ten silver coins.

"Pieces of eight! Pieces of eight!"

The little bird was startled by the outburst.

"Do you realize what this means, Whitecap?"

Whitecap looked dubious.

"It means we're near! Very near!"

Nicolas was determined to make the bird understand. "Treasure, Whitecap! It means there's treasure! Right here! Right below the waves!"

It was so simple a plan that Nicolas couldn't believe he'd not thought of it much earlier. He would hook his legs securely inside the boat, and, leaning on the gunwale for support, plunge his head underwater.

And then he would open his eyes.

And see!

Why, all this time he'd probably been floating over all the treasure in the world and he'd not even bothered to take a look. The golden cup and the pearls and the pieces of eight, why, they were as nothing compared to what might be down in these depths. According to Phineas and the others there were whole cities that had sunk beneath the waves, not to mention the ghostly armada of wrecks, their holds stuffed with gold and diamonds, not to mention the palaces of mermaids whose walls of mother-of-pearl were said to dazzle any eye and to soothe even the most savage appetite known to man.

Ship's Log - day ninety five - all this time wasted - when will i learn? - why have i spent all these days on the surface? - it is too dark now - but first thing tommorrow morning i will have a look

And so the next morning, with his feet hooked through one of the tangled nets, which was then tied to the heavy lead anchor of the *Cygnus*, Nicolas balanced himself, his stomach pressed firmly up against the edge of the boat—and without further ceremony, dunked his head into the sea.

His eyes stung painfully as he forced them open.

They were still burning as he emerged, only moments later, spluttering and gasping.

Yet such marvels as they had been witness to, he assured the little bird beside him in the boat, such riches as they had been filled with made all his foolhardy determination well worth it, and transmuted each and every pain and discomfort he'd endured into a priceless treasure in its own right.

"Diamonds!" he cried aloud to the bird, rubbing the stinging salt from his eyes, and tripping over the anchored net still wound around his ankles. "Living diamonds, Whitecap! Breathing and billowing everywhere, and burning golden stars!"

Well into the night, the boy regaled his calm companion with near-hysterical descriptions of the treasures that were now within their grasp. He'd no way of knowing, of course, that it was only the crystalline dance of bubbles in laughing ascent from his own mouth whose glimmer had so seduced him, that it was only the dully glowing chips of amber set into his own boat's hull that he'd seen shining against the strange blues and greens of the sea. Indeed, he'd bent so far over into the water that his face had been all but pressed up against the starboard wing of the *Cygnus* itself.

"I will dive!" he swore to the little black noddy, who'd drifted off to sleep. "I will enter the sea!"

And there was little time to update his Ship's Log after that.

First of all, he would need something to weigh him down and help him to descend. He quickly decided that net and anchor would serve the purpose, and carefully knotted the net so that he could slip it on and off around his waist when the time came.

That was easy.

Protecting his map against the moisture, however—and more importantly, his precious ash—these were problems that were more difficult to solve. Yet solve them he must, for he was convinced of the absolute necessity of bringing both of them along with him, no matter where he went.

For a whole day he sat puzzling out the problem.

"Of course!" he shouted to Whitecap the next morning, brandishing the bottle into which he had stuffed his map.

The bird fluttered backward, alarmed momentarily by the look in the boy's eyes. Nicolas seemed to be measuring the circumference of the little bird, comparing it to the narrow neck of the bottle in his hand. In all their long days together at sea, it was the only moment of strain in an otherwise idyllic relationship.

The next couple of days were rather windy, and so the process of decanting the valuable ash from cages to bottle was a delicate one. Nicolas huddled up in the bow, sheltering himself, careful not to squander a single grain of the fine gray powder. Whitecap, satisfied now that the boy had abandoned his passing inspiration to bottle him and take him along, grew bolder and bolder, finally finding a comfortable perch on the boy's knuckles as, pinch by pinch, the ash was tranferred into its new glass vessel.

"I'm so silly," babbled the boy, "I should have done this long ago." He shook his head in regret. "Why, who knows how much has already been lost? How much have I dropped or scattered? How much has already been blown away?" It was undeniable that the bottle, once he'd figured a way to seal it shut, would prove a far more practical container than his open-sided cages. "How can I have been so careless?" Nicolas reprimanded himself at regular intervals, working all night by the light of a waxing moon.

It was a few hours before dawn that he pressed the two pearls firmly into place, corking his two bottles—one bottle containing his ash, the other his map to treasure.

Before lying down to sleep until the sun rose, he took up his journal and wrote in it for the last time: *Ship's Log - day 100 - today at dawn - I will dive!*

That was all.

He would leave the Log behind, in the boat. Along with his shipmate, Whitecap.

The small white patch atop the otherwise black bird's head had become smudged with ash at some point during the previous day's work. Nicolas turned to the bird just before he dove, and in a wordless gesture of farewell, dipped his finger into the sea, and then tenderly dabbed at the soiled feathers atop the bird's head until their luster was restored.

Turning away, he took up his bottles.

And then he jumped, feet first, over the side of the boat.

The swan shattered with a splash, breaking apart in a froth and swirl, as wave after wave of wet feathers fell in upon themselves, foaming, and then disintegrated. Like the boy himself, it was swallowed up, and vanished without a trace.

Below the surface, in the empty heart of blue and the endless airless green, Nicolas struggled in dismay, wrestling as with an invisible adversary. He was sinking fast, too fast, and the dazzling diamonds that bubbled up to light the trail of his own escaping breath shot upward so swiftly that he could not close his hand over a single one. He was a helpless marionette, and they were its glittering strings, swaying and trembling above him, lengthening to infinity in their ascent to the rapidly receding surface of the sea.

Nicolas stared down at the darkening depths into which he was descending, blank depths devoid of all detail, depths from which he was expecting, at any moment, the emergence of a vast city of gems, or a ghostly wreck, its decks piled high with bricks of gold, its masts garlanded with pearls. But no such visions materialized. Only once, an enormous fish with fat silvery lips and swollen eyes loomed up close, then veered away again, absorbed back into that bottomless pool of shadows that was deepening too quickly from a watery twilight of slate-gray and turquoise to a drowned midnight of deep dark purple and black.

A terrible silence engulfed him.

Heavier than stone, it crushed the air from his lungs—and yet it was only such a brutally mounting pressure that could elicit from the suffocating boy those hallucinations he so desperately needed to survive his ordeal by water.

Nicolas did not resist.

Freely he abandoned himself to the dangerous rapture of the deep, surrendering, in the downward swirl of consciousness, to each and every image conjured by his breathless mind from this cruel density of deeper and deeper blue. Perhaps there *were* schools of fish, painted bright as parrots or clowns, crimson striped and yellow backed and blue bellied, swarms of them, enveloping him, where there had been nothing moments before. Perhaps there *were* huge masses of slick green tentacled weed and mountains of fanned and feathered and sharp-fingered corals laying suddenly exposed—the viscera of this sea that he split further and further open as he plunged like a knife into its living body of water. Or perhaps there was nothing. Nothing but a boy traveling down, straight down through a void, his head bursting, his eyes swelling in their sockets, his lungs filled with salt and syrup, convulsing.

"I'm drowning," it suddenly occurred to him.

130

He began to fumble madly with the heavy anchor netted around his waist, tearing at the knot. It was only when he saw the bottle rising past his face, with the map rolled up neatly inside, that he realized he'd made a mistake in his frenzied haste, and untied the wrong knot.

Nicolas opened his mouth in alarm.

Immediately he was choking on a flood of bitter saltwater.

Desperately frightened now, he managed to claw through the net at last. Recoiling instantly, violently, from the released anchor, he spun around, suddenly weightless, suspended between the downward plunge of his lost lead weight and the upward flight of his lost map to treasure. For that one moment, neither ascending nor descending, the boy could not tell up from down. It was a single moment of profound peace, the calm before the storm.

An instant later, the pearl, jarred from position, popped loose from the bottle full of ash—and what began as a little eddy round the narrow neck of the bottle, as seawater swirled in and ash swirled out, grew to a whirlpool of terrifying proportions.

Nicolas felt the whirling current grab him by his heels, spinning him in increasingly violent circles. And not only the clown and parrot fishes, not only the brain and fan and finger corals began spinning with him, but the faces of his fellow pirates spun somehow as well, leering out from beneath the spiraling jets of water and from within the pink and peach hollows of enormous whelks and conches. Some of them he recognized, but there were others—faces pale and horribly contorted, they seemed the drowning victims of some terrible shipwreck, already sucked down once to their watery graves, and rearising now, unwilling ghosts, from the ancient rotting hulls of their haunted homes at the bottom of the sea.

A screeching gull diving to catch a falling piece of eight. The bandage from his wounded foot. The masts and jagged timbers of splintered ships. The doorway to the tavern and the lighted windows that had flanked the dark town's crooked streets. The smell of his captain's warm shoulder. One of his own yellow slippers. Even a broad-winged eagle dizzily circling the very center of the whirlpool as if it were a mountain's inverted peak. Its momentum increasing insanely, it seemed nothing could escape the whirlpool's awful power. As if his own frantic breath were mingling with the dissolving ash to build and then moments later to demolish the most lavish of underwater kingdoms, whole cities of sand and coral arose, draped in tattered sails and stained with algae, and then fell, whole continents birthed and then dragged effortlessly from their moorings, the entire tempest glittering with all the forever unattainable treasure of an absolute vertigo.

Then, like a magic lamp calling its genie home, the bottle inhaled, and the point of the whirlpool passed through the round glass threshhold, and everything, Nicolas included, was funneled inside.

The pearl clicked back into place, and abruptly all was still.

Nicolas lay on his back, gasping, for several minutes, gobbling up deep mouthfuls of air. He could not clear his head and so could not even begin to explain to himself by what enchantment he found himself able to breath once more.

Rising to his feet at last, looking about in amazement, he could only conclude that he had, somehow, landed on the bottom of the sea, in a strange ruined city that had sprung up as if by magic from the dark ocean floor. As he wandered through the crumbling gray walls and towers of this strange underworld, it occurred to him that perhaps he had drowned after all and been left now to pace, for all eternity, the bloodless corridors of his own watery doom.

In the distance there were colors.

All around him in the distance he saw the flash and sparkle of another sort of city, softer and rounder, alive and palpitating in bursts of pink and bright yellow, of cream and teal and flickering scarlet, its doorways and windows opening and closing, waving and trembling. It was a city populated with a host of strange trancelike movements, a wriggling and scuttling, a wash and warp and swooning pulse, and over all a slow feeling of falling.

Nicolas crept forward, then strode more boldly in an effort to penetrate this other kingdom of tender tremors. His progress was rudely interrupted by a dull clunk on the head, which knocked him down and set the ground tilting beneath him. He looked to see just what it was that had blocked his path, but there was nothing there, nothing but the blue air and the kingdom of coral beckoning beyond.

Three times he rose to his feet, and three times he found himself colliding against the same invisible barrier. Fingering the bump that had arisen on his forehead, the boy resolved to proceed with more caution next time, leading with his outstretched arms, feeling his way with his hands, which were soon pressed up against a hard, smooth, transparent surface, a wall of glass that curved gradually like the sides of a bottle—the bottle in which, the boy was eventually forced to admit to himself, no matter how preposterous it seemed, both he and his ruined city of pirates were enclosed.

He looked down at himself to see if he'd shrunk somehow. Or was it that the bottle, one of his very own ale bottles, had somehow increased in size? But how? Nicolas gripped his head in his hands, squeezing, massaging his temples, trying to understand. But it was impossible to understand, here, underwater, where all seemed uncertain—where neither size, distance, or color stopped shifting long enough for their boundaries to be drawn or their measure to be taken.

Once again the boy was thrown from his feet, this time through no fault of his own. The wide green shell of a monstrous tortoise vanishing out beyond the glass wall warned of the ever-present danger of collisions over which he had no control. Indeed, balanced as it was upon a narrow ledge of rock, his drowned city lay in a far more precarious situation than he'd realized. Peering out through his curved window, he could see the cliffs of rock drop away sharply on all sides, plunging into shadows in which the foundations of this great sea still lay hidden far beneath him. Perhaps there is no bottom, he thought, perhaps it just goes on forever and ever, always falling.

As he raised his eyes from the awful depths, he caught sight of the starfish for the first time. "A blue starfish!" he cried, its image burning like the spark of a single blue explosion frozen in the prism of the deep.

It was enormous, spread out alongside its captive, a bit of tangled fishnet leashing the bottle to one of its long arms.

"Hello," the boy called foolishly, knocking on the glass, "you're very beautiful."

He paused for a moment, thinking.

"Will you let me go?" he asked, certain that the bottle, if set free, would be buoyed up to the surface by the air trapped within it. He knocked on the glass again. "If you would kindly let me go," he called, "then I can rise to the surface like any bubble."

It was no good petitioning the blue starfish, that was obvious, and so Nicolas took matters into his own hands, running up and down the ruined streets, despite the pain in his foot, crossing his drowned city of pirates from end to end, shaking it from side to side, trying to rock the bottle from its perch.

Suddenly the bottle gave a jerk and rolled over completely, sending the boy into a bouncing spin against its walls. For a moment it lay motionless, as if seeking the surface—and then, end over end, it began to rise—gaining speed as it went, flipping and twirling and toppling. Thrown violently through the streets of the rising city, Nicolas caught an occasional glimpse, outside, of the blue starfish, still tangled in the scrap of net, dragged along behind the bottle as it shot faster and faster upward.

Terrible pains charged through the boy's chest and head, and he felt as if he would faint. He tried to keep his eyes open, but the pressure in the bottle was so great it forced his lids closed. He was rolled up into a ball, with his face pressed between his knees and his arms curled to protect the back of his head, when the speeding bottle finally broke the surface of the water. There was a flood of light, and a roar like that within the mouth of a tidewater cave. Yet much to the boy's surprise and horror, the bottle went right on rising, tearing straight up into the sky.

Forcing his eyes open at last, the terrorized boy saw nothing but the blinding white of the clouds. Until he caught a glimpse of the cold flashing fire of that bright blue star that fell free only at the last minute. Landing with a light smack on the water, it hesitated there, floating, briefly, trembling, like a sign or a seal upon the mysterious gateway of the waves—which it promptly closed, as it sank, in the next moment, beneath them.

CHAPTER FIVE

A Certain Distance

"Let's fly."

The invitation came as something of a shock.

Watching the cold, clear water dripping tirelessly from leaf to leaf outside, the boy had scarcely moved a muscle or spoken a word in hours. The old man's voice startled him.

"Let's fly," repeated Gillam, ignoring the puzzled look on his upturned face.

They were crouched down in their makeshift shelter, a single slanting wall of thick oak and maple branches they'd hastily dragged into place beneath the shadow of a more and more threatening sky, and beneath which they'd been huddled silently now for hours, listening for hours to the steady rhythm of the rain falling all around them.

"But . . ."

Nicolas had never turned down an opportunity to swing through the bright air under the old man's expert guidance. There were warm sunny days when he virtually begged to be lifted up just one more time. But they were so far from the meadow now, all the way on the other side of the aviary, and the rain showed no signs at all of letting up. Squall after squall passed over them, their leafy wall shuddering with each new onslaught, leaking now in one place, now in another.

The boy could picture the meadow to himself in this rain, sodden and gray, its pale hibiscus blossoms bowed down with relentless moisture, their petals torn and transparent as soaked tissue. He could picture the bucket of sweetened water, sinking into the mud, overflowing. And the hummingbirds nowhere to be seen, huddled somewhere in their own improvised shelters, their nervous wings perfectly still, waiting.

"But the rain . . . "

"Fine weather for flying," the old man assured him.

"How will we get there, then, to the meadow?"

"The meadow? Why do we need to go there?"

"But . . . ?"

"We should be able to fly anywhere, my boy."

"Anywhere?"

"Anywhere at all."

Nicolas fell silent.

"Look!"

He tried to follow the trajectory of the old man's extended finger, but it kept darting back and forth and up and down, never pointing toward one place for more than a few seconds at a time.

"There! There! See how she dodges each raindrop!"

The boy caught sight of the lone swallow at last, dipping and weaving almost faster than the eye, flickering through the rain-stitched air.

"Fine weather for flying," swore the old man, delighted, as the dark sickle-shaped silhouette of the swallow swooped down almost all the way to the ground, then fluttered up once more, and disappeared from view.

"There's more than one way to do everything, my boy," said the old man, sighing to himself.

"Look," said Nicolas, tentatively, "th-there."

It was a leaf, caught up in a gust of wind.

"Precisely," said Gillam.

Nicolas was apprehensive, however, as to what might come next, for the old man was not, after all, immune to the occasional practical joke.

"And there are the machines," Gillam went on, "the flying machines."

He worked quickly and diligently, as usual, looking up only occasionally in an always swift and sure search for the necessary raw materials. Watching closely as the old man knotted and wove and spliced together his twigs and damp grasses, it was not long before Nicolas recognized the little hollow skeletons taking shape, remembering them from the tabletop in the dark swan coop where they'd lain, between larks' ribs and birch bark.

"Let me explain," mumbled Old Gillam.

Nicolas went on studying the silent man's hands as they spoke. From his pockets appeared bits of thread and moss, tiny splinters of wood, tufts of goose down, and seven types of resin. At one point he asked Nicolas to hold his machine for a moment, while he tore two patches of cloth from a corner of the boy's shirt and stitched them together with a needle he drew from the heel of his shoe.

"There," he said after he'd attached the little lung-shaped sail, checking to see that it was symmetrical.

There was scarcely time to admire his handiwork.

Once more Nicolas was busy following the old man's finger into the distance, watching as the tiny flying machine glided through the pelting rain, which passed right through its hollow body as it turned sharply in the wind and soared off into a grove of dripping trees.

"Of course," sighed the old man, "the mechanical method is often clumsy, and always, always complicated—and even, according to certain theories, quite dangerous."

Nicolas was still searching through the trees for some sign of the old man's mechanical marvel.

Gillam stood up and stretched his legs.

"He's going to lift me up now and run off into the rain and then he will trip and fall and we'll both roll over and over laughing in the mud."

But Old Gillam's motionlessness interrupted the boy's ecstatic reverie.

"Get up, my boy," commanded the old man in a whisper, "get up slowly, and as you rise pay attention to the ground, watch how it moves gradually farther and farther away."

Gillam's own head, the boy could see from the corner of his eye, was bowed down—he was following his own instructions, staring calmly at the ground at his feet.

When he did look up at last, Nicolas rising beside him, the old man could see by the blank expression on the boy's face that a far more dramatic lesson would be needed if his pupil were to be initiated into the mystery of flight once and for all.

"Do as I do," he said, and sank back down.

Nicolas quickly followed suit.

"This time press your nose right down against the earth," instructed the old man, "like this, with your eyes wide open. And then rise, even more slowly this time, and never take your eyes off the ground."

Such positioning was so awkward that Nicolas almost lost his balance, but he managed to do as he was told. Old Gillam chuckled as he reached out with one thumb to wipe the splotch of mud with which the earth had marked the tip of the boy's nose.

"The rest is all practice," he said, "and of course the remembering, remembering exactly what it is that you see."

"I don't understand," said Nicolas.

"It's an exercise, not a problem to be solved," the old man corrected him.

"Oh."

"Try it again."

Once more Nicolas almost toppled, but this time he wiped the mud from his nose himself.

"It's the difference between the mud on the end of your nose and that mud down there," said Gillam, pointing to the earth from which the boy had just rearisen.

Nicolas looked up at him.

"Aren't they the same?" he asked.

"Don't worry about those obvious secrets yet, they'll only confuse you. In fact,

140

don't think of it as flight at all. That will only make you dizzy or trap you with-in your own machine. Just think of it as creating a certain distance. Then you can go as high as you like."

The rain continued for hours, and there was little else to do but *exercise*, as Old Gillam called it. It wasn't until the boy's legs began to ache, from rising and crouching, up and down for hours on end, that Old Gillam decided it might at last be an appropriate time to try exercising the subtler muscles.

"You see that butterfly over there, sheltered beneath that broad leaf on the bot-tom branch of the youngest of the crab apple trees?"

Nicolas strained his eyes, finally locating the butterfly. It was resting motionless beneath its green umbrella, yet swaying up and down with the branch to which it clung every time a gust of wind shook the crown of the tree overhead.

"You see it?"

Nicolas nodded.

"It's yellow," he said, "with black diamonds on each wing."

"Yes," said Gillam, "that's the one. Now look *with it* at the ground beneath it as it bobs up and down."

"With it?"

"With *its* eyes, yes—look through the eyes of the butterfly itself, and watch the ground as though you were swaying there beneath that leaf in that rain."

"Do butterflies have eyes?" the boy wanted to know.

"Climb out of the machine," insisted Gillam, almost impatiently, "I'm try-ing to simplify this for you. You know, my boy, you can spend your whole life constructing wings—but you don't need wings to fly."

Nicolas did as he was told, trying hard to enter into the bob and sway of the butterfly suspended between wind and rain, watching the ground approach and then recede a certain slight distance, recording every detail of that trembling of earth in his mind's eye.

In the end, Old Gillam did sanction the use of wings of a sort. He sat per-fectly still in the damp shadows of their leaky shelter, eyes closed and yet open, soaring out over the rainy fields and forests of the aviary. Nicolas sat beside him, soaring as best he could, but with one slight difference: on either side of him his extended arms waved gently winglike, undulating up and down through the misty air. "Perhaps it *will* help you concentrate," Gillam had conceded.

An hour later, he spoke once more.

"What do you see?"

"The streams," said the boy, "curving all gray and blue through the rain, and all connected . . . "

Nicolas was familiar already with every inch of the mud of the aviary on the tip of his nose. He knew that terrain by heart, knew each of those streams personally, had bent over each tributary of cool running water at one time or another to quench his thirst or rinse his hands or merely glance at his fragmented reflection.

But looking down from these heights, he saw a different set of streams now which did not satisfy his more intimate, more immediate thirst. It was another, larger thirst they roused in him, the thirst for connections—for these streams formed an elaborate network, a vast circulatory system that drained and fed every inch of the aviary.

"Like blue veins," said the boy, "and sometimes like the trail of ore through solid rock, suddenly forked and jagged like a damp gray or purple lightning."

There was nothing that was not transformed.

The tops of trees billowed beneath him like green and gold clouds, or waved like hair tangled underwater. The lakes opened up like giant eyes in the earth, perpetually staring. Even the scattered rooftops of the aviary's buildings took on a new character, mosaic, alphabetic, as if they spoke a secret language only decipherable by the stars or by one who dared travel toward them.

"The tops of things," Old Gillam muttered from his stillness, as the boy's arms beat with a steady, hypnotic rhythm high above the aviary on the very tip of his nose.

The wings of the albatross were tremendous.

They were stretched across the heavens above him like a long living roof, mercifully blotting out, for a time at least, the dizziest and most difficult gifts of the heights. For long periods, as he watched them, they remained perfectly still, a virtual horizon line—tilting slightly, gradually, now to one side and now to the other, as the bird shifted its weight in space, gently realigning itself with the currents of warm air coursing invisibly through the heavens.

Once in a great while, the wings would tense, and with a shuddering motion that seemed to well up from within, they would break forth from stillness like a wave from the sea, rising up and subsiding, once, perhaps twice or three times. The boy would feel the change in altitude echoing deep in the pit of his stomach.

It was during one such interval that Nicolas first caught sight of the eye of the albatross. With the barrier created by the great wing momentarily removed, he found himself staring directly into that soft shadowy cave in which the bird's eye, protected from the glare of the sun on the sea, was nestled, glistening and alert, constantly scanning the surface below for signs of life, for prey. He'd no trouble picturing the fateful dive of the albatross. Attracted by the splash of his bottle as it broke the surface of the waves, it had swooped down, quickly snatching up a bit of the torn net looped round the glass, then soaring immediately upward again, pilgrim in tow.

"Perhaps the net is caught now, tangled around its beak, and the albatross cannot let go," the boy muttered, as new fears began to assail him.

He knew that an albatross could fly over the sea for months on end without landing, even sleeping on the wing. And though he'd never been told the tales, there rose up in him, instinctually, the legendary sailors' awe of this great bird. After all, when two travelers meet in the middle of a vast desert where no other creature dares venture, how else should or could they approach one another except trembling with a fearful respect? They have lost the habit of intimacy, both of them, and yet their long lonely journeys are somehow parallel, and so brothers they are and brothers they will remain.

And no matter how much they are strangers, brother never harms brother without the direst of consequences.

"We two-legged creatures," he heard his own ancient mariner's voice whispering in his head, "we share a common religion."

Nicolas knew then that he must trust this bird implicitly—and he soon grew used to the vibrations of its flight, its tilts and dips, its swings and shudders. It was only a matter of time before he found that he could actually stand on the flying ground within the bottle, and even walk. And as usual, the moment he began to walk, he began to search, this time for what he had lost—which was everything.

"Everything," he sighed, "I've lost everything," listing in his head all those things that had been sacrificed, from swans and slippers to ash and map and pride, "and still I am no closer to the Phoenix than when I began." Indeed, his heart was still so heavy he was amazed that the albatross, as strong and powerful a bird as it was, did not sink back down into the sea beneath the weight of such a burden.

No sooner did the boy feel the first tear welling up in his eyes than he felt a sharp sting where it froze against his skin. Reaching up to pluck the frozen tear from his cheek, scrutinizing the tiny droplet of ice between his fingertips, he realized suddenly how cold it had become inside the bottle. Examining the walls of his glass ship, he saw a pattern of ice crystals blossoming on its inner surface, white bursts and ice-blue blooms that fractured all that lay beyond them, splintering the surface of the sea far below.

It was vast, that sea, an empty plain. Gazing down through the icy wall of his glass prison, he searched for some sign of the track he had followed across it. "Nothing," he whispered, remembering how often he had scrawled that very word in his Ship's Log, "nothing." For unlike the plains of earth, this plain could not be plowed or furrowed, it suffered no scars or footprints, it left no trace at all of the passage of its pilgrims.

Nicolas raised his eyes to find that the frozen tear had already melted in his hands. He plucked another from the skin of his cheek. Turning it around and around between his fingers, he watched as it grew smaller and smaller, shedding layers, like a pearl in reverse, finally dissolving completely, only to reappear moments later as a fresh irritation in his sad and tired eye, as yet another tear.

In the end, more than anything else, it was the need to stay warm that kept him pacing furiously up and down the streets of his flying ruin. Whether or not he was still searching for anything was impossible to say. But he never stopped moving. Despite the pain in his swollen foot, he went on tramping back and forth, ducking fallen timbers, climbing over piles of rubble, charging through dark doorways and vaulting from the cold, abandoned sills of empty windows.

It was a curious, asymmetrical, hammering step that he slipped into, unconsciously—stamping down hard with his good right foot to generate sufficient heat to stop him from shivering, then touching the ground lightly, scarcely at all, with his left foot, protecting his wound from its own weight. It became a sort of dance, his body speaking clearly and without inhibition of both aspiration and dilemma, advance and retreat.

Powerless to stop, he danced on till he dropped in exhaustion to the ground.

By then he was far too tired to notice the change that his dance had wrought in this gloomy city, how the repeated hammering of his steps had unmistakeably altered it. So constant kneading will lighten dough and make it rise. So the steady pressure of a flame will raise a cloud of steam from a weight of water, or the burden of a million years will hatch a gem from a ton of earth. So a series of blows will crush a stone to bits, and those bits to smaller bits, and those smaller bits to dust, to finer and finer dusts, to powder and salt and ash. So each of the boy's steps, whether he knew it or not, went on refining the grey city, lightening it, whitening it.

The stars rushed out so suddenly and with such urgency that Nicolas was frightened. It was the first time since his flight began that he'd dared to look straight up, really up, beyond the albatross, who was becoming no more than a shadow of movement as the dark of night deepened all around him. At first he was too dizzy to focus, too filled with groundless fear, his eyes charging in all directions at once, burned successively by each point of light they encountered. By the time the sky was black and the lamps of the stars were at their brightest and fiercest, the boy found that he was actually out of breath, as if he'd been racing from one corner of the cornerless heavens to another, trying desperately to count the lights.

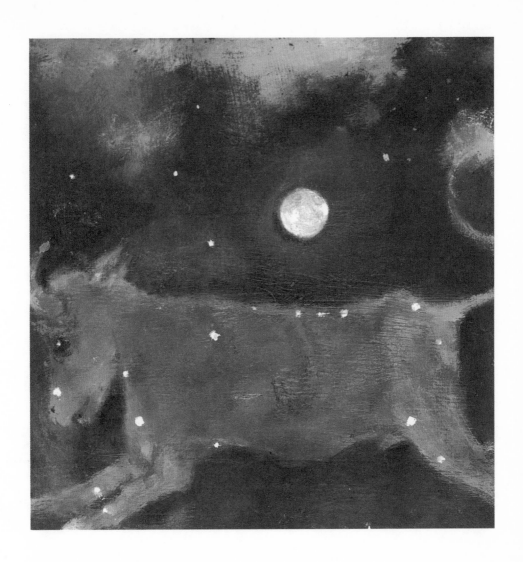

Quickly, prudently, he slipped into the protective embrace of his technique, sitting perfectly still, extending his arms and allowing them to rise and fall gently on either side of his body. Suspended at midnight in the sky, however, one cannot possibly locate one's habitual ground. And so Nicolas let go of that ground completely, intent only on observing and, most important of all, as Old Gillam had taught him, on remembering whatever it was, grounded or groundless, that he was able to see.

All night he stared at the stars, constellating them within himself.

Pegasus, the winged horse, charged out at him first. Like a great sparkling wind hurled through the darkened heavens, it seemed to pass right through his body, humming, glowing, like a wave of electricity. A thousand other pictures swept through him in its wake, crowding his eye, each one breaking apart into another thousand and then another thousand million tales of the light.

There are two fishes in this dark sea, said his spiraling eye, bound together for the length of night and light; and there is a bull, its body disappearing beneath these dark waves, its gold-tipped horns afloat and shining like twin islands. There is the hero, Hercules, his labors ended at last, his body pricked by sword-points of a distant fire that both consumes and heals his world-of-wounds night after night. There, said the sails of his heart suddenly, there are the flashing wings of Columba, Noah's dove, never again to return to this world-of-wounds that burns along with its heros. And there, whispered his blindman's ear, there is the echo of the golden splash of broken-hearted Cygnus, the heavenly swan, its head still bowed to the waters of the river, still hunting, peering beneath those waves that once closed with a hiss and a murmur over the flaming hair of its fallen friend. Was it a river of fire now, or a river of darkness, and did it begin, or did it end, there, at the heavy foot of that other, more impatient hunter, great Orion, with his club and his blade? Staring at the burning spark that marked the hunter's upraised foot, Nicolas suddenly felt a bright stab of pain in his own left foot. Looking down, he thought he sensed a strand of tiny lights wending its way down his bent leg to cluster and swirl around his wound until it glowed like a constellation itself.

In the blink of an eye, the light from the wound vanished.

That was how it was.

One picture opened right up into another, and another, many of them opening right up into the bottle and into the boy himself.

There was no telling where it might end.

At times the stars seemed but a curtain designed to obscure for him what lay behind them. And yet at other times their bright curtain seemed to open for him of its own accord. Ever since Nicolas had been sucked up underwater into the glass bottle, he'd had to give up, once and for all, all those notions of size and measure and border and body, all those map-reading techniques on which he'd previously relied. What was unlikely, what was improbable, what was physically impossible—all these things were becoming a matter of course.

What was larger could fit easily into what was smaller. Obviously. How else could he have found himself trapped within his own ale bottle?

Down was up, of course! And up down.

And in a bottle flying through the air on the wings of an albatross, at dawn, a boy awakes, confused, but hardly surprised any longer, to find that inside his glass cage a fine white snow is falling lightly all around him.

"*Zephyr*," whispered Nicolas, reading, as he brushed the fine white powder from the small rectangular brass plate—and he knew that he had found his pirate ship at last.

That the mysterious flying city rose up, in fact, from the hull of a ship, as if built upon it—this he had suspected for some time. He'd already stumbled upon what he imagined could be nothing other than its splintered mast. He'd already slipped through several perfectly round low windows that could be nothing other than portholes. But it was not until, after hours of wading through deepening snows, and stumbling accidentally over what remained of the wrecked ship's bow, that he finally confirmed his suspicions—wiping away its covering of frost and flake to reveal the tarnished nameplate buried below.

"*Zephyr*," he repeated, with the deepest of sighs, and the lost sails of the abandoned ship swelled for the first time in innumerable centuries, the vessel rechristened and then launched with a breath as warm and gentle as its breezy name-sake. At the same time, the wings of the albatross trembled slightly, then arched, then fell with a whoosh through the air. The ship in the bottle swept forward into the clouds.

"I'm always searching for *something*," the boy had been complaining to himself earlier that morning, not yet realizing that it never was or would be anything more or less than his ash, his own ashes, that he'd perpetually seek and find. Had he known too soon, perhaps he'd have given up his search. Perhaps the ash might not have been sufficiently refined. Had he known his pinch of precious dust to be already in his possession, perhaps he would have called off his search and thus stolen it from himself. Perhaps the Pilgrim would have stopped walking, refusing to take the next necessary step. For each of his steps, the tired tread and the sprightly swagger, the forward march as well as the empty loops and limping ellipses, all of them, not only this last painful and powerful stamping step, this desperate dance—*all* were necessary to insure that the ash be ground to the proper texture and tint. In fact, every-thing in this flying bottle—city, ship, snow, his own more and more subtle body, each was composed of one and the same precious ash—precious for the very reason that one can never lose it even when it is lost, or find it even when it is found.

And so it was on a ship white as snow, in a city white as snow, in a bottle colder and even clearer than ice, that he added a new step to his repertoire, a quiet step, a motionless step—as he lay back, the palest of pilgrims, floating fear-lessly in the air, staring up at the shifting shapes of the clouds overhead, freeing their images, step by step, with his calm, cool eye.

That first time he saw his ship *outside*, the ribbed wet silk of its single sail bil-lowing, overflowing with the very clouds in which its journey was bathed—that first time he thought it merely a reflection on the inner surface of the glass. Even after careful examination, he couldn't be certain if it was the same ship, his own, or another, if it was inside, or out.

He could hear Gillam's laughter as clearly as he could see the ghostly *Zephyr* gliding through the clouds.

"A problem that just can*not* be solved," smiled the old man's voice in his head, "and there is such a thing, my boy—*that* problem is no longer a problem at all, but rather the firm foundation of dream."

"Now relax, and tell me what you see," the boy demanded of himself, filling in for his absent teacher.

"I see two fishes," he said aloud, answering himself, playing two parts at once, while outside the clouds played all others.

Nicolas recognized the two fishes, their forms similar but not identical to those starry skeletons he'd seen swimming in the sea of darkness last night. Perhaps the change they'd undergone was due in part to the changed aspect of the sea itself, for it was a roiling, aggressive sea through which they now swam, a tumultuous sea of bold and enormous clouds, their bruised backs and bellies constantly transformed through their continual collisions with one another. It was through this phantasmagoric battleground of air and moisture that the two imperturbable fish swam, in opposite directions, yet parallel. One was moving one way, and one was moving the other, and yet their eyes were focused on precisely the same point.

A crack of thunder split the air, and the snow inside the bottle eddied around Nicolas as he jerked upright with a start and a swift sharp intake of breath. Peering through the whirl and clash of displaced snowflakes, the boy's widened eyes and quickened breathing tumbled forward, gradually tracing, in the storm of movement outside, the outlines of another, more distant whirl and clash. There was a snarling in the clouds and, moments later, the forms of two savage dogs burst forth, each rearing up on its hind legs to tear at the other with its bared teeth.

Apparently the elements were at war with one another.

And yet he felt no fear.

As a matter of fact, Nicolas noticed at that point that he felt very little at all, not even the cold, not even the accustomed pain in his wounded foot.

"I'm numb," he realized, as the surprise of the thunder subsided and his breath slipped back into a steady rhythm. "Numb," he repeated to himself, dreamily, sensing as yet only the protection that such a state could afford him, still ignorant of its attendant dangers.

"Perhaps they are not at war at all," reconsidered the boy, eyeing those grimacing partners in the clouds, "perhaps it is only a sort of dance."

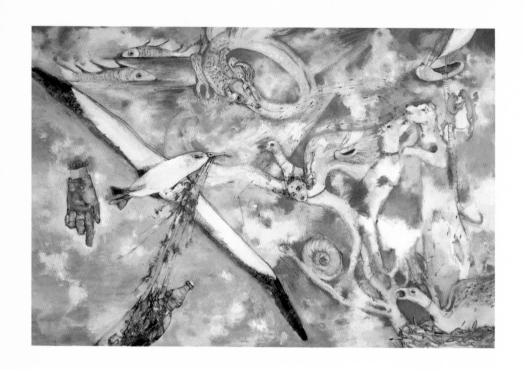

Gradually he became aware of the fact that any change in the rhythm of his breathing seemed to result in a corresponding change outside in the sky—as if he could control or at least influence certain aspects of the drama by turning his own heat up or down.

Nicolas stared at the dogs for hours, and right before his eyes he saw them change, their bodies rearranged, bits and pieces of the bodies of other animals transposed over their own, their heads suddenly maned like lions, their tails suddenly lengthening like serpents, their paws curling like the talons of birds of prey while their snouts narrowed into sharp beaks with which they pecked at one another's eyes. Their colors changed as well, moving through every shade of slate and blue, then blushing through the spectrum of fruit and flesh into smoky lavender, ultimately dividing, at sunset, into a white so pure and a red so bright and bloody that the boy had to turn his eyes away.

For days the pageant continued unfolding, always new, always different— unlike that other drama of stars and darkness that seemed, in contrast, of an absolute stability, resuming every night unchanged.

Sometimes Nicolas lay on his back in his bed of soft snow, looking out through his window at the clouds all morning and all afternoon. Other times, he ignored the patterns outside, choosing instead to watch and wander within his vessel. It was certainly easier to walk now, the numbing cold all but eliminating the agonizing pain in his foot, and taking advantage of this reprieve he became far more thorough in his investigations.

So thorough had he become, in fact, that on the morning that he discovered the ladder, he was surprised more than anything else. "How could I have missed it," he wondered. It rose straight up from the city, towering high above its highest buildings, reaching right up to the roof of the bottle itself, stopping only inches from the inner surface of the glass.

Nicolas began to climb immediately, of course.

But old and weathered as the ladder was, its wood warped and rotting, the rungs upon which he stood gave way within moments, snapping and splintering, sending him tumbling down into the streets of the city below. The boy grew more careful after that, testing each rung with his weight as he ascended.

157

It wasn't long before he'd found a new vantage point from which to watch the cloud-play outside.

Sometimes, early in the morning, before the frost had melted from the walls of the bottle, he'd balance himself on the uppermost rung of the ladder and with the palm of one hand flat against the cold glass he'd clear away a little circle of ice about the size of his own head, and then lean with his nose pressed up against the bottle, watching the changes in the clouds outside until his legs grew so tired he could no longer stand.

It was on one such morning that he first saw the bird nesting in one corner of the sky. Its body was indistinct at first, the mists of which it was composed thin and feathery one moment and then thick and opaque the next. Its royal bearing reminded him initially of one of Old Gillam's mute swans as it slid quietly across the smooth surface of the sparkling lake of memory.

This peaceful impression swiftly passed. The boy's eyes suddenly filled with fire, as a single ray of sunlight breaking through the clouds illuminated the bird's nest. From that burning nest, rising simultaneously with the boy's excitement, a second bird emerged like a shadow from out of the first, its great wide white wings pushing aside the darker, heavier clouds in its path, propeling the bird up, and up, and up, even as the single word, "Phoenix!" rose in perfect harmony along with it from the boy's heart and hovered silently on his trembling lips.

Nicolas steadied himself on the ladder as the sun disappeared, almost immediately, retreating back into the mists that had enshrouded it for days. The fire in the nest was extinguished in a single instant, and the bird that had arisen halted as if anchored in its flight by that other bird still struggling to retain its form in the perpetual shifting of feather and fog.

"Fly! Fly!" the boy cried out to the bird whose name he'd never quite managed to utter aloud, so quickly had his soaring hopes condensed and then evaporated in these clouds.

For a moment neither bird moved, each locked in place, one above and one below, uneasily balanced—one the leaf and one the root of a tree whose connecting branches were swallowed up, seconds later, by a fresh tide of clouds, a chaos of fresh shapes and forms that obliterated both birds entirely and sent the boy, discouraged, back down the ladder, one step at a time, to what out of habit he had come to consider the ground.

For the rest of the day he wandered disconsolately through the snowy ruins, convinced all over again of the pointlessness of his quest, reminding himself again and again of just how little he really knew of this fabulous Phoenix if even now, after all his searching, he could still mistake a bit of sun-gilded cloud for the true medicine for all pain and passion and sorrow.

Hours later, having tunneled deep under the snow to enter the hollow of the hull of the old wrecked ship in the bottle, Nicolas made another unexpected discovery, this one even more startling than that of the ladder.

The cask itself was so small, so unassuming, so encrusted with rust and ice that he might easily have overlooked it had he not tripped right over it, stubbing his toe. And so difficult was it to open that, had he not been feeling so irritable after his disappointment in the clouds, had he not been so unwilling to concede even the tiniest of defeats after such a vast and crushing blow as he had been dealt that morning in the sky, he might have just abandoned the closed casket without even looking back, and without ever having released the pale fire that lay locked up inside.

The transparent flame that leapt up from the treasure within as he finally tore the heavy iron lid from its rusted hinges flickered and danced across the boy's features, indistinguishable from his astonishment. The fire seemed to spread, illuminating the shadowy hollow of the hull, igniting each crystal of ice and flake of snow. Inside the chest a pile of gems glowed, fiercely paternal, at the nucleus of all these lesser lamps that its mere presence had kindled.

"Diamonds!" gasped Nicolas, his eyes flashing with their light.

Eager as he was, it was still quite some time before he summoned enough courage to reach out and touch one of the gleaming stones.

He'd always pictured the pirate's triumph as a far more unruly and jubilant affair. But the very thought of actually scooping up a handful of *this* unearthed treasure and letting it run gleefully through his fingers left him cold. Merely to return the silent stare of each and every one of the gems seemed celebration enough.

"I shall never let them out of my sight," he swore aloud, still addicted to oath-taking.

His eyes were already tired by the time he noticed the small torn piece of pressed linen wedged into one of the seams of the chest's discarded lid. The writing was crooked, cramped, and nearly impossible to read, the words and letters jumbled up right on top of one another. Here was a storyteller, thought Nicolas, with no space or time or tools, but only a long story that must be told.

"To those . . . only . . . who seek the diamond . . . body and . . . to no . . . others do we speak of a . . . valley of . . . ser . . . pents," Nicolas began reading at the top of the page of cluttered text, ". . . a deep valley . . . of diamonds infested . . . with . . . deadly serpents."

"Serpents," shuddered the boy, remembering. His eyes could scarcely penetrate the fearful shadows conjured by the words before him and he leaned in closer to the pile of luminous jewels, using them to light his way as he tunneled through the document's dark, forbidding scrawl.

"Know that he who would . . . acquire . . . the lean the . . . hard . . . the gem that cuts . . . the . . . gem . . . "

Nicolas stopped, confused, doubling back and rereading.

Perhaps, he thought, where the linen is folded and torn there were other words, words that are missing now.

"The gem that cuts . . . the . . . gem, the gem that cuts the gem," he repeated, and then read on, ". . . must first throw . . . the flesh . . . pieces into . . . the valley and to he who seeks the . . . unearthed . . . treasure . . . let him hereby be . . . gravely . . . warned but to he . . . who . . . rather seeketh the . . . body glittering . . . to he and no . . . other do we . . . speak of . . . how the diamonds adhere . . . faithfully . . . to . . . the pieces of flesh . . . "

He turned the stiff linen over. There was more.

" . . . this have we seen . . . with . . . our own eyes and know . . . to be . . . true and know you too that the vultures . . . "

Nicolas looked up for a moment, swallowing his breath.

" . . . the *vultures* . . . will . . . come and carry the flesh . . . back . . . to the top of the gorge and . . . there the diamonds . . . are . . . retrieved by the grace of our . . . lord . . . reddened on this fourth . . . day in . . . the year . . . of . . . "

Here the document broke off entirely.

But this did not deter the boy, who flipped the sheet once more and began to read the entire message again, and then again, trying to piece together the images into a single decipherable whole.

It was hard work lugging the casket of diamonds out from the *Zephyr*'s abandoned hold, dragging it through the high drifts of snow, up into the daylight. It was even more arduous a task to hoist it up on his slim shoulders and then clamber to the top of the ladder without spilling a single shining stone. Yet that is precisely what Nicolas learned to do, for he had sworn once more, sworn this time never to let the diamonds out of his sight—and so he bore his gleaming burden with him, gladly, or at least patiently, wherever he went.

The serpent, when it appeared, did not surprise him.

In fact, he'd been expecting it to show itself. He'd been almost impatient, sensing for some time now that along with so many other things its poison too must be hidden somewhere in these fantastic clouds. Every morning he settled down on the top rung of the ladder, with his treasure chest balanced beside him, gazing out fearlessly into the clouds, fortified by his new-found wealth, confident now that no new disappointment could jar him from his diamond heights.

And then one morning there it was, waiting for him as he settled down atop the ladder with both jewels and eyes raised to heaven.

"You!" was all he said.

As if on cue, signaled by the boy's voice, the serpent began to move, the clouds of which it was composed beginning, slowly at first, to slide, seething with a motion that promised expansion but only gradually, through convulsion. It was as if the clouds were turning back in upon themselves, turning themselves continually inside out. Nicolas watched the line of the serpent's back stretch, arch, and curl, its head creeping closer and closer to its tail, its tail curling as well, to meet the lethally opened jaws halfway.

He felt the pain of the bite in his own body.

Was it only a wind, that shudder passing through the monster's flesh as its fangs sank deeper and deeper into its own defenseless tail? Was it only a wind passing through those clouds he questioned daily? Or was it indeed the celestial agony of the great beast, its own poison flooding through its own veins, closing the circle of its own fate, forging another perfect link in the indestructible chain that bound it to another destiny both greater and smaller than its own?

Nicolas checked the serpent's eyes to see if it had been blinded, like he, by the riddle of its own mortality. But its eyes were adamant, opened wide and glinting. Were they the boy's diamonds reflected on the inner glass? Or had the gems' million-year-old carbon been reconstituted in one circular moment of vision that lay beyond the glass entirely?

Nicolas scanned the cloud-wracked sky for some sign of the nervous circles of those dark birds of prey he knew could not be far away from this most exquisite of all corpses. Just before twilight there was a fresh convulsion in the circle of clouds that still described the serpent. Something was sprouting from the monster's bent back. The boy had no trouble recognizing the strong, skillful wings of a vulture.

"But, but it's the same creature!" he exclaimed as the winged serpent carried its own self and its own diamond eyes high up to the top of its own cloud and vanished into the encroaching darkness. As night fell, the Pilgrim came yet another step closer to understanding, or experiencing, the unspeakable unity of the ash, the quintessential *one* devouring itself within or beyond every painfully heroic dream of dilemma.

Then all went black.

In the morning, it was a cold and lonely vigil on which they embarked, Nicolas and his clear, colorless gems. Each time a shape started to congeal outside in the clouds, it somehow checked its own forward momentum, reversing itself just before the threshold of its emergent body—and the ever-expectant boy was left with nothing but a few beads of moisture condensing inside, or a bit of dried seaweed still clinging outside, to the glass wall of the flying bottle.

He spent hours watching nothing but the large, lazy wings of the albatross, nearly expressionless as usual. He even turned his attention back, for the first time in days, to the surface of the sea below.

Only once, briefly, the ghostly *Zephyr* reappeared in the clouds, its smooth white sail puffed up bravely with a fragment of the great empty spaces through which it soared.

"What can I do?" the boy called out to the ship vanishing in the clouds, feeling at last the impotence of his great wealth.

"Nicolas! Nicolas!"

The sound of Old Gillam's voice startled him.

He'd been drifting off over the aviary, stunned by the silvery eyes of its many bright, unblinking lakes far below. It had been a cloudless afternoon, and he'd been able to see for miles in every direction.

"A fine afternoon for flying," as Gillam would have put it.

Yet when he came to his senses, startled by the old man's voice, he found himself still inside the bottle, the pearl that sealed its narrow mouth still lodged firmly in place, and the sea of clouds through which he sailed still hesitating, still holding back.

He'd never forgotten that afternoon in the aviary.

He'd been exercising his subtle muscles alone, in a clearing deep in the woods, and he'd slipped into a trance higher than any other he'd ever experienced. Later on Gillam had told him that he'd even ceased waving his arms, that he'd been sitting perfectly still when the old man finally located him, and that it had taken hours to revive him and draw him back down to earth.

"You must be careful now," he'd reprimanded the boy, "now that you're more skillfull."

Nicolas was shivering uncontrollably, both in his reverie and, now, in the bottle.

The old man threw a blanket around his shoulders, a blanket that smelt faintly of the meadow, of the shallow roots of grasses, of honeysuckle and manure.

He looked him straight in the eye.

"Listen to me, my boy," he spoke earnestly.

Nicolas was trying to stop shivering.

"It can be disastrous to be stuck in the sky," warned Old Gillam.

And then he reached out and pulled the boy into his arms, embracing him with every bit of the warmth in his body.

After a few minutes he held out his hand.

"Here," he said, "stare deeply into this . . . "

To Nicolas, shivering and alone now in his glass ship in the sky, even the memory of that simple gift the old man had pressed into his cold palm made him feel safer, warmer.

"It's the shell of the snail," he'd whispered.

Which even now might explain this sudden swirl and eddy in the clouds outside the glass, which distracted the boy from the nagging emptiness that had begun to assail him and inspired him to bolder and bolder feats of acrobatics as he twisted and turned this way and that, left and right and up and down, in a determined effort to coax some concrete form from this pattern that remained, as yet, but an abstraction in space. He was dizzy as an amateur pilot by the time the spiral led him at last to its creation.

"It *is* the shell of a snail," he whispered. He could even identify the snail's body now, that pale moist sliver of mist stretched out like a worm beneath the delicate burden of vertigo upon its back. "But how did he know?"

Nicolas didn't recall the moment when he actually lost his footing on the ladder. That he'd grown increasingly dizzy, that the eye of the spiral of the shell of the sluggish snail had seemed to draw him in, that he'd surrendered, willingly, to it—all this he could not deny. He'd a vague memory, as well, of being surprised by the long rope ladder he saw dangling from the hull of the ghostly *Zephyr* as it coasted, one last time, through the most distant clouds. But as for the fall itself, it wasn't until the wood had splintered and the heavy chest full of diamonds had been catapulted through the air, striking the glass wall of the bottle near his head, that his clearest memories of descent began.

He heard the crack. That was the beginning of it.

Then he saw it, slicing through the glass like the trail of a shooting star frozen momentarily in space.

With a rush of cold air, then, and a furious blast of snowy ash and flake, the bottle split in two, like an egg, and everything it contained came pouring out into the air. The lonely albatross soared off into a distant silence with nothing but a weightless scrap of empty fishnet caught up in its beak.

Nicolas was certain he had plunged right into the center of those clouds that

164

swirled around to build the beautiful shell of the snail, for he was spiraling madly as he dropped down, faster and faster.

There was a humming and a buzzing in his ears that grew louder and louder the further and the faster he fell.

And in the air all around him—a bright flash and sparkle, a cloudburst, perhaps, a million beads of moisture released at last from the wrack overhead, or perhaps a violent scattering of shining stones, a shower of diamonds.

Or was it only the fragments of the shattered glass of the bottle, plummeting, down, along with him, to earth?

The boy couldn't help but reach out, even as he fell, grasping at the air itself, trying to salvage something, anything—a bead of moisture, a shining stone, a shard of glass.

Head over heels he cartwheeled through the sky, hands opening and closing.

The ragged man seated on the shore of the otherwise deserted island was singing as he worked, his hands busy scraping at the rough surface of the gnarled and knotted piece of wood that had washed up onto the sand with that morning's tide.

"Frail boat, I sink into the sea," sang the marooned pilot, his voice trembling with obvious emotion as he repeated the words he knew so well, "still water's dark, still water's deep . . . "

But then for some reason this morning he began to improvise, adding new verses to the song, verses he'd never heard before, although they sounded as familiar and natural as his own breathing the moment the words fell from his lips.

"The cradle tips," he sang, "the darkness sighs . . . "

The man's busy hands fell suddenly still as he went on singing.

"A tumbling child wakes in my eyes . . . "

He let the piece of driftwood fall to the ground, and looked up, staring off into the depths of the sky.

"Still water flows . . . " he sang on in a voice that was barely audible. And then he saw it, far in the distance, even as his breath closed around the final phrase of music, " . . . still water flies."

It was a boy.

A boy falling from the sky.

A boy tumbling to earth.

And all around him, lights flashed and sparkled, falling as well.

"A shower of diamonds," marveled the solitary man through his clenched teeth, doubting his own eyes, "a rain of stars."

He sat as if hypnotized until this strange weather ended.

And then, as the tumbling child disappeared into the treetops below, he rose to his feet and strode slowly and resolutely from the shore into the interior of the island, singing softly to himself.

CHAPTER SIX

The Fall

The splash that Nicolas had been awaiting was all wrong. It was rough instead of smooth, warm instead of cold, and it was green, bright green, instead of blue, deep blue. Not to mention the riot of birdsong that followed so closely upon impact as to be virtually inseparable from it. And that buzzing in his ears.

It was some time before he realized that his difficulty in breathing was caused not by the fact that he was once more submerged, underwater, but only that he was holding his breath, drowning himself in anticipation of a struggle that never came. When he gasped at last, mouth opened wide, it was the taste and smell of fresh green leaves that oriented him instantly. "Land!" he cried aloud, for there could be no mistaking that flavor of meadow and field and hillside, just as there could be no mistaking the firm, familiar embrace of home and hearth.

Nicolas tried to move. Instantly the air all around him erupted in a noisy, high-pitched flutter, as if alive. It seemed, indeed, as if every nervous inch of space were winged.

He'd been away for so long that it was necessary, as he recovered his senses, to reassemble the natural world, piece by piece: the countless leaves of the tree into which he'd crash-landed, the restless wings of the weaver birds whose dozens of hanging nests his unexpected fall had disturbed, the warm breeze that ceaselessly rustled both wing and leaf as well as every fragrant atom of the air. It was an exquisite puzzle, this island, this earth, no two pieces of which were quite alike.

He was caught fast in the limbs of the tree, dangling upside down, his bruised legs hooked around one of its branches. It was an uncomfortable position. Yet trying to extricate himself, straighten a knee, untwist an ankle or dislodge a foot, he was easily distracted by each fresh new detail of the reemergent earth. Often he ceased struggling altogether. Often he just hung there, mesmerized by the quivering lattice of branches, by a bird's yellow tailfeather, by the hundreds of apples hanging, just like him, from the boughs of this bountiful tree.

Nor was he daunted by his painfully closed fists when it first occurred to him to reach out and pick one of the ripe apples. He merely chose one nearer to his face, and, leaning out, stretching, extending his neck as far as possible, he pressed his lips, then his teeth, up against the bright tough skin of the fruit, and bit down into it without even removing it from its branch. All thoughts of his crippled hands, and of what it might be that they clutched almost involuntarily, were banished from his mind as he heard the snap of the apple's firm flesh giving way, its tart juices flooding his mouth and his throat with an almost burning delight.

He was already devouring his third apple when he heard the song drifting toward him from somewhere below and beyond. He stopped chewing immediately. It was as if the breeze had wrapped itself around a bit of music, and like a scrap of dried leaf the melody rose and fell, carried along with all the other notes that any wind perpetually assembles and scatters.

Right beside him, crowds of noisy weaver birds were busy squabbling over the few remaining bits of fruit still clinging to the apple cores he'd left dangling, pale as stripped skeletons, from their leafy branches.

"Sssshhhh," he hissed, shaking the tree, frightening them.

They rose momentarily up into the air, then realighted, noisier than ever, many of them right on top of the boy. He hung there, motionless, bits of apple

stuck to his sticky lips and chin, listening as the haunting melody carried forward by the breeze took on a distinctly human tone, a voice, and soon after that a body, the singer himself emerging through the thickets of trees below and stopping in his tracks, staring up at this boy draped from the top of the enormous apple tree, covered with birds.

"So then," he exclaimed, relieved, "I'm not a madman after all! And you are real! And you have really fallen from the sky!"

Nicolas wasted no time.

"That song!" he shouted down to the man from the treetop.

"Song?"

"You were singing," insisted the boy, "you were singing just now as you arrived!"

"Aye lad, it's true," conceded the man, "it's true that I'm often singing to myself, that I love to sing . . . "

"The Requiem!" crowed Nicolas.

"Well . . . yes . . . "

"The Drinking Song!"

"Yes, certainly, that too sometimes. First a requiem and then a drinking song. And then a preparation for harvest."

"A what?"

"A Hymn for the Planting."

"The planting?"

"And you the biggest seed of all," mumbled the only witness of the boy's fall to earth, chuckling to himself.

"Where am I?" Nicolas remembered to ask at last.

"Don't you want to get down from up there?"

The man had already begun to climb the apple tree, negotiating its branches with a graceful strength that astonished the boy, appearing right beside him in a matter of moments.

"Lift your legs," he instructed, "now," as he bent back one of the larger limbs pinning the boy in place. Nicolas did as he was told, but then almost tumbled to the ground, unable, as he was, to reach out and catch onto anything to support himself given the clumsiness of his still stubbornly closed fists.

"Hang on!" cried the man, catching the boy just before he fell.

Nicolas held up his fingerless hands.

"I can't . . . I . . . "

The man nodded, questioning him no further, holding him tightly around the waist from then on. "Be careful of the hive," he warned as they descended, one leafy bough at a time.

"The hive?"

Nicolas waited until he felt his feet planted firmly on the ground, then looked back up, peering into the living labyrinth of leaves and branches. He'd little trouble locating the enormous spiral lodged in the largest and lowest fork of the apple tree's thick trunk. It was a huge snail shell, its hidden hollow alive with a tireless buzz and bustle of bees.

Lowering his eyes, the boy watched as the man bent down to the ground and picked up one of the apple cores that their descent had knocked loose from its branch.

"Ahhhh, I see you've already tasted of our fruits," he remarked with a warm and knowing smile, "so then you've not much to fear from the bees. They have a nasty sting, you know."

The boy eyed the busy hive once again, more warily.

"But then you've already been stung by our apples," he went on, explaining, "and there are many who say that the sting of a suncrisp or a bluepearl or an unripe pippin is far sharper than that of any angry bee, and almost as sweet as its honey."

"Who are you?" Nicolas asked abruptly, for he'd suddenly a sneaking suspicion that they'd met somewhere before, he and this ragged man with his strong, graceful limbs and warm, friendly voice.

"Come," said the man, heading off into the trees, beginning once more to sing softly to himself of the tipped cradle and the fallen child. Nicolas tried to follow but soon stumbled, tumbling, along with the child in the eye of the man's song, to the ground—his wounded foot unable to bear his weight for more than a moment or two.

The man turned and helped the boy back up onto his feet.

"It's no use," said the young Pilgrim, "I can't walk."

"Nonsense," said the man, "you need a crutch, that's all," and he set to work immediately. Nicolas sat right where he'd fallen, watching and waiting. Once more his companion began singing to himself.

"A Hymn for the Planting?" interrupted the boy.

"Yes . . . well . . . " the man rambled on as he fitted the wooden pieces of the crutch expertly into place, " . . . a requiem then a drinking song then a planting hymn, but in the end, no more than a poor pilot's tune, for it's always the same poor pilot that sings it, though his destination keeps changing and adding to the words afresh with each new twist and turn of the old path."

"Poor pilot," Nicolas was whispering to himself, when the name suddenly burst forth from his lips with the force of a revelation.

"Pal'nurus!"

"And you must be Nic'las," was all the pilot said.

Nicolas didn't know which was stranger, that the drowned pilot of pirates' legend was here, alive, safe and sound and healthy, or that this very same pilot somehow knew *his own* name. He didn't know which question to ask first.

"Try it," said Palinurus, handing him the completed crutch.

The boy struggled to his feet.

"But I thought you'd drowned, I thought you'd fallen overboard and—"

"Yes," said Palinurus as they got under way, "at first I thought I *had* fallen."

He reached out to help the boy, holding him securely beneath one shoulder whenever the terrain grew too irregular or the slope too steep.

"But looking back on it—and I've had plenty of time to go over it again and again in my mind since I washed ashore here on this island—well, looking back, I've become more and more convinced that I didn't fall at all, no, I'm sure now that I jumped, actually jumped right overboard, right into the sea."

"But so did I!" shouted the boy.

"Yes?"

"Yes!"

"Well then, it's a wonder our paths never crossed before."

"How did you know my name?" Nicolas at last got around to asking.

"Your name? Why, from the tales, of course—there's few travelers whose names don't surface sooner or later in a room full of yarning sailors."

"Tales about me?"

"Certainly, if you're the boy they call Nic'las."

"I am! I am!"

"Tales about you, then," the pilot assured him.

"But what—"

Nicolas took a nasty spill just then, despite all precautions, his useless hands doing little to break his fall.

"You're sure you don't want to open your hands?" asked the pilot, frankly, but respectfully.

Nicolas shook his head emphatically no.

"There we go," said Palinurus, lifting him to his feet once more and handing him his crutch.

"What sort of tales?" Nicolas went on once he'd caught his breath.

"Well, they say . . . "

The pilot stopped, crouched down, and stared directly into the boy's eyes.

"Yes," he said, "it's true."

"What's true?"

"They say your eyes burn like the eyes in the tail of that peacock that few men, much less a boy, have ever survived a glimpse of."

"They say that?"

"They do."

Palinurus went on walking.

"They even sing of it," he added over his shoulder, and once more began humming softly to himself.

Nicolas limped on in silence for a few minutes.

"They say that *you* were betrayed by sleep," he said at last.

"What dreamer hasn't been?" was all the drowned pilot replied.

And once more they walked on without speaking.

"Let's stop here for a moment," said Palinurus, "I want to check my map."

"Map?"

"Yes," said the pilot, drawing a bottle from the folds of his rags, a bottle containing a single neatly rolled piece of parchment.

The boy's eyes widened. "Where did you get that?" he snapped.

"My map?"

"*Your* map?"

"Why, it washed ashore one day, not long after I did, tossed right up onto the beach in the foam of the surf."

"Let me see it!"

The boy's tone had become almost belligerent.

Palinurus carefully extracted the parchment from the bottle. Before he'd even finished unrolling it, Nicolas staked his desperate claim.

"But it's mine! It's my map! The map I lost when I dove into the sea, you must believe me! I put it into that bottle to protect it but then I lost it, it floated away when I—"

"Now hold on a second, lad, you haven't even looked at it yet."

"But it's mine! It's mine! It must be mine, and now I've found it again and—"

"Eyes that burn like the depths in a peacock's tail." That was all the pilot muttered, staring, as he passed the hotly contested piece of parchment to the excited Pilgrim.

"But . . ."

The fire in the boy's eyes lost its heat and its brilliance almost instantly.

"But there were morning glories, here," he protested, smoothing the edges of the wrinkled paper with the knuckles of his closed hands, "these flowers were blue before, they were bright blue." Whereas the flowers that decorated the borders of this map were, despite the ravages of fading and staining, quite obviously white.

"Lilies," said Palinurus.

The boy's eyes roved over the map in frustration.

"And the volcano," he complained, turning the map around and around, "where is the volcano?"

"This?" asked Palinurus, mystified, pointing to a small red triangle in the upper right-hand corner.

"But it should be over here, in the inverted waves of the sea!"

"A volcano," marveled the pilot, for he'd never been able to decipher that particular symbol, despite the days and weeks and months he'd spent poring over the mysterious messages with which the map was covered.

"And what is this in the center?"

"That's the aviary of course" said Palinurus, more sure of himself now.

"The aviary!" cried Nicolas, stunned to find his home, which he'd not even recognized, occupying so central a position on the map.

"But then where is the Garden of Jewels? It's the Garden of Jewels that should lie in the center!"

"The Garden of Jewels! Why, it's right here, right here . . ."

"Where?"

"Here, here, right here on this island! No need for a map to find that!"

"Here?"

"Beyond one of the seven gates in the outer garden wall."

Nicolas was thoroughly confused by these blatant topographical inconsistencies. He was still reluctant to admit that this map was not his own.

"They're almost identical, but they're so different."

"One is mine," explained the pilot, calmly, "one is yours."

He lifted the parchment gently from the boy's lap.

"Two maps," he went on, "two maps of one world."

"But—"

"After all," Palinurus persisted, "how did you arrive here?"

"Through the air."

"And I from the sea."

He paused.

"So of course our worlds are rearranged, lad. That's the only reason one man can teach anything to another."

The boy fell silent for a moment, as the pilot crouched over what was undeniably *his* map.

"What are you looking for?" Nicolas asked suddenly.

"There's a hill somewhere nearby. I don't spend that much time here in the wilds, I come only to collect the honey, but I know there's a high crest from which you'll be able to see most of the cultivated portions of the island. It'll save you a lot of painful walking."

"No, no, I mean what are you *searching* for?"

"Hmm?"

Palinurus looked up and saw the boy's eyes burning brightly once again.

"Ahhh, I see, you mean what's in the center, in the aviary."

"In the aviary!"

"Yes, where Argent, the great swan oracle, is said to nest and to sing."

Nicolas was struck dumb.

"What are *you* looking for?" asked the pilot.

It took a moment for the boy to find his voice again.

"The Phoenix," he answered at last.

"Phoenix, Phoenix, now let me see," mumbled Palinurus, preoccupied with his map, "it's some sort of bird, a rare sort of parrot, isn't it? One that repeats itself endlessly? Ah, here we are!" He'd located his advantageously placed hillside and rose now to his feet, rolling up the map and stuffing it back inside its bottle, paying no attention at all to the indignation written all over the boy's face. "It's not far," he assured him.

Half an hour later, pausing in the midst of a dense forest of old red maples, Palinurus pulled a small, circular object out from beneath the tattered sash knotted about his waist, letting it rest flat in the palm of his extended hand.

"What is that?" asked Nicolas.

"My compass," answered the pilot. "Here in the uncleared forest it sometimes grows difficult to steer with no view of the six hills to guide one."

"The six hills?"

"I'll point them out when we get there."

In the meantime, Nicolas took a closer look at the object lying in the man's palm.

"But what do these characters stand for?" he asked, indicating the figures that marked the dial's cardinal points.

"The elements," replied the pilot.

"But what about the directions, what about north and south, and east, and west?"

"What about them?"

"I thought that a compass—"

"I've been at my own helm my whole life, lad, and I've never steered by any other means than these four elements laid out around this dial. Give me fire, give me water, give me air, and give me earth—and I'll find my way where I'm going sure enough, every time. Oh, I've been lost alright, that I won't deny. And likely as not there's plenty of shorter routes than many that I've taken."

He turned to the boy and smiled.

"But give me the longest distance between two points any day," he laughed, "and I'll still get there, and with a tale or two more to tell than anyone else."

Laughing, he tucked the compass back into his waistband.

"Come now," he said, "this way."

Nicolas limped after him.

"He's dead, you know," announced the boy a few minutes later.

"Who's dead?"

Nicolas hesitated.

"Argent, the swan."

"And yet they say he still sings," said the pilot, undismayed, as they emerged at last from the forest.

The burst of sunlight was blinding at first.

"There," cried Palinurus, squinting, and pointing to the bright horizon, "there, the six hills!"

"You've traveled that far?" Nicolas asked the pilot.

"Oh, no," he replied, "I only use them to navigate by, just like I learned to use the stars when I was lost at sea."

Nicolas was gazing off at the hills. To a boy who'd just returned from the stars themselves, they seemed far less inaccessible than this landed pirate would lead him to believe.

"Shall we go on?" asked the pilot.

But Nicolas scarcely heard him. His eyes were wandering, following the dark blue path of a river in the distance, winding across a wide open plain, disappearing into the hills beyond.

"I think . . . " he informed his companion at last, pointing, or saluting, with his closed fist, "I think *that* hill, on the right, is the volcano."

The pilot's jaw dropped.

"The red triangle," he whispered, as he glared at a pair of red hills on the horizon, "but which one?"

"I'm not sure," muttered the boy, his eyes still wandering, "but I think perhaps that river, there—I think that is the river beside which the Queen lies sleeping."

For a moment the two travelers stood staring off into the distance, Palinurus eyeing the potentially fiery slopes of his familiar landmark as if for the very first time, while Nicolas studied the flocks of birds hovering all along the course of the distant river, birds whose progress paralleled the river's so closely that it seemed to the boy almost as if their dark silhouettes were its very current.

A strange restlessness overtook both wanderers. Without exchanging a word they began to move forward, continuing on in silence until they'd reached the crest of the hill from which Palinurus had promised the crippled boy his panoramic view of the island's tamed wilderness.

Nicolas was the first to break the silence.

"What are we standing in?" he asked

"Apple blossoms."

Just over the edge of the ridge, where the firm ground fell away, another ground was rising, congealing at their feet like wine-stained clouds, clinging to the precipice in waves of pink foam.

"You're back up in the treetops again," explained the pilot. "We both are. You see, the whole cliffside below us here is terraced and planted, it's a single steep apple orchard, an agricultural marvel, just one of many."

"And it was you who—?"

"Me?" laughed Palinurus. "Oh, no, lad, no, the apples have been here in this garden a lot longer than I have."

A breeze sent a gust of soft pink petals eddying across the boy's bare feet, tickling his sore and swollen toes.

"Most of the trees are in full bloom now," explained the pilot. "Later there'll be fruit, mountains of fruit."

Far below them, the sea of apple blossoms subsided until, at the very bottom of the cliff, no more than a single ring of trees remained. Yet even in that circle of no more than half a dozen it seemed to Nicolas as if no shade of pink were entirely absent—from the flash under a flamingo's wing, and the wink of an infant's fingertips, to the tougher magenta of torn plum skins and crushed berries.

"Is that a wall?" Nicolas asked abruptly, his eyes instinctively seeking out the bleached clay and mud-brick of color's more neutral ground, exhausted as they were by the profusion of pinks, and wary of moving on just yet to the burst of greens and the wash and sweep of yellows and all the rest of the almost alarming fertility of this island's sun-drenched palette.

"A wall, yes," replied Palinurus, "you see? There's one of the doors, one of the seven doors that lead, perhaps, to the Garden of Jewels."

There was already too much to see. Nicolas made no attempt to locate that door of which the pilot spoke. He was content, for the moment, merely to follow the lazily winding course of the wall itself, realizing too late that what seemed a simple path through the landscape was ultimately more of a labyrinth—for the course of the wall was interrupted at every moment by bolder and bolder details, explosions of living color, from arched battlements of trellised roses, red and yellow and deafening white, to hedges of flaming azalea and thick purple drapes of fuchsia and wisteria. And then all pretence of peace or predictability was shattered, once and for all, by the boy's discovery of what looked like a caravan of horses proceeding slowly and methodically along the *top* of the meandering wall.

"Horses?"

Palinurus nodded.

"It's a lot sturdier than it looks from here," he assured Nicolas, "and a lot higher. There's no way to see over it once you're down there. That's why I wanted to bring you here."

"It's a road," Nicolas marveled as he caught sight, at closer range, of a horse and cart, a bright green overflowing cart, rounding one curve of the wall. Even closer, even clearer, at a point where the top of the wall split and fell in a cascade of steps into the garden's interior, there stood two gray mules in shiny blue jackets, munching contentedly on a few tufts of mint or thistle sprouting up from the cracks in their elevated highway.

"What's in the cart?"

"The cart?"

"There, the green cart, on top of the wall."

"Ah, seeds," answered the pilot, and before the boy could think twice, trying to catch him off-guard, he quickly asked, "What is that in your hands?"

"It's what's left of my—" Nicolas interrupted himself.

"I saw you reaching out as you fell," confessed the pilot. "I saw you grabbing at the sudden sparkle in the air."

"It's all I have left," mumbled the boy, his voice fading as he went on. "Diamonds, perhaps, perhaps only glass, but I have sworn . . . "

"I understand," said Palinurus.

"You do?"

"Or at least I understand now, after all my days and nights here, on this island, in this garden." With a sweeping gesture the pilot drew the boy's attention back to all the intricacies of the landscape blossoming before them. "All of this," he said, "might have fit in the hand at one time."

So passionate were his words that for a moment the boy could picture the entire island cradled in the palm of the pilot's hand.

"There's nothing here, or anywhere, that can't be traced back to its seed," the pilot went on, as Nicolas followed the slow but steady progress of the horse and its green cart along the top of the wall, "and what every seed needs, first and foremost, is a dark and hidden place, a refuge, a shelter, in which to enter into its own strength and power."

Nicolas was suddenly conscious of a pulsing heat, radiating outward, from within his tightly closed fists.

From out of nowhere, it seemed, the pilot now produced a handful of the as-if magical seeds in question. Many of them the boy recognized, the tiny brown pearls of the appleseeds, for instance, the black and white splinters of the marigold, the cupped nuts and papery wings of the oak and the maple. But there were others that were brand-new to him.

"And this one?" he found himself asking over and over again.

"The dark spruce over there just beyond the wall."

"And this one?"

"Cabbages," said Palinurus, and pointed, "that whole field there is planted with them, though they've only just begun to sprout."

One by one the seeds in the man's hand were paired up with the gloriously ripened fruits of their seclusion, which were flourishing now in every corner of this vast garden outspread before the eyes of the two kindred travelers. There were pear and peach and sunflower, alfalfa and thyme and wild blueberry, hops and honeysuckle and hemp and hydrangea. His eyes darting back and forth repeatedly, from land to hand, Nicolas was scarcely able to distinguish any longer between those lines that furrowed the fields beyond and those that criss-crossed the pilot's palm.

"And this one?"

"This one is magnolia," said the pilot, pointing to an immense tree rising up in the center of the ring of apple blossoms at the bottom of the cliff. The boy stared into the tree's tremendous canopy of green light and green shade. "All of this," he reminded himself, echoing the pilot's words, "all of this might have fit in my hand at one time." Looking down at his hands, then once more in awe at the lush green majesty of the ancient magnolia, the boy felt suddenly further from the goal of his quest than ever, as if all of his tireless searching had yielded no more than this impatient yearning, always the same, whether imprisoned in a buried seed or hidden in a frustrated boy's clenched fists.

Suddenly, Nicolas gasped.

"You've seen the lion," said Palinurus, knowingly.

"Lion?"

"Nesting high in the magnolia."

"But, but how, but, it's green!" Nicolas finally managed to blurt out through his confusion.

"Yes," agreed the pilot, matter-of-factly, "it's the green lion."

The lion had been so effectively camouflaged by the foliage of the tree that initially the boy had looked right at it, or through it, without even noticing it. But then it had turned its head to face him, materializing all at once before his eyes. Though they stood too far away to hear its roar, its mouth had opened impossibly wide, and Nicolas felt the force of that inaudible cry echoing deep inside himself, in every cell of his own body.

"Since w-when . . . since when do lions, e-e-even *green* lions, nest in trees?"

"Since when do seeds rest in quilted beds?" countered the pilot, pointing out the strange patchwork that the boy had not yet noticed covering the ground beneath the magnolia. Once more Nicolas could not believe his eyes.

Palinurus was laughing.

It was as if a blanket had been spread out on the turf below the tree, squares of some loose light fabric stitched together, each one a different shade of an approaching dusk, a gradual lullabye of blue and violet, then charcoal, then black. Scattered across its surface, a flock of dark ducks had gathered as if for a picnic, attempting to peel back the occasional corner or poke right through the loosened weave, impatient for a taste of the tender bulbs buried beneath.

The boy questioned his companion with his eyes.

Palinurus shrugged.

"The Field of Sleep," he said, "or at least that's what it's called on *my* map."

Nicolas was silent.

"Here, let's plant one of these," suggested the pilot, crouching down without waiting for a response, and burrowing into the dark, damp soil with his thumb and his forefinger.

"What sort of seed is that?"

"Don't know exactly."

Nicolas studied the seed Palinurus had deposited gently inside a hollow of earth at their feet. It resembled the seed of a marigold. But while the latter was half black, half white, this one seemed poised to explore the realm between two different poles, a realm in which it was not black but rather red that was opposed to white.

Palinurus covered the seed, patting the earth affectionately back into place as he spoke. "Everything has its own unique point of departure," he reminded the boy, "its own unique seed."

He rose to his feet, brushing the loose dirt from his hands.

"It looks like a grave," said Nicolas, staring down at the little mound of packed earth, "a tiny grave."

"Mmm-hmm," the pilot agreed.

"I wonder," mused the boy, half aloud, "I wonder what sort of seed it is."

"By their fruits you shall know them," intoned the farming pirate.

Nicolas glanced up just in time to see the green lion atop the magnolia tree roaring soundlessly once again, the yawning of its jaws once more accentuating the ache of that abyss of desire deep inside him.

"But I want to know," he whispered, "*now.*"

"You see that little white house?"

Palinurus was pointing into the distance, far beyond the magnolia and the apple blossoms and the Field of Sleep.

"There?"

"No, no, that's only a chicken coop," the pilot corrected him, "not so far. There, right near that grove of tall poplars, the round house just at the edge of the ravine."

"It's a gazebo?"

"Exactly," said Palinurus, "that's where we're headed, that's where we'll sleep tonight."

He looked down at the boy's swollen foot.

"You think you can make it?"

"I'll try," said Nicolas.

They'd scrambled down the cliff as best they could, given the boy's lack of agility, and were working their way past the ring of apple trees. Nicolas had slowed his pace, to catch his breath, and was watching a group of cows that were grazing in the dry yellow grass near the picnicking ducks, when, quite unexpectedly, he caught sight of a human figure, a woman, crouched down amid the herd. She's milking them, he told himself, and would have thought no more about it had one of the cows not shifted position just then, affording him a clearer view.

"Look!" he shouted, turning to the pilot.

By the time he'd turned back, however, only a moment later, the woman had vanished.

"There was a woman, there, there," he insisted.

"Yes?"

"And she had no clothes on," spluttered the boy, "none at all."

From out of the corner of one eye, in the open cabbage patch, Nicolas caught a clearer glimpse of another figure, a man this time. He was hunched over the plowed earth, harnessed to some sort of machine, a primitive rake or harrow, which he dragged along behind him as he trudged up and down the field's long, shallow furrows. He, too, was naked.

The boy turned to his companion, then back again to the naked man at work—only to find that, just like the woman, the figure had vanished.

"But I saw them!" he insisted.

"You saw them, yes," agreed the pilot, "just as I have seen them many times, *many* times, but always only for an instant, always just like *that*," he snapped his fingers, "always just around a corner or just beyond a hedge or just about to disappear into the densest thicket of trees, always vanishing in the blink of an eye."

Nicolas had stopped walking.

He was looking down at himself, at the dark soft moons of his nipples, at his tender young sex dangling between his legs, at the downy hair frosting the tops of his pale thighs.

"I'm naked too!" he cried. Attempting to cover his body with his crutch, he succeeded only in unfooting himself and falling, landing on his bare backside on the ground, blushing scarlet.

Palinurus tried not to laugh.

"A fine figure of a boy," were the only words he could squeeze out through his smile.

Nicolas refused to go on until some sort of rudimentary clothing could be improvised, a grass skirt, perhaps, or a broad-leaved loincloth, scratchy birch-bark kneepads or maybe a breastplate and codpiece of dried mud. In the end there was even a helmet fashioned from the inverted bowl of an abandoned bird's nest, a hat that the pilot, still trying to restrain his laughter, placed personally upon the boy's head. "Marvelous!" he cried out again and again, complimenting the boy profusely as they resumed their trek across the island to the sanctuary of the gazebo.

"I can't be certain," said the pilot as they walked, "but I believe it's *they* who do most of the work around here." The boy's eyes were darting nervously, on constant alert for even the slightest sign of the naked couple. "I've never seen anyone else at all," the pilot went on. "In all my days here on this island, they are the only other people I've ever laid eyes on . . ."

He paused.

" . . . until *your* arrival, that is."

"Why didn't you tell me I was naked?" asked the boy.

"Oh, there'll be plenty of clothes when we get there, lad, don't you worry."

"When we get where?"

"To the temple, the gazebo," he said. "Why, there's a whole wardrobe there, everything your body might desire, and all made with my own two true hands."

Nicolas eyed the man's rags with suspicion.

"Ah, I know what you're thinking. Why these torn rags if the closet's so rich and full? I don't know, perhaps I'm just tired of it all, tired of buttons and laces and seams. There are days when even a piece of the finest silk seems to press against my skin like an iron suit of armor." He sighed. "Even the lightest of feathers, at certain moments, can weigh a man down—bending his knees, crushing him to the ground. I don't know. Perhaps it's just time for me to move on."

That night Palinurus stretched out on the hard marble floor of the gazebo while Nicolas lay curled up above him on its arched marble bench, both of them collapsed there for hours, tired, but unable to sleep.

"There's Columba," whispered the boy, pointing up to the stars twinkling in the dark sky.

"And in here as well," whispered the pilot, "listen."

Overhead, in the bronze eaves of the temple roof, a pair of doves were cooing with that calm expectancy they'd carried with them from the broad, warped beams of the ark in which they'd gathered, just like this, long ago.

"I'd almost forgotten," said Palinurus, sitting up suddenly.

Overhead, there was a soft flutter of wings as he drew his hand out from the shadows.

"More seeds?" asked Nicolas, looking down into the open palm.

"A fragment of blue eggshell," recited Palinurus, "and a piece of bone, and a pinch of salt."

In his mind's eye, the boy saw those last precious scraps of blue eggshell he'd tossed defiantly over his shoulder at the foot of the volcano. He'd known far less of the nature of seeds at the time, or he mightn't have squandered them so. He might have stayed and tended his garden of sorrows, watering it with tears, instead of moving on in such haste.

But that was alright, he decided.

There was plenty of room for both the weed and the wheat, for both the wild and the willed.

"I know all about the blue eggs," he assured his friend, "ahead *and* behind."

He could feel it all over again, that strange sensation of being followed, shadowed, and yet unable to turn around. It had been a long time since he'd given any thought at all to the winged gray boy. And suddenly now, this quality things had of fading in the memory terrified him. He closed his eyes tightly, trying to summon up the face of dear Old Gillam, worrying and fretting over every elusive feature and detail.

"I don't understand," he grumbled, a bit of his old defiance returning. "I don't understand what makes you call that crummy old shell a seed anyhow."

"It's easier to understand when they aren't broken," said the pilot, trying to simplify things for the boy. With his finger he drew a circle in the air, conjuring the clearly invisible egg in its entirety.

"And that," scoffed Nicolas, nodding toward the object that lay alongside the shell in the man's hand, "that's nothing but an old bone."

"Hard seed of a dead-man," swore Palinurus, "with all its secrets locked up tight."

Nicolas bent down closer, staring at the bone.

"They say," Palinurus went on, warming to his tale like the drunken pirate he once was, "they say that the bones of drowned sailors guard their galleys' sunken treasure until a million years of ocean grinds them at last to paste and powder. And even then they still haunt the depths and can thicken and swirl like a fog, blinding anyone who dares approach too close to the terrible secret of their wealth."

"And this," asked the boy, more humbly now, "is this a seed as well?"

On the tip of one moistened knuckle he carried a few grains of salt from the man's palm up to his tongue.

"Mother of all flavors," said the pilot, and he closed his hand, which promptly vanished back into the shadows along with the three most mysterious seeds of all.

Nicolas sat up.

"I've some to show as well," he exclaimed, remembering.

He bared his shoulder, thrusting it forward—offering his companion a bright armful of burning red berries, the crimson pips of the flaming pomegranate glowing even in the darkness.

"Ahhh, I'd wondered," said Palinurus, "I'd wondered where your tattoo was, you having been to the sea and all." He was lying of course, for he'd already noticed the marks on the boy's skin. Among true pirates, however, gawking at such pictures uninvited was considered an almost unforgivable display of bad manners.

Free now to satisfy his curiosity, he reached out, gripping the boy's arm, his face moving in eagerly, closer and closer, the whites of his eyes reddened as if by lantern light, so palpable was the fire lit by the bright ink under the young Pilgrim's skin.

For a long time he did not speak.

"Into the earth, then," he whispered at last, hoarsely, breaking his silence as if from the depths of a trance, "underground."

Nicolas felt uneasy at the change that had come over his friend, and he dared not interrupt.

"Into the earth," the pilot droned on, "into a world from which you can look up and see the roots of things dangling, penetrating the loam and the coal like veins of ore, creeping through the black rock of the under-sky like branches of slow-moving lightning illuminating the grave. Take good care that you return, lad. Take care you don't forget to close the circle, to pay the boatman, to replace the stone in the mouth, to open *and* shut the torn curtain of howling . . . "

Waiting far too long for his guide to continue, the boy was finally forced to conclude that the man had fallen sound asleep, the dreamlike flicker of the burning pomegranate now gilding the dull lids rather than the bright whites of his eyes. The boy did not want to disturb the weary pilot, and so for quite some time, an hour, perhaps, he just sat where he was while the man, still gripping his arm, still studying his tattoo through closed lids, sank deeper and deeper into sleep, his breathing growing more and more regular. It was not until he'd begun, at last, to snore, that Nicolas deemed it politic to move—gently disengaging himself, and creeping quietly back to his perch, to his bench, curling up on the curved slab of marble. His helmet slipped sideways across his brow the moment he lay down, the tattered nest cradling his head now, protecting it from the stone of the bench. It was a perfect pillow, and almost immediately the boy fell into a sleep so deep that he did not hear Palinurus arise early the next morning and tiptoe out of the temple and off through the trees in the direction of the red hill on the horizon.

When he did finally wake, the sun was already high in the sky, and Palinurus was nowhere to be seen—nowhere, that is, until the boy, in a moment of inspired desperation, turned toward what might have been a volcano on the horizon, and caught sight of his fugitive pilot at once, despite the vast distance that already separated them. Far out on the bright green alluvial plain, near the blue banks of the winding river, he saw him. And like the river, the man himself seemed mysteriously allied to those flocks of birds hovering above them both, flocks that had increased in size overnight and that seemed now like a dark wind at his heels.

I don't know, the boy repeated to himself, reconstructing the pilot's words, *perhaps it's just time for me to move on.* "Please don't go . . . " he couldn't help whispering aloud, and he watched until the birds had obscured the figure of the man entirely, then sighed and turned away.

Wasting no more time, he set about getting dressed, stripping off his makeshift garments and crawling, naked, on his hands and knees, around the base of the gazebo, searching for access to the storerooms beneath the temple floor. It was there that the pilot had assured him he would find a lavish wardrobe, though they'd been too tired last night to open the closets, agreeing that it would be better to wait until the light of morning.

Palinurus had told the truth.

Delighted, astounded, and yet at the same time aware that his cheeks were wet with tears of loneliness, the boy pulled garment after garment out from the temple's deep cellars, trying each one on yet unable to decide which to wear. Each was of a design more ingenious than the next, and, much to his amazement, each one fit him perfectly.

He finally settled on a pair of bright green leggings crocheted from soft fern and a sleeveless blouse made from two giant purple cabbage leaves secured on either side by a tough zigzagged lacing of green twig and horse hair. Over this, after long deliberation, he chose a breastplate, its broken seashells pressed and baked into a hardened paste of iridescent clay and crushed violets. And though he was faced with a fantastic array of hats, conical and floral, feathered and furred, some brimmed and some tasseled, still others crested or quilted or veiled—in the end, for sentimental reasons, the boy just could not part with his helmet. It took him well over an hour, given his nearly useless hands, to construct a single strap from the stem of a rose, scraping off its thorns with a rock and then looping it through the straw of the old nest and fastening it beneath his chin.

It was already past midday by the time he'd completed his preparations. Beginning to fold and stack the clothing scattered around, he stopped himself—there was no real reason, after all, to return the shirts and hats and breeches and blouses and vests to the temple's dark cellars. Besides, spread out on the grass all around him, the empty clothes made him feel as if he were not quite alone. For a long time the boy just stood there among his army of invisible pilgrims, unable to drag himself away from such strangely reassuring company. And yet he knew that he must not linger any longer. More than half the day was gone already, he reminded himself, and there had been no moon in the sky last night, which meant that he must return to the gazebo before dark unless he was willing to risk getting lost on the island, a dangerous prospect at this point. It was the pink of apple blossoms, still visible, even from afar, that he chose as his target. Hoisting his weight up onto his crutch and straightening his helmet, he set off to get a closer look at some of the marvels of this island he'd seen, as yet, only from a safe height and a comfortable distance.

He was hungry by the time he reached the ring of trees at the foot of the terraced orchard on the cliff. He was looking forward to the sweet tart taste of their ripe apples. But he'd forgotten that the trees, blooming as they were, had not yet put forth a single piece of fruit. Forced to forage elsewhere, harvesting a handful of parsley and a few crisp baby carrots for his meal, he continued on as he ate, not stopping until he stood amid the cows, still grazing contentedly where he'd seen them the day before.

Of course he'd returned hoping for another glimpse of the naked man and woman. "I'm certain to see them just when I least expect to," he assured himself, recalling the trustworthy pilot's testimony yet underestimating the difficulty of trying not to expect what one anticipates above all else. He looked *only* over his shoulder, *only* out of the corner of his eye. Neither of them appeared.

A few minutes later he stood in the shade of the magnolia tree, as close to its trunk as he could get without trespassing on the silken checkerboard of the Field of Sleep. Peering up through its branches, he waved at the green lion in its nest, trying to divert its attention. Now that he stood within earshot he was eager to hear the roar he'd only felt before. The lion, however, ignored him, and after an hour or more of useless shouts and signals, the boy gave up.

Tired already, discouraged, his arm sore and almost bleeding where it chafed against the rough wood of the crutch, Nicolas decided to turn back, heading dejectedly for the gazebo. "It's already so late," he grumbled to himself, frowning at the lengthening shadows of afternoon, regretting the shortness of a day that seemed all but wasted.

Leaving behind the lion and the cows, emerging from the ring of apple trees, he decided to steer a course closer to the garden wall so as not to lose his way. Stopping to pick a spray of the bright orange azalea planted along its base, he suddenly became conscious of the sound of rushing water beyond the high palisade. Looking around for its source, he found himself face to face with a door fashioned from the same violet clay as his breastplate and flanked by two shutters blue as polished turquoise. "One of the doors," he recalled the words of his pilot, "one of the seven doors that lead, perhaps, to the Garden of Jewels."

He knocked only once, timidly. It was only a slight touch, a tap, and yet the door swung wide open immediately, admitting him into the interior of the walled garden for the first time.

The song of the water was irresistible. Without hesitating he followed the little trough that ran right past his feet, limping along its course as swiftly as he could, not stopping until he'd reached the edge of the fountain into which its clear stream was pouring, water striking water, ringing and sparkling.

Nicolas bent over the large square basin of the fountain, panting with thirst for that limpid water that lay far beyond his reach. It was deep, this basin, deep as a well, the stones of its damp inner wall slick and glistening with gray-green moss.

On the far side of the fountain he spied a rope and a pulley, and, scrambling around the rim of the basin, he reached out for it with his closed hands, pressing the rope between his wrists and pulling on it as hard as he could. When the dented copper bucket at last appeared over the rim of the well, overflowing, the boy practically dunked his whole head into it, splashing and gasping, as he swallowed great gulps of cool, delicious water.

Raising his head, dripping wet, wiping the water from his eyes, he suddenly recoiled.

In his haste he'd not even noticed the little island that rose up in the center of the fountain. It was a sort of cage, a ruined or unfinished shrine or tabernacle of green slate and granite within which stood a single barren tree, its limbs blackened as if baptized by a blast of raging fire. It was not the tree, however, that had startled him, but rather the snake stretched out, motionless, along one of its dark dead branches.

"You again!" he cried out.

At the sound of the boy's voice, the serpent suddenly raised its head with a sharp hiss, slithered down the limb to which it had been clinging, and disappeared into a hole at the base of the trunk. There, at the root of the tree, on each of the four flat sides of the pedestal from which it emerged, the boy discovered the following inscription, the same inscription repeated four times, facing four different directions:

> *You, who are thirsty, come hither.*
> *If, by chance, the fountain fails*
> *The goddess has, by degrees,*
> *Prepared the everlasting waters.*

The shadows falling across the words of the inscription, deepening the color of the stone, obscuring the incised letters, warned Nicolas of the dark, moonless night soon to come—and the added possibility of the presence of living serpents inhabiting this island did nothing to calm his fears as he hobbled back out of

192

the garden, closing the door behind him. It was even later than he'd thought, and within moments he was no longer able to make out the form of the gazebo in the gathering gloom, no matter how hard he strained his eyes.

To make matters worse, he tripped and fell. Just when he least expected it, he tripped right over the naked couple, who lay in the shadows beneath a small hedge of forsythia and witch hazel, embracing.

"My crutch!" he cried out as he hit the ground.

Knocked from his hands, it had disappeared almost as fast as the surprised lovers: their bare buttocks flashing through the trees, that was the last glimpse he had of them. And then it was night, a black night through which, unable to locate his crutch, he was forced to crawl for hours—until he arrived, finally, miraculously, back at the sanctuary of the gazebo. Safe at last, he sprawled right out in the grass at the foot of the temple, surrounded by that crowd of clothing in which he'd dressed the open field earlier that day.

He was sound asleep almost before his pillow, its strap broken, slipped once more into place.

"Come *on*!" whined the boy, impatiently.

The mule just stared at him, every once in a while bursting into a hilarious chorus of honks and grunts, baring its teeth, flapping its wet pink lips, and shaking its head from side to side as if in refusal.

It had seemed like a brilliant idea, the only idea possible. There simply was no other solution. He could not take another step, not one. The crooked branch with which he had replaced his lost crutch was already cracking beneath his weight. It was almost useless. His foot was growing more and more swollen by the hour. Was he to crawl, then, on his hands and knees, through the remaining six doors? Perhaps. But only if he had to.

"Come on!" shouted the boy.

It was merely a matter of negotiating the last half of this steep stairway, for he was certain that if he could only coax the mule down a little further, all his problems would be solved. "Just another step, just one, just try, please," he implored the beast, who stood paralyzed with fear halfway down the narrow flight of stairs, unable to summon enough courage to move in either direction, either down to the ground or back up to the top of the wall.

"Well, if *I* can walk," shouted the boy, angry now, "if *I* can scale this wall to fetch you, and in my condition, the least you could do is—"

Nicolas turned away, in disgust, from the pile of offal that had appeared on the stone step beneath the rump of the terrified beast.

"Move!" he commanded a moment later, and brought what was left of his useless walking stick crashing down, hard, across the animal's back. With a sudden cry of pain, the bewildered mule jerked forward, its hooves slipping over the edge of the next step, the next, and the next, powerless to stop itself, clattering all the way down to the grass below, in which it stood, a moment later, staring up at the boy as if nothing had happened. Nicolas exhaled, took a step or two, then slipped in the pile of shit, and slid down the stairs on his back. Lying stunned in the grass, he looked up into the wide, innocent eyes of the mule, not knowing whether to cry or laugh.

"I'm sorry I hit you," he said, as he struggled up, wiping his soiled foot clean on the grass, fingering his bruised spine.

The mule honked once, and spit, then fell silent, while Nicolas set about examining the little blue vest strapped around its back and belly. It was a saddlebag, he discovered, lined on both sides with an array of pockets and pouches that would come in quite handy on a journey, such as his own, of indeterminate length.

"Let's see," he mumbled to the mule, turning to face the wall, "how do we get out of here?" A few yards in front of him he spied an unfamiliar door, black, with dull, unpolished shutters, rough and gray as cement.

The boy suddenly felt like a thief, caught red-handed.

He'd come to this island to enter the Garden of Jewels, of that there could no longer be any doubt. And the pilot had told him that in order to do so he must pass through the seven gates in the garden wall. The pilot had not, however, said anything about climbing over that wall, which was exactly what he had done. He found himself standing now, staring at the inside of a gate he hadn't actually passed through at all. "This is all wrong," fretted the boy, worried lest his entire quest be jeopardized by some such minor infraction or trespass. So, gritting his teeth, he managed to limp out of the garden, out through the black door, turning on his heels then and counting to ten, before reentering, this time in the proper manner, through the second door, which he pretended never to have seen before.

The mule had not moved. It stood waiting for him, with a look on its face that was a supremely patient blend of the puzzled and the amused, that look of humility in the eyes of a creature who is perfectly content to remain forever confused. There's got to be more than this, thought Nicolas to himself, looking back and forth from the mule to the door, checking to see if he'd missed something between them.

A high-pitched squeal, awful to hear, abruptly redirected the boy's attention to a rickety scaffold that was barely standing and might have fallen over completely had it not been leaning into the wall for support. From beneath its slanting wooden roof, as he watched, several fat pinkish creatures came trundling toward him, snorting among themselves.

"Pigs?" asked Nicolas.

That awful squeal tortured the air once more, as the pigs chased one another with surprising speed and agility back into their pen.

"Pigs," repeated the boy, snorting himself, as he struggled to a sitting position astride the mule.

The mule just stood there, refusing to move.

"Come on!" he cried, kicking its flanks to make it go, guiding it out through the door, cutting across the cabbage patch and turning to the right. It was familiar ground already, he was indeed backtracking, but he'd quickly made up his mind, after the anti-climactic swine behind door number two, to postpone his search for the next door, the third, and satisfy instead a different appetite. He was confident, now that he rode in style and comfort on the back of this beast he'd tamed with his own bare stumps of hands, that he could find his way all the way back to the wilds on the far side of the cliff—back to that enormous apple tree whose fruits he'd been so soon seduced by, and back, at last, to the spiral of that hive whose honey he'd not yet had the chance to taste.

"I'm hungry," he explained to the mule, speaking its language at last, loud and clear.

It was a long way, and several times they wandered lost in the forest, until a saving glimpse of one of the six hills through the trees oriented the boy or a faint scent of fermenting apples beckoned the mule. Despite all their difficulties, however, and their differences, there was no denying that they made a handsome couple, boy and mule. Nicolas had made certain of that. Even from a distance he'd admired the bright blue of the mule's vest. When he'd dressed himself that morning he'd chosen something blue as well, donning a loose shift of overlapping jays' wings, gathered at the neck and waist with bunches of dried gentian and lavender and lobelia.

Even the always preoccupied weaver birds interrupted their work to pay their respects, rising up in unison like a single puff of gold dust in a wind, as the blue boy and his blue mule hobbled into the little clearing beneath the apple tree.

An hour later the pockets of the mule's vest were loaded down with apples of every variety: empire apples and gala apples and melrose and wealthy apples, bright red winesaps, handfuls of tiny crab apples and green-streaked lady apples, shiny spartans and firesides, ten or twelve bold rome beauties, and even a single early maiden blush, the bloodless skin of its cheeks still pale and yellow.

"All these different apples growing from the same tree," Nicolas exclaimed to the mule, who was busy munching on the discarded cores that littered the ground at its feet, "and while all the other trees are still in bloom, without a single piece of fruit on their branches."

The mule smacked its lips and swallowed.

"It must be a sacred tree," the boy concluded.

Right at that moment an enormous gob of thick, golden honey struck the top of his head with a dull splat.

"You see?" he cried, dropping to his knees beneath the overflowing hive. The mule leaned over, stretching its neck, and began to lick the sweet, sticky crown from the boy's head.

"How will I ever get up there?" Nicolas wondered aloud, staring at the hive wedged in the fork of the apple tree.

Some time and several falls later, standing painfully on the toes of his good foot, balanced precariously on the mule's back, and reminding himself over and over again to resist even a single glance into the spiral of the shell that protected the hive lest he grow dizzy and tumble once more to the ground, he managed to thrust his hand at last into its molten depths and withdraw it, dripping and buzzing, laden with honey and haloed by bees. Quickly he crouched down, catching the syrup in one of the saddlebags, the largest, which he'd prepared earlier, lining it with a double layer of waxy green cabbage leaves.

Four, five, six times he repeated the process, until the pouch was nearly full. But then on his seventh try, one of the thousands of bees that had been relatively co-operative and slow to anger charged the innocent mule, and, landing on its snout, stung the very tip of its nose. Instantly, the mule cried out, kicked its heels, and ran, sending the boy toppling to the ground in a sticky heap.

Nicolas was unable to establish any sort of rapport between the bees and the mule after that, though he tried repeatedly. "Now don't worry," he would whisper into the mule's trembling ear, attempting to lure him over to a hedge or flowerbed alive with the furiously busy insects. Or he would gently pluck a single gardenia or an apple blossom within which one of the drunken bees was rolling around and around, bathing in nectar, its legs twitching in ecstasy. He would tenderly offer the flower to the mule, holding it up to its still swollen nose. Instantly the animal would shy away, running, then stopping, looking back over its shoulder at the boy in annoyance.

Nicolas would have abandoned such efforts at reconciliation entirely were it not for the fact that when they left the clearing at last, heading back toward the walled garden at the base of the cliff, the bees followed. They'd already been underway for some time when it occurred to the boy that the incessant buzzing of the hive had not diminished at all. Turning, he'd seen the long wavering column of bees that stretched out behind them, their ranks occasionally breaking, yet always reforming, extending as far back as the eye could see. "You'll just have to get used to them," he told the mule, finding it necessary to raise his voice above the buzz and hum of their escort.

Much later, passing once more through the hoop of blossoming apple trees, Nicolas signaled abruptly for the mule to stop.

"Wait," he said, certain they'd not pass this way again.

Behind them, the bees obeyed as well, their wings whirring, flying in place. "There's one more thing."

Dropping to the ground, he crawled, on all fours, over to the hem of the Field of Sleep, and, lifting one corner of its quilt, he plunged his fist into the loose soil, uprooting several of the bulbs that lay sleeping there, cradling them as softly as possible in the crook of his arm so as not to wake them as he crept back to the mule. The animal eyed him, suspiciously, as he stuffed the three bulbs, clotted with damp earth, into one of the apple-filled pouches.

Suddenly, behind him, there was a terrible commotion. The flock of ducks, to which Nicolas had paid scant attention, interrupted their picnic the moment they realized what had happened and began quacking their complaints in no uncertain terms, protesting this impetuous harvest or theft, the spoils of which they had not been offered even the tiniest share of. In one long straggling line they came waddling after the boy.

It was several minutes, tripping and falling and crawling, before Nicolas managed to overtake the terrified mule and hurl himself across its back. Yet even then, the ducks kept on coming. It soon became apparent that, like the bees, they intended to stay, to stick close to him through thick and thin, wherever this journey might lead them.

It was a strange and noisy caravan, boy and mule and ducks and bees, that wound through the fields of cabbage and carrot and parsley, along the garden wall, stopping, before they reached the gazebo, in the meadow that sloped down gently to the ravine.

"I think it's better if we just go on from here in the morning," said Nicolas, turning to the mule, which lay on its side not far away, nibbling an apple. They'd sufficent clothes and provisions, after all, there was no need to return to the gazebo, and the boy was suddenly anxious that they had wasted far too much time already.

It was quiet for the first time in hours. The caravan had settled down for the night, the bees forming several separate swarms on adjacent tree branches, the ducks plopping down wherever they stood, their heads dropping to their breasts. Off in the distance the honk and wheeze of a lone mule echoed across the open meadow.

"It's your friend," said the boy, "maybe," for there'd been two of them atop the wall, and one had been left behind.

The mule had stopped chewing and pricked up its ears.

Nicolas sighed.

"Perhaps he misses you," he suggested, and both he and the beast stared off into the darkness in the direction of the animal's cry, but all was silent now, peaceful and faintly glowing under the slightest sliver of a new moon just beginning to blossom in the sky.

The boy sighed again, lying down flat on his back and closing his eyes.

"You know?" he said, "there are days now, days when I forget about the Phoenix entirely, when I don't even give it a thought, not one thought, from morning till night."

For some time the boy had been aware of the steadily increasing heat within his still stubbornly closed hands, and he brought them up close to his face now, feeling the warmth of their fire on his cheeks.

"Yet," he went on, "it's really the only thing that I desire, and every single step I take leads me nowhere else."

He let his hands drop to his chest.

"Isn't that strange?"

Once more, he took a deep breath, rolling over onto his side.

"Isn't that the strangest thing of all?" he asked again, even though he could tell, judging by the sound of its breathing in the darkness, that the mule had fallen asleep and was no longer listening, and so could not answer even if it had been able to.

The third door did not look like a door at all, at least not like either of the two doors that had preceded it. It seemed more of a hatch, hardly high enough for a boy, much less a man, to pass through. Set low into the wall, and tilting, as if it led not through, but down, underground, it was split into two warped panels, one side frosted with dull green mold, the other brown with rust.

Its stiffened hinges buckled and screeched as he pulled open one panel, and hesitated before opening the other.

At first he could see nothing. Slipping his head cautiously into the shadows, letting his eyes adjust, he could just barely make out a short crooked series of steps, cut right into the hard packed earth. They seemed to descend and rise up again, almost immediately, as if the door led into a tunnel that dipped down beneath the foundation of the garden wall and came up and out again on the other side.

Stepping down, gingerly, the boy's nostrils were immediately assaulted by a gritty sour smell that stung his eyes and throat. It was this acrid odor, he was certain, that discouraged the bees and the ducks, who'd refused to follow. The mule had been discouraged as well, though for a different reason, balking at the very first sign of a flight of stairs.

Thus, once again, the crippled Pilgrim who'd already sworn so many times that he'd never be able to take another painful step took another painful step, several of them, a dozen or more, down into the little tunnel, and then up again into the thick gray light that hung like a shroud over this part of the garden, a sullen haze that was the result, the boy soon discovered, of a series of small fires, scattered here and there in front of him, belching smoke.

Nicolas tried to investigate more closely. He was curious to know just what it was that was being burned. But the shifting of the wind kept driving the stinging smoke right into his eyes, blinding him, forcing him to retreat.

In fact, the fires seemed to be burning without any flame at all. That much he could see from a distance. Most seemed no more than low smoldering heaps, seething with smoke, like wet wood or ash. Several of them looked as if they issued from nothing but the flat surface of the ground itself, their smoke rising up like a cloud of muddy steam released from some hidden cleft in the earth.

Nicolas felt a chill run through his body. It was oddly disconcerting, this gray garden, almost funereal. It seemed so out of place on the otherwise bright and beautiful island. He was repelled, and yet at the same time there was something so intimately familiar about the odor of the fires that he could not quite put it behind him. It was still with him, later, long after he'd reemerged through the

200

little tunnel and closed the hatch securely, rejoining his caravan. Hours passed before he realized why it was that he recognized the smell.

It was his foot, of course!

His wounded foot!

He was loathe to admit it, but for several days now he'd been aware that the puffy blue-black flesh all around the edges of his wound had begun to stink.

And thus try as he might—to leave the distressing implications of this somber burning ground behind him, to concentrate instead on the more comforting light and life of the rest of the landscape—he could not entirely succeed. The odor of that smoke accompanied him just as faithfully as his buzzing bees and his perpetually squabbling ducks, following close behind him like a pestilential wind nipping at his bruised and stinking heels.

Nicolas turned the corner with great relief. The sharp bend of the wall effectively blotted out the terrain already explored behind him, releasing him into a whole new landscape. At last he was entering virgin territory.

It wasn't long afterward that he began to hear voices. It's only bee-hum or duck-talk, he told himself, it's only the song of water running and babbling once again. But he could not quite convince himself.

He signaled the mule to stop and for a long while sat listening, and looking. "What's that?" he wondered aloud, noticing, for the first time, a ring of broad leafy trees in the distance. They seemed to have been planted there deliberately, so unnaturally precise was their arrangement, and studying them more closely, Nicolas saw that they enclosed a wide circular field of some sort, a pale sandy crater or arena along whose perimeter the surrounding terrain seemed to rise up in one continuous wind-blown dune.

His imagination sparked, there was nothing he would have liked better than to change course immediately, to steer toward this strange wild amphitheater in the distance. But he had to make a choice. The voices were growing more and more persistent. It was becoming apparent that they beckoned, not from the distance, but from quite nearby, from just beyond the garden wall. "It's probably too far away anyway," he muttered, rationalizing, tearing his eyes from the horizon and forcing them to rest atop the mule's head, between its tensed ears. With a sigh of dismay, Nicolas was forced to admit to himself that there were far too many places on this earth for one boy to visit, and that he would have to grow accustomed to passing many of them by without ever having entered into their secrets. As his caravan began to move forward once again, he waved one hand, briefly, over his shoulder, and in a scarcely audible voice whispered, "Goodbye," without looking back.

Instantly, as if in reply, a whole series of giggling "Hellos" erupted in shrill falsetto from the base of the wall alongside which the mule had stopped in blank-eyed surprise.

Nicolas stared down at the chorus of wild pansies, their scraggly purple, white, and yellow petals ruffled by the wind.

"Well, don't just stand there, come on in."

"Did you *say* something?" Nicolas asked, almost embarrassed to be taking part in such a conversation. Neither Palinurus nor the map had mentioned anything about talking with flowers. From over the top of the high wall there spilled a wave of barely suppressed laughter, rippling through the air.

"The door! The door!" wheedled the pansies, flopping their bright heads from side to side as if their necks were broken.

"Sssshhh," someone was whispering behind the wall.

"The door!" repeated the pansies. "Open it! Open it!"

Nicolas had barely noticed the door, and he'd hardly time to examine it now, with its heavy iron grill and intricately carved lintel—for the mule, intoxicated by a sudden heavy sweetness in the air, had already pressed its nose up against the thick wooden panel and pushed its way inside. Wave after wave of laughter rolled over them as the caravan passed through the fourth door, through snicker and chortle and titter and hoot, right into the continual comment of the gossiping herb garden beyond.

"Welcome! Welcome!"

"Oh, put your trumpets away, we've heard it all before."

The boy's head spun in all directions, but there were so many voices blaring from so many bugles of flowers and broad cymbals of clashing leaves that he couldn't be sure from which of them the fanfare or its retraction had originated.

"Look at the clothes on 'em!"

"Quite the dandy, I should say."

"And the ass dressed up to match."

"Well, I never . . ."

"Jay feathers and gentian and—"

There was a sharp intake of breath behind him, then a whoosh and swat as a long spike full of lavender came spanking down on the rump of the bewildered mule, missing the boy by less than an inch.

"Why, that's my cousin on my sister's side," accused the lavender, "there, around his neck, all plucked and dried."

"Speaking of plucked and dried, when's the last time you looked at your own reflection in the pond?" teased an adjacent mullein.

"Oh, and I suppose you call *those* flowers?" snapped the lavender. "Why, I've seen nicer ears on a mule!"

"On this mule right here!" goaded a third voice.

"Donkey ears! Donkey ears!" erupted the entire garden.

It seemed to the boy as if it were much more than a breeze suddenly tangling the spikes of lavender and the tall yellow steeples of mullein. And there must have been more than a million tiny pink flowers in the carpet of wild thyme beneath them, each one of which started giggling so uproariously that the ground itself seemed to shift under the mule's hooves, sending it running right across the garden, crashing through the curlicues and arabesques of its neatly manicured beds, trampling a low hedge of hyssop, flattening a bright yellow primrose or two, knocking the blossoms from the long stems of a row of columbine.

"Stupid ass!" threatened a clump of monkshood, nearly trampled as well, its clusters of blue helmets shaking ominously. "Why, I oughtta . . ."

"You ought to what?"

Laughing at the moody blue monk's poisonous threats, it was a single towering angelica that rose to the rescue—its stem climbing a full six feet into the air, topped by a huge globe of milky green flowers, a single spherical snowflake the sun was powerless to melt.

It was almost impossible to keep track of who was arguing about what, or what was arguing about who, for there were so many petty disputes going on at once, and every herb in the garden was more than willing to interfere in every other herb's silly business.

"Pay no attention to them, boy," he heard a whisper, "they don't get out much."

Nicolas had managed to stay astride the mule as it fled, but in the shade of a few isolated horse chestnuts, the beast had stopped so short that the boy was finally thrown from its back. As the animal munched contentedly on the fruit littered beneath the trees, the grounded Pilgrim busied himself picking those very same spiny green fruits from his backside and looking about to see what plant it was that was whispering at him now.

Sprouting from a crack in the garden wall, Nicolas spied a lone dandelion.

"That's the trouble with roots," it was whispering, as if wary of being over-heard, "they tend to—"

But it was too late.

"What are you doing in here?"

"Scat!"

"Filthy weed!"

"Scamp!"

"Tramp!"

The dandelion wasn't whispering anymore.

"Stick-in-the-muds," it hooted, at the top of its voice.

"Vagabond!" came the reply.

"Been nowhere! Done nothing!" taunted the dandelion, waving its cottony head. Its yellow flower had long since faded and dissolved to a single round puff of feathery seed.

"Orphan!"

"Drifter!"

"Hobo!"

"Homebodies," scoffed the weed.

"You'll tug on the wrong root, one day," cried the mandrake.

"Charlatan!" shouted the dandelion, quickly lowering its voice and confiding in the boy. "I didn't like the sound of that at all. Would you do me a little favor and just breathe on my—"

"Who let the riffraff in here, anyway?"

"Who left the door open?"

"That's what I'd like to know!"

"Must have been that stupid boy."

"Come on!" hissed the weed, insistent, "just one breath, just one, that's all! I can't take this another minute."

Nicolas had played this game many times in the meadows of the aviary, and he leaned down now and blew lightly on the dandelion, making a wish as its head burst instantly into a fluff of seed, flying off in every direction at once.

"Don't bother to get up, I'll see myself out," the flying seeds called to the rest of the garden, laughing with a hundred voices at once, and then dissolving to silence.

"And then there were none," sneered all the herbs in unison.

"Travel!" exclaimed the fragrant yellow flowers of a shrub whose branches looped and twisted around every other plant in its vicinity. "I really don't see what all the fuss is about."

"Old bag," whispered a few stalks of dill among themselves.

"Old maid," tittered every dewy blue blossom of rosemary.

"For fifty years I've not set a foot outside these walls and—"

Nicolas didn't mean to interrupt, but he just couldn't contain his excitement on recognizing the old shrub's sweet perfume.

"Honeysuckle!" he cried out, delighted, snapping off one of its blossoms and crushing it between his fingers.

"Ouch!"

"Little brat!"

"That's right! You'd better run!"

For Nicolas had scampered away, backwards, tripping over a stone and landing flat on his back in a large clump of amaranth, or "love-lies-bleeding," as she preferred to refer to herself with her customary melodrama—never tiring of reminding the other plants that when their flowers had already dried and fallen to the ground, her long crimson tufts would still retain the vigorous red hue of youth.

"I am," she would pronounce from time to time, whether any one was listening or not, "immortal."

And every herb within earshot would groan.

Nicolas stood up, wiping the ruddy juice of the crushed amaranth from his hands, its blood staining the blue feathers of his tunic purple where it touched them.

"Whew, will you look at his foot."

"Ugghh."

"And the stink!"

"I was wondering where that came from."

"Go stand in the yarrow, boy."

"You think?"

"I think it's too late even for that."

"Far too late."

"It's awful."

"Too awful."

"Sweep him out of here, please," they begged the heather, but she was too busy nursing her own wounds, bruised by the hooves of the mule as it ambled across the garden toward the boy, its belly swollen with chestnuts.

"Which war?" asked the yarrow, shaking its long stalks from side to side in regret.

"War?" asked the boy.

"What war was it in which you received such a terrible wound?"

"War?" asked the boy again.

"He's not very bright, is he?" muttered one mint to another.

"But I'm no warrior," objected Nicolas, "I'm a pilgrim."

"Aha!"

"Just another weed!"

"What did I tell you?"

"I knew it!"

"I told you so!"

"No, I told you!"

"Scat," spat the lavender, still seething.

"Travel," scoffed the honeysuckle once more, tightening its grip on everything.

The boy did not have to be convinced to leave. Mounting the mule, he began a halting procession through the hedged aisles and paths and cruel cul-de-sacs of the relentlessly gossiping garden, picking up the other members of his caravan as he went, luring the ducks out from their lovely lemon-scented haven amid the verbena, stopping in a patch of bright sunlight near the door, near a mound of borage upon whose hairy stems and bright blue drooping flowers all of his bees as well as many others besides had converged in one drunken buzzing crowd.

"Psssst."

Nicolas ignored the whisper at first, tired of all this talk.

"Pssst, before you go . . ."

Almost directly beneath the mule, several clusters of bright flowers were quivering, twinkling like five-pointed pink stars.

"It isn't much, but it's the best I can do."

Casually, the mule lowered its head, gripping half of the whispering plant between its teeth, tearing it from the earth and then turning, as if to pass it along to the boy.

"You need to see a doctor," insisted the centaurea plant.

"A doctor?"

"In a dream."

Nicolas stared at the pink flowers drooping from the mule's mouth.

"What's your name?"

"Sssshh, not so loud," warned the herb, "if the others knew they'd be angry."

Over his shoulder Nicolas could hear the rest of the herbs busy teasing the water mint, questioning her virtue.

"Trollop!"

"Bed-hopper!"

It was common knowledge that many of the garden's other mints were hybrids sprung from her own restless seed.

"They're really *all* weeds, you know," the centaurea went on whispering, "they just don't like to admit it. And the dandelion's no different. Oh, he's traveled, certainly, but still he's got a deeper root than many."

Nicolas had harvested his share of dandelions and knew this to be the truth.

"Now hurry, before they hear us, for my leaves and flowers may bring you at least some temporary relief until you . . . "

The mule had already started toward the door.

"But who are you?" Nicolas asked again, interrupting.

"You *are* like him, in many ways you *are* like him."

"Like who?"

"Like the ancient one. He too was part man, part horse."

"But we're neither," cried Nicolas, "we're neither man nor horse, don't you see?"

"He too was wounded when I met him."

"But we're only a boy, a boy on a mule!"

Anxious to leave the garden now, the mule was walking faster and faster, almost breaking into a trot.

"And perhaps I shall be able to heal you as well."

"But—"

"Sssshhh, you are almost through the gate, and I shan't be able to talk once you are on the other side. Now listen carefully and do just as I say—"

The flowers in the mule's mouth suddenly wilted and fell silent as the shadow of the door's lintel fell across the boy's lap. And then, as they crossed the threshold, a deafening hum bore down upon him, overwhelming every other sound. Every single bee in the garden had risen up into the air at once, buzzing furiously, many of them so drunk that they bumped right into one another as they swarmed out through the open gate, attempting to fall into formation behind him.

By the time Nicolas had recovered his senses enough to reach out for the gift of pink flowers, the mule had already lost its patience, had already chewed and swallowed.

Behind them the heavy wooden door banged shut.

The boy paid no attention at all to the shrieks and curses of the wild pansies as first the hard hooves of the mule and then the broad flapping feet of the ducks flattened their bright colors into the earth. What a relief it was to have silenced that garden full of obnoxious voices, to have left it far behind him without so much as a backward glance.

"They were right, though," the boy thought to himself, looking down at his wounded foot and wrinkling up his nose as he continued on his way—neither warrior nor centaur, but only humble pilgrim, only a stubborn boy on his stubborn mule.

"They were right," the thought kept haunting him.

As he reached up to cover his nose with his fist, trying to escape from the stink of his own rotting flesh, he noticed for the first time the blood that had begun to seep out from beneath the fingers of his clenched hands and trickle down his wrists and arms.

There could no longer be any doubt that the boy was reaching the limit of his endurance. Stopping with increasing frequency, devouring apple after apple in an attempt to revive his flagging strength, it began to dawn on him, slowly at first and then with a growing dread, that there was indeed a point beyond which his body could not be pushed. Those last few mouthfuls of honey remaining in his saddlebags, potent as they were, could only revive him for an hour or two, before the weakness and the dizziness returned, blotting out all else.

"I've passed through such places before," the boy tried to tell himself, gritting his teeth, desperately attempting to situate the misery somewhere outside, on the map. But he knew this was different. He knew by the odor of death, by the lapses of memory. He knew by that cold fire in his clenched hands, which no longer warmed but froze. And he knew most of all by the mouth of his wound.

Rocking back and forth on the mule, hour after hour, it seemed to him, in his near-delirium, as if the wound were opening wider and wider as he stared down at it, as if it were drawing breath, drawing more breath than he in fact, inhaling greedily.

Perhaps, had the very next door, the fifth, not proved such a trial of just that strength he no longer possessed, he might have held on longer. For hours he'd battled against the terrible wind that pressed against that door, hurling all his weight repeatedly against the implacable barrier. A single foot was all he managed to slip through the gap he'd opened, a single wounded foot whose numb and swollen toe he touched, briefly, to the turf on the other side—before the violence of the wind once more overwhelmed him, forcing the door closed.

He'd no idea what lay behind it, in the garden beyond. Surely nothing could have survived such a violent gale, surely the garden was empty, swept clean, erased, polished, smooth as glass.

"I'll never know," he mumbled to himself, his voice trembling.

Draping himself across the back of the mule as best he could, lying crossways on his belly, with his eyes on the ground, he wondered if he had indeed qualified to move on to the next door, and then the next, the last, beyond which he pictured the Garden of Jewels that lay awaiting, at this point, no more than its pilgrim's wasted corpse.

Nicolas did not know how much time had passed, days or nights, perhaps weeks, perhaps only hours—perhaps only a single painful minute exaggerated and distorted by his tormented senses. He'd no idea how long the mule had been standing still. But when he did, suddenly, become aware of the fact that they were no longer moving, he looked up, twisting his head around, to see a doorway, the sixth, behind him. The mule had already passed through the gate on its own, unbeknownst to him, and then stopped, unable or unwilling to proceed any further.

"Is it night?" Nicolas asked.

Shadows lay so thick and close upon him that he could feel their pressure against his skin. He had to lift up the darkness like a tent around him as he struggled into an upright position on the mule's back, searching for some clue as to his whereabouts.

It was only then that he realized, with a shock, that the doorway was brilliantly aglow, a bright slab of daylight floating in the twilight that engulfed him.

Nicolas turned from the doorway and peered deeper into the dark garden, quickly discerning, even through the shadows, the reason for the mule's refusal to continue. Rising up, directly in front of him, blocking all else from sight, was an enormous stairway, so steep, so massive, that he gasped aloud as his eyes climbed, one at a time, its thousands and thousands of steps, steps that disappeared high over his head, vanishing in this gloom beyond the sixth door.

No wonder the mule stood paralyzed, faced as it was with such an awful climb.

Yet there was something else as well, something barring access to the stairway. It was a statue of some sort, or so the boy thought, a figure, frozen, bewitched by that same gloomy stillness that made even the mule, even the boy himself, appear carved from the same block of dead, gray stone.

It did not occur to Nicolas to wonder why the mule bowed its head so tenderly to the stone figure at the foot of the stairs, why it sniffed and listened with such caution, and why it shuddered then and trembled beneath him. It was only a horse, a stone horse collapsed on the ground, on its side, its stone legs jutting out sharply, bent and buckled like the broken masts of a beached wreck. Until a single puff of steam, one feeble breath, animated the statue at last, revealing to the boy that this stone, this horse, was a living thing. Suddenly Nicolas recognized the black horse which, along with its dark rider, had been lost or abandoned long ago. He would have wept, had the well within him not run dry.

The horse was dying, its last gasps condensing in the gloom. Some of the bees, deprived of even the slightest trace of sweetness here in this grim garden, were immediately attracted by the warm white flower of its breath already evaporating into darkness, and they converged around the steaming nostrils of the horse, clustering frantically.

"No!" the boy cried aloud.

He waved one arm through the air to frighten the bees, which rose up, scattered, and reformed again instantly. Again the boy waved, and again, and the bees scattered and returned, scattered and returned. One bee, more confused than the others and buzzing angrily, landed on the rump of the mule, and, without a moment's hesitation, plunged its stinger all the way into the poor beast's much-abused flesh. Instantly the mule leapt into the air, right over the

lamed horse, and, with Nicolas clinging desperately to its neck, it began running up the towering staircase before it even knew what it was doing.

The frightened creature stopped only once, gazing anxiously up into deepening shadows, then turning its head and staring down the way it had come, its ears twitching, as if trying to expel those vibrations buzzing up from far below. Caught between two terrors, one not yet known, the other a painful memory as real as the thorn in its flesh, the mule had no choice but to continue on and on, climbing higher and higher.

It did not, however, climb alone. The ducks, after lengthy deliberation, had chosen to follow. Slowly, comically, their short legs and wide flat feet negotiating the stairs with great difficulty, often falling back two or three steps for every one they advanced, they clambered on and up, pursuing the terrified mule. Nicolas turned once and saw them trailing down the length of the entire stairway, tumbling and squawking, like a line of drunken sentries, the dark feathers of their uniforms in chaotic disarray. Beyond them, through the bright rectangle of the open doorway, poured all the brilliance of the island's beautiful springtime colors.

"Stop!" he suddenly cried to the mule.

The naked figures of a man and a woman had flashed by, chasing one another like two enormous colorless butterflies, traversing in an instant the steadily shrinking doorway full of bright garden and then vanishing.

Nicolas turned away from the light, desolate, letting his head sink down onto the mule's neck, burying his face in its coarse hair, gripping the beast tightly with both his arms and his legs to prevent himself from sliding to either one side or the other.

Hours passed, and still the mule went on climbing. And then all at once it stopped. The boy looked up, and though at first he could not see it, he could sense it, blocking their path. A door. One vast, heavy door.

Was it the seventh? The last?

Perhaps he had lost count, perhaps he had already passed through hundreds of doors as he lay all but unconscious across the mule's back. And even if it *were* the seventh, the gateway to the Garden of Jewels, how would he ever, weak as he was, force his way through such an impenetrable barrier? Of all the doors this one was surely the most immovable. It was tremendous, monumental. An unassailable fortress of a door that dwarfed not only he and his mule but the enormous stairway up which they had climbed as well.

The mule began to honk and wheeze, crying like a trapped child. Nicolas tried to dismount gracefully, to land on his feet, but his legs were numb and he fell to his knees instead. He was convinced that every moment might be his last and so allowed himself only a single shallow and painful breath before placing his clenched fists against the surface of the monstrous door and pushing with all his might.

With a rustle and a whisper, the entire door warped, curled, and tipped forward. Like a sheet of paper in a wind, it tilted and spun around, then drifted off, fluttering, into darkness. The startled boy had to brake himself with his fists, grinding them into the rough stone across which he slid, scraping the skin from his knuckles. Less than an inch beyond his hands, the ground dropped away completely, and, peering down over the edge, Nicolas found himself staring into a bottomless black abyss.

"Don't!" he warned the mule, seeing the beast raise one foot as if about to take a step and cross this last threshold. All around them crowds of nervous ducks were piling up everywhere, as one by one they reached the top step and tumbled, exhausted, onto the little stone plateau that was far too small to hold them all.

Nicolas leaned out over the precipice, trembling, staring down into the void below.

"There's something down there," he whispered to the mule.

Glimmers.

Gleams.

Glints.

Like the eyes of wild animals hunting in the dark, thought the boy with a shudder.

Or like diamonds in the night.

"I don't suppose," he mumbled moments later, as he unfastened the blue vest containing what little provisions he had left, "I don't suppose you'd like to come along."

The whites of the mule's sorrowful eyes glowed violet in the shadows that swirled up from the abyss.

For a moment Nicolas held the vest poised over the depths, hesitating, and then he dropped it. And listened. But no sound of impact ever reached his ears. Perhaps the object went on falling and falling, forever, perhaps it was falling still. Or perhaps the thud of its landing could not be heard above the nervous squawking of the throng of ducks, many of which were now struggling for a place to sit or stand up on the emptied back of the mule—who had, as usual, merely exhanged one burden for another.

"I'm sorry," said the boy, tenderly.

And then he turned his back to the beast, and jumped.

There was nothing else to do, no other way to go on.

He jumped right off the little stone pedestal, into blackness, with no thought of the consequences.

The braying of the abandoned mule had faded to silence, as had the raucous quacking of the ducks, and still he went on falling, and falling, down, down, down, the only sound the rush of dark air roaring past his ears.

He landed hard, but in something soft.

Thick, wet soil it felt like, loam or peat, rich with the smell of manure and the slime and sweat of swollen earthworms.

He heard a sudden crack and lay perfectly still. I've broken my legs, he concluded, calmly. Then he fainted from the pain.

When he regained consciousness he tried at first to move, tried lifting himself up onto his elbows at least, but even this effort was too much for him and he fell back, sinking into the cool dark soil, which seemed to welcome him.

"Perhaps I am dead," it occurred to him, "dead and buried."

And then he thought no more about it.

Rather, like a true pilgrim, he busied himself only with his progress, continuing on his way with the only part of his body he could still move at all—his eyes. Staring, face to face with nothing, these eyes were once more able to coax from the blackness those glimmers of light, those glints and gleams, those jewels of the night. More like sparks now, their colors were subtle, possessing all the clear, cold transparency of the diamond, yet burning at the same time with flashes of every imaginable hue.

Floating embers, drops of boiling ocean, blinks of a golden eye, chips of shattered sapphire, the heartbeat of steel, jade tears, the ringing of tiny emerald bells, and a gust of crushed opals. No gem was missing, no two were alike. And every one was separated by a gulf of darkness as deep as the terrible silence of the colors of their light.

Nicolas felt as if he were being drained, as if his body had opened, somehow, as if his blood vessels no longer circled around neatly feeding their own tail but shot off like garnet arrows of light, pouring him into the distance. A storm of red vulcan dust, his own blood released, swept past his face, scraping and stinging his skin like sand. While his soul, an amber shower, rained down upon the garden, penetrating the other jewels with its wandering light.

"Perhaps if I try to eat something," whispered the boy, as if the mule still stood tethered just a few yards away.

The blue vest, he discovered, almost by accident, was lying right beside him. Without raising himself from the ground, he rummaged blindly through its pockets with his fists, finding neither a drop of honey nor a single apple but only those tender bulbs he'd uprooted from the Field of Sleep beneath the magnolia tree. They'd not wilted at all but seemed on the contrary firm and fresh, and Nicolas pushed them, one after another into his mouth, chewing and swallowing mechanically. Their flesh was bitter. It stung his lips and his tongue. It made his head ache, and his throat pucker and heave.

As for reviving him, restoring his strength, their effect was quite the opposite, their narcotic paralyzing even his pilgrims of eyes, calling them back from the garden's more distant gems to those that glowed more intimately in his own unfolding hands.

They *were* unfolding.

His hands were opening at last.

He was not conscious of making any effort. Yet, one by one, his fingers were uncurling, extending, slowly, all by themselves, with a will and a motion all their own.

Nicolas caught only a glimpse of what he'd carried for so long in his clenched fists. He was lying on his back, with his arms and broken legs outstretched, and he had forced his head up, pressing his chin to his chest, watching the moving fingers of his hands as if they were not part of his body at all, as if they were some other, alien animal, quite distinct from him.

The palms, he could see, were covered with dried blood. The sharp cuts made by the tightly clenched jewels had long since healed, but their spilled blood had imparted its crimson hue to the diamonds pressed into the two fields of tender flesh. The heat and pressure of a tireless grip had fused the two together, and in those torn hands, which the boy could no longer claim as his own, lay two perfect rubies.

His heavy head, impossible to support any longer, snapped back, plopping into the wet soil.

Two scarlet halos were all that he could still see of the blood-red stones glowing in the darkness. Then even that glow faded. Once more the boy's hands seemed to be moving on their own, sinking this time, deeper and deeper into the loose soil in which they lay, until the two ruby seeds were completely buried.

His breath, coming in short gasps until then, suddenly relaxed its rhythm, slowed and deepened.

And though he lay on his back with his eyes fixed on nothing but the blackness above him, still he saw his own gray and swollen foot in front of him, he saw the wound slit open and close, open and close, like the eye of one soon to be dreaming or the lips of a whisperer of dangerous secrets.

It frightened him. As did the continued movements of his hands beneath the surface of the soil. His fingers seemed to be lengthening, tendril-like, creeping deeper and deeper, splitting and sprouting and branching off in every direction at once.

He tried to look back, to find again all those remarkable places he'd passed through on his way to this ghostly abyss, this deep and empty Garden of Jewels. But it had all fled, all but the long stairway, whose image gradually replaced that of his wounded foot in the blackness before his eyes.

It flashed across the darkness like a jagged bolt of lightning, turned to stone.

At its base the lamed black horse, its entire head encrusted with bees, one pulsing mass of buzzing insects. At its peak a lost and lonely mule, helpless, all but buried beneath the noisy burlesque of a crowd of hysterical ducks.

And between them, the bridge, of steps.

Sublime *and* ridiculous, the vision frightened and embarrassed him, and it was only the stubborn braying of the stranded mule that he was left with, in the end, when his eyes closed and then failed to reopen.

P a r t   T h r e e

THE GARDEN
OF JEWELS

CHAPTER SEVEN

Through the Torn Curtain
of Howling

"Welcome!" said the dog.

It seemed to Nicolas as if the beast's head had popped right out of his wound.

"Step right up! Step in! Come! Come! Hurry!" the dog howled as the deep blue curtain parted. "You've been so busy travelling, you've had no time to get started."

The boy felt the branch begin to give way, he paused, then inched out further, and still further.

"Excuse me, your majesty, but I was wondering which way . . ."

The Queen's eyes snapped open and at the same time there was a loud crack beneath him. Nicolas leapt at the last possible moment and found himself sailing through the tree-tops for what seemed like hours before landing, on all fours, on the far side of the towering kingdom of effort, on the threshold of the castle of deeply sleeping beauty.

On the steps of the ruined palace, what remained of the once powerful royal guard sat, ever vigilant, guarding the last of the palace treasure.

"Twenty-one cats," cried Nicolas, remembering that he had counted them. He was still busy counting their treasured rubies when one of the cats interrupted him.

"These rubies are not prisoners," the feline insisted. "They are the jewels in the Queen's crown, after it comes tumbling down."

Far below him, the stripes of the circus tents began to spin like the spokes of a wheel. "One step at a time, one step at a time," he whispered to himself, keeping his eyes locked straight ahead, trying to steady himself, to control his dizziness.

Nearly drowned out by snatches of calliope music drifting up from the tents below, he thought he heard someone urgently calling.

"Nicolaas! Nicolaaaas!"

But he was afraid to look down.

"The little, greasy orange ones, now there's a good deal," wheezed the first horned man. "For two kronen, a gruber, and a half sack of snuff I'd let you have a whole barrel of 'em."

"But the long blues," barked the second horned man, "they're a better bargain. And fresher too. Here, smell."

Nicolas recoiled in disgust at the odor. He wanted to ask the price of a pair of the red potted ones but when he tried to speak all he could make were awful squeaking and snorting sounds.

"He doesn't like the long blues," grumbled the second horned man.

"Nor the greasy orange ones," snarled the first horned man.

"What does he know?" said the second.

"What does he know?" agreed the first.

The boy's eyes never left the ferry as it approached slowly from the far bank of the river.

"I want to cross," he said, clambering aboard immediately, the little skiff rocking dangerously.

"That'll cost you," said the boatman.

It wasn't until they were in midstream that the man turned to Nicolas between strokes of his paddle and asked, "Have you made the *other* arrangements?"

"What arrangements?"

"For your return," said the man. "How is it that you'll be crossing back over when the time comes?"

Nicolas shook his head.

"I don't know."

"Ahhh," sighed the boatman, "*that* bridge," and he paddled on in silence.

"Nicolaas! Nicolaaaas!"

"But why do you bring me gifts?" asked Nicolas uneasily.
"Will you not accept them?"
The boy glared at the giftbearers mistrustfully.
"We have travelled so far."
"And for so long."
"We are your humble serpents."

Rubbing the sleep from his eyes, he marveled at the bright blues and pinks of countless blossoms, hypnotized by the flashing ripples of the cold, clear stream and the tireless wings of the darting hummingbirds.

"I have returned," he dared to whisper aloud, "I am back home, in the meadow, in the aviary."

The boy covered his eyes, gently, with one hand. The whole enchanting scene was swiftly swallowed up in darkness, vanishing like a dream. The voice of the boatman came back to him as he sat perfectly still, in deep melancholy, unable to lift his hand from his darkened eyes.

"Whitecap!"

The little bird was fluttering, frantic, its tiny wings beating against the iron bars of its cage.

"I promise I'll return for you," cried the boy, as he turned to the window and stared out at the sun, which was black as a drop of ink and growing steadily larger, threatening to engulf him completely.

Nicolas scarcely recognized his own voice.

"Beautiful black sun," he says, as the walls of the room dissolve around him and the sudden cry of a raven echoes from over the far horizon.

CHAPTER EIGHT

In the Raven's Head

There was something tapping gently against his shoulder. It sent a current of images surging through his eyes, images that vanished a moment later when the tapping had ceased.

"Where am I?"

The tapping began again, and again his eyes were filled with a beautiful violence of light, pink and blue and violet bursts and blooms, flashing fluorescent wings, cool electric water—until once more the tapping withdrew and the light subsided. Yet this time certain images persisted, echoing through his head, and he opened his eyes and his mouth in surprise, recognizing them.

"I remember now," he mumbled.

"Good," he heard a barely audible whisper behind him.

"The Garden of Jewels . . . finally I . . . did I finally . . . ?"

"Inside you will have only what you remember," the voice continued, louder and clearer now. "Nothing else will be permitted to enter with you."

241

The tapping, when it resumed this time, was firmer.

Once more the bursts of memory's light.

 "There were flowers everywhere," said the boy. "When I woke there were bright blues, bright pinks, and they were climbing . . . like . . . like a curtain of ladders trembling, blossoming. And hummingbirds stitching in and out, scarlet, violet. Oh, to have slept for so long, and then to wake in such a beautiful garden."

Nicolas turned his head just far enough and just in time to see the long blue staff as it lifted from his shoulder.

"But then—?"

His eyes opened and closed, painfully.

"But how did I—?"

Again the blue staff descended, making contact. The boy clapped one hand to his face, covered his eyes, uncovered them again quickly, covered them, uncovered them, again and again. "There's a light within everything," he marveled, "such a hungry splash of light, a spark, exploding its own shell, and the new colors all ascending, always ascending, and their heights are humming like a transparent engine of wings."

Behind him the voice was clearer than ever now.

"Like the breath escaping from a child asleep?" came the suggestion. "Like that bit of breath passed through a prism?"

"Yes," said the boy.

"Ahhh," said the Raven, withdrawing his long blue staff once more, "but we're getting ahead of ourselves—inside they will know better than I what to do with this effervescence of color."

"They've gone now," muttered the boy, "the colors have gone now . . . "

For the first time he turned his head all the way around in order to see who he was speaking with. Confronted with the red hot iron of the Raven's expressionless eye, however, he turned away again, shivering with fear. This time he remembered without the aid of the dark bird's magical blue staff.

"But I hadn't awoken at all," he cried, "it was a trick, a trap, the long bars of bright flowers were suddenly hard and black and barren, their stems rising and falling at one another, crisscrossing, tighter and tighter, weaving a cage, a room, imprisoning me . . . and . . . and . . . "

He turned once more, bravely, glaring at the Raven in distrust.

" . . . and you . . . you were there!"

"We met there, yes."

Nicolas bowed his head, closing his eyes so tightly that a thousand tiny intersecting wrinkles appeared, like a nest, around each tensed socket.

"But how did I get there," he croaked, "and how did I get here?"

"How you got there is your own affair," said the Raven, "but as for how you got here, that is quite simple. I brought you here myself."

"It was a terrible place," the boy was moaning, his eyes still clamped shut, "it was cold, and I felt sick to my stomach, standing by the only window, looking out, the sun black in the sky, like a dark round hole in the air. I tried to crack the glass of the window with my head, I did, I tried to escape. But each time my head hit the glass I went numb and couldn't feel a thing, and nothing changed, and I couldn't get out, I couldn't get out!"

He opened his eyes, emerging from the deathly cold cage of the room.

"Tell me how we got here."

"You opened the book."

"The book?"

"I had to insist."

"What book?"

"The book lying on the table, alongside—" the Raven stopped himself, "but I have said too much already."

"The book," Nicolas was mumbling, trying to remember, "the book lying alongside the . . . the . . . "

"Don't worry about it now, not now," said the Raven. "Later, inside, they will know better than I how to organize all these dark intersecting lines."

"Inside where?"

"Inside the cave."

With his blue staff and his long slender black beak, the Raven pointed to a dark doorway cut into the exposed face of a wall of rock a few yards away. Nicolas was gripped with dread, and he deliberately looked away from the dark threshold.

"What's in there?" he whispered.

"All that you can remember," explained the Raven for the second time, "and no more."

"And I must enter?" asked the boy fearfully.

"Empty-handed," intoned the Raven.

"But my . . . my . . . "

Nicolas fell silent.

For the first time since his journey had begun he could scarcely remember what it was that it was so important that he call his own. *My* swanbags, *my* ash, *my* bottle, *my* diamonds, he chanted to himself, flipping swiftly through the whole catalogue of painful transformations.

"My rubies!" he said at last, remembering. A moment later his confusion began all over again. "But where are they?"

"Do you remember them?"

"Yes, of course!"

"Then you will be able to bring them inside."

"But where . . . ?"

"Whether you can find them or not. Now, close your eyes!"

Nicolas did as he was told, so imperious was this dark bird's command. He felt the familiar tap on his shoulder, and instantly a vast rambling ruin of a stairway materialized within his eyes, its stones cracked and worn, crumbling from rubble to dust. He gasped as he caught sight of the abandoned rubies, perched on those distant steps, blood-red and glowing. And then the blue staff was lifted, shifted, until once more it pointed directly into the cave's dark mouth, which promptly swallowed up the entire stairway, engulfing it as if it had never been there at all.

Nicolas was more frightened then ever, and still refused to let his eyes, wide open now, cross the darkened threshold.

"I *must* enter?" he asked, his voice faltering.

"If you wish to be healed," was the Raven's terse reply.

The boy had forgotten all about his wound. So much had happened and in so many places so remote from his understanding that he was only gradually able to join one end of his broken path to the other, and even then there remained enormous gaps and blanks and blind spots, even then all sense of continuity seemed to have been lost forever.

"But, but I thought my legs were broken."

The Raven said nothing.

"I thought that I was dead, and buried."

Still the Raven said nothing.

"I thought that I was burning or drowning or rising or falling, that I was balanced high on a wire the width of a river in the sky, or trapped like my own image in a mirror. I thought that I was dreaming, yes, and that I had awoken back home, back in the aviary, in the meadow, in springtime, with morning glories, and hummingbirds, and . . . "

Slowly, quietly, tears began to pour from the boy's eyes.

"I thought that I had been found in a nest in a forest by a kind and wise old man who taught me how and when to fly."

For several long minutes the Raven remained still and silent, while Nicolas went on weeping.

"Inside," he whispered at last, "they will know far better than I just how to harvest all these tears."

"And the Phoenix," sighed the boy, trying to dry his eyes, "the Phoenix whose feathers are a deep purple, perhaps, and whose neck is perhaps golden, whose head is perhaps crowned with an exquisite crest . . . "

"Perhaps," agreed the Raven.

"The Phoenix," the boy sighed on, "a single one of whose feathers is, perhaps, the only medicine for all passion and all pain . . . "

"And all sorrow," concluded the Raven.

"I thought, I dreamed, that I was searching for such a fabulous bird."

"And indeed you are," whispered the Raven, in earnest, "indeed you are."

Nicolas made up his mind, then and there, to enter the cave, and, raising his head, he fixed his eyes directly upon the dark gateway cut into the stone, staring intently.

"The eyes alone can never pierce the veil," insisted the Raven.

"I must enter," vowed the boy.

"Yes."

Immediately the darkness in the depths of the entryway began to stir, to open. "Who's that?" asked the boy abruptly.

From out of the cave a figure had emerged into the bright light and stood staring now in his direction, shading his eyes from the glare of the sun.

"They're waiting for you," was all the Raven would say.

Nicolas watched as the figure before the cave turned, like a sentry, and began to reenter the shadows. Though he'd scarcely felt the single tap of the blue staff against his stooped shoulder, it had nonetheless already worked its magic deep within his eyes. "Wings," he cried aloud, catching sight, just before the sentry vanished, of the tips of a pair of folded wings dragging along the ground behind him, brushing his heels as he vanished into the cave.

"I've . . . I've seen him before . . . but before he was . . . " The boy's perplexity was increased still further by a pair of objects he caught sight of on the ground beside him. "And what are these?" he mumbled.

"Your luggage," said the Raven.

"But they're like buildings," marveled the boy, looking more closely, "like tiny buildings."

Suddenly he gasped.

"You have a powerful memory," explained the Raven, before the boy's speechless surprise could subside.

Nicolas gazed in wonder at the miniature swan coops beside him, accurate in every detail, right down to the doorways through which he and the old man had passed countless times.

"It will be of great value to you, inside, this powerful memory. You will be healed deeply."

"I can bring them with me?" begged Nicolas, still not understanding, still reaching out with his hands.

"You already have," the Raven assured him, at the same time firmly pushing the boy's hands away with the tip of his long powerful staff.

Nicolas turned away in dismay.

"Who are they?" he asked, indicating two men he now noticed behind him, one mounted on a horse and the other perched on a low stool beside him, both of them busy as if with preparations for a journey.

"The wounded or the healed," said the Raven simply, "we go by no other names here."

Nicolas twisted around to study the two men more closely.

"The man astride the horse lost an eye in a fight with a thief in the night," explained the Raven, "and has been looking for something ever since." The boy said nothing as he stared at the crimson bandage angled across the man's expressionless face. "The other man is a singer, and a deaf-mute."

"But how can he possibly—?"

"And you," interrupted the Raven, "you are a lamed pilgrim, are you not, a cripple forever walking?"

Nicolas dropped his eyes to his own wound. At some point in time, he couldn't imagine when or where, it had been rebandaged, but the tight white linen with which it was bound could scarcely hide the foul-smelling blood that seeped through its folds and stained the cloth with its poison.

"Can you stand?"

"I think so," said the boy.

"You must leave the crutches behind," the Raven reminded him, "you must enter empty-handed."

"But where did they come from?" Nicolas had not even been aware of the fact that, though he was kneeling, he was still leaning forward against the two sturdy crutches for support.

"I don't know where they came from," confessed the Raven, "but inside they will be far more able than I to offer the proper thanksgiving for all of these inexplicable gifts of the moment."

Attempting to rise, Nicolas began to tip backward, but the Raven was behind him, catching him as he fell. The boy could feel the bird's dark, shiny feathers brush against his skin. They were cold and sent a shiver down his spine.

He felt the bird's dark wings begin to enfold him.

He felt himself begin to rise into the air.

"No," he said, pulling away, and almost stumbling, "I will not be carried."

His breath came in short sharp gusts.

"I will walk," he proclaimed.

And the Raven nodded, and might even have smiled had its beak been built to bend and curve in that direction, had its muscles been more highly adapted to the acrobatics of sentiment. As it was, the bird merely stood looking on, silent as the grave, while the boy rose to his feet, and, tottering, discarded first his crutches and then his clothes.

"Empty," he whispered.

One step at a time, the Pilgrim crossed the little expanse of turf that separated him from the mouth of the cave, the Raven following right behind, hovering close with his staff but not touching him. Only at the last moment, as the shadows began to fall across the naked boy, clothing him in the blackness of the tomb, only then did the Raven intercede, tapping one shoulder one last time—a single tap that coincided with the sound of the swan coop door, which admitted the boy, and his dreams, and then slammed shut— leaving nothing behind it but a rough hole hollowed out in a wall of solid stone.

"Don't dawdle, young man."

The darkness, inside, lasted only for an instant.

"Come, come, don't just stand there gawking, there'll be plenty of time to look around once we've set to work."

The interior of the cave was suddenly flooded with a light so bright it dazzled the boy's eyes. Before he could focus, there were hands gripping him, grasping and guiding. And voices.

"Move him over a little, to the right."

"Here?"

"Yes, thaaaat's better, much better."

Someone was tugging at the cloth wrapped around his foot.

"Now, you see? Isn't that more comfortable?"

Nicolas couldn't answer, and didn't even know if the question was addressed to him anyway.

"Oh, dear, will you look at that . . . "

"Shall I burn the linen?"

"Definitely—but soak it first, and then separate the waters."

He reached up, groping for his eyes, rubbing them.

"Now hold his leg."

"Like that?"

"Yes, but tightly, try to keep it still."

The first thing that emerged from the fanfare of shapes and colors was the doorway through which he had entered. For a moment it hung in front of his face like a bright picture on a dark wall, a portrait of the daylight he had left behind, its faded greens and lost yellows tinged with an inevitable sadness. Expecting to see the Raven standing at the threshhold, right where he'd left him, Nicolas was amazed by the presence, instead, of a white horse.

"My horse!" he cried out.

"This may hurt."

"But it's my horse, it has returned at last, it has come to—" a sharp and sudden stab of pain cut the boy short. "Owwwwww!"

Glaring down at his foot, he saw, for a moment, only a broad feathery blur of blue. In the next moment, a moment of focus, there appeared the head of a bird, enormous, a bird with bright blue feathers and bright lavender arms where its wings should have been, a bird in a wide puffy skirt that seemed to be stained at regular intervals by crushed strawberries, a bird with dark moist eyes and a pale orange beak from which dangled one long wriggling worm. With a shock, Nicolas realized that the worm had just been plucked, by this strange bird, from the poisonous depths of his wound.

He stared into the bird's glistening eye as it tossed its head back, flipping the worm all the way into its mouth and swallowing.

"The early bird always gets it," she chirped, "first come, first served."

The boy's jaw dropped.

"And you, you'll catch nothing but flies that way."

Nicolas closed his mouth so fast that his teeth clacked.

"Allow me to introduce myself," said the big blue bird, "I'm Beryl. And this is the Bear."

Nicolas turned his head slowly, until he was face to face with a big brown bear in a yellow tunic that stared back at him quizzically, yet with an eye far kinder than the eye of the brisk blue bird, who, even as she spoke, reached out to lift a sharp, lethal-looking instrument from a nearby tabletop.

"Everyone else you already know," she chirped, and made a swift incision in his left foot just above the shin.

"Ouch!" cried the boy, and turned, instinctively, to the Bear, who smiled slightly, and nodded, patting him gently with one large flat paw.

"What do you mean, everyone else?" Nicolas managed to croak.

"Your horse, for instance," mumbled Beryl, busy cleaning her sharp surgical steel.

"Yes, my horse," sighed the boy, and turned his eager eyes back to where the white horse still stood, motionless, gazing inside.

"But where is the Raven, what happened to—"

"The black becomes white, the white becomes black," the bird was humming to herself.

"Do you mean that—?"

"And then there's your shadow," she added, changing tools.

Nicolas inhaled swiftly as his gaze met that of his hidden companion, who stood, facing him at last, in the middle of the cave, in the halo of light cast by his outspread wings, each feather of which was aglow with the quiet color seeping in through the adjacent doorway, each a pale private fire of reflected daylight. Though the strange boy's complexion seemed still dim and dark, in stark contrast to his illuminated wings, this time Nicolas was reminded, not of ash, but rather of dust, the tiny particles of dust hidden in a ray of sunlight, particles that, just like this shadow-boy's body, might suddenly, as the light shifted, erupt in brilliance and bright form.

"You have to understand something." Once more Beryl's sharp steel prepared to stab into the boy's tender flesh. "Something about color . . ."

"Owww!"

" . . . about its transformations . . ."

"Owwwwww!"

This time she was scraping at his skin with what looked like a tiny brass fork.

" . . . transformations that are nothing if not continuous."

"You're hurting me," whimpered the boy.

"According to *all* the Philosophers, *without* exception—once it has begun, the suffering must continue on to its natural end," insisted the blue bird, raising the instrument of torture in her right hand. "Otherwise all is lost, all is squandered, all is but waste."

The Bear's broad brown paw went on patting his leg, strong, yet gentle. "You must have patience with Miss Beryl," he whispered into the boy's ear, speaking for the first time, "and you must trust her." The Bear leaned in closer and closer, until Nicolas could feel the warm sticky moisture of its nose pressed right up against his cheek. "You *must* trust her, for there is no wiser Mistress of the Art than she."

Another sharp jab caused the boy to howl in pain. The howl echoed through the cave, as if the walls of the chamber were howling right back at him.

"Nature may be assisted, even accelerated," proclaimed his strange surgeon, raising her voice above the howling echo, "but never, never outwitted, never omitted."

The Bear whispered once again in the boy's ear, "Of course I'll admit that her bedside manner leaves something, well, something to be desired."

Looking down, Nicolas could see that he was indeed resting on a bed or cot of some sort, propped up against a cushion or two with his legs stretched out, exposed and defenseless, in front of him.

"Is she a doctor?" whispered the boy.

The Bear nodded.

"We shall need nine incisions, ten all together, counting the wound itself," Beryl was explaining.

But Nicolas was no longer really listening. He'd begun to feel painfully dizzy and had been forced to close his eyes for a moment—surprised to find, once he'd reopened them, that his entire leg, all the way up to the knee, had turned a deep shade of blue.

"There's something else you need to understand," Beryl began, sharpening the tool in her hand as she spoke, "something else about the colors—"

"There was a dog!" Nicolas suddenly blurted out, interrupting.

"Mmmm-hmm," grunted Beryl.

And then stabbed once more.

Again Nicolas howled.

And two more times, in quick succession, the knife or needle entered his flesh.

"The Hound," said Beryl, counting the tears in the boy's flesh at the same time, "six, seven, eight . . . this next one will do it . . . "

"Oooooooooowww!"

"There," said Beryl, her sharp tool clattering down on the marble tabletop, "*now* you may enter."

Nicolas was staring down at the blued flesh of his leg in alarm. It seemed to be swelling right before his eyes, each tiny incision itching and stinging, oozing a drop or two of bright red blood.

"But remember," warned the bird, "when you enter, it is not *he* that is howling, don't make that mistake. In the end it isn't the Hound that howls, but you, for it is you, the Philosophers agree unanimously, who gives the Hound his voice."

"Now I remember . . . " mumbled the boy.

"Well, then, get on with it," insisted Beryl.

"It wasn't until I'd passed *through*, and turned back to look at him, that I realized he was the same dog, the dog who'd always sat quietly beside the Queen and the gateway of dream. But the howling had stopped by then. Once I stood on the other side everything grew silent, and it was in that silence that I recognized him, when I turned around—"

"Yes, of course, of course," Beryl interrupted him, "but you are moving too fast, you are rushing the passage. According to the Philosophers it is when we are between, neither on one side nor the other, it is then when we are most likely to effect a true transformation. So it is the actual entering I'd have you recall and not all these *this sides* and *that sides*, aghh, you pilgrims with your destinations, they won't hold water here, not for a moment, now go back outside and enter again and this time tell me what you see during the act of migration."

Nicolas gazed down at his wound, already exhausted by the effort of recollection.

"I want you to feel the color of everything," concluded Beryl.

Nicolas said nothing.

"Here, let me help you."

She produced a small torch and held it so that its beam of bright white light fell directly onto the boy's blue foot, illuminating the pink slit of his wound, isolating it from the other smaller incisions with which it was now surrounded, thanks to Miss Beryl's Harsh Art.

"Was it a curtain?" the boy wondered aloud.

"It was the Thin Blue Skin of the Apprentice while he was staring up at the sky," prompted Beryl.

"But . . . but that was me. I was the boy staring up at the sky . . . straight up . . . " Nicolas began to speak, haltingly at first. And then he went on, speaking faster and faster, gaining momentum, until his own words seemed to make less and less sense to him, and to make less and less sense of what he realized more and more vividly had been a dream, the beginning of a long dream.

"I'm a boy . . . a boy flying a kite . . . through the smooth dry folds of blue that brush up against me on both sides on all sides like cold papers of snow hammered by a deepening night-weight in which violets bloom as they dissolve."

"Beautiful," said the Bear.

"Beautiful," agreed Beryl, "now into the breach."

Nicolas spoke as one hypnotized.

"Red fountain of life raising cliffs of sponge," he said.

"Inner ear of the king's last ruby melting," he said.

And then he said, "She was blue, so blue, the starfish, unbearably blue, but overturned beneath the surface the bright muscle of her underbelly exposed a million pink shallow embraces unexpectedly prolonged, a whirlpool of arterial wells yielding warmth."

"Ohh, I've got goosebumps," chirped Miss Beryl.

There was a long silence.

"What's going on?" asked the boy, as if he had just awoken.

"You have released them," said Beryl, indicating the brood of small black birds that had sprung up like frantic seedlings in front of the Bear, whose strong soft arms encircled them.

"I have?"

"Well, I'll admit that things are a little out of control, but there's a time and place for everything, or so the Philosophers joke in private, and every action provokes a reaction, every entry an emergence, no matter how hard they are to pair up later. After all, if your shadow can arise from a fragment of blue eggshell heedlessly discarded over your shoulder, then certainly four baby black swans can emerge through a torn blue curtain rustled by the passing breath of poetry."

Nicolas could only follow about half of what Beryl was saying, and he told her so.

"Well, if you like we can move on to lines now, which can be explained, but mind you that does *not* mean that we will leave colors behind, not at all, for a change in color, even a slight one, can crucially alter any angle of intersection and throw off even the most seasoned of calculations."

"Lines?" mumbled the boy, following her only so far.

"Lines! Lines! Yes!"

Beryl's wide purple hands flailed as she spoke, drawing invisible figures in the air.

"Like the lines on your palms or the stripes of the circus tents! Lines! Long straight connectors and conductors, the marks on your maps to treasure, the consecutive steps of your endless flights of stairs! Your ropes, your roads, your rules!"

Dipping one finger into a jar of sticky red paste, Beryl quickly reached out and painted a simple linear pattern on the bare skin of the boy's torso.

"Lines," echoed the boy, thinking along them.

"Yes, lines to weave with, lines to climb, lines to cross, outlines, horizon lines,

waistlines, straight lines, curved lines. . . ."

"I was balanced on a line, far above the circus, far above the earth," Nicolas began to stutter, "but I was in two places, I was in both places, I was up *and* down, I saw myself below myself, far below, with a different long thin line gripped in both my hands."

"Parallel lines," explained Beryl.

"And the worm! There was a worm just like the one you tore from my foot."

"Living lines," explained Beryl.

Something suddenly clouded the boy's brow.

"Can a line, well, can a line be . . . be coiled?"

"Like the precision of a serpent, yes."

"Then—?"

"Yes, Nicolas, you were bitten by a certain line."

The boy spoke slowly now, and with tremendous effort.

"And I have been traveling along another one."

"Bravo!" cried Beryl, clapping her extravagantly purple hands together with a loud smack.

"Bravo," whispered the Bear at the same time.

"Ahh, how I love the long strong bare lines of trees on a cold morning," purred the Mistress of the Suddenly Soothing Art, "they are branching tributaries of a frozen river flowing toward a zenith of sky."

"There were cats in those trees," said Nicolas.

"Yes?"

"Yes, I remember, because I counted them, yes, there were twenty-one cats, most of them stretched right out along the branches."

Beryl waited patiently for Nicolas to fall into the colors *between* the branches of the trees. It did not take him long.

"Look!" he cried out, pointing.

The Queen of All the Shepherds was staring right at him. She hovered like a cloud or a castle in the air, just beyond the trees, veiled by their branches. "And she is crowned," cried the boy, "at last the Queen is crowned—or at least I thought she was, until I realized that her crown was not . . . not a thing, but . . . but . . . actually a place."

"A place where you have already been," whispered the Bear.

"How did I get there?"

"It doesn't matter," said Beryl, "just go there."

Nicolas let his eyes see both the crown atop the Queen's head and the temple that arose from the hilltop directly behind her.

"If I could climb onto the top of her head, and stand on my toes," he reasoned, "then perhaps I would at least be able to see over the crest and into the interior of the temple."

"Sight lines," explained Beryl, "lines of approach."

"But how . . . ?"

"Did you ever see a cat walk the line?"

"I'm not sure," said the boy.

"Cat lines," Beryl explained. "You really must study them, so silent and smooth, lean as a breeze, and as supple—a quick, steady tapering and a sudden flare, then nothing, stillness, perhaps for centuries, and finally a single soft step, perfectly on course."

She stared at him in silence.

"Become a cat," she said finally, with a casual shrug.

"That black one there," suggested the Bear.

 Nicolas stared at the blackest cat of his dream, all four of its legs fully extended, its body stretched out along one vertical length of tree trunk, close enough to the shoulder of the Queen to jump and land safely if and when the time came.

"And from her shoulder to the top of her head," calculated Beryl, as if able to read the boy's thoughts, "is such a negligible distance for one, like you, who's already traveled so far."

"What is that?" asked Nicolas, referring to the object Beryl had just plucked from a nearby shelf.

"A bone," she answered.

Once more she stuck her finger into the red paste, this time tracing out the arcs of the boy's ribs with her simple paintbrush.

"Internal lines," she explained, "bones."

"It has a hole in it," said the boy, pointing to the bone.

"For the Bear's Breath," said Beryl.

The Bear nodded.

"Are you ready?" asked the Mysterious Mistress of the Metamorphic Art, wiping her finger on her skirt, adding a fresh red stain to the many already there.

"Yes," both boy and beast answered at the same time.

The Bear had already shifted position, his brood of baby black swans momentarily regrouping. He was crouched down now over the boy's infected foot, as Beryl handed him the carefully designed instrument. Placing it in front of his snout, he leaned in closer and exhaled through the hole in its center several times. Nicolas could feel the Bear's Breath that passed through the bone. It was hot, and it tingled as it touched the edges of his wound.

A sudden stretch and reach of the muscles in his hips and his shoulders forced a sigh of physical exhilaration from the boy. He arched his back and blinked. He saw, in a strange flickering green light, the features of the Queen, magnified, sliding right by him, like an unmoored reflection drifting by on the surface of a swift moving stream. Then beneath him there was only blackness, the black of her hair merging with the black of his fur, indistinguishable. A soft, low, intoxicating vibration began to rise up from deep in the heart of his throat. He blinked again, and again—each time the whole world burst like a bubble before his eyes.

Curled up contentedly, purring black on black, it was an hour, perhaps longer, perhaps much longer, before he bothered to remember why he'd come.

Finally he roused himself, yawning.

And stretched.

Up.

Poised atop the head of the Queen like a dark living crown, like a bolt of sleepy black lightning returning quietly to the sky—from the crest of such a dark and royal wave—he was indeed able to pierce the veil of the temple on the hilltop and gaze deep inside with his sharp, sleepy eyes.

"Well?" was all Beryl said.

"My rubies," said the black cat.

The vast ruined stairway that materialized within the boy's cat's eye tumbled from high to low or from low to high—but the lines of its old stone steps remained bound one to another, one after the other, like the pages of a book.

"Lines, or angles, of ascent or descent," explained Beryl.

But the black cat wasn't listening and was possessed by its own private geometry anyway, a geometry apparently taught right inside the sacred precincts of the temple itself, there on its ruined terraces and across its written-in-stone slopes. Like lazily rebellious musical notes that have drifted idly from their duly assigned lines on the staff, there were cats strewn every which way on the temple-stair, making a gentle mockery of its melody, deflecting the permanent order of its steps. And there was a stream of water as well, water whose restless cascade of colors Beryl had already warned could so easily alter angles and render approximate each and every act of calculation.

"The Priestesses are out exercising their rubies in the cool ruined air," remarked the Bear with obvious delight.

"There's more than two," the boy meowed, confused by so many rubies, "there are others . . . "

"Oh yes, there's hundreds, thousands, perhaps. Why, they say the temple adepts tend the largest herd of rubies in the underworld, rubies more plentiful than there are seeds in up to a million pomegranates."

The rubies, thought Nicolas, are not mine at all, but rather the jewels in the Queen's crown.

He'd begun, gently, to ease his way back out of the black cat, and it was while he was caught in between, half-cat and half-boy, that Beryl began to speak. It *was* her voice, he was sure of that, and yet it seemed to come from so far away, from somewhere deep within the temple's inner walls. As she spoke, every one of the cats turned toward the source of the sound of her words and sat, serenely, staring.

"At the foot of the stairs you lie wounded and asleep, wretched and dreaming. The burning path of venom has blazed a trail for you through painful thicket, baleful bramble. Everything is born from a wound. When you awake the Green Lion must walk without its feet, and you must sacrifice to the Crowned Ape. No food for three days, and on the fourth day eat nothing but the last pinch of salt. And you should, according to the Philosophers, drink plenty of fluids. Pay at each gate. Next!"

Nicolas found himself deposited abruptly back on his bed.

He had the distinct impression that he'd surprised Beryl somehow, interrupted her. She seemed self-conscious, as if she were trying to conceal something. He became convinced that she had been inserting something into his foot.

"Back so soon," she said.

There was an unmistakable tone of sarcasm in her voice.

"How long was I gone?" asked the boy.

"Twelve hours," whispered the Bear.

"Quite a catnap," chirped Beryl.

"What did you put in my wound?" he confronted her.

"Eggs," said Beryl.

"Seeds," whispered the Bear.

"What you don't seem to realize is that we have turned your wound into one big incubator."

Nicolas pictured the large white-washed incubators back in the aviary, with their dozens of tiny drawers and cramped compartments full of high-pitched peeps and squeaks of hunger. He looked down at his blue swollen leg.

"I don't know what you're talking about," he said.

"Well, there's a lot of things you don't know," drawled Beryl, teasing out each word. "For instance, I'll bet that you don't know, hmmm, let me see . . . ah, what would you say if I told you that I knew the old man?"

"What!"

"I knew him quite well, actually."

Nicolas was sure he'd misunderstood.

"Old Gillam," she mused, "it was he who made this skirt for me. Why, I'm surprised you don't recognize his workmanship. Didn't you once own a similarly berried pair of yellow slippers, Nicolas?"

The boy was speechless.

"Intersecting lines," sighed Beryl, "ahhh, yes. You know certain of the most ancient Philosophers claimed that *all* lines *do* eventually intersect. But only the eye of the needle, they said, holding to the golden thread of their sacred science, truly sees the weaving of *that* world."

The entire cave seemed suddenly to crowd in around the boy, swirling like memory at its most violent.

"Intersecting lines," repeated Beryl.

"I didn't notice before," Nicolas mumbled in shock, when he spied the Urn of Blue Powder, then the bowl of cracked blue eggshells waiting for the mortar and the pestle, and those hollow wicker frames—were they bird cages? were they flying machines? and weren't those the tiny ribs of the meadowlark? Such an intimate jumble of jars and baskets, of basins and bottles and boxes! His head continued to spin as object after object became entangled in the web of recollection.

"King!" he cried out, "and Queen!"

Catching sight of the two swans convinced him, beyond all doubt, that he was indeed back home, back inside the old swan coop, back inside the old man's private laboratory. As he watched the slow, stately gestures of the two elegant swans, he found himself sliding back into the warmth of an afternoon spent wandering along the lush green banks of a long, lost lake. He couldn't help but smile to himself, remembering. And yet, at the same time, remembering, he couldn't help but cry.

"Uh-oh," said Beryl, "time for the harvest already."

"What are you talking about," snapped the boy, tears streaming down his cheeks, "why didn't you tell me—?"

"I'm telling you now. I've done nothing but tell you."

"Then tell me how I got here! How did I get back?"

"Understanding the colors," said Beryl, trying to stay calm.

"Why didn't you tell me where I—?"

"Then explaining the intersecting lines," she took one deep breath, "or at least trying to."

"And where is Old Gillam?" sobbed the boy, "Where—?"

"And now, so soon," chirped Beryl, "the harvest."

"Where?" shouted the boy, "Where? Where?"

"Look, we still have a few more lines to go here, but we can do a quick weave, if you cooperate, and then you can grieve to your heart's content. But we do not want the harvest to be premature."

Nicolas was breathing heavily, but he'd stopped shouting and was listening once again.

"Let's try a little question and answer," suggested Beryl. She turned to the Bear, and said, urgently, "Get the bowl!"

The Bear hurried across the cave, or the coop, returning with a wide glass bowl.

"Polish it," said Beryl.

The Bear did as he was told.

"Now concentrate," Beryl said to Nicolas, passing him the bowl at the same time, placing it in his hands and positioning it beneath his chin. The first one of many tears to come splashed and streaked down the curved glass, falling right on target.

"Now don't move," Beryl insisted.

She cleared her throat.

"*Question*: What did the Queen of All the Shepherds tell you when you asked her for directions?"

Nicolas did not answer.

"You did ask her for directions?"

"I always ask her for directions," said the boy, his lips pressed tightly against each word as he uttered it.

"Well then, what did she say—this time, in your dream?"

He was trying to remember.

"*Question*: Where did you tell her you wanted to go?"

A terrible struggle was going on inside the Pilgrim, dragging him in two different directions at once, pulling him apart.

"*Question*: Did you seek directions to the Phoenix? Is that what you asked her?"

"I . . . I . . ."

"Is that what you asked her?"

"I . . ."

"*Question*: Where were you headed?"

"She . . . she told me . . ."

"*Question*: Where were you sent?"

"She . . . she . . . she t-told me that I must cross the river!" Nicolas blurted out at last.

"The dividing line," explained Beryl.

Already enough tears had been shed to form a small pool in the bottom of the bowl, which was trembling in the boy's hands.

"But . . . but . . . with what will you pay the boatman?" asked Nicolas.

"Excuse me?" said Beryl.

"She said I must pay the man on the boat, the man on the shore, the man with the poles and the oars."

"Ah, yes," said Beryl, "lines of exchange."

"But I have nothing, nothing, not even . . . "

"So she sent you to the marketplace."

"How did you know?"

"It's a well-traveled route," explained Beryl, "a familiar line."

"I tried to choose wisely," swore Nicolas.

"But beyond that door there were nothing but pigs." Nicolas was indignant.

"No, I mean, yes—"

"Yes, pigs!" Beryl was laughing.

"It's not funny!" shouted Nicolas.

"No Bear's Breath and Bone needed for that transformation," she cackled, but her laughter stopped suddenly when she noticed the dangerous tilt of the bowl in the boy's hands.

"Be careful!" she and the Bear shouted simultaneously.

"And that awful smell," the boy was whining, oblivious to the warning, "the smell of death, things dead and decaying."

"Be careful!" Beryl cried again, louder, reprimanding him. "You must hold the bowl in position, at all times! No sorrows will be wasted here, not in *my* laboratory."

"I don't remember anything else," snapped the boy.

"Don't sulk," the bird snapped right back.

"And besides," he huffed and puffed, "why must I return to all these places, why must I go back when I want to go on? How else will I ever reach the fabulous Phoenix?"

The boy fell silent for a moment.

"Why do you keep turning me around?" he demanded to know.

"*The Question!*" cried Beryl, exultant.

"Good question," whispered the Bear at the same time.

"Now," said Beryl, rubbing her hands together, "how about the rope?"

"The rope?"

"The tightrope high above the tops of the pleasure tents," teased the Mistress of the Reversible Art, "which side of the river is that on?"

Nicolas was terribly confused.

"On that side, no, on the other side, on . . . I . . . "

"*Question*," boomed Beryl. "In which direction do you walk the rope?"

"I . . . or . . . "

"Nicolas," she said, lowering her voice suddenly, looking deep into his eyes, curling her hands around his, helping him to bear the burden of the bowl rapidly filling with tears, "Nicolas, even the most ancient Philosophers are vexingly contradictory on this point, and age after age, the harder we apply ourselves to its study, the more perplexed we become."

"It's true," whispered the Bear.

"Listen," said Beryl, and she began to read, with the aid of an enormous magnifying glass, from a book that was far too heavy to lift from the floor at her feet, "*. . . and thus faced as we are once again, with the problem of the opposites, we say but this, that each line arrives only as its own return. And then we blow out the candle, and fall silent. Sometimes for minutes. Sometimes for millennia. We are the most ancient Philosophers.*"

Nicolas was staring down into the bowl, into the pool of tears, which had grown just large enough to capture his reflection.

"In other words, every line leads in two directions at once," came a whisper.

Beryl looked down her beak at the Bear.

"And you would presume to paraphrase the Philosophers?"

"Ohh, yes," said the Bear, "as often as I can."

And then he executed a quick, comical curtsy.

A moment of stiff shock swiftly gave way to delight as the customary reserve maintained by the Mistress of the Masks of the Art gave way like a dam, burst by a flood of warm and contagious laughter.

"Ohhh, you are truly the wisest of the wise old circus bears," she proclaimed, slapping him on the back. The Bear was grinning from ear to ear—happy to be back in the ring again, still up to his old tricks.

"But we've forgotten all about our patient," said Beryl, trying to recover her composure, "here we are laughing while he sits and weeps."

It was a contradiction Nicolas did not need to have pointed out to him. Slumped down on his increasingly uncomfortable cot, collecting his tears in the glass bowl, listening to their laughter, he had already decided, once and for all, that he was *the* most miserable of creatures.

"Now, now, where were we?" said Beryl, still chuckling.

"Or where *are* we?" snapped the boy.

"Now don't get testy with me, young man. You can walk right out of here anytime you want."

She gave his swollen blue foot a quick pinch.

"Oowwwww!"

"And we'll see how far you get," she muttered under her breath.

Nicolas hung his head and said nothing.

"I am only trying to give you some sense of direction," explained Beryl.

Nicolas looked up but still said nothing.

The Bear cleared his throat and tapped the petulant boy on the shoulder.

"In other words," he said, speaking slowly and clearly, "every line, as well as every *road,* runs in two directions at once."

Nicolas opened his eyes wide, and then wider.

"She sent me back," he mumbled to himself.

"What was that?"

"She sent me back," repeated the boy, more emphatically, his voice filling with amazement.

Beryl seemed to be holding her breath.

"I asked her to tell me the way to the Phoenix, and she sent me back, back to the aviary, back here to the swan coop, to—"

Nicolas interrupted himself.

"Have I been deceived?" he asked.

"No . . . no . . . " Beryl hemmed and hawed, "that's not really possible in a dream . . . "

She paused to think.

"According to certain of the Philosophers," she said at last, "deception is indispensable so long as we are to remain in the operating theater. There are even instructions in certain of their books for the manufacture of a complicated mechanical rose that spits at, and sometimes even bites, the hapless gardener who by chance or design draws too near to its great beauty."

She paused, as if listening to the laughter of the Philosophers echoing through the distant ages of burlesque.

"And," she went on at last, almost smiling, "among those adepts who wrote exclusively on the nature of the sacrifice, there were those who insisted that the first sacrifice must always be the Truth, the known Truth."

"Why?" asked Nicolas.

"For Nature loves to hide," said Beryl, "and beginning from Nature as we do, we must thus begin with what is hidden—we must turn the known truth around by a subtle manipulation of the chemicals, or a contradiction in terms."

Beryl looked the boy directly in the eye.

"Or, when all else fails, by a rude practical joke, or a lie."

The Bear suddenly cried out, distorting his voice into the high silly squeak of a master of the art of vaudeville, at the same time crossing his arms exaggeratedly across his chest and pointing in two different directions at once. "Whichwaydidhego?" he howled.

"I dunno," squawked Beryl, joining in the charade.

But no one laughed.

"I just don't know," said Beryl, her tone deadly serious once again.

"And I don't know either," whispered the Bear.

"You see it is precisely such a simple *I don't know* with which we must, according to the Philosophers, begin the great work." Beryl sighed so deeply that the walls of the cave seemed to breathe in and out along with her. "Still anyone who deserves to be called a Philosopher at all," she admitted, "would have to agree that of all the deceptions, it is the linear deception that is surely the most excruciating, involving, as it invariably does, such a massive displacement of momentum. Such turnarounds can prove catastrophic and would certainly be avoided at all costs, were they not absolutely necessary, Nicolas."

Nicolas sighed, hoping that the worst was over.

"Feel free to weep now," said Beryl softly, "you may certainly weep now for as long as you like." And that is just what Nicolas did, filling bowl after bowl with his tears, bowls the Bear dutifully emptied and replaced, pouring their contents into a large copper kettle beneath which Beryl was busy building a fire.

Nicolas smelled the smoke and then saw the flame. Not long afterward he heard the low rumble and hiss of the tears in the kettle as they were brought to a boil. Soon an enormous cloud of steam appeared in the air above the seething cauldron. He watched carefully and quietly as Beryl and the Bear affixed a concave metal hood in place above the kettle, which intercepted the evaporating tears as they rose up and up and up. They condensed against its curved copper heaven and clung there for as long as they could, until their returning weight caused them to fall back once again into the sea of sorrow still boiling furiously below.

Nicolas looked down into his bowl, staring at the surface of the pool of fallen tears.

Nicolas looked up again at the steam of tears rising and condensing high above the fiery depths of the kettle.

He looked down again.

And then up.

Then down.

Up.

Down.

Up.

"The Harvest of Infinite Tears," announced Beryl, sensing the boy's fascination with the vertical apparatus of this crying game.

The Bear lifted the bowl from the boy's hands and emptied it into the kettle, quickly replacing it.

"So now we know that you were turned around in your dream," said Beryl.

"Or that I am still turning around, around and around, in my dreams," suggested the boy.

"We know now that every dream returns through its future," concluded Beryl.

"And that all nostalgia is heaven bent," whispered the Bear.

Nicolas looked up sharply.

"But that is just what—"

"Sssshhhh," said the Bear.

"That's just what he used to say about the—"

"Ssssshhh," said Beryl.

"Is something wrong?" asked Nicolas, concerned.

Both of them were crouched down beside the kettle, leaning in as close as the heat would allow, as if listening for something.

For several minutes no one spoke. Or, rather, no matter how many times Nicolas tried to speak, he was hushed immediately.

"What are you—?"

"Sssshhhhh."

"Listen."

"But what should I—?"

"Sssshhhhh."

"Listen."

Each of his questions met with the same response.

Until he gave up entirely and just sat, silent.

It remained so quiet for so long that the boy became conscious of certain sounds he hadn't noticed before. There was the sound of tears falling—ringing, like coins tossed into a well, each one singing as it struck the rim of the glass bowl or the surface of the pool. There was the dull thunder of the tears boiling. And there was the hiss, as well, of steam rising, and then another, heavier hiss, of steam cooling, and then falling—falling back to the sound of tears falling once again. All these sounds were mixed up with the waves of his own labored breathing, with the crackle of the fire, with the occasional "Ssshhhh" of the two mysterious technicians crouched down beside the kettle, regulating the heat.

Suddenly, quietly, Nicolas whispered.

"I hear it."

Both Beryl and the Bear nodded emphatically, ecstatically, at the same time bringing their fingers up to their lips, urgently demanding silence.

"The swan song," said Nicolas, "I hear it . . . I hear it . . . "

Time seemed to stand still and rush by at the same moment.

It was as if he stood face to face with his own reflection, as if each of them took a step forward, passing right through one another, like planes of light. Each then found themselves standing face to face with themselves once again, for there were an infinite number of mirrors and thus an infinite number of selves, as in the depths of a diamond where reflection embraces reflection in a world without end.

For a moment, Nicolas had a vivid impression of sunlight flashing upon water, of bright lines etched in the still surface of a lake, of the crystallizing ripples left by the graceful glide of a disappearing swan. For a single heartbeat its feathers blazed with the clearest of fires, burning with a slow silver glare.

"Argent," called the boy.

Then darkness.

And the next thing he knew Beryl was shaking him by the shoulders, as if awakening him. The fire under the cauldron had been extinguished, the bowl in his hands had been set aside. Reaching up to touch his face, he found that his tears had ceased flowing, that his cheeks were dry as dust.

"Time to bring the harvest to market," said Beryl.

Nicolas looked down and was surprised to see that his leg was no longer blue. It had been wrapped in some sort of thin silver foil.

"What's on my foot?"

"Never mind." Beryl grabbed his hand. "Here," she said, and placed something into his open palm.

Nicolas looked closely at the little pile of white granules.

He looked up at Beryl, then at the Bear.

"What is it?"

"It's the first pinch of salt."

"Salt?"

"The prescribed tribute of tears," explained Beryl, "minus all that messy moisture. With it you can return to the marketplace, and there you will at last be able to purchase the blue coin with which to pay the boatman."

"The boatman?"

"Don't tell me you've forgotten already?" fretted the Mistress of the Art of Embarkation. "The boatman! The man with the long poles and the oars."

Nicolas remembered now but grew somewhat reluctant when he remembered, as well, the terrible odor of the marketplace, and the unfortunate condition in which he'd found himself on his last visit.

"Must I return *there?*" he moaned.

And despite his fervent hopes that the worst was already over, it was precisely *there* that he soon found himself, right back in that stinking square, standing once more in front of the foul worthless wares of the rude little horned men.

"Speak up," barked one all in black, "speak up or I'll sew your lips shut once and for all with a needle and sharp thread of red ants."

Nicolas shivered with fear, taking the threat quite seriously, but found he could not utter a word—for no matter how hard he tried to speak, all he managed to do was snort, like a pig.

Everyone laughed without smiling. The whole square erupted in a mirthless cackling. And then, without warning, something struck him on the side of the head with a loud, greasy splaaaat.

"Blubber for the cry-baby," howled a second horned man.

Nicolas snorted again, trying to protest, provoking another wave of cruel laughter.

"Oh, why did I have to come back here?" he was shrieking to himself, "what if I am trapped, if they will not let me leave, what if—"

Suddenly he remembered the pinch of salt that Beryl and the kindly Bear had armed him with. He opened his hand, and the tiny white pyramid that rose up from his pink palm sent a tremor of surprise and excitement through the entire marketplace. Darting in quickly, it was the horned man all in black who snatched the prize, his bright red tongue flickering like flame as he greedily licked the salt from his sticky fingers.

"Spice of fallen kings!" he panted, "so you are no beginner after all, but already rich with the great losses!"

The other horned man had grabbed the thief's already empty hand and was licking the dirty gnarled fingers himself, searching for one last succulent grain of the rare spice.

"Are you pig, then, or prince?" wheezed the dark man, pulling his hand away and belching.

"Neither," insisted Nicolas, shocked by the sound of his own voice, which had returned unexpectedly. "Neither. I am pilgrim."

"And you wish to cross the river," came a reply.

The marketplace had vanished.

"But—"

"And what will you give to me if I take you across the river?"

"But they did not pay me," cried the boy, in a panic, "they did not pay me for my salt!"

"Everyone must pay before they can cross the river."

"But I left the market with nothing, nothing, I tell you. I have nothing at all. Look."

The boy turned his pockets inside out.

"And that's when I saw it," he said.

"Saw what?" asked Beryl, ignoring the protests of the dog and crashing right through the gates of dream in her berry-stained tutu.

"The shell," he answered, "a piece of the blue eggshell. It must have been left there from . . . "

"The blue coin," explained Beryl, "payment for the harvest."

"It must have come with me all the way from the aviary."

The boatman held out his hand.

"What took you so long?"

"But I was—"

"I've been waiting here forever."

"But I—"

"I suppose now that I'm dead you have no use for me."

"But—"

"Or perhaps you were just afraid, hmm, frightened of a little death, just like all the others, afraid that a bit of it might rub off on you?"

Nicolas no longer even tried to reply.

"What could you have been thinking? Running off and leaving me like that, all alone on the cold, cold ground without so much as a few fistfuls of soil to cover me or a heavy coin or two to close the lids of my eyes."

Something was terribly wrong.

"But I suppose you had places to go and people to meet, I suppose the whole world is your nest now, never mind this old bag of straw that used to be a wise man, let the scarecrow lie there, it's already served its purpose, no crows left for it to frighten now anyway, and what the birds and beasts don't nibble away, well, the wind will scatter that out of sight soon enough."

Nicolas could hold his tongue no longer.

"But it was *you* who sent me away!"

"Me!"

"It was you who prepared me, and clothed me for a journey."

The old man appeared to be thinking for a moment.

"Ah, yes, so I did, so I did," he said. "Never mind."

Suddenly he vanished.

Nicolas turned around in circles, but he was alone.

"Nicolaaaaas!"

Old Gillam's voice rang out across hills and through valleys.

"Nicolaaaaaaaaaas!"

The boy whirled madly, this way and that, trembling with frustration.

"Oooooover heeeeeere!"

Suddenly the old man was right next to him, floating in the air right in front of his face—and cupped in his extended hand was a bit of clear water, a tiny lake in which floated two tiny white specks of swans. Gillam quickly closed his hand into a fist and the lake vanished.

Then he started to laugh.

So eager was the boy for some sign, any sign of Gillam's warmth and affection, that he laughed right along with him, willing to absorb any insult whatsoever, just so long as he could share in even a fraction of the old man's good cheer.

"A lot has happened, eh, my boy?" The apparition had moored itself to his shoulder, the old man's extended arm tensing and then sagging like any old rope fastening a boat to a shore. "A lot of water under the bridge, yes?"

Nicolas nodded, afraid to speak lest he shatter the old man's increasingly benign mood. But it was shattered soon enough.

"Hey there, sailor! Remember me?"

Once more Miss Beryl came crashing audaciously right through the gates of dream.

"Why Beryl, you old witch, you," bellowed the dead man, "why, I haven't seen you since . . . since . . . "

"Since you went head over heels off the bow of that ship and were swallowed up in the sea."

"A long time," he said, "a long, long time."

"Too long," she insisted.

"What are you doing here?" the boy demanded to know.

Beryl ignored him.

"And you never told me you were a sailor," accused Nicolas, turning back to his beloved apparition.

The old man stared at him, squinting.

"You know? You look familiar, somehow."

Nicolas was dumbfounded.

"Haven't we met somewhere before . . . on an island somewhere in the great sea . . . "

"He means the great sea of—"

Nicolas did not give Beryl time to explain.

"You stay out of this!" he shouted, "This is *my* dream!"

"Who are you talking to, my boy?"

Beryl had vanished.

"I just w-wanted to be alone with you."

"We *are* alone," said the apparition.

"I . . . I . . . I just wanted to . . . apologize to you," muttered the boy. "I wanted to apologize for taking so long. I mean, I never dreamed it would be so difficult to find—"

"Now, now, you don't have to—"

"But don't you see, I do!"

The boy was adamant.

"I never thought that I would be gone for so long," he said.

"How bad is your wound?" asked Old Gillam.

"Very bad," answered Nicolas.

"What wound?" asked Gillam, pointing.

The boy looked down and, much to his astonishment, saw that his foot bore no trace of injury.

"What's taking you so long?" demanded the apparition.

"Huh?"

"What're you waiting for, get going, get going."

"But I've only just returned."

"Don't be an idiot! You haven't even left yet!"

All at once Nicolas grew conscious of the fact that he was weighed down by some sort of baggage. Glancing down, he recognized the shape and the texture of his two precious swan bags, but not their color—for they were not bright and white now, but rather dark and dull as lead, and suddenly almost too heavy to lift.

"Get going, get going," cried the old man, raising his hand from the boy's shoulder, breaking contact, and beginning, immediately, to drift away.

"Why did you never tell me you were a sailor, why did you never tell me you had been to sea?" Nicolas cried after him.

"On a ship," moaned the vanishing apparition.

"A pilot?" cried the boy.

"Only a sail," came the distant reply, "only a sail on the great sea . . . "

Far off in the distance, as far as the horizon, Nicolas saw vultures circling.

"He's gone," said the boy aloud, turning away with a shudder.

"Don't oversimplify," said Beryl.

"But he's gone, he's gone already," whined Nicolas. "It's taken so long for memory to find him again, through the curtain, above the circus, across the river, all that effort and now he's gone."

"You sound awfully sure of yourself for someone still caught beneath the wing of sleep."

"What's that?" the boy asked abruptly.

For he'd heard music, distant music.

"The Lullabye," whispered the Bear into his ear.

"But it's the same tune that's been following me all the way from—"

Nicolas stopped to listen.

"The cradle tips, the darkness sighs . . . " went the verse, "still water flows, still water flies." But, as usual, there were new words. "And caught beneath the wing of sleep . . . "

"You have to understand something about the Immortals," said Beryl, "something about—"

"Look!" said Nicolas, pointing.

Someone or something was approaching.

"Something about their willingness to change sides," Beryl went on, ignoring him. She had begun pulling and tearing at the foil that was wrapped tightly around the boy's foot. "According to the Philosophers," she said, "one must remain constantly on guard against taking them too literally. The center around which their words spin with such demonic speed is no longer located within themselves at all and so is defined in a manner that must remain indecipherable to anyone still laboriously drawing breath around a passionate personal nucleus."

"Look!" repeated the boy.

"Are you listening?" Beryl wanted to know.

"Yes," Nicolas assured her, "I'm listening, but I'm looking also."

"Bravo," whispered the Bear.

"For instance," Beryl went on, "both kindness *and* cruelty, without the gravitational pull of their accustomed nucleus, tend to mutate, taking on a different shape altogether when thus robbed of all reference."

"Look," whispered Nicolas, "they're carrying something."

Though the figures were still too distant for the eye to define, their song was distinct. Though light and invisible as a breeze, it still brushed right up against the sensitive skin of the ear.

"Caught beneath the wing of sleep . . . " Nicolas mouthed the words to himself as he heard them, "I cling . . . "

"And thus," Beryl continued, "robbed of all reference—"

"So what are you telling me?" snapped Nicolas, interrupting "that *nothing is real?* That it's all an illusion and I should just sit right down, right here, right now, and never take another step since I'm not really moving anyway?"

"On the contrary," Beryl assured him, "or exactly."

"*Nothing* means two different things in your sentence," prompted the Bear.

Nicolas scoffed, annoyed to see that even the Bear was joining in this rhetorical game, and he tuned his ears back to the mysterious song in the wind.

"The Requiem," the Bear conceded this time, as the invisible song whispered the same phrase as before into the boy's ear, more insistently now, "and caught beneath the wing of sleep . . . I cling . . . to . . . "

"To what?" the boy whispered to himself.

"According to the Philosophers," Beryl was still rambling on and on, "the theorem that *nothing is real,* when taken to mean that none of the things in the sense that you habitually use them are real, could perhaps be proven to be true in many, if not all, cases. The Philosophers refer to this as the constantly challenging experiment of negation. However, if one were to interpret this *nothing* as *one* thing as well, and not merely as the many *no-things* or lost certainties of a valuable life of experiments in the operating theater, if you mean by nothing the monadic loss, the sum total of the many tiny losses, then you have passed beyond the disorientation of negation into the experiment of affirmation, where that *one* thing, *nothing, is* indeed real, and where a body need be given to only that one proposition, a proposition that can always be proved, every time, in exactly the same way under exactly the same set of infinite circumstances, for in the realm of affirmation Truth is one and yet it is many and yet it is not at all in a continuously emptying spiral of hosanna in the highest!"

Beryl burst out laughing.

"Ah," she said as soon as she could recover herself, "you must admit sometimes it seems as if there is no bird at all underneath all those fabulous feathers. And surely you must see now how hard it is for the Immortals, how hard it is for them to express themselves to us, how painfully difficult it must be for them to enter and center themselves in our operating theater, no matter how well equipped with larks' ribs and boiling tears and berried slippers and philosophical treatises and exquisite flying corpses it may be?"

The figures that had been approaching for so long and from so far away had arrived at last. So dazzled was the boy by their exquisite crowns and bright robes glittering in the sun, and by their deafening cries of exultation, that it was several moments before he had to face the unpleasant fact that beneath all the fanfare and finery there lurked four leering serpents, slithering toward him across the ground, each bearing one of the four corners of a litter laden with that mercurial treasure whose wealth of significances he was at last coming to view as inescapable. Now, apparently, it was the treasure itself that had become the one seeking, and he, in turn, the one sought for.

"Bid welcome to the four kings," instructed Beryl, solemnly.

"Welcome" whispered the Bear, four times.

"How did they find me?" was all Nicolas wanted to know, as he eyed the serpents warily.

"It's not easy to perform a pilgrimage to a moving target," taunted Beryl. "You should know that."

The first of the four serpent-kings reared up, raising its head high into the air as if preparing to strike.

Nicolas recoiled.

"Don't be rude," whispered the Bear.

"They have come all this way to offer praise," whispered Beryl. "Listen well, for it will be your turn soon enough."

"I saw the fire burning at the end of the world, illuminating the night sky with its fountain of agonized desire," hissed the serpent king. "Know that it was the power of but one of its dying embers, gathered in the proper time and season, wrapped in linen along with a single grain of wheat, and placed beneath my pillow, that graced me, in a dream, with a vision of my guiding star—along whose path of lightning I have come at last, to offer my gift to the orphaned child of the flame, son of the sweat of the philosophical salamander."

"Is he talking to me?" Nicolas whispered.

"Who else?" Beryl replied.

"From my kingdom of the setting sun I have brought you these golden lines in which all flame lies tamed and concealed."

Nicolas quickly recognized the sticks, one clearly notched, as the tools with which Old Gillam had long ago taught him how to make fire.

"But these are only—"

A moment of pain robbed him of his voice. Before he could confirm his suspicions that he had indeed been bitten by this serpent, the second serpent-king had already arisen and begun to speak.

"I saw the blue star," it said, "shining like the glory flower on the waters. I followed it, night and day, until I found you, here, in the distillery. I have brought you a basin of the coolest, clearest water that the depth of my kingdom has to offer, and I have carried it across great deserts without spilling or drinking a drop. All hail the *filius philosophorum,* bastard son of the most ancient of waters!"

Nicolas recognized this gift also. It was the basin in which he had been bathed, alongside his captain, in the tavern by the sea. Yet once again before he could comment or object, a shriek of pain stole the words from his trembling lips. This time, however, he was certain that he saw the serpent dart forward and strike his foot with its fangs.

The third serpent was quickly approaching. Rising up higher than the others, swaying in the air as if charmed by some music audible only to itself, it told its tale.

"A simpler star, one of the many with which the heavens have been littered since the beginning of time, was the star that led me here. Long years I traveled, never taking my eyes from the sky."

"My map!" cried Nicolas, even before the gift had been formally presented.

"And when the star fell at last, I marked the moment here on this piece of parchment, which I humbly offer to you now, wreathed in the glory flowers of early morning. May it one day beckon and guide you to the borders of my own far kingdom of sharp pointed snows, where, with open wings, we shall welcome you, son of the clear air, fruit of the belly of wind, last gasp of the Philosophers and their only child."

"Such an extravagant style," Beryl was whispering delightedly to the Bear. "I never tire of it."

"Masters of the *Royal* Art," the Bear reminded her.

"Precisely," she agreed.

Once more the boy's struggle to speak was unsuccessful, stunned as he was by the pain of the third serpent-king's bite.

A strange sensation in the lower half of his body caused him to look down at his repeatedly wounded foot. At first it seemed to him as if his entire left leg had come alive—and it was several moments before he realized the truth, that the fourth and final serpent-king had, all along, been approaching far more stealthily and secretively than his three companions, that it had slithered along the ground right up to his foot, that it had begun to climb until, by now, it was already wound tightly around his leg, still rising in a steady spiral, further and further up his body.

Now it was sliding up his belly and across his chest.

Nicolas shuddered at the touch of its cold, clammy skin against his own.

Then, just before it reached his chin, it stopped and raised its head. "I have never seen my guiding star," it hissed, "but I know that it is there, for once upon a time I gave to a blind man a willow stick and a pan full of sand in which he drew for me its likeness."

Nicolas could feel the grip of the serpent-king tightening around his leg.

"I have traveled with my ear to the ground, listening always to the roar of the river of roots far below me."

Tighter and tighter it held him in its embrace.

"The metals were my only hope. I placed my trust in their deaf and dumb perfection and traveled on with only my blind sandcastle of a star to guide me."

Nicolas felt as if his leg were about to burst.

"And now, oh son of man, I have seen the spark of bright pain erupt, in its own season: in the nutmeg and the coal, in the honey and the emerald and the weed, in the captive cider, in the apple itself."

The excruciating pressure seemed to be released all at once. The numbness that followed felt almost pleasant.

Then there was the sting of the bite, which he'd been expecting this time.

"Well," he heard Beryl sighing, casually, as if nothing out of the ordinary had taken place, "someone will have to get to work putting away all these gifts and things, so I guess it may as well be me."

"B-but those are *my* gifts," he managed to moan, rising out of his ecstatically painful stupor.

"Ah, there we go," snorted the busy Mistress of the Self-Tidying Art, "it happens every time, just about now, the last spasms of the acquisitive child." She'd stopped in the middle of the cave, nearly stumbling beneath her burden of gifts, basin and golden wands and parchment and nutmegs and apples all spilling from her arms. "Look," she said, "they're merely the apparatus of the laboratory, the masks and costumes of the operating theater."

Continuing across the cave, she stopped at the far wall, dropping the jumbled heap of gifts on the ground at her feet. She bent down over an enormous wooden chest, trying to slide it far enough away from the wall to swing back its heavy lid and throw it wide open.

"So as usual I get to keep nothing at all," muttered the boy.

"None of these things," Beryl went on, panting, "none of them would be of any use to you now." She stopped to catch her breath. "Oh, no," she puffed, "not where you're going."

"Nothing at all," the boy was still muttering to himself.

"Nonsense," said Beryl, dismissing his fears with a flick of her thick purple wrist, "and besides, if you could just learn to cling to this *nothing* of yours as desperately as you hang on to all these other trinkets. But don't get me started on that again."

"Nicolas!"

Turning around to see who it was who'd called out his name, Nicolas felt for a moment as if he were looking into a mirror—but an old mirror, one badly in need of polishing, a mirror that was warped and smudged, its surface coated with layer upon layer of dust and grime.

"It's only me," said his reflection, and then he recognized the shadow boy, who'd been standing nearby all this time, unnoticed, of course, and unpolished, his image neglected, forgotten, eclipsed.

281

"Did you call me?"

"I invoked your name," said the winged boy.

Nicolas didn't know what to say.

Lowering his eyes nervously, he noticed that the tips of the boy's wings still dragged along the ground, that the feathers there were soiled by each step he took, that he was standing on them even as they spoke.

"You're trampling your wings," he said softly.

"Yes," said the shadow, "and my skin settles like dust and ash on the surface of all my brief moments of form."

"Why have you been following me?"

Nicolas's eyes widened in disbelief, and his voice faltered.

The strange boy had extended one gray, dusty hand, in the palm of which lay a blue egg, whole and absolutely perfect.

"Accept my humble offering," said his shadow, as he passed the treasure to Nicolas, steadying the boy's trembling hand with his own, letting the egg roll from one palm to the other, from the dark to the light, in a single unbroken gesture. "I am the fifth king," he explained, "and you are the son, not only of the Philosophers but of the gardener and the jeweler and the digger of graves."

"The fifth king," mumbled Nicolas in awe.

"Yes," said his shadow, "and I am your brother."

He kissed him, and vanished.

"High noon," announced Beryl, "no time for shadows."

Nicolas gazed in amazement at the beautiful blue egg.

"And that'll teach you to speak too soon, give me this, give me that, whining about nothing at all," she teased, "and just when you might be offering praise, singing psalms and hymns of wonder." She shook her head in exasperation. "Go on now, put it some place safe."

The boy looked up at her sharply.

"Yes, that's right, it's yours, it's all yours, no argument there, I mean, you're the one who laid it, after all, and fair is fair."

Nicolas went on staring at the egg.

"Come now, my greedy little healed child," cackled Beryl, bending over the heavy trunk once again, "come and help the big old Bear and the tired old ballerina of dream."

The Bear was already crossing the room to assist her.

"And when I woke up," mumbled Nicolas, his eyes sailing along the soft blue curves of the egg, "I was back in the aviary, in the meadow . . . "

"Young man!" shouted Beryl. "Put down that egg and get over here and help us!"

Nicolas was startled and nearly dropped his precious blue egg.

"Help? Me?" he stuttered, bewildered. "How can I possibly help?" He looked down at his foot, as if to explain "But—!"

"That's right!" crowed the blue bird.

"Good as new," cheered the Bear.

"Oh," objected Beryl, "*much* better than that!"

"Can I walk?"

"Can I walk, he asks me," groaned Beryl. "Of course you can walk! You can walk right over here like I've been asking you to for the past ten minutes and help us to lift this chest!"

Nicolas slid over to the edge of the cot and placed his feet one at a time on the ground, testing each one cautiously with his weight.

"I'm standing!" he cried a moment later.

"I'm waiting!" Beryl responded.

Depositing the egg gently down on his vacated cot, the boy began to walk across the cave. "I can't believe it," he laughed, hopping excitedly.

"Lift!" was Beryl's only reply.

And finally, though it was still too heavy to lift, even with all three of them straining together, they were able at least to drag the trunk across the floor and out into the center of the cave.

"There!" cried Beryl, immediately loosening the sturdy leather straps and iron latches that secured the lid. She was relieved to be so busy, for she was experiencing an unsettling burst of affection for this boy, especially now that they were nearing the conclusion of the great work, now that it seemed almost certain that their work was to be crowned with such sweet success. It was better, according to *some* of the Philosophers, not to make too much of an exhibition of this sort of sentimentality. Such displays, they argued, were unseemly in a serious surgeon. Never before in her long career had Beryl met with such a dangerous challenge to her nearly perfected armor of emotional restraint, and she was deeply grateful for the harmless distractions offered by these mundane tasks at hand.

She appeared to be completely absorbed in her work. Yet when, with an exaggerated flourish, she at last flung the lid of the chest wide open, she was in fact gazing intently at the expression of amazement on the boy's face.

I've never seen such vast eyes on any creature before, she thought to herself.

"Yes," she said aloud, to the boy, agreeing with his eyes, "the marvel of the Ten Thousand Things."

"Look!" cried Nicolas, intending to point out the yellow slippers perched on top of the pile of paraphernalia, but at the same moment dozens of other objects popped into focus—ale bottles and dandelion greens and a bushel or two of bright diamonds, honeysuckle flowers and long strips of silver birch bark, seashells and smoke and the plumes of a peacock, and there was the old torn burlap feedsack and one of the mule's bright blue saddlebags, there was a chain of gold and a lock and key of gold and even a crown of gold, and even the long narrow black blindfold, even a page or two torn from the abandoned ship's log—he didn't know what to point out first, so immense was this wealth heaped up before him.

As Beryl began to hurl things into the chest, he cried out once again.

"Look!" he pointed, "his wings!"

On the pile of gifts waiting to be tossed into the already overcrowded storage chest lay the discarded wings of the fifth king, bare and balding in a few patches, their feathers wilting.

Nicolas reached out for them, certain that they would fit perfectly on his own shoulders.

"Ah-ah-ah," warned Beryl, "property of the operating theater and not of its actors, no matter how skillfully trained."

More and more strongly, Nicolas got the feeling that everything within the walls of the cave was being drawn in, slowly but surely, to some sort of hidden magnetic center located within the open mouth of the cavernous chest of Ten Thousand Treasures. He couldn't see it, but he could feel it, a growing sense of urgency, of instability, all around him, as if the entire laboratory was tensed in resistance, refusing, like a rebellious genie, to return to the confines of its magic lamp. Beryl herself seemed at certain moments to be caught up in this tide of return. And then the hem of her berry-stained skirt became snagged on one sharp-toothed corner of the open trunk, and she almost lost her balance and toppled inside.

"Not so fast," she joked, and tore herself free.

Nicolas could hear the nervousness in her laugh.

"Don't forget these," said the Bear, plodding across the cave, by far the heaviest and most stable thing present. He was carrying something he had removed from the copper kettle.

"My—"

A murderous gaze from Beryl cut Nicolas short.

He took a deep breath.

"*The* swan bags," he said, "the two swan bags," and he watched passionately as they were tossed into the chest along with his beloved possessive adjective.

Once more he noticed, in alarm, that the edges of Beryl's skirt were quite clearly entering the chest. By now there was little doubt in the boy's mind just how it would all end.

"But I must go back!" he cried suddenly. "I must go back and free Whitecap from the cage before, before—"

"Who?" asked Beryl, hanging on to her skirt.

"Whitecap," said Nicolas. "He's trapped back in my dream in the cage, in the last room."

"Who is Whitecap?" she asked, exasperated, for she couldn't possibly be expected to keep track of every little detail of every patient's dream.

The boy neither answered nor waited for permission to be granted. He could see that Beryl was far too busy to object, busy dodging the jars and bottles that were beginning to come loose from their shelves and tabletops, many of them whizzing dangerously close to her as they were sucked into the apparently bottomless pit of the trunk.

"Don't be too long," she called.

Nicolas turned in time to see a handful of the surgeon's sharp knives and needles shoot like speeding arrows from one side of the cave to the other.

Beryl ducked.

"Don't dawdle," she insisted.

It was only at the last minute that he remembered his egg, and scurried back to his invalid's bed. "I'd better bring this with me," he said, cradling the gift of the fifth king gently in both his palms.

Thrilled as he was by the strength and stamina of his newly healed foot, he could scarcely contain his exhilaration, and found himself racing as fast as he could down the long, crooked hallway, through one open doorway after another, until he was once more trapped within the intersecting lines of the cold, caged room.

It was as he remembered it, cruel and claustrophobic.

The only thing that he couldn't understand was why he hadn't noticed, last time, the narrow doorway through which, this time, he had entered.

"You can come in that way," explained the Raven, as if reading his thoughts, "but you can't go out that way."

"Then how *will* I get out again?" asked the boy. "Tell me quickly. I am in a terrible hurry."

"There's only one way out," said the Raven, "the same way as before— nothing changes here."

Nicolas was silent for a moment.

"I opened the book," he mumbled to himself, remembering, "the book lying on the table . . . alongside . . . "

He stared down—there was the table, there was the book.

"It's the only way?"

The Raven nodded.

Raising his eyes, Nicolas found himself face to face with the imprisoned black noddy. It had poked its head out through the iron bars of its cage and was paying close attention to everything.

"Whitecap!"

The bird gave several high-pitched peeps.

"Whitecap, I'm sorry," crooned the boy.

Nothing in the room stirred but the little bird's head, which ticked rapidly from side to side, the white patch on its skull flashing like a beacon through the gloom of the dream.

"I'm sorry, but I was so sick last time I was here," babbled the boy, "so sick and confused, why, I didn't even recognize you at all until after I had already escaped."

Searching the tightly knit iron grid for an opening of some sort, he'd finally located two tiny little rusty hinges near its base.

"There now," he exclaimed, as he swung the metal gate back, opening up a space just large enough for the plump little black bird to squeeze through, "you're free now, and we can get back to the cave, for I want you to meet Miss Beryl and the Bear."

The bird flew straight out of the cage, circled the room twice, and landed on top of the boy's head. It peeped once, and then never spoke again.

"Now if we hurry, we can get back before—"

A loud clang startled Nicolas. Turning, he saw a bright golden crown rolling across the floor, clattering as it bounced off one wall, changed course and direction, rolled back out into the center of the room, and wobbled to a halt. Nicolas could feel the little bird hopping about  excitedly in his hair. A moment later there was a fresh commotion, a shriek overhead, and the next thing the boy knew there was a large black ape scrambling across the floor, apparently in pursuit of its crown.

"Lord of the realm," sighed the Raven.

Nicolas was about to ask a question.

"No comment," interrupted the stern black bird.

"I think we'd better get out of here," whispered the boy to the bird on his head, glancing down with a worried expression at his fragile blue egg, then over at the ape rudely wrestling with its ring of priceless gold.

He was already reaching for the cover of the book of passage.

"Hungry?" asked the Raven.

Nicolas hesitated for a moment.

With his long black beak the Raven indicated a little saucer that the boy hadn't noticed before.

"Where'd that come from?"

"You brought it with you," said the Raven.

Nicolas examined the contents of the saucer.

"Salt," he concluded.

"The last pinch," said the Raven.

"Ahhh."

"It's been three days," the Raven reminded him, "since you slept in the temple, since you've eaten . . . "

The boy's mouth began to water.

With the aid of one moistened finger he quickly managed to clean every grain of salt from the saucer. Or almost every grain. Hopping about on the saucer a moment later, Whitecap seemed to find at least a grain or two to satisfy himself.

Nicolas was impatient now to be on his way. Looking up at the cold, icy glass of the window through which he had once foolishly tried to escape, he congratulated himself on the progress he had made. He held his egg in one hand and reached with the other for the cover of the book.

It was heavy, far heavier than he'd expected. And once he'd flung it open, it seemed to set up a sort of vortex in the room, an expectant trembling similar to that unleashed back in the laboratory by the opening of the bottomless chest of Ten Thousand Treasures. This room, however, proved far more stoic, far more stable than either cave or coop. Here everything stood firm and immobile, withstanding the tide. Here nothing could be budged.

The tension in the air swiftly became unbearable.

"What happens next?" asked Nicolas.

"What usually happens when you open a book," said the Raven, "you begin to read."

Nicolas looked down at the words printed on the page before him.

"*Understand the colors,*" he read out loud.

He paused, taking a deep breath.

"*Explain the intersecting lines.*"

"It's very simple, really," said the Raven, "even though it's far more complicated than most things."

"I remember," said Nicolas.

"That is to say that despite the playful ease of all these images, one melting freely into the next, there can be no doubt that this is indeed the most difficult chapter of your book."

Whitecap was hopping about on the page, pecking at the paper, prospecting for another grain or two of leftover salt, and Nicolas had to brush him gently aside with the back of his hand in order to go on reading.

"*Harvest the sorrow,*" he recited, and then stopped, for he had reached the bottom of the page.

"Go on," said the Raven, "don't stop there!"

Nicolas looked up.

"Go on?"

"Of course!"

"But there is no more," insisted the boy.

"Turn the page," suggested the Raven, trying to be patient.

The scavenging noddy had to be brushed aside again before the boy could do as he was told.

He found only a single phrase on the next page.

"*Offer praise,*" he read, before the golden crown again slipped through the ape's excitable fingers and crashed to the floor.

"You may go now," said the Raven.

"What took you so long?" said Beryl.

Whitecap was flying in nervous circles around the roof of the cave.

"I was reading," said the boy.

A quick glance around convinced the boy that conditions within the cave had continued to deteriorate at a steadily accelerating pace. Most of the contents of the laboratory had already disappeared into the open trunk, and Nicolas got the distinct impression that in several places even the walls themselves had been breached. Beryl seemed to be involved in some sort of heated debate with the Bear, and a closer look revealed that she was actually anchored beside him—the enormous sash that had all along been knotted into a spectacular bow at the back of her skirt had been untied and was looped now, like a leash, around one of the heavier marble tables in order to prevent her from being swept back into the matrix of the Ten Thousand Things along with all of the other equipment that had been used to accomplish the great work.

"Usually she's gone already," said the Bear to the boy.

"He's tied me to this table," insisted Beryl.

"You asked me to," said the Bear.

"Ssshhhh."

Beryl tried to put her hand over the Bear's mouth, but he took several steps backwards, and, tethered as she was, she could not quite reach.

"You must be patient with Miss Beryl," whispered the Bear, "for it is a very Bashful Art of which she is the Undisputed Mistress."

"Oh you . . . " she spluttered.

"She's afraid to let you know how much she wanted to see you once more."

The boy couldn't see what all the fuss was about.

"According to the Philosophers," Beryl tried to explain, "such displays of affection should never be allowed to—"

Nicolas didn't think the Bear capable of interrupting anyone, but that is just what he did.

"And these Philosophers of yours, ancient or otherwise, were they not merely birds and bears and boys, just like you and me and young Nicolas here?"

"I don't see what that has to do with—"

"Maybe they were mistaken."

"Mistaken!"

Beryl was scandalized, but, like any scandal, this one had its unique and powerful attractions.

"Not about everything," the Bear defended his heresy, "just about some things, little things here or there, mistaken just like any bird or boy or bear may be from time to time."

Beryl was silent.

"And sometimes everything is born, not from a wound, but from a mistake."

"Untie me!" Beryl pretended to insist.

"Not until you tell him yourself," taunted the Bear.

"Oh, you really are the wickedest of the wicked old circus bears!" she swore.

Nicolas still didn't see what the trouble was, and so he came ingenuously to the rescue of both Beryl and the Bear.

"*I* should certainly have been disappointed, Miss Beryl," he said stiffly, with all the formal sincerity he could muster, "if you had not been waiting here for me when I returned."

Beryl whirled around to face him.

"Ohhhhh," she sighed, relaxing instantly, "oh, ohh, would you really have been disappointed, really?"

"Yes."

"Did you hear that?" she asked the Bear.

By now her whole body had gone so limp that it seemed no more than a blue and pink and purple pennant, flapping freely in the treasure chest's magnetic wind.

"Go on then, ask him," cajoled the Bear.

Beryl struggled to speak from her undisciplined heart.

"I . . . I . . . just wanted, oh no I can't, I can't—" she stopped herself.

The Bear laughed.

"I just wanted to hear you offer praise," whispered Beryl quickly.

"Praise?"

"Yes. You see, normally I am already gone," she gestured toward the laboratory's hungry closet, calling to her from across the room. "Normally I never get to hear the praises offered by my patients, for that comes later, when they are alone."

"You want me to offer praises *to you*? You want me to thank you for—?"

"Oh, goodness no, no, no, that's not it at all, it's not myself I care about, it's only the work. I'd never even dream of hanging a hymn around me that way, oh no."

"Then what?" asked the boy.

"Anything," cried Beryl, "you can praise anything. Why you've only just begun the fourth practice, you've so far to go in it, and I was just hoping that I might hear the tiniest bit."

"Anything?" asked Nicolas.

"Anything!" Beryl assured him, "Anything at all!"

Nicolas looked down.

"My egg?" he asked.

"Splendid!" cried Beryl.

Nicolas wasn't quite sure he knew just how one went about this activity of praising. He thought back to the impassioned speeches of the four serpent-kings, then recalled the simpler psalms of his brother, the fifth king.

"I haven't had much practice," he apologized.

"It doesn't matter, it doesn't matter," Beryl bubbled in anticipation, thrilled by this unexpected and unorthodox turn of events.

The boy collected himself and began.

"O blue pearl of my bruised and stinking heels," he stuttered.

Beryl gazed into his eyes as he spoke.

"O great beyond me that comes to meet me from behind me."

Nicolas felt more than a little bit ridiculous.

"Hurry," whispered the Bear, "we haven't much time."

"Ssshh," hissed Beryl.

But the boy could see for himself the little ragged tears that were appearing around Miss Beryl's waist, where the seams of her sash were beginning to split. Behind him he heard the distinct sound of galloping hoofbeats. The white horse had entered the cave at last and headed straight for the open trunk, into which it leapt and disappeared once and for all.

"O round blue lamp of the secret of shadows, blue trampled flame rising like a bubble to the surface of my childish sea of hand! O unforseen fruit of my gratefully misguided grasp!"

That's better, he thought to himself, but I'll have to work fast.

"Now I exult, O gem of future dusts, for I, high noon's healed infant, have made my joyful choice to remain always lost and always wandering through the terrors of the enchanted forest that runs around the rim of the first and only blue of the hidden and rejected nest."

"Oh," cried Beryl, "I knew it."

"Blue pearl, blue pool, blue eye of the scorned."

"I just knew it," cried Beryl once more.

"Thin blue skin of the apprentice meeting itself for the first time in the refuse and, and d-droppings of heaven—"

Nicolas stopped.

"Is that alright?" he whispered, for he thought perhaps he had gone a bit too far.

"Ahh," gushed Beryl, "it's marvelous, simply marvelous, just as I imagined it might be."

"Can I praise my foot, too?"

"Ahhh yes, yes . . . "

Beryl looked as if she might faint with rapture before she even had a chance to blow away and dissolve into the depths of the trunk.

Nicolas looked down at his strong and healthy feet. This'll be easy, he thought.

"O recurring step, first step, first and final—"

The satin sash, when it tore loose at last, made a noise so loud that Nicolas could not hear his own voice. All three of them, as well as the little black noddy still circling nervously around the cave, realized that the end had come at last.

"Oh, thank you Nicolas, thank you," cried Beryl, still hanging on by a few tough threads, "you are a lovely boy, just lovely, and it has been a privilege and a pleasure to have worked with you."

The Bear could hardly believe his ears.

The last few threads were snapping one by one.

"I feel as if I might even like to kiss you farewell," Beryl sang out, surprising even herself, "but then I'm afraid I might punch a hole right through your cheek with this silly sharp beak of mine—"

And then the last thread gave way, and all at once there was nothing but a blur of blue and purple before their eyes as Miss Beryl shot right out of her skirt and into the open trunk. A moment later there was a second, smaller storm, this one pink, as the last torn shreds of the tutu made a few quick orbits around the room before being swallowed up.

Not a single thread remained.

Frantically searching for some sign of Whitecap, Nicolas noticed with a shock that the walls of the cave had become so thin as to seem almost transparent. For a moment he felt as if he were back in his own ale bottle, trapped and flying.

"Give me your hand," he heard the Bear say.

Just then he caught sight of Whitecap sailing right past his face, backwards, sucked straight into the eye of the storm, tail-first.

"Give me your hand!" he heard once again, more urgently, and, reaching out, he felt the strong, warm grip of the retired old circus Bear at precisely the same instant as he heard the lid of the chest of the Ten Thousand briefly borrowed Treasures slam shut with a resounding thud.

Part Four

THE RETURN

CHAPTER NINE

The Great Goldman and His Flying City of the Sun

"Are you awake?"

Nicolas assumed that it must be the warmth or the darkness that had questioned him, and he did not bother to answer—until both warmth and darkness shifted and stretched, nearly crushing him.

"Hey!" he protested, "My egg!"

Instinctively, he hugged his treasure to his chest to protect it.

"Sorry."

Once more the warm shoulder of darkness seemed to stir.

"How long have I been sleeping?" yawned the boy.

"For a season," yawned the darkness in reply.

Nicolas felt something tickling his nose, and, reaching up to scratch, he found himself tugging at a handful of warm fur.

"Ouch!"

It was his turn to apologize now, and he was about to, when the entire night rose up onto four dark heavy legs and began to move off, slowly, leaving the boy curled up alone on the bare ground, on the damp floor of a small cave. Through its low doorway the first rays of earliest morning light were just beginning to penetrate.

"Let's get out of here," mumbled the darkness, swaying heavily, staggering toward the mouth of the cave.

For a moment the boy was plunged back into blackness as the big warm body of the Bear, passing out of the cave, filled the entire doorway, blocking the light. Then the shadow lifted, and once more the chill glow of dawn seeped back inside. From far away a trickle of birdsong approached.

Nicolas sat up, listening, with his egg in his lap. He smiled. And then he leapt up so fast that he bumped his head, hard, on the low ceiling of the cave. But it didn't matter—because it wasn't his head he was concerned with, it was his foot. He tested it again and again, leaning on it with all his weight, stamping harder and harder, his smile broadening with each successive step. So it *is* true, he assured himself. "Wait for me!" he cried out in triumph, and rushed out through the mouth of the cave.

After a few leaps and sprints around the clearing, he stopped to catch his breath. Catching sight of the beast's footprints, he proceeded more methodically, placing his feet, right, left, right, left, inside each of the impressions that the Bear's paws had left in the soft damp soil of the forest floor.

"What happened to you?" he asked in shock, once he'd caught up with his friend.

"New coat," said the Bear. "Like it?"

Nicolas scarcely recognized him. The solid dependable brown of the Bear's fur had vanished in the glare of an unexpected polar white.

"But how . . . ?"

"Oh, we've crossed over, that's all—you know, the white becomes black and the black becomes white. Or at least that's the way Miss Beryl would approach it." The Bear was hunched over, clawing at the dirt with his long sharp nails, digging for something. "But it really rarely seems that complex to me." He paused and looked up. "What can I say? I always hibernate in old clothes."

The boy had another surprise coming. When the Bear finally finished his excavations, straightened up, and held out his paws, the treasure he offered for inspection was neither the tangled root nor the few fat squashed termites that might have been expected but instead a pair of purple leotards and a pale pink crinoline.

"No need to get dressed up in the dark time," said the Bear, "but once those lights come up! Well! You know, despite all I've been through, and I've been through a lot, I've never really been able to give up show business once and for all. It's in my blood, I suppose. That's why I've saved all these old circus outfits over the years. Sure, Miss Beryl thinks they're all moth-balled back in the big trunk, but you know she's never worked for the kind of magicians I have, she knows nothing about the false bottom or the revolving wall. I've got dozens of secret hiding places in every single one of the forests I've ever foraged through."

The Bear was already crashing off through the underbrush.

"Come on," he called over his shoulder, "these'll do for me, but we'll have to find something for you to wear."

Nicolas ran after him.

An hour later they sat on the ground amid a heap of brightly colored clothing, trying to decide.

"How about this one?"

The Bear held up a pair of baggy yellow satin pants torn under one knee.

"Or these?"

Nicolas eyed the enormous shoes, their split toes extending at least three feet out in front of their cracked heels.

They both burst out laughing.

"There's nothing wrong with playing the clown," the Bear assured him. And so the boy decided impulsively on the yellow satin pants with one tattered knee and a black top hat with only half a brim. The Bear had already slipped into the purple tights and the short flared pink skirt.

"That's more like it," he said.

Nicolas couldn't help but be reminded of that other wardrobe he'd discovered in the basement of the little gazebo. These costumes could scarcely compete with the garish ingenuity of those others. "I spread them all out on the hillside," he was telling the Bear, "and it was as if they came alive. You should have seen them. There were feathered skirts and—"

"Oh I know, I know," interrupted the Bear. "They were marvelous. I've been trying to get back there for ages."

"Get back where?"

"To the island of course, and to—"

"You mean you've been there?"

"Been there," laughed the Bear, "been there? Why, of course I've been there! I grew up there, I learned everything I know in the circus there!"

"What circus?" exclaimed the boy. Yet even as he spoke, he remembered that strange ring of trees in the distance, the mysterious arena that, much to his regret, he'd been unable to investigate further.

"You skipped the circus!" The Bear was scandalized. "You missed the very best part, the best fruit the island has to offer."

The Bear's mood had suddenly darkened.

"For years I've been trying to return," he sighed, "and now you tell me that you were there and you never even . . . " The look of dejection on the boy's face quickly forced him to forget his own sorrows, and he grabbed Nicolas playfully by the shoulders, laughing aloud as he spoke. "But what am I talking about? If you missed the circus that doesn't mean the circus has to miss you! Just look at us, we're already dressed for the part! It's the simplest thing in the world, my boy, all you need do is listen to me—I promise I'll tell you *all* about it, while we're walking."

"Yes!" insisted Nicolas.

"We'll have a grand old time!" sang the Bear.

"Yes! Yes!" agreed the boy, but then he hesitated. "We *will* head for the Phoenix, won't we?"

"Yes, of course, you'll set out for the Phoenix and I'll set out for the circus and we'll walk together!"

The Bear's enthusiasm left the boy little time for cold calculation as to the remarkable coincidence of the coordinates of all these urgent directions. Once they'd begun walking, their path seemed to flow forward with a momentum so pleasant and natural that it was impossible for the boy to entertain any notion whatsoever of going astray. On and on they traveled, walking and talking, sometimes the boy on all fours, like the Bear, sometimes the Bear upright on his hind legs, like the boy, trusting in the landscape to lead the way, to guide them through grove and glen, through thicket and ravine, across meadow and marsh and brook and stream.

With every word spoken by the Bear, however, another more surprising landscape was taking shape, a landscape superimposed upon this one. It was as if they were both printed on paper, like posters plastered to an old wall, circus and wilderness, one on top of the other on top of the other on top of the other, and through a tear in one was visible a fragment of another. One minute the sky was empty, beautiful, blue. Moments later, there were birds, flashing by at irregular intervals, and then suddenly there were clowns, tossed relentlessly up and down from the surface of a trampoline, or was it a carpet of wildflowers, that stretched from one side of the magical circus ring to the other.

"Sometimes the birds would collide with the clowns," laughed the Bear, "but most of the time they managed to get out of the way at the last moment. They seemed to be playing tricks on the poor old clowns, for the birds were clowns, too, at least in this act."

He'd stopped suddenly and was sniffing the air and the ground at his feet.

"What is it?" asked the boy.

"More souvenirs," winked the Bear, and began to dig.

Not long afterward, shaking free the few clods of earth and uprooted violets that still clung to its surface, the Bear withdrew a small paper sack from the loosened soil. "They're still here," he announced, as he tore open the sack and removed six or seven objects so tiny that Nicolas had to bend over his paw for a closer look.

"What are they?" he asked, still puzzled.

With one careful claw, the Bear pointed out a tiny red rubber bulb which reminded the boy of the eye dropper with which Old Gillam used to feed the swarms of hummingbirds back in the aviary's meadows. But the Bear had a different explanation, assuring the boy that he had seen this very bulb attached with a string to the beak of a particularly agile sparrow who'd performed with the old clowns in the circus many years ago.

301

"Peepo," said the Bear.

"Peepo?"

"That was his name," explained the Bear, "and this was his false nose."

Trying to picture such a facial arrangement on a sparrow, Nicolas began to laugh.

"Oh, he was a sly one, alright. He'd creep right up behind them, one after another, while they were trying to have their tea. They never learned, the old fools—they were always trying to live life on the trampoline as if floating in the air were no different than standing on the ground. It's no wonder little Peepo never tired of teasing them, darting in on his swift wings and honking that nose of his right into their big ears. It was a ridiculous sound. And every time they heard it—well, everything just went to pieces. One by one, the cups and saucers would go flying, and then they'd begin to bounce, and soon enough the old clowns themselves were flying and falling and bouncing, trying to catch their runaway cups of sweet tea, and then their chairs would join in, and their table, and finally their pots and spoons and bowls and even their precious cubes of sugar, their whole world bouncing up and down on the trampoline in such a confusion and chaos that, each time the act was performed, it seemed a wonder that Peepo had once more managed to escape unscathed, and yet he did, every time, darting in and out of it all, that red nose of his glowing brighter and brighter as the laughter and the applause reached a crescendo."

The Bear had begun walking again as he talked.

"Oh, he was extraordinary, little Peepo, a real trouper!"

Nicolas looked at the array of tiny costumes in the Bear's still extended paw.

"There were others," he guessed.

"There were hundreds of others," the Bear assured him. "The air above the trampoline was filled with little flying clowns. Of course, I could only save a few of their props and costumes."

Nicolas was able to identify a pair of tiny shiny blue shoes, an inch-long blond wig, braided, and a little set of false teeth, crooked as tossed confetti, the front two missing.

"To the audience, of course, it seemed a complete jumble, but it was really one of the most precisely choreographed acts in the entire circus. Not that there wasn't a certain amount of improvisation. The birds seemed to undergo a strange transformation once they actually slipped into their little clown suits. They became incapable of resisting even the most primitive forms of mischief. There wasn't a moment when one of them wasn't busy flying away with a hat here or unraveling the hem of a sleeve or a sweater there, distracting the old clowns in a thousand different ways. But never, mind you, never at the expense of the order of the act itself. It was they who held everything in place, right down to the guide wires that kept the trampoline stretched taut. I tell you, there wasn't a string in that entire circus that wasn't pulled or anchored somewhere along the line by a bird."

Nicolas felt sorry for the old clowns, but still he couldn't keep from laughing.

"Yes, their real trick," the Bear went on, "was negotiating this chaos they'd released. They had to, even if it meant sacrificing their own safety, they absolutely had to reach the corners of the old clowns' mouths. You see, there was one problem with the act, a problem with the clowns themselves—for they were so shell-shocked, so frustrated at having fallen once more for the same simple, stupid tricks, that at a certain point there was a real danger that their act would culminate in an expression of dismay or despair, or maybe even anger. The birds' real skill then was in catching hold of the corners of the mouths of the old fools and raising them up with their guide wires. Because it doesn't really qualify as a clown act at all unless it leaves the old fools smiling."

Something distracted the boy from the sound of the Bear's voice. He stopped, and looked down, at the ground, almost losing his balance. He hadn't been paying attention to the fact that they were crossing a small bridge, a series of pale stone arches over the edge of which his glance had inadvertently fallen, tumbling into a drained riverbed, all dry sand and gravel but for a thin stream of barely blue water, barely flowing.

The circus had vanished.

"Where are we?" Nicolas asked for the first time since they'd set out.

The Bear shrugged his big white shoulders.

From their vantage point on the bridge, Nicolas could see both the grove of trees from which they'd emerged a little while ago and the harsher and less hospitable expanses that were opening up now ahead of them. Staring for several minutes, in silence, out across low leathery hillsides and thorny hedges, where nothing stirred, where everything lay still and dry beneath a cloudless sky, the boy heaved a sigh of relief when the Bear began, once more, to speak, and to move forward.

"And what happened then, in the other rings?" he prompted, following close on his friend's heels, anxious to return to the bright fanfare of the circus.

"Oh there was only one ring," the Bear corrected him, "it was only a one-ring circus, although it seemed at times as if . . . "

The Bear had caught sight of something in the distance.

"Look," he cried, and began to scamper on ahead.

By the time Nicolas caught up with him he'd already finished digging.

"There," said the Bear, holding up the garment he'd unearthed, a pair of short trunks that bore the black and yellow markings of a leopard's spotted pelt. "Try them on," he insisted.

"Me?"

"Yes," laughed the Bear, "here, let me help you get out of those foolish yellow bloomers."

"But—"

"These will be much more becoming."

Nicolas was having trouble extricating himself from the limp folds of yellow satin and was awkwardly shifting his egg from hand to hand, worried lest it drop and break.

"Here, let me hold that," suggested the Bear.

"You'll be careful?"

"Of course."

Though the leopard trunks were a bit too large for Nicolas, they were soon fastened around his waist with a length of rope that kept them from falling down around his ankles when he walked.

Gently, the Bear passed the blue egg back to the boy.

And then, before they set off, he buried the pile of discarded yellow satin in the hole in the ground at their feet. "Fertilizer," he mumbled, as he patted the loose earth back into place with his broad heavy paws.

"The audience was always already deathly quiet, and yet it was an iron rule that the ritual call for silence nonetheless be sternly issued." The Bear hesitated for a moment. "*Ladies and Gentlemen, until the trick is completed and the performer is once more safely on the ground, we must request that you remain absolutely silent.*"

His deep voice echoed in the boy's ears.

"It was actually the first real solo I ever had," he confessed, suddenly bashful.

Nicolas had been wondering just when his friend the Bear would get around to tales of his own talents. Until now he'd proved strangely reticent in this regard, preferring to extol only the skill and daring of others.

"Sometimes I would add: *'Any distraction may prove fatal!'* "

"Bravo!" cried Nicolas.

"But, like I said, by that time it was already so quiet in the grandstand that you could hear a pin drop or a feather fall to the ground." The Bear cleared his throat. "I was very young at the time," he admitted, "and quite nervous. But then the more experienced I became, the more, well, the more interpretive freedom I was allowed with the text." Once more he cleared his throat. "For instance, sometimes I would say: *'Ladies and Gentlemen, please, be advised that your slightest sound may prove to be the single straw that breaks our Human Camel's back.'* Or sometimes I might say: *'Your absolute silence, Ladies and Gentlemen, is all our Mighty Atlas requests in return for that world he shoulders, now, before your very eyes, for one and for all.'*"

"Bravo! Bravo!" cheered Nicolas.

"But my greatest success of all came years later with this brief warning." There was a dramatic pause. "*His strength, good people, is in your silence. Ssshhhh.*"

"And then?" whispered the boy.

"Then I'd lower the megaphone, and go sit in the corner on my tall purple stool, and the trick would commence."

Nicolas had been trotting along abreast of the Bear, anxious not to miss a single word of his story—until the rope around his waist snapped, forcing him to stop and lift his sagging leopard trunks from around his knees before he tripped over them and fell flat on his face. It took him several minutes to find a safe place to rest his egg and then to re-knot the frayed ends of his belt.

Then, as he was running to catch up with the Bear, who hadn't even noticed the boy lagging behind, so involved was he in the climax of his tale, he saw something out of the corner of his eye that puzzled and disturbed him.

"The cave?" he mumbled to himself. "But how—?"

For a moment he paused, looking back at its dark mouth.

One nervous glance ahead, however, at the increasing separation between him and the Bear sent him running forward again in a panic. Besides, he insisted to himself, it was impossible, it couldn't be the same cave from which they'd started out this morning, it couldn't be that cave in which they'd slept through the long night before.

The Bear was gabbing away but stopped immediately when he heard the boy panting for breath at his side.

"What happened to you?"

"I almost lost my shorts," stuttered Nicolas, "and, and, then I . . . "

He fell awkwardly silent.

It couldn't possibly be the same cave, he reprimanded himself once more. Calling himself a fool, he vowed neither to think nor say another word about it, and begged the Bear to go on with his tale as if nothing at all had happened.

The Bear did not need to be coaxed.

"Well, by this time," he continued, "Mighty Floating Atlas was already balanced up on the whirling circle of birds."

"What whirling circle of birds?"

"You mean you missed that part?"

Nicolas nodded, apologetic.

"You mean I can tell it again?"

"Please."

"From the beginning?"

"Yes."

The Bear was delighted.

"You see, at first it was a single circle," he explained, "a circle of tiny bluebirds flying so swiftly around and around that the wings of one could scarcely be distinguished from the wings of another. Still they flew faster, faster and faster, until all that could be seen of them was one thin blue electric ring engraved in air."

Nicolas closed his eyes for a moment, trying to visualize the bluebirds.

"One by one, then, consecutively smaller circles of birds would enter, accelerate, and then fit themselves concentrically within the outer, larger rings, each ring of birds flying in a direction opposite to the ring adjacent to it."

He turned to Nicolas.

"Can you picture it?"

"Ummmm, I think if there were enough rings, and they were close enough together," mused the boy, closing his eyes again, "and they went on flying faster and faster and faster . . . "

His eyes popped open wide.

"You see it? You see it!" cried the Bear.

"It's solid, like a disc, like a flat blue disc suspended in the air!"

"And it was up onto this blue disc, onto this whirling circle of bluebirds that Mighty Floating Atlas was about to take a step . . . "

The Bear pointed to the boy's leopard trunks.

"When all of a sudden his belt snapped and his shorts came tumbling down."

"Noooo!"

"Only kidding," chuckled the Bear, "but those *were* his shorts, you know."

"But how did he stand? How could he keep from falling?"

"Well, it wouldn't be much of a circus act if everyone sitting in the grandstand could perform it as well as the man in the center of the ring, now would it?"

"I suppose not."

"*My* theory was always that it was the fact that the rings of birds were flying in alternating directions, that's what gave him his stability, his ground. If they'd all been flying in the same direction, I think, strong man or not, Mighty Floating Atlas would have had to change his name to Mighty Flying Atlas, for he would have been shot through the air over the heads of the spectators even faster than his twin brother, the Human Cannonball, in the act immediately following."

The boy's mouth was hanging wide open.

"But that was only the beginning."

"You mean there was more?"

"A Strongman has to lift something, doesn't he?"

"I guess so."

"And you could tell by his leopard trunks that he *was* a Strongman. They always wear leopard trunks."

"Oh," said Nicolas, looking down self-consciously at his own skinny arms and legs, and at the oversized trunks puckered up around his narrow waist.

"Some said it weighed a ton, others said two or three or even four. We never found any scale powerful enough to weigh it, so we never really knew for sure. All I do know is that it took twenty or more men to roll it in and out of the tent before and after the act. And if it began to tip, even slightly, everyone within sight just ran, terrified at the prospect of being squashed beneath it. Only Atlas himself could budge it then."

"What, what was it? Tell me!"

Nicolas was hopping up and down.

"The mirror."

"The mirror?"

"It was round, just like the circle of birds beneath him, and of identical dimensions."

"But what did he do with it?"

"He lifted it, of course," said the Bear, "he lifted it straight up over his head."

He gave the boy time to picture the marvel.

"And the remarkable thing was that when his arms were fully extended, it became a perfect mirror of the ground, the blue ground, that is, the whirling ground of birds upon which he was balanced. So that there were two circles, two blue whirling grounds, one above and one below, one a perfect reflection of the other, and our strong man stretched out between them in his black and yellow shorts, as stiff and as solid as the trunk of a great flowering tree, a tree in which root and fruit, ground and crown, were the same and yet different."

Once more the Bear gave the boy's imagination time to catch its breath.

"And that would be my cue," he said at last, "to slide off the purple stool in the corner and reenter the ring for my grand finale." He cupped his paws around his mouth like a megaphone. "*Ladies and Gentlemen!*" he bellowed, "*Mighty Floating Atlas! A Strong Flower of a Man!*"

He lowered his hands and sighed.

"The applause would be deafening."

Yet not nearly so deafening as that moment of recognition that caused the boy, for the second time now, to almost lose his balance. "Again!" was the only word he managed to squeeze from his mouth as he gazed down in shock at the dry banks of the riverbed below him. While another voice, not his own, was roaring in his head, "It's the same bridge! It's the same bridge! It's the same bridge!"

He turned to face the Bear, who'd stopped alongside him.

"It's the same bridge," he said aloud, at last.

The Bear only shrugged.

"Are we traveling in a circle?"

This time the Bear answered, but tersely. "In a ring," he said. And he began to walk again, crossing over the bridge and moving off casually through the dry countryside, his heavy feet leaving no tracks in the hard-packed red earth.

The boy's head was spinning in a circle, or a ring, all its own.

"The cave, the cave," he whispered aloud, "then it *was* the same, it *was* the same cave after all."

The Bear pretended not to hear him.

"And another thing," Nicolas went on, his voice gaining assurance, "just how long have we been walking? I mean, why doesn't it get darker, why doesn't the sun set?"

He looked straight up into the sky.

"It's been noon for hours and hours," he marveled, "hasn't it?"

It was true—for some time now the sun had been frozen at its zenith, directly overhead, in the center of the sky. The boy stopped walking and stood looking directly up into its burning eye.

"I've heard it said that only an eagle or a falcon can stare directly into the sun like that," said the Bear, "even though certain young men have been trying to do so for centuries."

310

Nicolas blinked in pain and lowered his gaze, rubbing the bright heat from his eyes with the back of his hand.

"There was even, once upon a time, a great trapeze artist, the greatest aerial magician of them all, who actually attempted, as part of his act, to pluck the sun right out of the heavens. I swear it to be the truth." The Bear shook his head, staring far off into the distance and smiling to himself. "Ahhhh," he sighed, "what an act that was!"

"What act?" asked the boy, still dousing the embers in his burnt eyes.

"The Great Goldman," said the Bear, "The Great Goldman and His Flying City of the Sun."

Nicolas couldn't believe his ears.

"City of the Sun!"

"*Flying* City of the Sun," repeated the Bear.

"But that is where the Phoenix returns with its ashes. It gathers them up and flys off to a City of the Sun!"

The boy was tugging impatiently at the edge of the Bear's pink skirt.

"Where is this City of the Sun?" he demanded to know.

"Well, for the Great Goldman it was—"

"That's where I want to go! There I shall certainly be able to find the Phoenix."

"For the Great Goldman it was wherever—"

"Where? Where is it?"

"I'm trying to tell you," laughed the Bear. He loved all forms of enthusiasm, even childish impatience. "I'm trying to tell you that for the Great Goldman it was wherever he'd had it positioned for that evening's performance."

"Had what positioned?"

"The sun! The sun!" said the Bear, beginning to walk once again. Without realizing it the boy was once more trotting eagerly alongside, listening. "It was round, as a rule, it was always something round," the Bear went on, "but that was about its only consistent detail. Oh, they came in all colors and sizes and materials, the suns of the Great Goldman. Sometimes it was an enormous piece of cardboard covered with foil and illuminated by the big top's main spotlight, sometimes it was one of the big yellow balls the elephants used to toss into the air with their trunks. And then sometimes it was smaller, sometimes just a bit of tinsel or glass, one time a pendant of crystal fastened around the neck of a beautiful young woman in gold sequins dangling by her teeth from a single wire high above the heads of the crowd."

Nicolas gasped.

"Sometimes it was a hoop of fire, or a silver thimble, or a single shining coin."

The Bear paused, turning to make sure he'd succeeded once more in capturing the boy's attention.

"But whatever it was," he went on, "it was always placed just a bit too far away, just far enough out of reach to cause the act's climactic trick to fail each and every time it was attempted."

"To fail?" whispered the boy.

"Oh, yes," the Bear assured him, "it was a circus tradition. It was what everyone waited for, whether they realized it or not. I always wondered what would have happened if the trick had succeeded, even once, after all those years of heroic failure. I wondered just how the audience would have reacted."

Nicolas didn't think he understood.

"Why do you look so surprised?" asked the Bear. "Surely you didn't think it was all about triumph! Not at all, my boy, not at all!"

He paused for a moment.

"In the end a circus is only about its acts!"

"Which acts?"

"Whichever of its acts one is performing—for they all engender their own risks, their own thrills, their own responsibilities, from broken bones to vertigo to humiliation, not to mention fame and fortune and sudden death."

"But what if one is only watching?"

"Well, then, one is performing the watching act," explained the Bear, "which is no exception to the rule."

Nicolas decided he'd had enough of high-flying circus philosophy for the moment. He decided it was high time to return to the ground.

"Are we walking in a circle or not?"

"We're in the ring, as I said before," answered the Bear, patiently. And then he fell silent, and walked on as if ignoring Nicolas, although the whole time he was watching him out of the corner of his eye, watching and waiting.

Five minutes later, as the Bear had anticipated, curiosity once more got the better of the boy.

"Tell me about the brilliant failures of the Great Goldman," he begged.

"First of all, it wasn't only *he* who failed," the Bear elaborated. "Oh, no, it was all his Citizens of the Sun, as they were called—for many of the other members of the troupe would make their own attempts on the sun before the Great Goldman himself finally launched that last, doomed, show-stopping effort."

The Bear looked deep into the boy's eyes.

"Have you ever really seen a trapeze act, Nicolas? The graceful arcs, the swift spins and reversals, the hands outstretched in empty space, the lonely moments of unsustainable flight, and then the sudden drops arrested in mid-air."

Nicolas had often witnessed the dramatic maneuvers of swarms of swallows at twilight or before a storm. He'd stared for hours at the spinning halos of butterflies drinking from the first flowering trees of spring. He'd been startled many times by the nearly vertical trajectory of a lark flushed up from the grass of a meadow.

"But they all have wings," the Bear reminded him, "whereas in the Flying City of the Sun of the circus it's only the wingless that fly, for it is only the wingless that can fall, and without the fall the flight is, according to an old circus proverb, no act at all."

"So that was the only qualification for citizenship," asked Nicolas warily, "winglessness?"

Whether he flew in or fell in, one way or another he knew that he must gain entry into this Falling Flying City of the Sun if he was ever going to find the fabulous Phoenix.

The Bear smiled.

"Why do you ask?"

"I was just wondering . . . " mumbled the boy.

"Over the years," the Bear went on slyly, "membership in the troupe grew to staggering proportions, and though not every Citizen of the Sun flew and fell every night, still, in any one performance there were enough daring attempts and failures to dazzle even the most jaded of spectators."

The Bear described one feat after another in glittering detail, from the desperate solos of lone men and women, with their back flips and double and triple somersaults and swift loops and pirouettes, to the more coordinated attempts of whole families trained since birth, of brave parents who willingly, night after night, would launch their only child out over the abyss like an arrow toward whatever had been chosen as that night's shining goal.

"Citizenship in this Flying City of the Sun cut across all other boundaries and borders," the Bear explained, "for guest citizens would arrive from thousands of miles away just to perform one time with the Great Goldman."

Nicolas watched the dark mouth of the familiar cave grow larger as they drew near it once again. He watched it recede into the distance as once more they passed it by. This time he could even make out their footprints in the soft earth at its threshhold. But he said nothing, so mesmerized was he by the Bear's words.

"Every day some new gypsy citizen would appear in the tent with a pair of tights and begin rehearsing. And even within the circus itself the constant defections would sometimes temporarily blur the lines between acts beyond recognition. I remember the night the juggler flew and fell. The sun was only an orange that evening, or a lemon, I forget which—the Great Goldman had been sleeping all day with a headache and so hadn't had time for more elaborate preparations. It didn't matter. Hanging upside down with his knees hooked over the bar, the juggler began to swing through the air, back and forth, with more and more force."

"What happened?"

"I don't really know," confessed the Bear, "but later on I was told that when he got close enough he actually tried to exchange one of the balls he was juggling for the sun, for the orange or the lemon or whatever it was in the spotlight. All I remember was the whole handful of colored balls raining down, and then a moment later, there was the body of the juggler himself, sprawled out in the net beside us."

"Us?"

"The fallen."

"But what do you mean by *us*? Were you in the net?"

"I was."

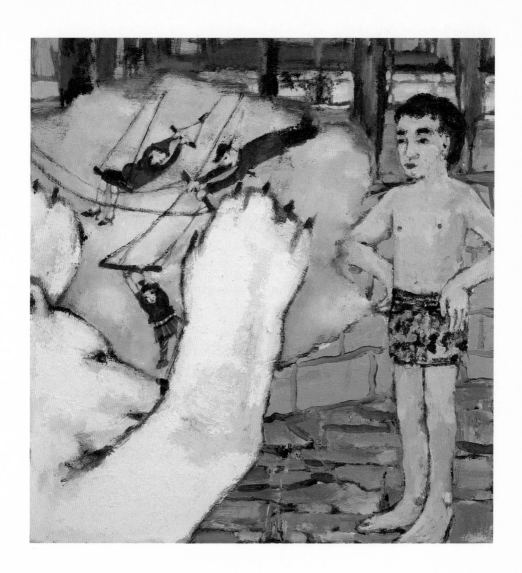

"You mean you . . . ?"

"I'm wingless, aren't I?" the Bear reminded him.

Nicolas tried to picture the heavy white Bear balanced on the bar of a trapeze, swinging through the air, as the song goes, with the greatest of ease.

"Oh, so you thought that citizenship was only open to men and women, hmmm, no animals need apply? On the contrary, the Flying City of the Sun was filled with creatures of all kinds. Even an occasional bear. Even an occasional bird."

"But—"

"So long as it agreed to have its wings bound before it left the ground. It was a matter of policy. The Great Goldman excluded no one, no one. It wasn't unusual for a member of the audience to jump up impulsively from his seat and volunteer right then and there—a child, an old man, a pregnant woman, a butcher or a baker or a chemist. The Flying City of the Sun gained all sorts of unlikely citizens that way. And no matter how preposterous the spectacle, no one ever laughed. There was no trace of ridicule in it. *The source of every stupid desire is profound*—that's what the Great Goldman always told us. And that's what all of us shared in common: desire, stupid or otherwise, who's to say? No, there were no fools in the Flying City of the Sun, only falling citizens. You wouldn't laugh at a shooting star, would you? Would you?"

"No."

"Well that's what we were in the end, shooting stars, as one after another we plummeted through the air, down into the net stretched out below us."

There was a moment of respectful silence.

"Not that we didn't laugh about it later," the Bear admitted, "but laughing *from* the net is a lot different than laughing *at* the net."

He allowed himself a chuckle or two.

"I suppose it's true that we may have cut a somewhat comical figure down there, at least to the untrained eye—snared and tangled up like a pack of broken fireflies, nursing our wounds, our sprains and bruises and extinguished lights. But by that time no one was even looking at us, we weren't even looking at ourselves, for all eyes were fixed above, awaiting that final spectacular performance, the rise and fall of the Great Goldman himself, whose consummate showmanship never disappointed."

For a short while they'd been traveling through the shade of some trees, that grove of trees from which they would soon emerge, Nicolas knew from previous experience on this circular path, at a point not too far distant from the little bridge. He was prepared to cross the bridge this time. He told himself that this time he would not be startled, that he would not lose his balance. But once the Bear began to describe the Great Goldman, Nicolas became so absorbed that once more he lost track of where he was.

"Five hundred pounds!" exclaimed the boy.

"And all in gold, from head to foot," the Bear whispered. "You could hear every heart in the crowd beating like the same drum as he struggled one heavy step at a time up the long rope ladder, climbing all the way to the roof of the tent."

"But how did such a fat man ever—?"

"Oh, it's a long story. You see, he grew up in the circus, he was born virtually under the spotlight, his mother entering labor just outside the ring, still in costume, during a short intermission. He was only six or seven years old when he became the circus fat boy, one of those freaks of nature that people can't resist paying so much money to see. It was a hard life, no doubt about it, even before his parents died. . . ."

"What did his parents do in the circus?"

"It was claimed that his father could, from fifty paces, slice the flame from a burning match with the blade of a knife hurled through the air," said the Bear. "And his mother," he went on far more reluctantly, "well, his mother . . . "

"They worked together?" whispered the boy.

The Bear nodded solemnly.

"Oh."

"It was a tragic accident from which his father never recovered. And after the old man's suicide, his orphaned son kept more and more to himself, retreating to his trailer soon after each show and seldom emerging until the following evening. Or at least that's what most of us thought. Legend has it, however, that the first time he performed on the trapeze was late at night, all alone, with no audience other than a few of the out-of-work clowns and local children who were paid to clean up the grandstand while the rest of us were sound asleep—

that is, until rumour of these lonely late night performances began to spread, until people began to look forward to them each night, until . . . well . . . but the rest is circus history."

The Bear fell silent.

"He was a sight to behold, the Great Goldman," he went on at last, "dazzling in his gilded tights, orbiting high above the heads of the crowd like an enormous golden planet swept from one end of the heavens to the other by the eternal rhythm of its desire. And when he fell! It was if we were all victims of some bewitchment. Our eyes remained glued to the heights, hypnotized, staring in silence at the sudden emptiness there."

The boy looked up, involuntarily, his vision burned by another eyeful of imperturbable sun.

"I remember one night in particular," said the Bear, "the night when the part of the sun was played by a monkey."

"By a monkey?"

"A chimpanzee," explained the Bear, "a chimpanzee perched on a platform high above the crowd, with a crown of gold on its head."

Nicolas gasped.

"'Ladies and gentlemen,' announced the Great Goldman from halfway up his rope ladder, 'tonight I will attempt a trick never before dreamed possible in this or any other circus, tonight I will attempt to pluck the crown of gold from the brow of the beast and return with it to earth.'"

"But my dream, my dream," insisted Nicolas, "the monkey in my dream!"

"Your dream," reprimanded the Bear, "haven't you learned yet that dreams are shared?"

Nicolas dropped his eyes in embarrassment.

"The crowd was even quieter than usual that night, not a single cough or sneeze disturbed the silence—until the chimpanzee caught sight of the great golden fat man ascending his ladder, and began to jump up and down and point, screeching and cackling, shaking his head from side to side, nearly dislodging the crown."

Nicolas could hear the cries of the excited chimp. It seemed to be laughing at him, at the Great Goldman, at everyone.

"And then the maestro began to swing," sighed the Bear. "Gripping the bar of his trapeze with one hand, he flung himself back and forth through the air, faster and faster, his momentum building, drawing him nearer and nearer to his goal. Perhaps this is the night, we all thought, perhaps this is at last the night that the sun will yield to its most ardent seeker. Faster and faster and still faster the Great Goldman hurled himself through space, the whole tent shaking beneath his tremendous weight, and louder and louder the chimp screamed and hooted, waving his arms and stamping his feet, flailing about like a mad child. So close he came each time, closer and closer and closer, until only a fraction of an inch lay between his outstretched hand and the bright golden crown, until only a hairsbreadth of empty space lay between him and his shining goal, just once more, just one more dip, just one more rise and one more stretch and then—"

A harsh voice cut the story short.

"It's the same bridge! It's the same bridge!"

For a moment the boy could see nothing at all. Everything seemed to be rushing by too quickly, as if he were the one who was falling from the roof of the circus tent.

"It's the same bridge!"

"Who—?"

Nicolas caught sight of the parrot a moment later, perched on the white stone wall of the bridge he and the Bear found themselves standing on for the third time.

"Not again?!"

"Where am I? Where am I? Where am I?" shrieked the parrot, ruffling its green feathers, cocking one sharp, cold eye in the boy's direction.

Exasperated, and dizzy, Nicolas sat right down on the ground.

"I can't go on! I can't! I can't!" taunted the bird.

In a flash the boy was up on his feet again, lunging at the parrot, which flapped into the air and resettled on the other side of the bridge.

"I can! I can! I can!" it squawked mercilessly.

"Where did you come from?" shouted the boy, lunging again.

"Can! Can't! Can! Can't! Can! Can't!"

This time the parrot settled down a safer distance away.

"Whooa now, my boy," warned the Bear, restraining him with one heavy paw, "calm yourself."

"Calm myself!" spluttered Nicolas, "how can I calm myself when, when, when—"

"I'm rising, I'm falling! I'm rising, I'm falling! I'm rising, I'm falling!" the obnoxious bird completed his sentence for him.

"How can I calm myself when I'm—"

"Up! Down! Up! Down! Up! Down!"

A look of surprise suddenly spread across the boy's face.

"Haven't we met somewhere before?" he barked.

The parrot regarded him first with one eye, then with the other.

"Who are you?"

"Who are you? Who are you? Who are you?"

"I know who I am!" shouted Nicolas.

"Who am I? Who am I? *Hoo-emm-aaiii?*"

The boy winced.

"Parrot! Pilgrim! Parrot! Pilgrim! Parrot! Pilgrim!"

Nicolas crouched down and picked up a stone, but the Bear caught his arm before he could throw it.

"Nicolas, you must calm down!" he laughed.

"But, but, but—it's the same bird—"

"It's the same bird! It's the same bird! It's the same bird!"

"The same bird as in the tavern!"

"Crown of gold! Crown of gold! Crown of gold!" screamed the parrot.

"You see?"

"Same crown! Same crown! Same crown!"

"It is! It is! It is!" shrieked the boy, his voice indistinguishable by now from that of the parrot.

"Well that's still no reason to get angry," insisted the Bear. "After all, I was in that tavern as well—don't you remember *me*?"

"You!"

"Certainly. I'd been kidnapped, shipped off to work in some gruesome two-bit carnival."

Suddenly Nicolas could picture the Bear, muzzled and chained to a table in the rear of the pirates' saloon.

"Doesn't *anything* happen for the first time?" he whined.

"Not in the ring," said the Bear, gently, as the parrot rose up into the air and landed on his broad shoulder. "There isn't a single gesture in the circus that isn't repeated over and over again."

"I'm flying! I'm falling! I'm flying! I'm falling! I'm flying! I'm falling!" echoed the parrot.

Nicolas exhaled so thoroughly that he seemed to shrink for a moment. And then he made a move so unexpected that even the wise old circus Bear, who thought he'd seen everything at least one thousand times, was shocked, for a moment, into paralysis. It was frightening, this impetuousness. Yet it also convinced the Bear, once he'd recovered from it, that this boy would indeed find whatever it was he was looking for.

"Well, then, if we are in the ring," Nicolas howled out, defiantly, "let's get on with the performance!"

And since his egg was already in his hand; and since it was round as he'd been taught all solar symbols must be; and since the only requirement of a true citizen, other than winglessness, was desire, stupid or otherwise—he simply tossed the precious blue egg straight up into the air, and, crying out "Watch me catch it!" he reached up into the sky for all that lay forever outside the confines of the circle.

It might have been a disaster.

Yet, though he failed to catch the egg, he did manage to collide with it and thus to soften its impact with the ground, breaking its fall enough to prevent the delicate blue shell from shattering into a million tiny pieces. Instead, it began to roll. Down the far side of the arched bridge it sped, faster and faster, the boy and the Bear in hot pursuit, and the parrot as well, flapping about in the air above them, chattering away, "Lost! Found! Lost! Found! Lost! Found!"

By the time it had rolled to a halt, the boy had already returned to his senses. Kneeling on the ground, he took the egg in his trembling hands, tenderly turning it around and around, inspecting the surface of his treasure for any tiny cracks or fractures. He couldn't believe that he had taken such a risk.

"What a fool I am" he mumbled.

"I'm blind! I can see! I'm blind! I can see! I'm blind! I can see!" cackled the parrot.

"I only wanted to . . ."

His voice trailed off.

"Not like that," was all the Bear had to say, and he began to claw at the patch of ground where the egg had come to rest. "If you really want to become a Citizen of the Flying City of the Sun, if you really want to fly with the rest of us and fall with the best of us, then you must put these on," he instructed, holding up the pair of plum-colored tights he'd unearthed, "and you must plan your failure—"

"But I'm not going to—"

"Or, or your *act*, what ever you choose to call it, you must plan it more carefully, more artfully."

Humbled by his near disaster, Nicolas did as he was told, squeezing into the pink and purple leotards. When it became clear that he was once more to use his precious blue egg for a target, however, he couldn't help but resist.

"But suppose I drop it?"

"It's a risk you'll just have to take."

"But—"

"You already risked it once, didn't you?"

"But that was different," stammered the boy, "I wasn't thinking."

"And that is precisely why you must risk it again," insisted the Bear, "more thoughtfully."

"Encore! Encore! Encore!" cheered the parrot.

In the end, they decided it would be most judicious to anchor the egg somehow, so that if the boy's grasp proved too weak or too clumsy, the egg would remain safe. Nicolas spied an abandoned nest in a nearby tree and suggested that the egg be set down, safe and sound, inside it.

"I can swing from that branch over there," he pointed. "I can swing from one branch to the other and lift the egg from out of the nest."

"Splendid!" agreed the Bear.

The boy climbed, hand over hand, from limb to limb, placing the egg in the nest, then positioning himself a carefully calculated distance away from it, drawing a diagram in his head, charting the course he would take from branch to branch. His heart was beating wildly, and he began to sweat.

"Are you ready?" asked the Bear.

Nicolas dropped down from a sitting position, sliding forward off the branch he'd chosen to launch himself from until he was hanging by both his hands. His body felt heavy as lead. He closed his eyes and took a deep breath.

"Are you ready?" repeated the Bear.

The Pilgrim's eyes were open again and he was staring down at his feet. They were dangling just below the frayed pink hem of his tights, as if pinned there, limp and useless. He mimed a few floating steps, wriggling his pale toes. Still he said nothing.

"Nicolas?"

No answer.

"Nicolas, are you ready?"

It was so quiet that the boy could hear every cramped muscle in his body creaking as he shifted his weight on the branch.

"Are you ready?" the Bear asked one last time.

"Yes," he whispered. "I'm ready."

Immediately, he began to swing: drawing his legs up and arching his hips backwards, displacing his weight, reversing it, extending his legs straight out in front of him, pointing his toes at the sky, back again, forward, back, forward.

"Shall I introduce you?" begged the Bear.

Gaining momentum, Nicolas nodded enthusiastically from the bar of his tree-top trapeze.

The Bear cleared his throat and cupped his hands around his mouth.

"Ladies and Gentlemen," rang out the solemn announcement.

"Ladies! Gentlemen! Ladies! Gentlemen!" the parrot could not keep from chiming in.

"Fools and Strong Men."

"Fools! Strong Men! Fools! Strong Men!" echoed the parrot.

"Your attention please!"

In his head the Bear had been preparing an elaborate speech, a poem about

the light of the blue sun and seeing what isn't there, about the eagle and the falcon, about hurtling through the air with a faith beyond compare, and much
more besides. He'd no doubt that the parrot would come to his aid, echoing the
crucial words, giving each rhyme its proper emphasis. It would possibly be his
finest piece of work. But the sudden shower of torn leaves falling down around
his shoulders caught him by surprise. Peering through the branches above he
could see that the boy was already accelerating at a rate that would leave no time
at all for fine and fancy phrases. "Head's up!" was all he managed to shout
before the boy's body was already hurtling through the air in the direction of the
nest.

Nicolas didn't remember letting go of the branch. There was a brief sensation
of rising, unattached. It thrilled him, and filled him with power, and yet it
couldn't have lasted for more than a second or two.

He was, for a moment, above the nest, looking down at the beautiful blue egg
resting peacefully in the center of its ring.

Then he began to drop.

And everything went wrong.

The rim of the nest was too close, the branch he'd chosen to break his fall was
too far away. And time moved so swiftly that there was no separating one
moment of miscalculation from another.

Of all the things that fell, Nicolas was by far the largest and the heaviest, and
so he fell the fastest, crashing through leaves and branches and thumping down
onto the hard ground, upright, on his backside.

"Ooooomphh."

The breath was knocked out of him and seemed to lie there for a moment on
the ground beside him.

Next came the nest.

Overturned, and empty, it plopped down directly atop his head like a lop-
sided crown.

Last of all, lightest of all, came his precious blue egg. If all of the other calami-
ties seemed to pass by in a single instant of lightning-like intensity, the fall of the
blue egg seemed, by contrast, to take hours, days, weeks, even years—each and
every moment of its descent frozen in its own blue time. Nicolas sat, stunned,

staring up at the egg as it dropped forever down. Nearly weightless, it couldn't have hit the ground with much force, and yet its impact seemed to shake the very earth beneath the boy, sending a crack not only through its own shell but through everything else in the world as well, including the heart of its devoted pilgrim.

The egg shattered.

Chips of its blue shell seemed to fly everywhere.

"I'll never be able to put it together again," screamed a voice inside the boy's head.

"One!" shrieked the parrot, "Many!" and then again, "One!" and again, "Many!" over and over again, "One! Many! One! Many! One! Many!" Its voice multiplied until there were a hundred parrots, a thousand, a chorus, a jungle of parrots, pouring in through the shattered gate of the egg of the City of the Sun, surrounding Nicolas, swallowing him up within their storm of shrill cries. A moment later the storm of voices took on a shape, a body. It seemed to swell and lift, gusting up into the air over the boy's head, rolling over and spinning into itself, congealing. Then once again it dipped and dropped, covering him, pressing him down, but gently, as if it were a sail swollen with wave upon wave of wind.

He'd been caught up in storms before. He'd been swept down the slopes of a volcano and reduced to ash by the flames of his own desire. He'd been sucked under water and bottled by his own thirst. He'd nearly been devoured by the vortex of his own dreams dispersing, nearly disappearing along with the Art and its Mistress into the matrix of the Ten Thousand Things.

But this was different. In this wind he felt neither the heat of desire nor the ache of thirst, and there was no trace of that crippling nostalgia for vanished dreams. This wind was soft, somehow, yes, that was it, it was soft, a wind so soft that despite its terrible force it brushed up against the skin of his face almost tenderly, almost like . . .

"Feathers!" howled Nicolas, "Feathers! Feathers!"

"Feathers! Feathers! Feathers!" cried a million parrots.

It was as if a bird had been born from the egg, but a bird without body, or a bird with every body, a bird all loose light feathers that, caught up in any bit of breath or breeze, would lift and clot and separate, changing shapes in an end-less effortless dance. No sooner had the boy realized the facts of this storm than the whole mass of feathers was sent tumbling off over the countryside by the gust of his gasp of surprise. Nicolas ran to catch up. He ran with all his strength. And yet each time he drew close enough to dive across its quivering threshold, the whirling currents of air set up by his sudden movements would change its shape entirely and send the whole storm of feathers reeling off in a new guise and a new direction.

He lost count of how many times he found himself spinning around madly inside the swirl of feathers, of how many times he then found himself marooned outside its protean embrace.

"One! One! One! There's only one!" the parrot would shriek at him as the feathers pulled away, sweeping over him in a single seething mass, floating off, leaving him behind. "There's only one in the whole wide world," he'd shriek back at the parrot. And maddened, he'd redouble his efforts, tumbling head-first into the storm, into that whirl of bright feathers where the one became the many, where a single parrot became a jungle of parrots, all of them taunting him at once, "House of cards! House of cards! House of cards!" as he reached out yet again, as yet again his hand returned empty, and yet again the entire storm scat-tered and collapsed around him, and then re-arose, hovering for a moment over his bowed head or scudding like a storm cloud off toward the horizon.

Several times he looked up to see the Bear standing not far away, applauding wildly.

"What shall I do?" Nicolas shouted to his friend.

"She'll make you fight," replied the Bear.

The boy was already running in the opposite direction, following the flight of feathers. He strained to hear the Bear's words over his shoulder.

"She'll force you to fight, for she can take the form of any bird, and all the waters, and the blinding heat of fire." The mass of feathers suddenly stopped short and veered around, returning now, speeding in his direction. "But you must hold on," he heard the Bear shouting as he entered the maelstrom.

"Hold on to what, to which, to—?"

"You must hold on," echoed the Bear's voice, "you must hold on to nothing . . ."

Seconds later Nicolas fell once again. He did not get up this time but simply lay flat on his back plucking at the million wings in the air that seemed to have come to rest right on top of him. He'd even time to catch his breath, time to watch more calmly how his hands failed each time, their desperate spasms repelling one feather after another, sending them flurrying out of reach in the wind generated by the violence of their gesture of desire. "You must hold on," he repeated to himself, "you must hold on to nothing." With a shock, the boy realized that it was only when his hands remained completely still that the feathers came close enough to touch his skin. "Stop!" he told himself, but it was easier said than done.

"Stop! Just for a moment!" he begged that part of himself that never ceased.

"Please stop," he prayed.

In the end, it didn't take very long at all. The Pilgrim lay flat on his back with both his arms stretched up into the stormy air above him, his hands wide open and motionless. And even after he felt the feather land on his palm, he remained perfectly still for a moment longer. Even when he did at last begin to curl his fingers, closing them into a fist, he did so slowly, slowly, slowly—until that last moment, when they snapped shut like the jaws of a snake.

There was a terrible commotion overhead, a painful stretching, a rending and tearing, as the whole storm of feathers began to rise straight up into the air. Nicolas felt an incredible pressure in the palm of his hand, as if it were from this one point that the storm was pulling away, struggling to be set free, as if it were at this point and no other that it was still attached.

"Hold on," he told himself, "hold on."

As he watched, arms raised, one fist clenched within the other, the entire sky seemed to lift like a layer of skin, wrinkling up, puckering and shrinking as it withdrew. Like an old dry rag it suddenly caught the breeze and began to billow and flap, inflating and deflating, as it sailed heavenward.

A ray of sunlight struck the edge of the distant storm cloud that it was swiftly becoming, and Nicolas gasped.

He felt a sudden stab of pain in his hand, as if something had been plucked free at last, like a thorn, from his flesh. At the same instant from out of the cloud emerged a head, or two heads, or two hundred heads, and eyes and arms and legs, or claws and a snout and a beak, or waves of salt, or wings, or tongues of violet flame, a golden neck, and a most exquisite crest. It was a bird or a beast, it was an open book, it was the machinery of flight, a great goddess, or a cold shower of naked gems. It was all the waters and the blinding heat of fire. It was a hand beckoning, a hand waving farewell. It was only a bit of sun gilded cloud, only a phantom, a patch of light and moisture drifting, shifting shapes on a clear or a cloudy day above one boy's passionately clenched hands.

"The Phoenix," whispered Nicolas.

There was a rumble of thunder and a flash of lightning, and suddenly it began to rain. Water poured down from the sky. Within moments Nicolas could hear the gurgle of streams rising in their underground reservoirs, irrigating the parched land. Looking up he saw only a single streak of color, the track of the vanishing parrot. The rest was fog and mist, a curtain of falling rain, nothing more.

He closed his eyes and let the rain spatter off his cheeks and forehead, let it puddle round his eyes and run in through his parted lips.

Pressed up against the palm of his hand he could feel the hard rib of the single central quill, and on either side the soft wings, their rows of fine fiber, tough as silk, neatly combed.

From somewhere directly behind him he heard a single, low, good-natured laugh.

"Well. It's a fine feather."

Nicolas jumped to his feet and turned around sharply, slipping and sliding in the mud, nearly falling back down, expecting to see . . .

But it was only the Bear, standing right beside him, his fur soaked and matted, his wilted pink skirt dripping with rain. He stared at the boy, mouth clenched, lips trembling in a feeble attempt to suppress his emotion—until he could control himself no longer, and burst out laughing.

A moment later, Nicolas joined in.

CHAPTER TEN

Requiem

"White as snow, pink blossoms bright," chanted the boy softly, "then fields of green, then golden light." He often addressed the feather thus, with the little poem he'd composed for it, inspired by its bands of color. Sometimes, late at night, blinded by the darkness, he'd only have to recite his little poem and the feather would appear right before his eyes, its colors clear and bright, as if the sun were shining directly upon it. Such intimacy, however, engendered certain expectations, and thus certain inevitable frustrations. *Show me the way to return,* he asked the feather every night, and yet every morning he and the Bear set out once again, wandering aimlessly, lost, still so far from home. It was as if even after all these days and nights of travel together, the secret of the feather's medicine was still locked up tight inside it, like the voice one cannot quite hear in a dream.

Nicolas was troubled.

For the past week he'd been awakened each morning by a sharp stab of pain

in his shoulder, and this morning the pain had been accompanied by a drop of bright red blood that stained the tip of his finger and the sleeve of his shirt. What he feared most was that this pain in his shoulder was merely the herald of another wound, the next, and that nothing had really changed after all. Removing his feather now from his pocket, he stared at it as he walked along, brooding. All passion and pain, he thought to himself, and all sorrow . . .

"But you promised," he said aloud then, gazing down at the feather in his hand, "you did promise, didn't you?"

The sun was just rising, and its first rays falling across the ground at his feet revealed to the Pilgrim that he could not proceed any further along this particular path. Indeed, so intently had he been contemplating the feather held up in front of his face that he'd nearly walked, like a perfect fool, right off the edge of a cliff.

"I thought there would be no more falling," he whispered to the feather, gripping it with both his hands. "I thought that everything would be different now."

"You're talking to yourself again," said the Bear, approaching from somewhere behind him. He was breathing heavily. "You must have set out even earlier than usual this morning. It's taken me forever to catch up."

"But I've hardly traveled at all. I've been standing here for most of the morning."

"Maybe I'm just slowing down," sighed the Bear, "getting old and all that . . . "

"We can't go any farther anyway," grumbled Nicolas, "not on this path."

He pointed with the tip of his feather to the edge of the cliff.

The Bear looked down, then up, then off into the distance.

"I was bleeding this morning," mumbled the boy.

"Hm?"

"I was bleeding this morning when I woke up."

Nicolas poked one finger through a tear in his shirtsleeve.

"It's your tattoo," said the Bear.

"How do you know?"

"I tried to chase him away earlier, before you were awake, but he must have returned again when I dozed back off."

"Chase who away?"

"Peepo."

"Peepo?"

"Yes."

"You mean the sparrow, the sparrow from the circus with the—"

"The one and only."

"But what—"

"He was pecking at your tattoo," explained the Bear, "trying to steal one of the seeds of the pomegranate."

Nicolas was examining the tiny red scab in the center of the picture painted on his skin.

"But why would he do that?"

"I suppose he was hungry," shrugged the Bear. "I suppose maybe he thought the seeds were real. Unless it was just another of his practical jokes."

Nicolas felt as if his friend knew a lot more than he was saying.

"Perhaps he was trying to do another clown another favor," added the Bear at last, smiling coyly.

"But it hurt so much it woke me up."

"Yes."

"And he was trying to steal something from me."

"Yes."

"Pain and theft, you call that a favor?"

The Bear didn't answer. For a long while they stood staring silently off into the distance, finally deciding to spend the rest of the day and night right there in the soft grass at the edge of the cliff and begin backtracking the next morning, searching for an alternate route.

"Perhaps he was only acting on behalf of someone or something else," suggested the Bear hours later, aware that Nicolas had been thinking of nothing else all afternoon.

"Like who?"

"Or what." The Bear's tone was solemn. "Perhaps it's the pain itself that is trying—"

"The pain itself," interrupted Nicolas, doubtful, "you think the pain itself is trying to steal something from me!"

"Perhaps it is only taking what belongs to it, what you have neglected to offer it."

And with that, the Bear fell obstinately silent.

The next morning they set out, walking all day, directionless it seemed, unable to choose one path over another. "Sometimes I feel as if I'll never find my way back to the aviary," lamented the boy, "sometimes I feel as if I'll never see it again."

"Oh, I know," agreed the Bear, "these return journeys, they are endless, you don't have to remind me. I've been trying to return to the island for I don't know how long."

That evening, as they were preparing for sleep, Nicolas finally asked the Bear about the sacrifice.

"What is it that I have neglected to offer?"

"Perhaps you should let the little bird be your guide."

"The thief itself?"

"Thieves and guides often travel in close company, Nicolas."

The boy looked down at his tattoo, thinking.

"One seed of the pomegranate," he mumbled.

The Bear took a deep breath.

"First fruit of the dead," he said. "I'm sure you've heard *that* story."

As the boy's eyes began to close, he could taste the bittersweet juice of the pierced seed bleeding across his tongue.

"Nicolas," whispered the Bear gravely, "dream carefully tonight. I think we are very close to the aviary, very close indeed."

But the boy scarcely had time to heed the Bear's advice, for no sooner had he fallen asleep than a brush of swift wings against his cheek and a sharp pain in his shoulder alerted him to the presence of the infernally talented sparrow. "Gotcha!" he cried out, leaping to his feet. Immediately the little bird darted away with Nicolas in hot pursuit. The Bear awoke with a start, then a groan, and by the time he'd clambered to his feet both boy and bird were already growing small in the distance.

"Wait for me!" he cried, and tumbled after them.

Even in the dream, if it *was* a dream, the boy held the feather out in front of him as he traveled—leading with it, like a pilot with his compass, listening with it like a writer with his pen, like a painter with her brush—measuring everything according to its snow white and blossom bright and field of green and golden light.

He ran all night, crashing and stumbling through the dark, the wings of the bird beating the air always just ahead of him, just out of reach—until the sun began to rise over the horizon, and the mischievous sparrow at last came to a halt, settling down upon the branch of a tree with the purloined pip of the pomegranate clenched firmly in its beak. Nicolas stumbled to a halt, and then stared as a flock of great blue herons whirled around in the sky over his head and glided down to earth, landing in a pool of shallow water a few yards away from where he stood in shocked silence. When he looked back, the sparrow had vanished.

"Are *all* the oracles to fall silent then?" whispered the boy.

"Ultimately," said the Bear, who'd caught up with him at last.

As if a veil had been lifted from his eyes, the boy suddenly became conscious of the familiar configuration of stream and sandbar and cypress, the sweet odor of root and drowned grass, the call of bittern, woodpecker, and jay. "I know this place," he whispered to himself, incredulous. "I know this place better than any other place on earth." He looked down at the feather trembling in his hands, then lifted his eyes, gazing around at the peaceful marshes of the aviary.

And then he began to run, splashing through the low-lying pools, hopping from one island of sand to another, startling the flock of herons, which rose up into the air as he approached, then reeled, returning, once he had passed.

"Come on!" he cried out, turning round and beckoning to the Bear, who bounded after him, as best he could.

With each step he took he felt himself growing lighter and lighter, and very soon he was as light as the feather he led with. Several times he even thought he could feel the old man's hands gripping him tightly beneath the shoulders, swinging him through the air—so effortlessly did he fly onward, so like a bird.

It was already dusk by the time they reached the swan coop, and the shadows seeking shelter beneath its eaves and around its walls cooled the boy's ardor and cautioned him, staying his hand before it reached out for the door that sealed the old man's tomb.

"Let's sit down for a while," whispered the Bear, tenderly, leading the boy by the hand to a small flight of crumbling stone steps a few paces away. Nicolas followed, though his head was turned, back, over his shoulder, trying to make out the familiar contours of the building before it sank into the rapidly deepening twilight.

"Something has grown up all around it," he said.

"Forests are like that," explained the Bear, pulling the boy gently down beside him. "They grow up around everything, always."

"I wish I could see."

"That's why we should rest now," urged the Bear, "and maybe even sleep."

"Oh, no, I couldn't sleep!"

"Well alright, we'll just rest then, we'll just sit if you like, we'll keep vigil here until morning."

"Yes," agreed the boy, "a vigil, until the morning."

The boy and the Bear sat quite still on the old stone stoop. It was on these very steps that Nicolas had spent his last evening with Gillam, watching as wave after wave of herons swept across the darkening sky, returning to their nests.

Nicolas crouched down, and with the sharp quill of his feather, he scratched a circle, slowly, in the dust at his feet.

"There," he said, wiping the dirt from the tip of his pen, "that was the last thing the old man said to me."

"An elegant farewell," observed the Bear.

"And a map for my journey," marveled the Pilgrim. "He always thought of everything."

For a moment or two Nicolas wept, quietly. Thus their vigil began.

As the hours of shadow rolled on over them, they began talking more and more, the boy's mood expanding and then contracting, now solemn, now joyous, now cautious, now curious, changing from word to word and moment to moment. The Bear was so exhausted that several times he might have drifted right off to sleep, with his chin on his chest, were it not for the sound of the boy's voice.

Initially Nicolas spoke almost exclusively of the aviary, and of the old man. Yet, as the night wore on, he began to speak of other things, of other places and people, recalling bits and pieces of the adventures that had befallen him within that ring the old man had drawn in the dust on the night before departure.

Nicolas didn't know what made the Sumerian appear in his memory just when he did. He seemed to enter unannounced. It occurred to the boy that perhaps the Bear might know what had become of him.

"*He* has returned home as well," the Bear said, "and long before you—that is, if the tales told of him are to be believed. He is a great king once again, they say. He has resumed his crown and his mantle and rebuilt his city walls, which had fallen into ruin in his absence."

"The Walls of Uruk," whispered the boy to himself.

"They say he is the wisest of rulers now—his laws written in dark, rough stone, but his tales of travel carved in polished tablets of lapis lazuli."

"Did you ever see his tattoo?"

"Yes, I saw it once or twice."

"A broken heart," declared the boy.

The Bear nodded.

"You know that he asked about you . . . "

"About me?"

"Yes, many times, they say."

"What did he say?"

"Well, he never knew your name . . . '*Whatever became of that boy,*' he'd muse from time to time, '*the boy with the empty bird cages, the boy tattooed with the glowing brain of death.*'"

"The what?"

"The glowing brain of death," repeated the Bear, "that's how he always referred to the pomegranate. He was a great admirer of your tattoo, you know, envious even, or so tavern gossip would have it."

"Envious? Of me?"

The Bear fell silent for a long while.

"Ah, yes," he sighed at last. "You've all returned, all you wearied pilgrims. Sometimes it seems as if everyone will return, everyone but me."

Nicolas tried, with his pale, thin arm, to encircle his friend's broad shoulder. The Bear turned to the boy and smiled. "Not that I'm complaining," he apologized.

"But you could stay here, with me . . . "

The Bear shook his head, patting Nicolas affectionately on one knee. "No," he said, resolutely, "if I'm to sleep at the side of the road every night, then sleep there I will, and soundly too—so as to get an early start each morning."

"A *relatively* early start," teased the boy, for he'd heard his friend snoring contentedly through many a dawn.

The Bear laughed and shrugged.

"After all," he said, "that's show business."

"Life in the ring," mumbled the boy, staring down.

Neither of them spoke for a long time after that. They might even have dozed off for a moment or two, or for much longer. Neither seemed to notice the gray ghosts and pale blue mists gradually softening the sharp black edges of the night. "Look," said Nicolas suddenly, pointing first to the ground and only later to the sky. It was, indeed, onto the dust below that the first ray of sunlight had cast its first swift shadow of the day: it was the shadow of a bird, and it passed right into the charmed circle scrawled upon the ground at their feet, right through its center and out the other side.

"It's dawn," said the boy, raising his head, pointing to the sunlight beginning to filter through the trees.

"It's time," said the Bear.

Turning immediately to face the old man's tomb, Nicolas was amazed to find the whitewashed walls of the coop buried beneath a dense thicket of vines. He had to hack his way through its loops and twists and tangles for almost an hour before he caught even a glimpse of the door of the old swan coop. By that time the blossoms had opened all the way, a brilliant army of blue trumpets, heralding the sun. The thousands of birds that inhabited the thicket of morning glories had burst into song, their chorus swelled by the buzzing of those hordes of bees who'd penetrated deep into the twisted blue forest to build their hidden hives. Every particle of this mountain of flowers was vibrating, alive.

With a path cleared at last, with his hand touching the door, pressed flat up against the whitewashed wooden panel, Nicolas turned to the Bear.

"I think I should go in alone," he said.

The Bear nodded in agreement.

One light push was all that was needed, and the door to the coop swung open without a sound, a single ray of sunlight penetrating its gloomy interior. Nicolas took one step forward, then hesitated.

"My feather," he reminded himself, for he had pocketed his treasure in order to wrestle more effectively with the many arms of the morning glory. Once he held the feather securely in his hand again, however, he strode boldly into the tomb, closing the door behind him and disappearing, along with the ray of light, inside.

It took him several minutes to orient himself in the dark. He found the stub of candle and the tin of matches he remembered Old Gillam always kept on a ledge above the door. The candlelight was weak, the flame flickering in his trembling hands. Even so, he could see that everything was lying just where it had been left.

The boy raised his eyes to the roof. In many places it had caved in completely, crushed by the grip of the flowering vine. Something soft and wet struck Nicolas on the head and began to drip down his neck and between his shoulderblades. "Honey," he said, reaching behind him and bringing one sticky fingertip up to his face, examining it by candlelight. What he'd thought was a large section of the original roof directly over his head was actually a series of elaborately constructed beehives, a whole city of them, two or three hundred, each one banked up against the other. Another heavy drop fell from the shadows overhead, this one hissing as it struck the candle, almost extinguishing its flame. Nicolas took a step or two to one side, surprised to find the floor of the coop so sticky that he had to struggle to lift each foot.

"A river of honey," he marveled, as he crouched down to investigate, his eyes tracing the course of the sweet heavy stream, which apparently crossed the coop from one end to the other. On the far bank of the river of honey, Nicolas knelt down at last, feather in hand, beside the body of the old man.

For over an hour, the Bear had been sitting patiently outside on the stone stoop, waiting for some sign or signal from the boy. He was concerned and yet did not want to interrupt or interfere.

Another hour passed and still he heard nothing.

The Bear paced for a while, then sat back down again. Another hour passed. And another.

The boy's voice, when it finally rose up from the tomb, seemed to breach the walls of its fortress in a million places at once, escaping like smoke through the dense tangle of blue flowers.

The Bear recognized the fugitive music at once. He sat motionless, eyes closed, hands clasped tightly to his breast, listening, as the boy sang the Requiem at last.

The flame's gone out.
It casts no light.
I cast myself
Into the night.
Frail boat I sink
Into the sea.
Still water's dark.
Still water's deep.

Asleep I fall.
Asleep I rise.
The cradle tips.
The darkness sighs.
A tumbling child
Wakes in my eyes.
Still water flows.
Still water flies.

And caught beneath
The wing of sleep,
I cling
To nothing
Rising.

This time when the door of the coop swung open, the ray of light penetrating the gloom seemed to pass out rather than enter in, darting forth from within the tomb itself. "You'll have to help," said the boy, standing barefoot on the glowing threshold.

The Bear rose to his feet, approaching cautiously.

"I want to carry him outside."

"Out of the tomb?"

"To the meadow."

"Do you think that's wise?"

"It's what he wants."

The boy had already dragged the old man's body up to the door of the coop. Peering inside, the Bear could see the top of his head and one shoulder emerging from the shadows.

"You're much stronger than I," explained the boy. "You'll have to help me—*I* must carry the feather, so it is *you* who will have to carry the old man."

"I understand," said the Bear.

Nicolas slipped back into the darkness. After several minutes he called out, "Are you ready?"

"I've never done this sort of thing before."

The Bear straightened his pink skirt, brushing it free of a few bits of twig and leaf, ruffling its edges nervously.

"You can come in now," said Nicolas.

The Bear didn't move.

"I said you can come in now," repeated the boy.

"His eyes are open," said the Bear a few minutes later, looking down at the body in his arms, relieved to be back outside in the fresh air and sunlight. He was standing at the edge of the lake behind the swan coop, while Nicolas searched the banks for some sign of the little skiff that had always been moored nearby.

"I found it!" he called out moments later.

The boy boarded first and held the boat stationary, anchoring it with one oar stuck into the mud at the bottom of the lake while the Bear waded out and laid Old Gillam gently inside. The boat rocked and sank dangerously low in the water as the Bear himself clambered aboard, but it did not sink. They drifted until the water deepened, and then Nicolas began to row.

"His eyes are open," repeated the Bear, once they were halfway across the lake.

"Yes," said Nicolas. "I know."

Cramped as they were in the little boat, the Bear was sitting with the old man's head on his lap.

"And there's a sort of bruise on the back of his head, right at the top of his spine—a soft spot."

"Perhaps that's where the feather turned inward."

"What feather? Your feather?"

"No, the small white feather, that feather that turns round and enters the brain of the dying swan. After that there's nothing but song."

"Is he a swan, then?" asked the Bear.

"I wouldn't be surprised," said Nicolas.

The Bear looked down at the feather in the boy's hand.

"Are you the Phoenix, then?"

"In my wildest dreams," replied the boy, "perhaps."

He looked into his friend's eyes.

"And what are you?"

"A bear," said the Bear, and smiled, as the little boat scraped up against the far shore of the lake.

An hour later they stood at the edge of the meadow.

"Wait," said Nicolas, producing a pair of yellow slippers that had been tucked into the waistband of his pants. Maneuvering around the Bear, he placed the slippers carefully on the old man's feet, then motioned for the Bear to follow as he strolled off through the meadow.

Another hour had passed, and the Bear's arms were growing tired, though he did not complain, for this was one burden he could neither refuse nor regret. Once again Nicolas insisted that they stop. He looked confused, and was turning this way and that, muttering to himself, "I don't know, I don't know." Suddenly his face relaxed, the furrows melted from his brow, and his eyes began to shine.

"But Nicolas!" shouted the Bear, in alarm, as he saw the feather the boy had tossed up into the air catch the breeze and go sailing away. "Snow white and blossom

bright," chanted the boy, covering his eyes with his hands, "and green fields and golden light." An instant later, he dropped his hands and went chasing off after the feather, twirling and skipping back and forth along with it, laughing as he ran. "Now I'm teaching *you* to fly," the boy called to Old Gillam over his shoulder. The Bear began to run as well, struggling at first beneath the weight of the body entrusted to his arms. He was laughing by the time he caught up with the boy, who stood pointing at the patch of heather in which the feather had come to rest.

"This is the place," he said, retrieving his feather.

The Bear deposited the old man gently on the ground.

And that is where they left him—though not right away, for they sat there the rest of the day, alongside the body, chatting contentedly, dodging dragonflies and hummingbirds, picking wildflowers, and chewing on the tips of long, slender blades of sweet meadow grass.

"Where will you go after this?" asked the boy.

"I'm not sure," replied the Bear, "but I was wondering if you would let me borrow that little boat of yours."

Nicolas was overjoyed to have such a gift to give his friend.

"Well then, I guess I'll be on my way."

"Already?"

"It'll be dark in a couple of hours."

Nicolas hadn't realized it was so late.

"You'll just leave him here?" asked the Bear, rising to his feet.

"Yes," said the boy, rising to his feet as well.

Both stood silent then, looking down.

"That's just how I found him inside," said the boy, "as if he'd only just lain down, the moment before, to sleep, forever."

The lids of Old Gillam's eyes quivered, and then closed.

"If we row across together," said the boy, looking up, "then you can leave from the other shore. Do you mind?"

"Of course not," said the Bear.

As they were walking away, however, something startled the boy. What a strange birdcall, he thought to himself, and stopped for a moment, glancing around. The cry rang out again and again.

"What is that?"

The Bear had stopped also. He'd turned round, and was walking back toward the boy.

"Could it be . . . ?"

Crouching down behind Nicolas, his voice trailed off, and he began poking through the tangled carpet of grass and wildflowers as if searching for something.

"It is!" he exclaimed, his voice filled with wonder.

"It is what?"

"The Stone!" he gasped.

"What stone?"

The strange cry was still echoing across the meadow.

"The Pilgrim's Stone," said the Bear, "you stepped right on it—it always cries out when touched by the foot of a pilgrim. Have you never heard the legend of the touchstone of the true pilgrim?"

Sometimes it seemed to the boy a wail of lament, the keening of the trampled earth itself carried upward by the wind. At other times it seemed almost jubilant, a wild shout of celebration. Over and over again, at regular intervals, the cry of the stone rang out, part shriek, part exultation.

"Legend has it that once awakened by the footstep of a true pilgrim, the Stone will go on singing, crying out one time for each of the pilgrims destined, on some future day or night, to pass this way again."

The Bear paused.

"But the legend also says that the Stone was lost long ago and has never been heard from since."

"And it's been here in the meadow, in the aviary, all along," marveled the boy.

"And so the age of pilgrimage has not passed at all," swore the Bear, "as so many had feared."

Once they'd launched the skiff, he and the Bear sat listening to the cries of the Pilgrim's Stone, neither saying a word, as they drifted back across the lake. By the time they'd moored the boat out behind the empty tomb, the boy had already lost count of its cries, so vast were those herds of future pilgrims fated to follow in one another's footsteps.

Nicolas waved with his feather until his arm was too tired to hold up any longer. By that time the Bear's boat had long since disappeared from view.

And still the Stone went on calling out, herald of a pilgrimage that was apparently without end.

That night, curled up on the ground beneath the cedars, wrapped in their fragrance, using what remained of his old nest for a pillow, he lay, with his Pilgrim's Feather gripped in his hand, listening to the Pilgrim's Stone crying out tirelessly into the darkness of the future. He listened until he fell asleep and would have been listening still, at dawn, when he awoke, had it not been for the birds, whose voices drowned out the cries of their brethren, swallowing up the ages of pilgrims to come in wave after wave of *chirr-up* and *peeep* and *ta-weet*, burying them, like a treasure, in the winged heart of their own restless songs.